Our Secrets and Lies

SINÉAD MORIARTY

PENGUIN
IRELAND

PENGUIN IRELAND

UK | USA | Canada | Ireland | Australia
India | New Zealand | South Africa

Penguin Ireland is part of the Penguin Random House group of companies
whose addresses can be found at global.penguinrandomhouse.com.

First published 2018
001

Set in 13.5/16 pt Garamond MT Std
Typeset by Jouve (UK), Milton Keynes
Printed in Great Britain by Clays Ltd, St Ives plc

A CIP catalogue record for this book is available from the British Library

ISBN: 978–1–844–88405–6

www.greenpenguin.co.uk

Our Secrets and Lies

For all mothers

PART ONE

1999

I

'Do you think I am?' Lucy asked, wiping away tears with the back of her hand.

Sarah handed her a tissue. 'No,' she said, trying to sound more sure than she felt. Two weeks late was not good. Sarah had been a few days late, but never two whole weeks. 'I've been late before, nearly that long. It's probably stress,' she lied.

'We always used condoms, except that one time in Kerry when, well . . . we were really drunk and . . . Oh, God, Sarah, what am I going to do?' Lucy wailed.

Sarah chewed her lip. 'Look, if you want to find out for sure, you could do a pregnancy test,' she said. 'I bought two in the chemist on my way here, just in case.'

'Oh, no. I can't do that yet,' Lucy said. She was afraid, afraid that the test might show she was pregnant, and then what? What would Tom say? Would he dump her? Would he hate her? Would he support her? Would they go to London or Liverpool? Where was the best place to have an abortion? It had to be a false alarm – it just had to be.

Sarah took a deep breath and said, 'I think not knowing is worse. Maybe you should just do the test, and when it's negative, you can relax.'

Lucy could barely get the words out of her mouth. 'What if it's positive?'

Tears sprang into Sarah's eyes. 'Well . . . uhm . . . we'll just deal with it. Let's take it one step at a time, okay?'

'I'm scared.' Lucy covered her face with her hands.

Sarah leaned over and gave her friend a tight hug. 'Whatever happens, I'm here for you. I have a hundred and fifty quid saved. It's yours if you need it, although I'm sure you won't. Whatever . . . You know what I mean.'

Lucy pulled away from her friend. 'Thanks,' she said. She really meant it. Sarah was her rock. She didn't know how she'd cope without her, but she had to dig deep here and get to grips with what was happening. 'Okay,' she said, nodding. 'I'll do it.'

Sarah reached into her bag and handed Lucy the two tests. 'It's important that you do two. The first could be wrong.'

Lucy locked herself into the bathroom. Thankfully her parents were busy in the shop and her sister Jenny was at a friend's house. She sat down and stared at the tests. If they were positive, her life would be ruined. Even if Tom didn't dump her and went with her to England for an abortion, their relationship would be destroyed. Every time they looked at each other, they'd remember what they'd done. Lucy didn't think their relationship would survive it.

But, then, maybe it would – they were mad about each other, weren't they? Well, she loved him and in Kerry he had almost said he loved her. He hadn't actually spoken those words but he'd said, 'I'm mad about you,' and as far as Lucy was concerned, that was good enough.

Please, God, make it be negative, Lucy prayed, as she peed on the sticks and waited for the results.

Sarah knocked gently on the door. 'Are you finished? Can I come in? I don't think you should be alone.'

Lucy opened the door. Sarah looked at the two sticks. They sat in silence. The seconds felt like hours.

'I can't look – you'll have to tell me.' Lucy covered her eyes with her hands, then took them away.

Sarah peered at the sticks. Her face fell. Oh, Jesus. They

must be positive. For a split second Lucy thought Sarah was going to throw them into the bin, but this wasn't something they could sweep under the carpet and forget about. The news was going to change Lucy's life for ever.

'It's bad, isn't it?' Lucy said, into the heavy silence. Sarah was crying now. Oh, God. Her stomach lurched. She turned and threw up into the basin.

Sarah handed her a towel. They sat on the edge of the bath and cried.

'Hold on,' Sarah said suddenly. 'You might have a miscarriage. Loads of people do. Look at your mum. She had a few, didn't she, between you and Jenny?'

Lucy nodded, but they were clutching at straws. She sobbed into the towel while Sarah rubbed her back.

'Are you going to tell Tom or wait a bit?'

Lucy had no answer to that. She knew that as soon as she told Tom, everything would change for the worse. Her little bubble of happiness would explode. 'My family can never know. It would literally kill my dad. He'd be so disappointed in me.' She sobbed.

'Come on now, Billy adores you. Sure, he has you on a pedestal.'

'Exactly, and I'd fall very far down if he found out I was up the bloody duff.'

'No one needs to know,' Sarah said quietly. 'Only you, me and Tom.'

'What if I don't tell Tom?' Lucy said.

Sarah looked at her in confusion. 'What?'

Lucy sat up straight. 'What if I don't tell him? I'll just go to London, have an abortion, come back and forget the whole thing happened.'

Sarah's mouth hung open. 'Are you mental? You can't just have an abortion and pretend it never happened. It's not like returning a jacket you don't like. It's a big deal, Lucy. You need support. It's painful and serious and . . . and emotional and all that.'

'But it's the perfect solution. I won't lose Tom, my parents won't be upset and I'll just get on with my degree and my life.' Lucy was sure that was the correct plan of action. This way, she'd get to keep everything and everyone and no one would get hurt. Okay, she would, but she was strong, she'd deal with it.

'Lucy?' Sarah shook her gently by the shoulders. 'Stop it. This is madness. Tom needs to know. If you don't tell him, you'll have this huge secret between you and it'll cause problems. Besides, he'll know something's wrong. Darren always knows when I've got something on my mind and vice versa. You have to tell him.'

'But if I'm getting rid of it, why does he need to know?'

'Because it's his baby.'

'Don't call it that. It's not a baby, just a cluster of cells.'

Sarah glared at her. 'Jesus, Lucy.'

Lucy stuck her chin out defiantly. 'Well, it's true.'

Sarah shook her head. 'It's not right to keep Tom in the dark.'

'If this stupid country wasn't so bloody backward, I could have it done here in Dublin tomorrow and not have to travel over to England on my own.'

Sarah took her hand and squeezed it. 'I'll go with you, but it should be Tom and you know it.'

'Would you, really?' Lucy said.

'Of course.'

'Thanks. I'd be a complete mess without you, Sarah. Now I just need to figure out how to organize and pay for it.'

Over the next two weeks Lucy contacted abortion clinics in Liverpool because the flights there were much cheaper than to London. She reckoned she was about six weeks pregnant, so she wanted to get on with it.

She refused to allow any doubts to cloud her mind, and when she woke up with tears on her face and a wet pillow every morning, she ignored it. There was only one solution and this was it.

Sarah remained quiet whenever Lucy brought up the subject, so she kept the information flow to a minimum.

She'd tried to avoid Tom because she found being with him really difficult. After the second week of telling him she was too busy to see him, he chased after her as she tried to scurry away after a tutorial. He caught up with her in Front Square and grabbed her shoulder. 'Hey, what the hell is going on? I've barely seen you in the last couple of weeks. Why are you avoiding me? Are you annoyed with me? And don't say you're busy because you never used to be too busy to see me.'

Lucy couldn't look into those eyes. 'I'm sorry. Of course I want to see you. I'm just . . . busy.'

'Doing what?' Tom demanded.

'Studying and helping my parents out in the shop and stuff.'

'So everything between us is okay?'

'Yes, totally.'

'Well, can you come back to my rooms now? Killian's out so we can catch up properly.' Tom leaned in to kiss her. Lucy reared back. 'What the hell?' he said, sounding hurt.

'Sorry – I'm so sorry, I just . . . I have to go.'

She turned to walk away but he clutched her arm. 'No way. You're not going anywhere until you tell me what's going on. Have you met another guy? Are you cheating on me?'

Tears sprang into her eyes. 'No, God, no. I just . . . I . . .'

Tom's face darkened. 'What? Just spit it out. For Christ's sake, Lucy, if you want to break up, just say so. Don't avoid me like some child and pretend you're busy. Judging by your reaction when I tried to kiss you, you obviously don't want to be with me any more so just say so.'

Lucy could no longer hold back the tears, which flowed down her cheeks. 'No, Tom.' She reached up and kissed him. 'I don't want to break up with you. I just have some stuff going on.'

'What stuff?'

'Personal stuff.'

'So talk to me. I might be able to help. Isn't that what couples do? Talk to each other?'

Lucy shook her head. God, this was so hard. She hadn't expected to get so emotional and now she was blowing it. She had to get away from him but also make him understand she still wanted to be with him. She tried to calm down. 'You're right, but it's just kind of private. I can't talk about it.'

'Are you sick? You look very pale – are you okay?'

'I'm fine,' she managed to croak.

'Are your parents okay? Is it your sister? What is it? Stop blocking me out – talk to me.'

'I can't. Just leave it, Tom. Just leave me,' Lucy snapped. She had to get away before she broke and told him the truth.

'Fuck this.' Tom took a step back. 'It's obvious you don't want to be with me. You can't even look me in the eye. So I reckon you've done the dirt. I just wish you'd had the balls to tell me. I expected more from you, Lucy. I thought we had something special. Obviously I was wrong.' He turned and walked away.

'STOP!' Lucy shouted. 'Please stop. It's nothing like that. I love you.'

'What?' Tom turned back.

Lucy hadn't expected that to come out of her mouth. She was losing all control, but she did love him. 'I love you, Tom, and I want to be with you and I've never even looked at another boy.'

'So then what is it? Tell me!' Tom pleaded. 'I need to know so I can believe you.' He wiped a tear from her cheek. 'I promise to help you with whatever your problem is. Trust me, Lucy.'

Lucy finally allowed herself to look into those beautiful green eyes. She could trust him. He was Tom, her Tom. He'd help her.

'I'm pregnant.'

2

Tom stood at the window and looked out at the driving rain. Jesus, pregnant. There were a lot of things he'd thought Lucy might say to him, but that hadn't been one of them.

He'd felt as if he'd been shot. He hadn't been able to speak for a minute, and then when he'd looked into her pleading eyes, he'd known he had to say something nice. He'd muttered, 'We'll work it out,' but he hadn't really believed that.

How could he have been so stupid? That one bloody shag. Jesus, they'd had sex about ten times that weekend in Kerry. It was just that one time they'd been really drunk and he hadn't used a condom. One stupid little mistake and now this?

Tom knew Lucy was waiting for him to call her to say he'd got the money and could go with her to Liverpool next week. But he didn't have any money. He'd blown it all on their weekend in Kerry. He'd asked three of his mates to lend him some, but they were all skint too. Everyone was – it was the end of January so no one had any cash. There was no other way. He was going to have to ask his dad for the money. He'd say it was for a college trip or something. He'd figure out a bullshit story to tell Gabriel.

It had been only three days since Lucy had blurted it out but Tom felt as if he'd aged ten years. A baby! Christ. Tom just wanted the whole thing to be over and for his life to go back to normal. He was worried, though. Things were weird with Lucy now. Would this break them up?

Why did it have to happen? Things had been going great. He really liked her, and life had been good. But now this. An abortion. Everything was messed up. Would Lucy be different now? Would she blame him? Would she go mad after the abortion? There was a girl in St Jude's, in the year ahead of Tom, who had ended up drinking a bottle of vodka a day after having an abortion. She'd ended up in hospital, then rehab.

Still, though, that wouldn't happen to Lucy: she was sensible, smart, together. Tom would be there for her – he had to be. He wanted to help. He just had to get the money. He didn't want to lose her. Lucy was the best thing that had happened to him. Sure, he'd dated loads of girls, but none of them had captured his heart. They were all St Jude's girls and all kind of the same. But Lucy was different. She was so smart and focused and, best of all, loving and warm. She made Tom feel ten feet tall. When he was with her, he felt really, truly happy.

Tom craved affection, having grown up with just his dad for a companion. He hated being an only child. He envied people with big noisy families. It had always been just him and Gabriel for dinner. When he watched other dads hugging their sons he tried to picture Gabriel hugging him. The closest they'd come was on Tom's first day in Trinity when his father had put his arm on his shoulders and said, 'You have four years to become a man. You need to grow up, son, come out of here with a good degree and don't let the family name down.'

That was it. That was as warm and fuzzy as Gabriel Harrington-Black ever got. Tom knew it was partly because his heart had broken when his wife died. Everyone said she had been Gabriel's true love. Tom had been ten months old at the time so he had no recollection of her. On the rare moments he allowed himself to think about his mother, it made him desperately sad.

But Lucy hugged him all the time and told him she was proud of him and that he was amazing to be so 'normal' despite having no mum and a distant father. She made Tom feel like he wasn't a failure, like he mattered, and he couldn't get enough of it. It had only been five months but he was falling for Lucy, falling fast and hard.

No, it would be okay. He'd ask for the money tonight, when he met Gabriel for dinner, and he'd get it and give it to Lucy and they'd go to England and come back and be normal again. It would be okay. It would all work out. It had to.

Tom watched his father enter the restaurant. Gabriel stood at the entrance as the manager rushed over to welcome him. He handed him his cashmere coat and looked around. Spotting Tom at their usual table, he nodded in his direction. As he made his way towards his son several people greeted him. Gabriel's booming voice echoed around the room.

'Yes, tough case, but he got what he deserved . . . Hello, good to see you still have an appetite after your client went down . . . I might join you for a cognac later, I'm meeting my son, he's in Trinity studying law, chip off the old block . . .'

Tom cringed as his father strutted about the place as if he owned it. He had not inherited Gabriel's supreme confidence. He braced himself for what was to come. Gabriel didn't like his son to overspend his allowance, and Tom knew he was not going to like being asked for more money.

Gabriel shook Tom's hand and sat down opposite him. Tom had made sure to sit with his back to the room so Gabriel could see who was in the restaurant. His father liked to see and be seen.

'Well, Tom, how are things?'

'Good, thanks.'

'Studying hard, I hope.'

'Yes.'

'Glad to hear it. I expect much better results this year. No son of mine is going to leave Trinity with anything less than a two-one degree. Of course I'd like to see you get a first, as I did, but I doubt that's going to happen.'

Tom said nothing.

Gabriel waved the waiter over. 'I'll have the sirloin steak, make sure the steak is bloody. I certainly don't want it overcooked but neither do I want it blue. My son will have the same, and we'll have a bottle of the Barolo.'

The Barolo was seventy pounds. Tom needed four hundred for the abortion. Lucy had paid for the flights and a cheap hotel for one night. He tried to build up the courage to ask for the money. When the Barolo was poured, he gulped a glass.

'Good Lord, Tom! An expensive red wine is to be savoured, not thrown back like beer.' Gabriel swirled his wine in his glass. 'You're becoming feral since you moved into rooms. Is that boy you're sharing with a bad influence?'

'Killian is great.'

'Mmm.' Gabriel wrinkled his nose. 'I would have preferred you to be with one of your St Jude's pals.'

'Killian's a good roommate, Dad. I have enough friends from St Jude's. I think it's important to make new ones too.'

'Of course it is, as long as they're the right sort. You want to befriend the people who will be the influencers of the future. I met Daniel Johnson when I was a student in Trinity. He went on to be the youngest man to become a Supreme Court judge. These are the people you should be palling about with. Not some fellow called Killian from Limerick who rows and studies sociology. What in God's name is he going to do with that degree? Utter nonsense.'

Although Tom disagreed with his father, he certainly wasn't

going to get into an argument about the merits of sociology. Besides, Gabriel only respected people who studied law, medicine or accounting. Anything else was 'utter rubbish'.

Gabriel lifted his steak knife and cut through the juicy meat. Tom watched as the blood oozed onto the plate. He felt sick. He had to say something about the money.

'You all right, Tom?' his father asked. 'You look a bit peaky. A good steak should sort you out. Eat up.'

Tom put a piece into his mouth and tried to swallow it, but his mouth was dry. He had a large sip of Barolo to wash it down, then took the plunge. 'Actually, Dad, I need to ask a favour.'

'Go on.' Gabriel sat back. He was looking directly at Tom.

'Well, the thing is, there's this trip coming up, you know a kind of class-bonding thing, and I need some money for it.'

'I give you a generous monthly allowance.'

'Yes, I know. I'm just a bit short as it's almost the end of the month.'

Gabriel shrugged. 'So wait six days and pay for it when your February allowance goes through.'

Tom cleared his throat. 'I have to pay for it tomorrow. It's the closing date.'

'Where exactly are you going?'

'West. Connemara. One of those adventure-type weekends.'

'With your law class?'

'Yes.'

'How much is it?'

Tom felt a drip of sweat run down his back. How was he going to convince his father that a weekend in Connemara cost four hundred pounds?

'Four hundred.'

Gabriel put down his wine glass. 'Four hundred pounds to go to Connemara for two days?'

'Yeah.' Tom busied himself cutting his steak and avoiding his father's razor-like stare. 'It's some fancy new place. They have all new state-of-the-art equipment, so it's a bit pricey.'

Gabriel nodded. 'I see.'

'Yeah, so I know it's a lot to ask, but I'll pay you back obviously. In fact, you can deduct it from my allowance next month.'

'That would leave you with fifty pounds to live on for a month.'

'I can manage on beans and toast. It'll do me good.' Tom patted his stomach.

'You need to eat more, not less. Are all of the class going?'

Tom swallowed a piece of steak. 'Almost.'

Gabriel raised his eyebrows. 'I find it difficult to believe that so many students would be willing to pay such an extortionate amount of money to go on a trip.'

Tom shrugged. 'Yeah, well, it's supposed to be awesome, so . . .'

Gabriel placed his elbows on the table and leant forward. He was giving Tom 'the stare', as if he was looking into his son's soul. Tom shifted in his seat. He thought guilt must be written all over his face.

'Tom, I was a barrister for over thirty years before becoming a judge and I can tell when someone is lying even before they've lied, just by their body language. So why don't you stop this farcical charade and tell me what the money is really for?'

Tom stopped breathing. Oh, God, what was he going to say? If he made up another lie, his father would know.

'Whatever it is, Tom, I would appreciate it if you did not lie to me. I find it extremely irritating. Be a man. Tell the truth. What is the money for?'

Tom held up his hands. 'Please don't freak out. I'm really

sorry, but I've got a girl pregnant and I need it for an abortion.'

Gabriel cursed under his breath. Leaning right across the table, he hissed, 'Are you sure it's yours?'

'Yes, absolutely. God, of course. Lucy is my girlfriend. We've been together five months. She's amazing, you'd love her. She came first in our class last year. She's very smart and really nice too.'

'Well, she can't be that intelligent if she got herself pregnant, now can she?'

'It was my fault, really.'

Gabriel inhaled deeply. 'You stupid fool.'

'I know. I'm sorry.' Tom felt his voice shaking. He had to keep it together – his father hated when he got emotional.

'I can't believe you've got yourself into this mess. Did I not tell you after your embarrassing exam results last year to focus on books and not skirts?'

'Yes. I'm sorry.'

'Who is this girl? A St Jude's girl? Do I know her father?'

Tom shook his head. 'You don't know her family or anything. Her dad owns a shop on Violet Road.'

'Christ, Tom.' Gabriel looked disgusted. 'Where is she going for the termination?'

'Liverpool. Lucy set it all up. It's cheaper than London.'

'So the shopkeeper's daughter is having a cheap abortion in Liverpool.'

'Yes.'

'I don't think so,' Gabriel hissed. 'Are you really that stupid? If anything goes wrong with this termination, it will come back to you and then me. If it's not properly performed she could die, get an infection or be barren for life. I'm not having some slut calling to my door demanding compensation for a botched abortion. Christ, Tom, use that bloody brain of yours. This has to be done properly. There is no way in hell she's having it done cheaply in some back-alley clinic. I'll find one with reputable doctors and organize it properly. You will not be going with her. From now on you will have no further contact with her. Do you understand?'

'What? I can't do that! I have to go with her! It's my fault, too. And I promised I'd be there for her.'

Gabriel grabbed Tom's arm. He held it in a vice-like grip. Tom wanted to pull away, but knew he couldn't. He'd never seen his father so angry. 'Listen to me, you idiot. This girl will be looked after by the best medical people, at my expense. Because of me, she won't have any complications or problems. She will have the termination, come back, get on with her life and keep her mouth shut. You will step away and get on with yours. I do not want anyone to know that my son had any involvement in a termination. When you're looking for a job in a top law firm in a crowded market, competing against graduates who are a lot smarter than you, you do not want your employers to know that you're the moron who got some tramp pregnant and was involved in an abortion.'

Tom was able to pull his hand back as Gabriel released his grip. 'Please don't call her a tramp,' he said, his voice shaking. 'Her name is Lucy Murphy. I understand what you're saying and I really appreciate your help, but I can't let Lucy go through this alone. It wouldn't be right. No one needs to know. She'll never tell anyone. She's a lovely person, honestly. You'd like her.'

Gabriel slammed his fist on the table, making the glasses jump. 'Like her? Have you lost your mind? I never want to set eyes on the little tramp. If she'd kept her legs shut, we wouldn't be in this mess.'

'Jesus, Dad, it's my fault too.'

'I am well aware of that, Tom, and you will pay for your

mistake. Your time living on campus is over. You are going to move back home immediately and I will be keeping a very close eye on you for the next year and a half until you graduate with honours.' Gabriel pushed his plate away. 'I've lost my appetite.'

Tom had to try once more to make him see sense. He couldn't abandon Lucy. She'd be terrified going to England on her own.

'Please, I'll do everything you ask, but I have to insist that I go with Lucy. I won't leave her on her own.'

Gabriel threw two hundred pounds onto the table and stood up. 'Listen to me very carefully, Tom. You will not be going anywhere with this girl. I will arrange for her to have the best care. If you attempt to go with her, I will cut you off financially and never speak to you again. I am trying to protect you and do what's best for the girl. Do not cross me on this, Tom. You've got yourself into an unholy mess and you're lucky to have me to get you out of it. One day you might even have the grace to thank me. Now, be back home with all of your things within the hour.' Gabriel strode out of the restaurant, leaving Tom open-mouthed.

Tom collected his coat and headed back to his rooms to pack. He'd have to call Lucy and tell her the new plan. He'd try to make it sound like a good thing – the best clinic, proper medical care and all that. He'd leave the part where he had to tell her she was going alone until the end.

3

Lucy woke to the sound of her sister Jenny shouting: 'It's a bloody house party, Dad, not an underground rave. You're going to make me a social outcast. I'll end up living with you for the rest of my life. I'll be a shrivelled-up old spinster sitting in the corner watching TV with you and Mum.'

'Your Christmas report was a feckin' disgrace, so you're not going to any parties and that's the end of it,' Billy roared.

Lucy heard a door slam and heavy footsteps on the stairs. Her bedroom door was flung open and Jenny threw herself onto the bed. 'I hate my life and I hate you.'

'Gee, thanks, what did I do?' Lucy asked.

Jenny sat up. 'You were a bloody A student, that's what. Why couldn't you have been thick and got rubbish results in your exams? It would have made life a lot easier for me. But you had to go and be a bloody genius and get into law and now Mum and Dad expect me to go to college too.'

Lucy snorted. 'I'm hardly a genius – I just work hard. To be fair, Jenny, your report was pretty bad and it wasn't just the exam results. Almost all the teachers said you weren't making much of an effort.'

'Except art, where I got an A. Does anyone ever remember that? All Dad says is "Where the hell will drawing get you?" It's so bloody annoying. I want to be a make-up artist, always have and always will, and nothing is going to change my mind.'

'Fine. You can do that when you leave school, but in the meantime try a bit harder in the other subjects too.'

Jenny rolled over and put one of Lucy's cushions over her head. 'They're all so boring. Who cares about the stupid Tudors and fat, ugly King Henry the Eighth and his nine million wives? How can knowing about that help me in life? Seriously, how?'

Lucy sat up and leant over to sip some water from the bottle beside her bed. She tried not to retch. 'Look, it doesn't matter what you think, you have to go to school and learn. You only have two years left and then you're free. Just try a bit harder.'

Jenny glared at her sister. Lucy knew she was thinking it was easy for her to say. Lucy liked studying. She always had her head stuck in a book. Even that time they went on holidays in France to the camping site. The photos showed Jenny whizzing down the slide into the swimming pool while she sat under a tree reading. 'I really hate it, Lucy. It all seems so pointless. I just want to get the hell out of this stupid place and do what I want and see the world and be a massively successful make-up artist and work on movies and live in LA with a swimming pool in my garden.'

'You can make the next two years easy or difficult. If Mum and Dad see you're trying, they'll get off your back and let you go to parties.'

Jenny punched the cushion. 'I really want to go. Jeff Long is going to be there and I know he fancies me, but if I'm not there, Louise might hop on him. Will you talk to Mum and Dad – *pleeeeease*, Lucy? If you tell them they should let me go, they'll probably agree. Everything you say is like gold to them. Lucy the law goddess.'

Lucy looked away. Goddess, my arse. If her sister only knew the mess she was in. Lucy the genius was up the duff. 'I'll have a go,' she said, with a sigh, 'but I'm not promising anything.' She got up and pulled a backpack from under her bed.

'Are you packing for your weekend with Tom?' Jenny asked.

Lucy tried to smile. She'd told so many lies in the last few weeks her head was spinning. 'Yes, and not a word to Mum and Dad. I told them I was going away with a few girlfriends from college.'

Jenny shrugged. 'If you persuade them to let me go to the party, my lips will be sealed.'

'I'll do my best,' Lucy said, as she packed a tracksuit and hoodie into her bag.

'Jeez, aren't you going to pack some sexy clothes for your dirty weekend? A tracksuit? Seriously? Are you trying to scare him off? I thought you were mad about him,' Jenny said.

Lucy paused. She so badly wanted to tell Jenny, but she knew her sister wouldn't be able to hide it. Jenny wore her emotions on her sleeve. Besides, she was only sixteen and Lucy didn't want her to know what an idiot her big sister was.

'Is he really gorgeous?' Jenny asked.

Lucy smiled. 'Yes, he really is.'

'Lucky you. I want to have sex with a hot boy.'

'Don't be ridiculous, you're barely sixteen. Seriously, Jenny, don't do anything stupid.' Her sister was so impulsive and at times reckless that she might end up pregnant too. 'Do not have sex,' she snapped.

'Okay, keep your hair on. God, you're so grumpy, these days. I thought Tom had dumped you. What's going on? Is everything really all right?'

Lucy had to try to behave normally and hide her fear. She didn't want her family to know anything. She had to protect them. 'Yes, it's fine. I just want you to be careful, that's all.'

Jenny twirled her long, highlighted hair. 'Well, it's a bit difficult to have sex when your parents lock you up.'

Lucy said nothing. She thought Jenny was hard on their parents. All they wanted was the best for their kids. Her dad

and mum worked long hours in the shop and had sent them to a good local school and paid for piano lessons and tennis classes and dance classes for the girls. All they expected in return was for their daughters to work hard and not mess up. Lucy didn't think it was much to ask, yet she had messed up. She had made a huge mistake and she had to fix it. She would not let her parents down, not after all they had sacrificed to give her a wonderful life.

Jenny sighed. 'You're no fun, these days. I'm going to listen to my new Shania Twain CD.' As she flounced out of the door she said, 'If I was going on a dirty weekend with my gorgeous boyfriend, I'd be in a really good mood, not a grump.'

Lucy continued to pack. What did you need for an abortion? She presumed comfortable clothes and a warm coat. She was worried about everything. Most of all Tom.

His dad had basically locked him up since he'd asked him for the money for the abortion. He knew his schedule and demanded that Tom come straight home after his lectures. He was like a tyrant and Tom seemed to be terrified of him. Whenever Lucy called him at home, the answering machine switched on. The only time she'd seen him in the last two weeks was in college, but it was difficult to talk with everyone around, and when they did sneak away for coffee, Tom seemed distant and distracted.

He'd barely been able to look her in the eye for the last week. Lucy kept trying to reassure him and tell him everything would be okay. But then yesterday Tom had got really emotional and said he was afraid things wouldn't work out: Lucy had no idea what his father was like and how much pressure he was putting on him.

'Pressure to do what?' Lucy had asked. 'I'm having an abortion, what more does he want?'

Tom bit his lip. 'He's just a nightmare.'

'We'll pay him back the money and then he can't hold any of this over you,' Lucy said.

Tom reached out and took her hand. 'I just want you to know that I love you and I'm sorry about all this mess.'

Lucy squeezed his hand. He loved her! The words she'd been waiting to hear. Her heart soared. Tom loved her. It was all going to be okay. 'I love you too. We'll be fine. This will all be over soon.'

She was due to meet Tom that afternoon to get all the information from him. If everything was in place, they'd go as quickly as possible, which was why she wanted to be packed and ready. Apparently his father had organized everything and booked them flights and a top clinic in London. Lucy was relieved that she would be in good hands. She'd been terrified of having a cheap abortion.

She finished packing and went downstairs to get something to eat, hoping she wouldn't throw it up.

In the kitchen, her dad was humming one of his olde-worlde Irish tunes while he cooked. The door from the kitchen to the shop was open. Lucy hated it left open. If anyone came into the shop and walked up to the counter, they could see into the kitchen and into their private life.

It was bad enough having the family business attached to the house so you never got away from it, but letting people snoop into your kitchen – her mum, Jenny and Lucy all hated it. Billy told them they were silly and that it was a very practical way for him to be able to slip out of the shop and make himself food or coffee without missing any customers.

Billy turned when he heard Lucy come in. 'Thank God it's you and not that sister of yours. She's in big trouble. I'm telling you, no daughter of mine is going to waste a good education. I'd have killed to go to a decent school. And I wouldn't mind but she has you as an example, her own sister in third-year law in Trinity and top of the class. How can she not want to follow that?'

Lucy forced a smile. If Billy ever found out that his precious daughter was a stupid idiot who had got herself pregnant, he'd die of disappointment. Every time Lucy looked at her father, she knew she was making the right decision. Her mum would support her, no matter what, but Billy was so proud of having a daughter in college and doing law that he almost burst every time he told someone.

She hated lying to them and keeping secrets. She'd never had to before. She had always had a brilliant relationship with her parents, which was why she found Tom and Gabriel's so odd and sad. Her parents had always supported her and cheered her on. Granted she'd been an A student who'd never given them anything to worry about . . . until now.

She couldn't wait for the abortion to be over. She'd bury the secret deep inside and forget it ever happened. Lucy was not going to let this bump in the road ruin her plan to graduate first in her class and work for the top law firm in Ireland. She planned to be a partner by the time she was thirty. She had it all mapped out and secretly she hoped that maybe Tom would be by her side in work and life.

Lucy poured herself a glass of orange juice. 'Me and Jenny are different, Dad. She's not as into studying as I was. Maybe you're putting a bit too much pressure on her.'

'Pressure?' Billy waved a wooden spoon in the air. 'She's lazy, that's what she is, and I won't have it. Now, enough about her, it's bad for my blood pressure. What do you fancy for breakfast? I'm making scrambled egg.'

Lucy felt bile rise in her throat. 'I'm actually not that hungry. I think I'll just have toast. Where's Mum?'

'She's in the shop.'

Billy spooned some of his egg onto a plate and sat down opposite Lucy. 'So you're off on a class trip for a few days tomorrow?'

Lucy nodded, keeping her head down so as not to be caught blushing. She'd always been a terrible liar. Jenny was a lot smoother at it. 'I'm heading early in the morning and I'll be back on Sunday night.'

'Is it all people from your law class?'

'Yes.'

'Isn't it great you've made such good friends? Is that fella you're seeing going?'

'No,' Lucy lied. 'Just girls.'

'Good. I wouldn't want some fella trying to take advantage of you. You're a lovely girl with a brilliant future ahead of you. Don't get distracted by fellas or any of that other stuff,' Billy said.

Lucy nibbled her toast, saying nothing.

'Mind you, it's not you I've to worry about, it's that lunatic sister of yours. She needs to be reined in. She's kicking up a storm about some party she wants to go to.'

Lucy looked up. 'Maybe you should let her go, Dad.'

'No feckin' way. Her report was a disaster.'

'I know, but locking her up isn't the answer. She'll make your life hell. Why don't you use it as a bargaining tool? Tell her she can go if she studies for three hours every day of the last week of the holidays.'

Billy sat back and pointed his fork at his daughter. 'Now that is a brilliant idea. You're some girl, Lucy, honestly, not only smart but sensible too.'

'Aw, shucks! Well, if you say so . . .' She grinned. It was nice to have her dad's praise. She felt so bad about her mistake, and she was so worried about Tom and the abortion that it was soothing to let her father's love wash over her.

Tina walked through from the shop. 'Billy, Mr O'Brien is here with the deliveries. He needs a hand.'

'That fella's as useless as the day he was born,' Billy muttered, but stood up and went through to the shop.

Tina closed the door and sat down at the kitchen table. She picked up Billy's half-drunk coffee and finished it. 'Well, pet,' she said, looking at Lucy. 'What's going on with you?'

Lucy reddened. 'Nothing.'

Her mother sighed. 'Lucy, I know you. Something's been bothering you for a while. Talk to me.'

Lucy felt herself crack. She longed to throw herself into her mother's arms and tell her everything. She dug her nails into her thighs to stop herself doing just that. She would not burden her mother with this when there was no need. In three days she'd be back to her old self. She lied, but kept it close to the truth. 'I'm fine, Mum. I just . . . I've just had a problem with Tom, but it's sorted, honestly. It's all going to be fine.'

'All right, Lucy, but I want you to know that, whatever it is, I'm here for you. I love you and I'll always support you, no matter what. Okay?'

Lucy nodded, not trusting herself to speak. She jumped up to put her glass and plate into the dishwasher, then scurried out of the room. If she didn't get out of there, her mother's kindness would break her wide open.

4

Lucy glanced at her watch. It was ten past four. Where was Tom? From her seat in the window of the Little Spoon she could see people rushing up and down the road, dodging the winter rain.

A shadow fell across the table. She looked up. It was Damien, her classmate from law. 'Hi,' she said.

'Hi.' He took off his coat and sat down beside her at the small table. 'Can I get you another coffee?'

'Uhm, well, I'm actually meeting Tom now so . . .' Lucy didn't want to be rude, but she needed him to leave so she and Tom were free to talk. Besides, Tom didn't like Damien. He thought he was a boring geek, as did most of the class. Damien was super-bright: he'd come second in the class, just behind Lucy, last year. He'd always been really nice to her. Tom said it was because he had a crush on her and she kind of knew that was true, but she didn't find him attractive. He wasn't good-looking but neither was he bad-looking, he just wasn't her type. He was too intense.

Damien shook his head. 'Tom can't make it. He asked me to give you this.'

Lucy frowned. What was he talking about? 'What?'

'I'm as surprised as you. Tom barely speaks to me. But I found it pushed under the door of my rooms when I woke up this morning and figured it was important to you. Look.' Damien handed her a note in Tom's handwriting:

Damien, I'm due to meet Lucy at 4 p.m. in the Little Spoon. Can you please go and give her this note? It's REALLY important. I can't make it because of my dad. Long story. But can you please make sure she gets this note? She'll be waiting for me. Thanks, Tom.

Lucy took the envelope from Damien's outstretched hand. She opened it and pulled out a note.

Don't hate me, Dad has locked me up. I can't go with you, he won't let me. He promised me it's all organized – a driver will pick you up in London and drive you to the clinic. You'll be staying overnight in a hotel and then a car will pick you up and drive you back to the airport. I'm so sorry, Lucy. I've spent two days fighting with him but he won't let me go. I'll be waiting for you at the airport when you get back and I'll be by your side after, I promise. I just can't go to London. I'm so sorry. I love you. Tom

A sob escaped her. Damien reached over. 'Hey, are you okay? Is it bad news? What did he say?'

Lucy bit down hard on her lip. How could she explain to Damien that her boyfriend had just left her to abort their baby alone? How could he do that? How could he let his father walk all over him?

'Lucy, talk to me. Please.'

Lucy found her voice. She needed to take control of the situation. It wouldn't help for Damien to find out. 'It's just a little issue Tom and I are having. It'll sort itself out.'

Damien looked worried. 'Lucy, you've gone green. You're the colour of an unripe banana. It's clearly not a small issue. What's going on? Maybe I can help. Is he treating you badly? You deserve to be with someone who appreciates you, not upsets you.'

Lucy put the envelope into her handbag. 'It's fine, Damien.

Please just forget about it. Thanks for bringing me the note. It was important.'

'Let me take you home at least. You really don't look well.'

Lucy fought back tears. 'I really appreciate it, but honestly, I'm fine. I have to go.' She pulled on her coat and turned to leave, then turned back to him and said, 'Please don't tell anyone about this. It's kind of private. Tom shouldn't have got you involved.'

Damien shrugged. 'You're the only person in the class I really talk to, so your secret is safe with me.'

Lucy smiled, then bent down and kissed his cheek. 'Thanks, Damien. You're a great friend.'

Gabriel stood outside the grotty little coffee shop and peered in. He saw a young girl who fitted Tom's description of Lucy. She was kissing another boy – clearly a girl who got about the place.

Sighing, he threw open the door and strode over to the table. She was pretty enough, long brown hair, petite, but nothing special. Tom was an idiot. Evidently she saw his son as her ticket to the good life. Over my dead body, thought Gabriel.

'Are you Lucy Murphy?'

Lucy and Damien looked around. A tall, imposing man with grey hair and an expensive navy coat stood before them.

'Yes, I'm Lucy.'

She had rather striking brown eyes. They made her jump from average-looking to very pretty. That was what Tom must have fallen for, Gabriel thought.

'I'm Tom's father.'

'You're Gabriel Harrington-Black.' Damien flushed. 'It's an honour to meet you, sir. I'm a fellow law student of Tom and Lucy's. Damien, Damien O'Neill. Delighted to meet you. I'm a huge fan, the sentencing of –'

Gabriel held up his hand. 'Could you leave us, please? I have a matter I need to discuss with Miss Murphy.'

'Right, of course, I'll be off.' Damien left quickly, looking utterly star-struck.

Gabriel brushed Damien's seat and sat down. 'Is he another of your boyfriends?'

Lucy felt herself blushing bright red. 'Oh, gosh, no. He's just a classmate. It's very nice to meet you, sir.' She proffered her hand, which Gabriel took and crushed in his own.

Lucy pulled hers back. God, this was so awkward. She had no idea what to say.

'I presume you know why I'm here?' he asked.

'Not really. I was expecting Tom.'

'Yes, well, Tom won't be coming. This is a most unfortunate business.'

'I'm really sorry. It just . . . Well, we were careless that one time and I'm just sorry.'

He glared at her. 'It's a little late for apologies.' Fishing in the inside pocket of his coat, he produced a thick envelope. He handed it to Lucy. 'Inside this envelope you will find a return ticket to London and an appointment at an excellent clinic.'

'Thank you. I really appreciate you helping us out, it's very decent of you. Tom and I are so grateful.'

Gabriel's lip curled into what was supposed to look like a smile. 'Miss Murphy, people make mistakes and get themselves into hot spots. But there is always a solution. The key here is to have this mess sorted out quickly and discreetly so you can put it all behind you. Go to London, terminate this pregnancy and never speak of it again. Move on with your life. I hear you're a bright girl, and no girl with an ounce of a brain wants to have a child while she's in university. I also think you and Tom should stay away from each other, let things cool down a bit. I understand you're in the same class, but in a group of eighty students I'm sure you can avoid him easily enough.'

Lucy felt as if she'd been slapped. 'What . . . what do you mean? Tom's my boyfriend . . . We're a couple.'

Gabriel pursed his lips. 'I strongly recommend a cooling-off period. Give each other some space to move on from this. Look, Tom is easily distracted and I didn't spend a fortune on my son's private education to have him do badly in university. Tom is a boy who needs to focus on his books to do well. I've told him that I want him to concentrate on one thing only this year, getting good results, which means he won't have time for relationships.'

'I won't distract him, I promise. In fact, I'll help him study. I love Tom and –'

Gabriel's hand curled into a fist on the table. 'Don't be ridiculous. This is a silly college romance that has gone very wrong and caused a lot of trouble. Now be sensible, forget about Tom, let him concentrate on his studies and you concentrate on yours.'

Lucy swallowed hard. She had to make him see that this was love, real love. 'I understand you're upset about the mess we've got ourselves into, but we really do love each other, and I know it may sound silly but it's very real, I promise you.'

Gabriel stared coldly at her. 'I have to get to court. Listen closely so there is no misunderstanding. I'm not asking you to stay away from Tom, I'm ordering you to.' He stood up to leave.

Lucy felt her shame and humiliation turn to anger. 'I'm sorry, but I won't.'

'Excuse me?'

'You heard me. I will not stop seeing Tom. I'm mad about him and he's mad about me.'

'Keep your voice down,' he hissed. 'I have just arranged

for you to have the best medical care available. You should be on your knees thanking me, you ungrateful girl.'

She put the envelope on the table. 'Here, take it,' she said, her voice shaking.

Gabriel picked it up and handed it back to her. She refused it.

'I'm not leaving until you guarantee that you will go through with this termination. I don't want you changing your mind or trying to convince my son that having a child with you is a good idea. No stupid girl with loose morals is going to drag my son down.'

The thought of keeping the baby had never entered Lucy's mind. She couldn't have a baby: she was only twenty-one. She'd have to drop out of college or defer, and all of her goals and plans would be changed.

'I'm waiting.' Gabriel held the envelope out to her.

'No.' Lucy was surprised to hear herself say it, but she suddenly felt filled with conviction.

'No?' Gabriel's face went bright red.

Lucy could see that he was shaken. The thought of her not getting rid of the baby was freaking him out. Good. She wanted to rattle him, the bastard. 'If I decide to change my mind, that's my prerogative.'

Gabriel put the envelope on the table and said very quietly into her ear, 'Do not cross me, or I promise you, you'll regret it for the rest of your life.'

He turned and stalked out of the café, leaving the envelope on the table in front of Lucy.

Lucy felt adrenalin pumping through her veins. She had stood up to him. She had rattled him, too. Good. Let him have a few sleepless nights wondering if she'd had the abortion or not. Of course she was going to have it, but it was nice to see him wrong-footed. What a bully. She felt sorry for

Tom, growing up with him as a father. Although, she thought angrily, that didn't excuse him abandoning her.

The adrenalin soon drained out of her and Lucy felt really alone. Her hands were trembling as she put the envelope into her bag. She wanted to weep. She needed to talk to someone, to process what had just happened. She knew where she had to go.

Lucy hurried past the shop, hoping her father wouldn't see her through the window, and ran up the road to Sarah's house. Her mind was spinning. Tom had said he loved her but he wasn't coming with her. Then again, he had promised to be there for her afterwards. She was feeling so many different emotions and couldn't make sense of anything.

She went to the back door of Sarah's house and found her friend in the kitchen. She could see Sarah's mum through the glass door. She was, as usual, plonked in front of the TV, watching soap operas.

Since Sarah's dad had walked out all those years ago, Mrs Hannigan had become a very bitter woman. Between Sarah's dad and Gabriel, Lucy felt incredibly lucky to have her lovely parents. Billy and Tina were worlds apart from Tom's and Sarah's.

'Oh, my God!' Sarah exclaimed. 'You look awful. What happened?'

'Can we go to your room? I need to talk to you,' Lucy said, fighting back tears.

Sarah ushered her upstairs and locked her bedroom door behind them. 'Okay, tell me what's happened.'

'God, it's a mess.' Lucy collapsed onto the bed, crying. When she'd calmed down enough to talk, she filled Sarah in on the whole encounter.

'*What?*' Sarah was in shock. 'He actually came in and threatened you and basically called you a slut? Oh, my God, what a psycho.'

'It was awful, Sarah. He's so intimidating. I was actually really scared.'

'Yeah, but you stood up to him, which is more than Tom did.'

'I know, but I kind of understand Tom more now. If I'd grown up with Gabriel as a dad, I might not stand up to him. He's a bully to the core. And Tom really did want to come with me.' Lucy wanted to defend him. She wanted to think well of him, although it was hard right now.

'So why doesn't he?' Sarah asked.

'Well, when Tom told his dad, Gabriel totally freaked out and said he'd pay for me to have proper medical care because he wants to make sure I don't die or get an infection, but he ordered Tom to stay at home. He's kind of locked him up since he found out. But Tom said he'd collect me from the airport when I get back.'

Sarah felt her blood boiling. Collect her from the airport? Big bloody deal. Was this guy for real? Sarah looked at Lucy, her lovely friend. Lucy, the strong, brilliant, determined one, the one who never put a foot wrong. The girl everyone in the neighbourhood knew as Lucy Murphy, the straight-A student. The Lucy Sarah was facing now looked shattered, frightened and alone. Sarah wanted to hunt Tom down and kill him.

She had to be honest with her friend. 'Lucy, it's not fair for you to go on your own. It's not right. Tom should be with you.' She thought he was a spineless git for saying he couldn't go. What kind of bullshit excuse was *My dad won't let me*?

Sarah knew that Darren would never let her have an abortion on her own. He'd be there, holding her hand all the way. Darren was her rock. He'd never let her down. Lucy deserved better than this. But Sarah didn't want to upset her friend any more than she already was.

Lucy began to cry again.

'Look, Lucy, if he really can't go, we'll go without him.'

'You'll still come with me?'

'Of course,' Sarah said. 'There's no way on earth I'd let you go through all that by yourself.'

'Thank you so much,' Lucy said, her voice shaky with relief.

'But do you still want to do it? You told Gabriel you weren't going to. Have you changed your mind?'

Lucy shook her head. 'I was just angry with him and wanted to say no to him and piss him off. But I have to do it, Sarah. I mean, it's the only way out, isn't it?'

Sarah said nothing. She watched her friend, trying to gauge her thoughts.

'Yeah,' Lucy said, nodding to herself. 'We'll go and just get it done.'

'All right. So what are the arrangements, then?' Sarah asked.

Lucy picked up her bag and took out Gabriel's envelope. Even looking at it brought back an image of his glowering face and made her feel ill. She opened it and looked at the tickets.

'Flight tomorrow at twelve forty-five,' she said. 'Can you get away without your mum going mad?'

'Yeah, that won't be a problem.'

Lucy looked at the brochure included with the tickets. 'It's a clinic in Marylebone Lane,' she said, reading it. 'Looks really nice. And the hotel is . . .' she pulled out another piece of paper '. . . the Village Hotel. Looks very nice too.' Her eyes welled. 'I guess if I'm going to do it, I might as well do it in style. God, Sarah, I can't believe this is happening.' She broke down in tears.

Sarah pulled her into a hug, holding her tightly. If she ever she got her hands on that Tom, she'd tell him exactly what she thought of him.

5

Lucy tiptoed down the stairs, not wanting to meet anyone before she left. She didn't want to have to lie any more, she just wanted to go.

The door from the shop opened and Tina looked into the kitchen. 'You're off then, love?'

Lucy nodded.

Tina walked over and gave her a hug. Then she looked directly into Lucy's eyes. 'Okay, pet, but please remember, if you change your mind and decide that this class trip isn't for you, I'm here for you. Don't do anything that feels wrong. All right?'

Lucy didn't trust herself to speak. Did Tina know? Had she guessed? 'I won't be gone long, Mum,' she said. 'I'll be home on Sunday.'

'I'll be waiting for you.'

Lucy kissed her mother's cheek. She felt like her heart was breaking. She had never, ever thought things would turn out like this. It was like a nightmare, but soon she'd wake up and it would all be over.

The two young women sat in the busy airport bar, nursing coffees.

'I didn't know what to pack for an abortion trip,' Sarah said. 'I kept packing and unpacking. Eventually I just put in jeans and a sweatshirt. I doubt we'll be going clubbing.'

'Clubbing?' Lucy looked at her friend and a bubble rose in her throat. She began to laugh. It was slightly hysterical and exploded out of her chest like a blessed relief from all of her worry. Sarah joined in and they were soon creased over.

Lucy wiped tears from her eyes. 'God, Sarah, I needed that.'

'Me too. I was so scared this morning that my mum, who barely notices I exist, actually asked me if I was all right.'

'I think my mum knows,' Lucy admitted. 'She said to me this morning, "If you change your mind, I'm here for you." She knows I'm not going on a class trip.'

'Did it make you reconsider?' Sarah asked.

'God, no. There is no way I can have a baby. I need to finish my degree and get into a top firm, which means signing over my life to them. You have to be a slave to your job to climb the ladder.'

'I know, but you also need to be one hundred per cent sure before you go ahead. I mean, if you have any doubts, we can postpone,' Sarah said.

Lucy shook her head. 'I still want to go ahead. It's the only way to sort out this mess. But it's weird – since Gabriel attacked me yesterday I feel really protective of the baby. It's as if I have to look after it and keep it safe from that horrible man. I know it sounds mad, but it's . . . It's a strange feeling.'

'Lucy, you could change your mind and keep the baby,' Sarah said. 'It would be complicated and difficult, and you'd have to take a year out of college, but you could go back after, finish your degree and still have a great career. Lots of women do it and you have two great parents who love you and will support you. I'll help out too.'

Lucy bit her lip. 'No way. I can't do it to my dad. He'd die of shame and disappointment. He's worked so hard to give us a good life and he's so proud that I'm studying law in Trinity and coming top of the class. It would just kill him. I know it would.'

Sarah took her friend's hand in hers. 'Billy loves you. No matter what you do, that will never change. Yes, he probably will be upset and disappointed at first, but if you tell him you have a plan to defer for a year and then go back, and if you show him you're determined to do it all, he'll be okay. He adores you, Lucy. You can do no wrong in his eyes. You're really lucky.'

'But that's just it, Sarah, I know he has me on a pedestal and I can't disappoint him. It's not fair.'

'For goodness' sake, Lucy, your dad grew up in the inner city with nothing. Most of his old friends are in prison or selling drugs – a baby isn't going to kill him. You have two great parents, and even if they are upset, they'll get over it – they'll adore the baby and help you. If anyone can do it all, you can. You're the most focused and hard-working person I know. You can make this work.'

'What about Tom?' Lucy said.

What about Tom? Sarah thought grumpily. Where was he now? Hiding under his bed, the coward. 'Well, that's something I can't answer. How do you think he'd react if you told him you'd decided to keep the baby?'

Lucy paused. This conversation was ridiculous. She couldn't have a baby. She was twenty-one. She had her whole life mapped out. Besides, Tom would . . . Well, Tom would probably . . . What would Tom do? He'd said he loved her, he'd said he'd be there for her after the abortion, so would he be there for her if she had the baby? They'd never even discussed the possibility. Lucy had just told him she was getting rid of it and that was that. But he'd never argued against it. He'd just gone along and seemed happy enough.

But he loved her and she loved him, and it would be their baby. It could bring them closer. Maybe it would finally make him stand up to his father. If she deferred for a year, Tom could continue and graduate next year as planned. It wouldn't have to affect his life too much.

'I think Tom might be okay about it,' Lucy said. 'But it's ridiculous. I mean, where would we live? How would we support a baby?'

'Well, you could stay with your mum and dad while you were pregnant and finish this year in college, and Tom could get a job in the summer and make enough money to rent a little flat or move in with you when the baby is born or something.'

Lucy tried to imagine Tom living in her parents' house. It would be way too weird. They'd have to find a flat. But she could finish this third year of her law degree and she'd only have to defer her final year for twelve months. She could study while she was looking after the baby and get ahead on her year off so she'd do extra well in her exams and ace them.

Sarah bent towards her. 'I can see your mind whizzing. What are you thinking?'

Lucy felt lighter, less weighed down. She felt hopeful for the first time in weeks. Maybe Sarah was right. Maybe she should think about it. She could always go to the clinic next week. She needed to talk to Tom. She needed to talk to her parents. She needed to be honest and stop lying and keeping secrets. Maybe she could be a mum and a successful lawyer. Why not? Look at Hillary Clinton: she'd had a baby and was a super-successful lawyer.

Sarah poked her. 'Talk to me, what's going on in that head of yours?'

Lucy turned to her. 'I still think the abortion is the best solution, but I'm not sure any more. Maybe I could do it, Sarah. I know you think Tom's a shit for not coming with me, but he does love me and I never gave him the chance to discuss keeping the baby. I love him and he loves me, and it would only be a year for me to take off. I guess maybe it could work out. I don't know. My head is spinning.'

They heard an announcement on the Tannoy that the flight to London was now boarding. The two girls looked at each other.

Sarah stood up and held out her hand. 'Come on, let's get you home. Call Tom, talk to him, then talk to your parents. You'll figure it all out, but it's better to be honest than sneaking around behind everyone's backs. Whatever you decide, I'm with you. If you decide you do want to go to England, I'll go with you. All the way.'

Lucy took Sarah's hand and stood up. 'Okay,' she said. 'This might be crazy, but it kind of feels right.' She glanced at the boarding gate. 'Let's get out of here.'

6

Lucy went back to Sarah's house and tried to phone Tom. It rang out. The answering machine must have been full. She decided to leave her bag at Sarah's and head into college to see if she could find him. She needed to talk to him, to see what he thought of her plan B. Would he tell her she was insane? Her heart was fluttering with anxiety.

Lucy trudged around Trinity for hours. She went to all the libraries, communal spaces, coffee shops, pubs and restaurants in the area, but there was no sign of Tom. She bumped into several of his friends, but no one had seen or heard from him in days.

After hours of walking she was exhausted. She had barely slept the night before. She felt like crying. Where the hell was Tom? She needed to talk to him. She tried calling his house phone at least twenty times, but it rang out every time. Damn it.

She was worn out and emotionally drained. She wanted desperately to talk to Tom but she'd have to wait until she saw him at lectures on Monday morning. Could she wait that long to tell her parents, though? She'd have to hide at Sarah's until Sunday night and pretend she was on her class trip. Or . . . she could go home now and just tell the truth. Lucy decided that she couldn't spend the weekend hiding and lying. She just couldn't do it any more. She needed to go home.

Billy looked up from his newspaper when the shop bell rang, expecting a customer. He was very surprised to see his daughter. 'Did something happen? Why are you back so early?'

Lucy had held it together until then, but when she saw her father's loving face, she put her bag on the floor, covered her face with her hands and began to sob.

Billy rushed around the counter to her. 'What's wrong, pet? You poor thing, what happened? Come on into the house and I'll make you a nice cup of tea.'

Billy opened the door to the kitchen and called Tina. 'Lucy's back, and she's fierce upset.' He sat her in a chair and handed her one of the big handkerchiefs he always carried in his pocket. 'What went wrong, love?'

Tina came in. When she saw Lucy, she stopped. Her eyes filled with tears. 'You came back,' she said.

Lucy nodded. Tina went over and pulled her daughter into her arms. Lucy buried her head in her mother's shoulder and cried her eyes out. All of her worries and fears flooded out.

Billy turned around with the tea. 'What's going on? Jesus, Lucy, are you all right? Was it some boy? Did that Tom fella break up with you?'

Tina shushed him with a look. She rubbed Lucy's back. 'We're here, love. We're here. When you're ready, just tell us everything.'

Tina told Billy to put a 'Back in 30 minutes' sign up on the shop door. By the time he returned, Lucy had finally stopped crying and was sipping her tea.

Billy sat down. 'Would someone like to tell me what the hell is going on?'

Under the table, Tina held her hand and squeezed it.

'I'm really sorry to let you both down but . . . I've got myself into a bit of trouble . . . I messed up . . . I made a stupid mistake . . . and –'

'What? Jesus, spit it out before I have a heart attack,' Billy urged her.

'I'm pregnant.'

'Oh, Jesus.' Billy's hand flew to his mouth. 'Oh, Lucy, no.'

Lucy began to cry again when she saw her father's crest-fallen face.

'It's okay, Lucy, we're here for you.' Tina glared at Billy.

'I'm so sorry, Dad. I know I've let you down badly.'

'Have you considered your options?' Tina asked her.

Lucy nodded. 'I wasn't going on a class trip this weekend. I was supposed to be flying to London to have an abortion, but I just couldn't do it. I'm not saying I won't, I'm just not sure. I mean, I guess I could defer for a year if I decided to keep the baby.'

'Hold on.' Billy thumped the table. 'Where is this fellow, whatshisname – Tom? Huh? Why isn't he here? Where does he stand in all this? He got you into this mess.'

Lucy didn't want them to think badly of Tom, but it was tricky to try to defend him. A man like Billy, who had never let anyone push him around, would not understand how Tom couldn't stand up to his father. 'Tom loves me and he said he'll be there for me,' she fudged.

'What really matters,' Tina said, 'is what you want.'

'I'm not sure,' Lucy said.

'But you can't give up everything you've worked so hard to achieve.' Billy fought back tears. 'You're top of the class. You're a genius, you can't go having a baby now. All you ever wanted was to be a lawyer and you're doing so well.'

'Yes, Billy, but if she wants to keep the baby, she could defer for one year, as she said, then go back and finish her degree. It would only be a year out and we can help her and support her with the baby.'

'We run our own business. How can we help raise a child?'

'We'll manage. I can do less hours in the shop and help look after the baby while Lucy studies.' To Lucy, her mother said, 'I'll look after the baby and let you away back to college to finish your degree. If you really want to keep it, that's wonderful. A child is a blessing – look at how much joy you and your sister have given us.'

'Lucy has. Jenny's given me pain in my arse mostly.' Billy sniffed.

'Stop that. Life would be less colourful without Jenny,' Tina said. 'And Lucy doesn't have to give up anything. She might have to defer, but what's a year in a lifetime?'

At that moment Lucy loved her mother more than she'd thought possible.

'I suppose that's true,' Billy admitted. 'It would only be a year and sure that's nothing. The child can be here with us during the day while you're at lectures and . . . Yes, I suppose we could work it out. But where will you live?'

'They can live here until they find their feet,' Tina said firmly.

'With Tom and all?' Billy said.

'Yes, we'll figure it all out,' Tina assured him.

'Well, I want to meet this Tom fella. I want him to come here and talk to us like a man. I want him to look me in the eye and tell me he's going to take care of you and the baby. If he doesn't, I'll hunt him down and wring his neck.'

'Yes, of course. I'll get him to call in,' Lucy said. 'Do you really think I can do it? Keep the baby and be a lawyer too?'

'You can do anything you put your mind to, Lucy,' Tina said.

'It won't be easy, but I promise you this. I will not let you give up your dream. You're going to follow your path, baby or no baby,' Billy said.

'I love you,' Lucy cried, and threw her arms around them.

'You're the best parents in the world. If I can be half the mother to this child, it'll be very lucky.'

Lucy sat on Jenny's bed and watched her sister applying highlighter to her cheekbones.

'Pregnant? You? St Lucy? I still cannot actually believe it. You're supposed to be the intelligent one in the family. If I got up the duff, Mum and Dad probably wouldn't be surprised, but you! No wonder they're walking around like zombies.'

'Stop. I feel bad enough as it is.'

Lucy getting pregnant was a disaster for Jenny. Her parents were already over-protective and barely let her go to any discos or house parties. Now that her saint of a sister had fallen from grace – or, let's be honest, had thrown herself off a cliff – Jenny's life would be hell.

Her parents would never let her out. Every time she left the house they'd be thinking, Is she having sex with a boy? Is she going to come home pregnant like her sister? If Lucy could get pregnant, they would see very little hope for stupid non-academic Jenny. She would probably end up becoming a nun, just to get out of the house, or else she'd stay here, eating chocolate to help with her misery and loneliness, get really fat, watch TV all day and eventually, when she was found dead, three weeks after her actual death, they'd have to take the roof off the house and lift her out with a crane and build one of those oversized coffins to bury her massive body in. People would shake their heads and say, 'She was once a hot blonde with great legs and look at her now.' And it would be Lucy's fault.

Jenny looked at her sister. She wanted to hate her but it was impossible. Poor Lucy was a wreck. Her eyes were red and puffy from crying and she had big black bags under them. She was also as pale as a ghost. 'You look like crap.'

'Gee, thanks.'

'Seriously, though, you need to make an effort. Let me do you up so you look hot when you see Tom in college tomorrow. You don't want him to think you've let yourself go and are one step away from a housecoat and slippers. He might dump you.'

'Tom's not going to dump me. He's promised to stay with me.'

'But are you really going to keep it?' Jenny thought she was mad. If Jenny got pregnant, she'd be over to the UK in a flash. Who the hell wanted a screaming brat ruining their lives? A baby was for ever. You were stuck with it – you couldn't hand it back – and then you'd worry about it for the rest of your life. Look at her mum and dad. They'd thought Lucy was sorted, twenty-one, in college, smart and sensible, and now they were crying about her pregnancy. They were pretending they were fine, for Lucy's sake, but Jenny had seen her mother's red eyes when she'd come into the kitchen that morning and found Billy sobbing into his coffee. They were completely gutted.

Lucy nodded. 'It's weird, but I feel so protective of the baby. It's as if I have to look after it and keep it safe. I know it sounds mad, but it's how I feel, and I think I can work it out. I'll just defer for a year, then go back and finish my degree.'

'Okay, it's your funeral. But I will not be minding your kid. Do not even think about using me as your babysitter. And if Tom does move in – which is, like, so weird – you are not allowed to have sex because the walls are thin and I do not want to have to listen to you two going at it.'

Lucy laughed. 'Let's take one step at a time.'

'Okay, but I'm just saying, straight up, no child-minding and no sex.'

'Thanks for your support, Jen!' Lucy punched her playfully.

Jenny finished doing her face. At least she'd succeeded in making her sister smile. But a baby? She was worried this Tom guy was going to let Lucy down. She had a bad feeling about him, really bad.

7

Gabriel stood outside the corner shop. A sign saying 'Murphy's' hung outside it. He rolled his eyes. Murphy, the commonest name in Ireland. Common name for a common girl.

The street was crammed full of semi-detached houses with small driveways, just about big enough to fit one car. He'd passed a park at the end of the road where a group of children were playing soccer. There seemed to be some sort of football club.

He peered through the window of the shop. It had overstuffed shelves and a huge sweet counter. Gabriel loathed corner shops where fat kids could buy more junk to shove into their faces. A small, bald man was leaning on the counter reading a newspaper. Probably the *Sun* or the *Daily Mail*, he thought.

He saw the door behind the counter open and Lucy came through. The conniving little bitch. Gabriel threw open the shop door and marched in.

'Well, well, well, here you are,' Gabriel said.

Lucy froze.

'Who's this?' Billy asked, looking at Lucy's shocked face.

'He's Tom's father.'

'Well, well, well yourself,' Billy said, as he closed his *Irish Independent* and puffed out his chest.

'Mr Murphy, I presume?' Gabriel asked.

'Yes, and you are?'

'Mr Harrington-Black.'

'Your son not with you, then? We're very keen to meet him.'

'Oh, I have no doubt you are,' Gabriel sneered. 'I need to speak to your daughter.'

'Speak away.' Billy crossed his arms.

'It's a rather delicate matter.'

'Would it have anything to do with your son getting my daughter pregnant?'

Gabriel rested a leather-gloved hand on the countertop. 'I think your daughter had a rather large role to play in her misfortune.'

'Your son needs to grow a backbone, come here and look me in the eye.'

Tina popped her head around the door. 'Lucy, your dinner's ready.'

'Come in, Tina, this is Tom's father. He came to speak to Lucy about the pregnancy.'

Gabriel barely acknowledged her. 'Your daughter has got herself into trouble and claims the child is my son's, although I'm not sure about that. From what I saw in the café the other day, she seems to be a very "friendly" girl. Still, I hate to see a young girl in trouble so I generously offered to help her to deal with the problem. She was due to have a termination yesterday in a top London clinic that I paid for, so you can imagine my surprise when the clinic called to say she never turned up.'

Gabriel tried to keep his voice even, but he was ready to wring the stupid girl's neck. He had sorted everything out and it appeared she hadn't gone through with it. There was no way a common slut was going to drag Tom down with her.

Billy folded his arms across his chest. 'She's changed her mind.'

'There is no changing of minds here. This isn't will-I-have-my-coffee-black-or-with-milk. This is a serious issue that needs to be dealt with quickly and efficiently.'

Tina rested a hand on Lucy's shoulder. 'I know exactly how serious an issue this is,' Tina said calmly, 'and if my daughter has decided that she wants to keep the baby, then that is what she'll do.'

Gabriel swallowed the rage rising in his chest. 'Let's be reasonable here. We both know keeping the baby is a ludicrous idea. You need to make her see sense. She'll ruin her life, her career, everything. She'll be a nothing, one of the thousands of single mothers leeching off the government for benefits.'

Billy leant forward. 'Now why would she be a single mother? Are you suggesting that your son is not going to stand up and be a man? Surely you're not telling me that he is going to leave my daughter alone to raise his child. Because I'm afraid that just won't wash. Your son is going to shoulder his responsibilities, show up every day and be a dad to this child and a supportive partner to my daughter.'

Gabriel stared Billy in the eye and said slowly, 'My son will have nothing to do with your gold-digging, manipulative, scheming daughter.'

Billy's eyes widened. 'What did you say?'

'Don't you think it slightly convenient that your ambitious daughter finds herself pregnant with the son of a Supreme Court judge, and that after pretending to agree to a termination suddenly changes her mind? She clearly thinks she can trap my son and ingratiate herself into my family but, I can assure you, that is never going to happen.'

Billy laughed. 'Do you know what I think? I think you're an arrogant prick. I think your son is a stupid, spineless coward and if you think I would let my beautiful and brilliant daughter near you, ever again, you're the one who is delusional. You know where the door is.'

Gabriel slammed his hand onto the counter. 'I am not leaving without a guarantee that she,' he jabbed a finger at

Lucy, 'is going to terminate this pregnancy and leave my son the hell alone.'

'Well, now, Mr Harrington-Black, you have two choices here. You can take yourself and your disgusting comments and accusations and walk out the door, or I can show you the door. Please believe me when I tell you that, while you might be taller than me, I grew up on the streets and I can beat you into a coma with two punches. And if you ever speak to or even look at my daughter again, I will come after you and kill you. Am I making myself clear?'

'Scum breeds scum,' Gabriel hissed, then turned on his heel and stormed out.

'Oh, my God,' Tina gasped. 'What a horrible man. Well done, Billy, you were brilliant.'

Billy turned to Lucy, who was crying silently. 'I'm telling you now, you are going to have this baby and I'm going to help you in any way I can. If Tom wants to be involved and come and live with us and help you raise the child, he is welcome. But I will never, ever have that bastard come near me or my family again.'

'Is Tom like that too?' Tina asked, her eyes full of concern.

'God, no,' Lucy said. 'He's the opposite, kind and generous and lovely.'

'Thank God for small mercies.' Tina kissed Lucy's forehead.

'Right, I'm closing up early. I need a drink after that.'

'Thanks, Dad.'

'For what?'

'For standing up to him and defending me and being, well, just . . . brilliant.'

Billy pulled her into his arms. 'Let's pray the baby has Murphy genes!'

8

Lucy dressed in the pink jumper Tom had told her he loved on her. What he'd actually said was 'You look beautiful in that jumper.' Whenever she wore it, she felt happy.

Jenny helped her with her make-up. 'Okay, you look good, fresh and healthy, not wrecked and knackered like you did half an hour ago.'

'Thanks, Jenny.'

'No problem, we want you looking nice when you tell him he's about to be a dad. He'll need to fancy you so he doesn't run away.'

'Stop! I'm nervous enough already.'

'He told you he loves you and that he'll stand by you. It'll be fine. Unless underneath all the niceness he has his dad's black soul.'

Lucy slapped her sister's arm. 'He has none of his father's characteristics.'

Jenny grinned. 'I still can't believe Dad threatened to punch him and kill him. It's kind of cool. I wish I'd seen him with his whole Bruce Willis vibe going on.'

'He was really great.'

'If only I'd been there – I'd have told Gabriel to go to hell and back.'

'I've no doubt you would.' Lucy smiled. 'I'd better go or I'll miss my bus. Wish me luck.'

'Good luck, and make sure you snog him before you tell him about the baby thing.'

*

Lucy sat in the Starbucks opposite the university and stirred two spoons of sugar into her coffee. She was exhausted and needed the caffeine and sugar rush. Tom hadn't turned up this morning to any of the lectures. Once again, she'd humiliated herself by asking everyone if they'd seen him. No one had. She'd eventually tracked down his best friend, Andy, who said he hadn't heard from Tom in days and was a bit worried. He said he'd drive over to Tom's house later so he could see him face to face to make sure everything was all right.

'Lucy?'

She looked up. Oh, God, it was Olivia, one of Tom's really annoying friends from St Jude's.

'Hi, how are you?' Olivia plonked herself down opposite Lucy. 'I heard the news.'

Lucy blushed. 'I'm fine.'

Olivia leant forward and, lowering her voice, said, 'It's pretty dramatic.'

'Well, it's all going to be fine.'

'Are you, like, okay about it?'

'It's not ideal, but yes.' Lucy smiled.

'Poor Tom, I heard he was upset.'

Lucy bristled. 'We both were, but it'll all work out for the best in the end.'

'Wow, you're tougher than you look. I mean, Tom's pretty great, don't you think?'

'Yes, I do.'

'So why did you change your mind?'

'Lots of reasons.'

'Tom said it was Gabriel's idea. I guess Gabriel wasn't too happy with you.'

Lucy wanted to smack Olivia. 'I don't really care what Gabriel thinks of me.'

'Really? He's kind of scary. He's always been so hard on Tom. Mind you, my father knew Gabriel back when they were boys in St Jude's and he says Gabriel was always very tough and that Gabriel's father was the same. You know Gabriel's father, Tom's grandfather, was the headmaster at St Jude's, don't you?'

Lucy hadn't known that and didn't care. Olivia seemed to think this was a big deal but Lucy couldn't have given a damn if Gabriel's father was the bloody president. Gabriel was a bully and she had zero interest in his father.

Olivia prattled on: 'He turned St Jude's around. It was always a top school, but Gabriel's father brought it to a whole new level. He was quite a maverick and ruled with an iron fist. Gabriel was apparently very keen to please his father and he ended up getting the best exam results in the whole country. My father says Gabriel is a genius, which explains a lot.'

It explains nothing, Lucy thought. If he was so bloody intelligent, why didn't he see that he was alienating his son and might never see or know his own grandchild?

Lucy hated the way the St Jude's crowd always thought stories about their 'special' school were so interesting. It was as if they were unable to peel themselves away from their school days, stand on their own two feet or have an individual thought. It was pathetic.

'It's kind of amazing that Tom turned out to be such a softie and a sweetie. My dad says Tom's mum was really nice. So sad she died so young.'

'Yes, it is.'

'I'm still in shock about you guys, though. Did Tom tell you he was going, because he didn't tell any of us?'

Going? What was she talking about?

'Was it a bad break-up? I presume you did it because he was very into you. He told me he was mad about you. To be honest, I was kind of surprised because you're not his usual type.'

Lucy frowned and held up her hand to shut Olivia up. 'We haven't broken up.'

'What?'

'Tom and I are together.'

Olivia looked puzzled. 'Well, why has he gone to New York to finish his law degree?'

'New York?' Lucy's head began to spin. 'What are you . . . New York?'

'Oh, my God, did you not know?' Olivia stared at her, clearly shocked. 'The only reason I found out is because my mum bumped into him on the flight yesterday. She said he was behaving really strangely. He told her he was going to finish his law degree in America because Gabriel thought it was better for him.'

Lucy was struggling to breathe. 'Are you sure it was him?'

Olivia nodded. 'I'm sorry, I really am. I presumed you'd broken up with him and that's why he'd gone. I . . . Do you need a glass of water? Lucy?'

Lucy gripped the table and stood up unsteadily on shaking legs. 'I need air.'

'Let me help you.'

'No,' Lucy snapped. 'You've done enough damage.'

She staggered out of the café and down the road, sobbing. How could he do this? How could he abandon her? Her heart was pounding as she tried to gulp in air. New York to finish his degree? Gabriel had obviously sent him away, far away from her, the social-climbing slut.

Oh, God. She bent over as pain stabbed in her stomach. She had to calm down – it was bad for the baby. She leant against the railings of a house and tried to control her breathing. She'd never, ever forgive Tom for being such a coward.

Never. Oh, what was she going to do? She was on her own now. Completely alone.

She dug her nails into her palms to stop the panic that was rising within her. She thought of the envelope, back in her bedroom, with the tickets that could still be used. She saw two futures before her, but now neither of them featured Tom, which hurt so badly. What should she do?

Lucy stared at the sky and felt a wave of hopelessness wash over her. This was crazy – how had this become her life? She wanted to lie down on the street and never get up again. But then she thought of her parents, of how good they were, and she thought of Gabriel talking to them as he had, the way he'd looked at them all, as if they were filth on his shoe. God, she hated him.

She put her hand on her stomach and took a deep breath. To hell with Tom and his bastard of a father. She'd show them. She'd be a great mother and a great lawyer and raise an amazing child. She would not fail. She was bloody well going to prove it to them all.

9

Billy sobbed into his handkerchief.

Tina patted him on the back. 'Calm yourself, Billy.'

'I can't, it's just . . .'

'I know, love, it's unbelievable.'

'How could she –' A sob prevented Billy finishing his sentence.

'She's something else,' Tina said.

Jenny came in, hair tousled, wearing her pyjamas. One look at her father stopped her dead in her tracks. 'Oh, God, what's going on? I can't take any more drama in this family. What has Lucy done now? Gone to Vegas and got married? Got a tattoo? Pierced her tongue? What?'

Tina grinned. 'Your sister's just called us. She went in to get her results this morning. She's only gone and got herself a first. She's top of the whole class.'

'A first in law. My daughter!' Billy's eyes shone. 'Billy Murphy from the inner city, who left school at fourteen, has a daughter who got a first in her third-year exams in law in Trinity College – no one would believe it. *I* can't believe it.'

Jenny put a slice of bread in the toaster and turned to her parents, arms folded. 'Great. Bloody brilliant. Now I'm going to look thick and useless no matter what I do. Why does she have to be an Einstein?'

'She deserves every bit of it,' Tina said. 'I never saw her study so hard. And to think she did it with everything that's going on. She really is incredible.'

Jenny turned to get the butter out of the fridge. She was

happy for Lucy, of course she was. God knew she deserved a lift after the last few months. But did she have to get a first? Now anything Jenny achieved would look rubbish compared to that.

Still, it was brilliant news for Lucy. Jenny didn't know how her sister had done it. The last few months had been so horrendous that she was amazed Lucy could concentrate on anything. Her strength had amazed them all.

'She sounded so happy,' Billy said. 'Like the old Lucy, happy and young. I told her to stay out for the day and night and have fun with her pals.'

Jenny snorted. Lucy's classmates would be throwing drinks down their necks and getting sloshed. They'd probably be drunk by lunchtime. What was Lucy going to do – sit in the pub beside them with her enormous bump, sipping lemonade?

'It'll give her a great lift. She needs the confidence boost,' Tina said.

'If I ever get my hands on that spineless little –'

'Don't go getting yourself all het up, Billy. It's bad for your heart,' Tina reminded him. 'We all feel the same way, but it is what it is and we need to deal with the situation ourselves.'

Jenny cut her toast with the breadknife and imagined sticking it into Tom's head. He was a useless fucker. How could he just leave her like that?

When Tom had left, Jenny had been worried that Lucy might do something mad like slit her wrists or something. She'd often heard her crying herself to sleep, and it made her sick to her bones to hear her brave sister so upset. Jenny was determined never, ever, ever to have unprotected sex with anyone, not even Joshua Jackson from *Dawson's Creek*, whom she was obsessed with. Nothing and no one was worth this.

Billy went into the shop to serve a customer. Tina was at the sink while Jenny finished her toast.

'Do you think she'll be able to cope, Mum?'

Tina stopped washing a cup. She had her back to Jenny. 'She has to, love. She doesn't have any choice. She'll have to muddle through and we'll all have to help. It's not going to be easy. One was going to be difficult, but two . . . Well, it makes things more complicated. But children are such a blessing and a joy too. Honestly, they are the greatest thing in the world.'

'We should have known it was twins – she got so huge so quickly,' Jenny said.

'All women have different bumps but, yes, she was very big very early on. Poor Lucy, if only . . . Well, no point in wishing for what isn't.'

'Do you think she'll be able to go back to college? Will you and Dad really be able to cope with twins and the shop?'

Tina faced her younger daughter. 'She has to, Jenny. She can't let this stop her achieving her dream. We all have to help her get there. That's what family's for, to help each other out in times of trouble. We'll find a way somehow.'

Jenny hoped her mum's plan didn't involve her having to change nappies or babysit on a Saturday night. Jenny didn't want to have zero social life and become an outcast just because her sister had got pregnant.

Tina sat down and put her hand on Jenny's arm. Uh-oh, a serious chat was coming.

'What's happened to Lucy is a lesson to you to be very careful when you meet boys and they want to take things to another level. You have to look after your own body and not trust them to. Do you understand?'

'You're telling me I should go on the pill if I'm having sex?'

Tina laughed. 'Yes, I suppose I am.'

'Don't worry, Mum. There's no way in hell that I'm going to end up pregnant.' And if I ever do, Jenny thought, I'll be on the first plane to England.

10

Lucy waddled along the street to Sarah's house. The sun was beating down and she was sweating profusely. She felt as if she was in a furnace. She was hot all the time and the warm weather was making it really hard to sleep and walk around. Then there was the weight of the babies pressing down on her bladder, making her feel like she needed to go to the loo every two minutes. Being pregnant sucked, but pregnant with twins was the worst. How could she be so unlucky?

She had just about got her head around having one baby when she'd found out it was two. It had pushed her over the edge. Even her mother had been shocked into silence at the ultrasound.

Lucy was exhausted and weepy all the time. She tried to pretend to her family that she was coping, but she wasn't. She cried herself to sleep every night. She prayed all day long that Tom would come back. How the hell could she cope with two babies alone? She longed for the old life, the one before Tom. How had one silly mistake cost her so much? She was the laughing stock of the university and her neighbourhood.

She could hear the locals in the shop whispering to each other. They clearly thought being pregnant had affected her hearing.

'She's huge.'

'Poor thing, her life is ruined.'

'Stupid girl, she had it all.'

'It's Billy I feel sorry for.'

'He was always boasting about her. Not much to boast about now.'

'I thought the younger one was the wild one.'

Lucy would grit her teeth, fake-smile and ask, 'Can I help you at all?' and the customers would fake-smile back. Tina said Lucy didn't have to work in the shop if it was too much, but Lucy had insisted on helping out. She wanted to do as much as she could before the babies arrived so that she wouldn't feel so guilty when her parents were flat out helping her to raise them.

Panic rose in her throat whenever she thought about after the birth. How would she even feed them? She'd decided not to breastfeed – it was too much. At least with bottles she could feed one and her mum could feed the other at the same time. And what about when she had finished her degree and was working? Would any guy ever look at her again? Who'd want to go out with someone who had two kids? Lucy'd never get married now. She'd end up on her own, living with her parents and her two fatherless kids. Lucy Murphy, the screw-up.

Her mum kept telling her she was beautiful and smart, and men would line up to be with her. She said that Lucy had to be optimistic and believe she would have the full and wonderful life she deserved. But Lucy wasn't so sure. What man wanted to raise someone else's twins?

Lucy stopped walking and wiped sweat from her forehead. She was tempted to lie down in Mrs Molloy's little front garden and go to sleep, she was so tired. Two hours of uninterrupted sleep had become a distant memory. Lucy wanted the twins out and her body back. She felt so big and disgusting. She didn't think she could do another month of this. It was really awful now.

'What you got in there? A watermelon?' a cheeky little boy shouted, as he pedalled by on his bicycle.

'King Kong more like,' his friend roared.

She shuffled up the road, down the path to Sarah's house and rang the bell. It was ridiculous: she was out of breath having walked barely a hundred yards.

'Hey, gorgeous.' Sarah grinned when she opened the door.

'I know you're trying to be nice, but I look like a sweaty whale.'

Sarah laughed. 'Let's just say you're not neat. But once they're out, you'll be back to yourself in no time. Look at your one Jane Seymour. She had twins a few years ago and she's so skinny now.'

'I feel like my body's been taken over by aliens. I want them to come out, but I'm scared of what it'll be like when they do.'

Sarah led her into the kitchen and got her a glass of cold water.

'Having one kid was frightening, but two? Seriously, is God having a laugh?' Lucy said miserably.

Sarah gazed at her best friend. She was like a different person. She had always been petite but now she had this massive bump, which looked so weird and unnatural.

Sarah didn't know why people said pregnancy was beautiful. The whole thing was putting her off wanting kids. Darren was mad keen to get married and start a family, but Sarah wasn't so sure. She was happy to get married – they'd been together since they were fifteen, so she knew he was the one. But a family? She wanted to open a hairdressing salon next year and a baby would just complicate things.

She didn't want to tell Lucy that Darren had proposed. She'd asked him to wait and not tell anyone until after the babies were born. It wouldn't be fair to shove her happiness in Lucy's face when she was having such a tough time.

Sarah said yet another silent prayer that Tom would feel guilty enough to come back. Darren reckoned he never would, but she didn't want to give up hope. It didn't matter if he didn't want to be with Lucy, but he needed to come back and give the poor babies a dad. Everyone deserved a dad. Sarah knew that better than most. It wasn't easy growing up without one. That was why she loved Darren so much: he looked after her and minded her and told her she was his princess. Darren would never leave her. Sarah was not going to end up like her mother, bitter and a man-hater. No way. Sarah was going to have a good life, with two solid parents for her kids, if she ever decided to have any.

She'd lied when Lucy had asked her if she'd found it difficult to grow up without a dad. She'd been lying about it all her life. She always pretended it had made no difference. She pretended she didn't care. But inside it hurt like hell to know she'd been rejected by her father. That he didn't even love her enough to contact her or send her birthday presents or a lousy Christmas card. He'd walked out and disappeared, just like Tom had, except Sarah's dad had waited until she was three to do it. She didn't know which was worse, to have your dad walk away before you were even born, like Tom had done, or when you were three and he knew you. They were both awful.

Sarah used to hear people say it was worse for her brother because he was five and a boy needed his father. But she thought that was rubbish. A girl needed her father just as much. She had always envied Lucy. Billy looked at her with such adoration – it was gorgeous. Billy thought the sun, moon and stars revolved around Lucy. Sarah had watched him at sports days, school plays and the school graduation ceremony . . . Whatever the occasion, Billy was always the first there, sitting in the front row, cheering and clapping. Sarah ached for that kind of love from a man.

She'd found it when she'd met Darren and she was never letting him go. Darren was the piece of her life that had been missing. He would look at his daughter the way Billy looked at Lucy. Darren would be a brilliant dad.

But Sarah had lied about it because Lucy didn't need to hear that. She'd told her that having a good mum was all a child needed, and that Lucy would be the most amazing mum in the world. Besides, the kids would have Billy, who would be an amazing granddad, so they'd have a positive male figure in their lives. That had seemed to make Lucy feel better.

'I do have some good news,' Lucy said. 'I got my results and I got a first.'

'What?' Sarah whooped. 'You are unbelievable! In the middle of all this crap you get yourself a first! Honestly, Lucy, you really are Wonder Woman! You can do anything.'

Lucy smiled. 'Dad hasn't stopped crying – he's over the moon. Mum cried too. At least I've been able to make them cry with happiness for once. It makes the guilt of the mess I've caused a little less horrible.'

'They adore you. You can never change that.'

I've certainly put their love to the test, Lucy thought grimly. 'Look at my ankles!' She swung her feet out from under the kitchen table. 'Huge.'

'It's just the pregnancy, don't worry. You'll be skinny Lucy again soon.'

'Jenny calls me Moby-Dick. To be honest, I was surprised she knew who the character was.' Lucy grinned.

'You're very hard on her. She's smart, you know. Not book smart like you, but street smart, and she really is brilliant with make-up.'

'I know, but where's that going to get her?'

'Where's hairdressing going to get me?'

'I didn't mean it like that. You're an amazing hairdresser and you're planning to open your own salon. You're going places fast. A lot faster than me, that's for sure. It's just that Jenny is kind of lazy. She just thinks she can do make-up and have a career. She seems to have forgotten the working-hard part. The part where you have to work for free and build up a portfolio and all that.'

She had a point. Jenny *was* lazy, but Sarah had seen how passionate she was about make-up. She recognized that passion: it was the way she'd felt about hair when she was sixteen. It was all she'd wanted to do. Her mother had badgered her into going to college and she'd had enough points to do an arts degree, but Sarah had put her foot down and said no. She'd gone straight into a salon and worked her way up. After only three years she was a senior stylist.

Lucy didn't understand because she wasn't creative, but Sarah could see that Jenny had lots of talent. 'Jenny will learn all that along the way. I just don't think your parents should force her to go to college. There's no point. She'll be miserable and probably wasting her time. She needs to do a make-up course at night and get experience during the day.'

'Well, you know what Dad's like about university. He's obsessed with us going and bettering ourselves. He hates the fact that he had to leave school at fourteen and he's worked so hard building up the business so we can have a better life than him. He's always wanted more for us . . .' Lucy's voice shook. 'I've let him down so badly. Sometimes I catch him looking at me and his face is so sad. I know this is killing him. I have to figure out a way to be a good mother and finish my degree. I can't blow it all. I have to make Dad proud of me again.'

'Come on,' Sarah said. 'This is just a bump in the road. You'll get back on track. Look at your exam results, for goodness' sake. Billy and Tina are so proud of you getting a first!

But, Lucy, you have to give yourself time. Take the year off and see how things go. You may need to take two years off. Don't put too much pressure on yourself.'

Lucy shook her head. 'There's no way I'm taking two years off. I'm already freaking about postponing for twelve months. I've done some reading over the summer, to try to get ahead and keep on top of things. I have to get a first in my finals. I want to prove to Dad and to Gabriel, Tom and everyone else, but most of all to myself, that I can do it. I have to, Sarah, I can't let this ruin my life.'

'You will do well in your finals and the babies won't ruin your life, but give yourself a break for the next few months. You've had a lot to deal with.'

Lucy twirled the water glass in her hands. She whispered, 'Do you think he'll come back? I keep hoping he will.'

Her friend looked so lost, Sarah thought. 'Sure, he might, but maybe best not to get your hopes up too much.'

A tear ran down Lucy's cheek. 'How could he do this to me? I'll never forgive him, Sarah, never. If he doesn't come back for the birth he's dead to me for ever.'

11

Jenny was in the shop with Lucy when it happened. Mrs Prendergast was complaining about the strawberries being overripe. She'd already given out about the bread only lasting three days before going mouldy and the ham being dry.

Jenny snatched back the strawberries. 'Well, Mrs Prendergast, maybe you'd be better off driving over to the supermarket if you're so unhappy with everything here.'

Mrs Prendergast frowned. 'Don't speak to me like that, you young pup. Isn't it bad enough your sister getting pregnant without you being rude and insolent too? Your poor father must be ashamed of you both.'

Jenny was sick of these judgemental old bitches gossiping about her sister. Who the hell were they to judge anyone? They all had their own secrets.

'My father is incredibly proud of us,' she said angrily, 'especially Lucy, who is a genius, which is more than I can say for your thick fool of a son who is so ugly that no girl will ever go near him, even though he spends all his time in school trying to feel girls up. So you'll be stuck looking at his disgusting face for the rest of your life.'

'What? I never . . . You horrible girl. My Greg is a lovely well-brought-up boy.'

'Greg is a pervert. I could take him to court for sexual abuse – he grabbed my boobs at least three times last year. He's the biggest loser in school. All the girls hate him and so do most of the boys.'

'Perhaps, young lady, if you didn't go around rolling

up your school skirt and behaving like a hussy, boys would leave you alone.'

'The best part of Greg's day is looking at my legs. Besides, he'd try to feel up a nun, he's that desperate. He's like a dog in heat. A really ugly dog that no one will ever touch.'

'Wash out your filthy mouth,' Mrs Prendergast hissed. 'You'll end up like your sister, a pregnant tramp.'

'Don't you *ever* call my sister a tramp. Lucy is the best person in the world. She made one tiny mistake. I'm sick of all you bitter old bitches spreading rumours about her. Now get out and don't ever come back here.'

'You're a disgrace. You'll both end up in the gutter.' Mrs Prendergast slammed the door as she left.

Jenny was shaking with rage. She kicked the counter hard. 'How dare she? I'm sick of those old biddies! I hate them all.'

'Jenny!' her sister exclaimed behind her.

'No, Lucy, I'm not going to feel guilty about what I said. I will not let anyone talk about you like that. It's not right.'

'Jenny . . .'

'And Greg is a disgusting perv, although Amanda Moran actually let him feel her up and she kissed him, the blind cow. But then again, she's got such bad acne that you can't see much of her face any more. It's like two eyes staring out from a pepperoni pizza.'

'Jenny, will you shut up?'

Jenny whirled around. 'What?'

Lucy was standing up, holding onto the wall. Below her was a puddle of water.

'Oh, my God! Is . . . Does that . . . Are you . . .?'

'Yes, I'm in labour and it's two weeks too early.' Lucy was crying.

'Sit down, I'll get Mum.' Jenny sprinted out of the shop,

through the kitchen and out to the back garden, where her mother was hanging the washing on the line.

'*Muuuuuum!* The babies are coming!' she roared.

Tina dropped a sheet and ran after her daughter. Reaching Lucy first, she wrapped her arms around her. 'It's okay, pet.'

'It's too early, Mum,' Lucy sobbed.

'It's fine. Twins often come early. Now, we'll get you into the car and fly up to the hospital. It'll be quicker than calling an ambulance.' To Jenny she said, 'Run up and get the red sports bag at the end of my bed. It's got everything we need. I had a feeling they might come early.'

Jenny sprinted off.

Lucy laid her head on her mother's shoulder. 'I'm scared.'

Tina kissed her. 'Everything is going to be okay. I'm here, sweetheart, and it's all going to be fine.'

Billy stared into the cot at the two beautiful babies sleeping side by side, one swaddled in a pink blanket, the other in blue. My grandchildren, he thought. Who would have thought I'd be a granddad at forty-seven?

'Aren't they precious?' Tina whispered.

'Magnificent,' Billy said, welling up.

'Lucy was so brave and brilliant. I was so proud of her,' Tina said. 'I'm so relieved everything went all right. I don't think she could have taken any complications. And six pounds each is a very good size. No wonder poor Lucy was so big. They're all going to be fine and that's all that matters.'

Billy put his arm around her. 'Aren't we lucky to have two healthy daughters and now two wonderful grandchildren?'

Tina smiled. 'I could happily have waited until my sixties to be a granny but, yes, we are lucky.'

Billy looked at his elder daughter, who was sleeping as soundly as the babies. Lucy was pale and there were dark purple circles under her eyes like two bruises. Poor pet, she needed her rest. What a year, Billy thought, what a bloody year.

He turned back to the babies. He made a silent oath that he would protect them until his dying day. He'd dragged himself out of the inner city but most of his friends had ended up in prison or worse. Billy knew what fighting was. He knew what hard work was. He knew how lucky he was to have got out of there and met a wonderful woman and had two beautiful girls.

He'd help Lucy to get back on her feet and finish her degree. He'd make damn sure she had the life she deserved. No stuck-up judge and his lowlife son were going to ruin it. No way, not on Billy's watch. And if that Tom fella ever darkened Lucy's door, Billy would break his scrawny, spineless neck. A man should stand up to his responsibilities, not run away, like a scared little kid. Everyone made mistakes, but you put up your hand and held yourself accountable. For all his posh background, the fella was a disgrace. As for his bully of a father, what kind of scumbag threatens a young pregnant girl? Billy doubted it was very judge-like behaviour.

Then again, Billy had grown up seeing people in authority behaving badly, from teachers to priests to policemen to judges. He knew fine well that no 'title' made you a decent person. No amount of letters after your name meant you were respectable. Actions were what mattered: how you behaved was the measure of the man you were, and by that standard Gabriel and Tom were at the very bottom of the barrel.

Billy watched as the baby boy's legs kicked the air. A little footballer maybe, he thought, and grinned at the idea. It was going to be fun having a grandson. He'd be able to kick a ball around with him and teach him boy things. Billy loved his girls, but it would be great to have a boy in the house.

Jenny came in carrying paper cups of coffee. 'This hospital is a dump. They don't even do cappuccinos. Can you believe it? And there are no cute doctors. They're all a zillion years old or women.'

Tina rolled her eyes. 'It's a hospital, Jenny, not a coffee shop or a disco.'

'I thought every hospital would have one Dr Ross, but none of them even looks like George Clooney's granddad.'

'You need to remember that *ER* is a TV show. Real doctors are normal-looking, not movie stars,' Tina said.

Billy took his coffee and moved away from their chatter towards Lucy. He drank some, welcoming the caffeine hit. He noticed Lucy stir. 'Hello, pet, how are you feeling?' he asked.

'Sore.' Lucy winced as she tried to sit up in the bed. Tina rushed over to help her.

'Did you have to get stitches? Will you have to sit on one of those doughnut cushions and wee in the bath for weeks?' Jenny asked.

'For the love of God.' Billy covered his ears.

'Stop that,' Tina snapped. 'Lucy had no stitches. She was wonderful.'

'That's good because Lorraine told me her aunt had to get loads of stitches and she was never the same down there again. Apparently it's just a big wide gap and she wees when she walks.'

'Jenny!' Tina glared at her. 'Enough.'

'I'm just saying Lucy's lucky.'

'Is it safe to listen?' Billy asked, taking his hands down. 'No more lady talk while I'm in the room, please. Thank God I'll have another fella in the house now.'

'Have you decided on names?' Jenny asked.

Lucy nodded. 'Yes, Dylan and Kelly.'

'Ooooh,' Tina and Billy said.

'You're such a lick-arse,' Jenny said.

'I think it's lovely that you named your son after my dad and your daughter after your mum's mum.' Billy ignored Jenny.

'I'm really touched,' Tina said. 'My mum was a lovely woman. She died far too young, and now this new Kelly will remind me of her.' She leant down to kiss Lucy.

'You should have called them Doug and Carol,' Jenny said.

Lucy sighed. 'I am not naming my kids after characters in *ER*.'

'But Doug is so hot!'

'What in God's name is she talking about?' Billy asked.

'Some television show,' Tina explained.

'Mum pretends she doesn't watch it, but she does.'

Tina laughed. 'Well, George Clooney does look very handsome in scrubs.'

Kelly began to cry, sounding like a kitten mewing. Tina picked her up and cuddled her. As Billy watched his wife, memories flooded back of her as a young mother, holding Lucy just after she was born. He wanted to weep. This was life, the circle of life. His lovely wife was holding her granddaughter. Billy's heart felt as if it would burst with love, for his wife, his daughters and now his two tiny grandchildren. To hell with Tom, these babies would grow up surrounded by love and that was all any child needed.

Now Dylan was crying too. Billy picked him up. 'Here, Dad.' Lucy held her hands out.

Billy placed her son gently in her arms. Lucy held him to her and put her cheek against his. He quietened immediately. Lucy closed her eyes.

'You're a natural,' Tina said.

Lucy opened her eyes and smiled, a proper smile, a real

one. Billy realized it was the first time he'd seen her happy in months. He'd remember this moment.

'So, this is all great and I'm thrilled for you, sis, but I'm starving. Can we go for food?' Jenny asked.

A midwife bustled in. 'Hello, everyone, congratulations. I'm just signing on for the evening. I'm Barbara, I'll be looking after you tonight. Now, how are the little dotes? How's Mum?'

'I'm tired but fine.'

'Sure, of course you're tired. I'm here to help. Now, folks, I need to run through a few things with Lucy and the dad. Is he here?'

'No,' Lucy said, her voice strong and clear. 'There is no dad. It's just me.'

Barbara didn't bat an eyelid. 'Well, let's get these little ones changed and I'll help you feed them.'

'See? Lucy's fine. She's got Barbara here so can we please go? We've been here for eight hours and I need proper food,' Jenny moaned.

Lucy looked up. 'Go on, Mum, honestly. Barbara will help me.'

'Absolutely. Sure that's what I'm here for,' Barbara chirped. 'Off you go and get some dinner. We'll see you in the morning. She's in good hands, don't worry a bit.'

'Are you sure?' Tina asked Lucy.

'Yes, Mum, honestly.'

Billy, Tina and Jenny hugged her, then one by one left the room. Tina asked one last time, 'Hundred per cent sure?'

Lucy smiled. 'Yes, go.'

Barbara showed Lucy how to change nappies, feed the babies and burp them. She said she'd show her how to bathe them the next day. Then she held Kelly and Lucy held Dylan and they fed them their bottles. Dylan gulped his down, burped and fell asleep.

'He's a real man,' Barbara said, laughing.

Kelly took a while to settle, and Lucy was glad Barbara was looking after her.

The midwife tucked them all in and told Lucy to press the call button if she needed any help or painkillers during the night. Lucy thought she might be in love with Barbara, she was so nice.

When the midwife left the room, Lucy gingerly swung her legs to the side of the bed and leant over the plastic bassinet where her two little angels were snuggled up side by side.

'Dylan and Kelly, I promise you that I will be the best mum I can be. I will love you so much that you won't even miss having a dad. I will protect you and mind you and give you the best life possible. I will do whatever I can to make up for your shitty dad running away. I'm young and I'm scared, but I'm smart and I'm strong, and I won't let you down and I will never, ever leave you. I'll make sure you don't make the mistakes I did. You're going to be successful and brilliant. I'm going to show Gabriel and Tom that I can be a great mother. You two are my world now. It's the three of us, for ever.'

12

Sarah held out her hand. Lucy gasped and pulled it up to her face. The ring was small but pretty. 'Oh, my God, it's beautiful! When did he propose?'

'A while ago,' Sarah admitted, 'but we wanted to wait and . . . well . . . we're going to get married in a month and I want you to be my bridesmaid.'

Lucy slapped a smile on her face. Bridesmaid? She'd barely lost any of her baby weight. The twins were only three weeks old and they were taking up all of her time. Some days she didn't even have time to wash. How the hell was she supposed to lose weight and fit into a bridesmaid's dress?

As if reading her mind Sarah said, 'You're the only bridesmaid, so you can wear anything you like. I won't make you wear some mint-green dress with matching shoes and bows. Honestly, you can choose your own outfit.'

Lucy now smiled properly. 'God, thanks. I was a bit worried there.'

Sarah laughed. 'I saw your fake-smile. Look, I know it's a bit soon after the babies, but Darren's mad keen to get married and start a family, so I may well be pushing a buggy around soon too.'

'That would be great,' Lucy said, grabbing her hand. 'We could help each other out.'

'Exactly.'

Lucy felt like crying. If Sarah had a baby, she wouldn't feel like such a failure. All right, Sarah would have done it the 'right way', but at least Lucy would have someone to talk to of her own age with a kid. She could moan about lack of sleep and how difficult she found it to settle Kelly after every feed, and how sometimes she wanted to put her in her cot and walk away.

She could tell Sarah how lonely she felt at night, when it was just her and the babies. Sometimes fear overwhelmed her. How was she going to cope? How could she raise them on her own? What was she going to tell them about their dad? Would she lie and say he'd died in a car crash? Would she say it was a one-night stand and she didn't know his name? Or would she tell them the truth – that he abandoned them, ran away like a coward and wanted nothing to do with them?

When she watched them sleeping and tried to figure out how to tell them why they had no dad, Lucy felt bereft. She didn't want them to know hurt or rejection. It wasn't fair. They were innocent little victims.

All of her other friends were either in college, had gone off travelling or were working in full-time jobs and busy all the time. At least with Sarah living so close by and having Sundays and Mondays off work, Lucy got to see her a lot.

'Where are you having it?'

'Well, with me saving to open my own salon and Darren saving for a house, we're pretty broke. Darren asked the football club if they'd give us the hall and they said yes. So, it'll be just a small wedding, nothing fancy.'

'It'll be great. You're brilliant together and I'm thrilled for you.' Lucy hugged her. 'What can I do to help?'

Sarah laughed. 'You can get some rest so you don't fall asleep at eight o'clock. You look exhausted. Are they up all night?'

Lucy nodded. 'Dylan's easy – he just eats and sleeps – but Kelly's hard work. She takes ages to digest her milk and cries all the time. Mum thinks she might be a bit colicky. It's hard work though at four in the morning when you've had no sleep and she's crying for an hour.'

Sarah peered at the sleeping baby. 'She looks so sweet there.'

'She's sweet when she's asleep! . . . Have you got your dress yet?'

'I got a gorgeous one from a second-hand shop in town. I've had it taken up and changed the sleeves, but it's really nice.'

'Good for you. And how's your mum? Is she happy for you?'

Sarah sighed. 'Mum's being her usual enthusiastic self. She told me I'm too young, too impulsive, that I don't know Darren well enough, that he'll let me down because all men are useless bastards, the usual cheerful chat. Honestly, she's wasted her whole life being bitter.'

Sarah's mother, Helen, was a sour woman. Lucy barely remembered her smiling. Everything was always wrong or awful or a disaster waiting to happen. It was amazing that Sarah had turned out to be so cheerful. Lucy reckoned that Sarah's drive to have her own business and succeed was because she'd watched her mother waste her life. Sarah had been talking about opening a hairdressing salon since she was thirteen.

Lucy was glad her best friend had Darren: he'd never let her down. She had chosen well, unlike Lucy and 'Tom the Tosser', as Jenny now called him.

'I'm going to ask Jenny to do my make-up as my wedding present,' Sarah said, 'and I hope you're okay with this but I was going to ask Billy to give me away. Would that be weird for you?'

'Not at all. He'll be delighted.' Lucy turned to tuck Dylan's blankets in. She didn't want Sarah to see her face. She was happy for Billy to give Sarah away, but Lucy knew that he would probably never give herself away. Who'd want to take on a woman with twins? It would be hard to see him walking Sarah up the aisle, knowing he'd never do it with his elder daughter.

But then again, Lucy had a brilliant dad and Sarah had none, so how could she be selfish about it? She gathered herself and turned back to Sarah. 'Let's go and tell him now. He'll be so chuffed.'

'Are you sure?'

'Totally.'

Just as they were heading downstairs, Kelly began to cry. 'You go ahead, I'll just settle her,' Lucy said.

While Lucy paced her bedroom floor trying to stop her baby girl crying, she heard whoops and cheers from downstairs. Her dad's voice carried up to her. 'I'd be honoured, Sarah. What a lovely thing to look forward to. Thank you.'

Lucy buried her face in her daughter's body and cried with her. Hearing the joy in her father's voice had cut her like a knife. She held Kelly and rocked her. She was sick of feeling useless and lost and miserable. There was something she could do about it, and she was bloody well going to do it.

13

Lucy's hand shook as she rang the buzzer beside the enormous black gates. She'd insisted on doing it alone. Jenny and Sarah were waiting for her in Sarah's car around the corner. She'd said she'd call them if she needed back-up.

'Who is it?' a familiar voice barked.

'It's Lucy Murphy. I'm here to find out where Tom is. He needs to know he has two beautiful babies.'

'What? How dare you come to my home? I told you to stay away from my son. I thought I'd made myself very clear. You are not fit to go near my son, or me for that matter. Don't ever contact us again, by any means.'

A sense of calm came over Lucy. She looked down at the two sweet faces in the buggy. Dylan cooed at her, and Kelly was sucking her thumb.

'If you don't open this gate, I will cause the loudest scene you could possibly imagine. I don't think you want your neighbours to see that, do you?'

'You wouldn't dare –'

'Watch me, GABRIEL,' she screamed into the speaker. 'LET ME IN OR ELSE!'

'Stop it this instant,' he roared. The black gates groaned and slowly began to roll back.

Taking a deep breath, Lucy pushed the double buggy through and up the driveway. Gabriel met her at the door. He looked the same, tall, broad and imposing.

Lucy pushed past him, wheeling the buggy into the vast

hall. It was cold and stark, like its owner. No soft rugs or furnishings, just cold white marble.

'That's enough, you can stop right there.' Gabriel closed the door. 'What do you want?'

'I want you to tell me how to get in touch with my babies' father.'

'My son has nothing to do with you or these poor unfortunate children.' He didn't even glance down at Dylan and Kelly.

'Tom needs to know,' Lucy said, her voice quivering. 'He needs to know that he has two beautiful children. He needs to take responsibility and stop hiding like a coward.'

Gabriel glared at her. 'My son is not a coward. He's just not going to get dragged down by some gold-digging hussy. Now take your offspring and get out of my house.'

'How can you do this? How can you deny your own grandchildren? Look at Kelly – she's the spitting image of Tom. She has his eyes. He needs to know, and they need a father.' Lucy felt a wave of emotion overwhelm her. She gripped the handles of the double buggy and willed herself not to cry.

Gabriel clicked his tongue impatiently. 'Tom was happy to leave. He didn't require much persuading – in fact, he practically ran onto the plane. What is it you really want? Money? Is that it? If I give you money, will you go away? How much to get you to crawl back under the rock you came from? Ten grand? Twenty?' He pulled a chequebook out of his breast pocket.

Lucy felt fury rise from within her. 'I don't want your filthy money. I wouldn't accept a cent from you. All I want is for Tom to know he has two beautiful children and to decide for himself if he'd like to be involved in their lives or take the spineless, pathetic decision to pretend they don't exist. You can keep your money.'

'My son is far away, living a good, respectable life. I got

him away from you and your mess. Now leave or I will throw you out. Go back to your corner shop and stay there.'

Lucy laughed bitterly. 'For all your success and money, you are the lowest form of human being I've ever met. A man who bullies his son and tried to bully a pregnant girl, a girl carrying his grandchildren, into having an abortion, then accuses her of being a slut. If I wanted to, I could go to the newspapers with this story. It's pretty salacious, don't you think? I could demand a paternity test and shame you and your coward of a son publicly. How do you think that would go down with your legal pals?'

Gabriel's face went puce. 'How dare you threaten me? You have no idea who you're talking to. If you cross me, I will destroy you and your father's business. You'll wish you'd never met me.'

Lucy laughed. 'I already wish I'd never met you. I also wish I'd never met your pathetic son. I was wondering how I'd explain to my children why they had no father and now I know exactly what I'm going to say. I'm going to tell them the truth. Their father was a weak man, bullied by his own father and too pathetic to stand up for himself.'

Gabriel's eyes were bulging and his face was twisted in anger. 'Get out of my house, you dirty little tramp. Those children will probably end up in foster care. You clearly can't even look after yourself. People like you shouldn't be allowed into university, whores looking for rich boys to trap. It makes me sick. I pity your children having a mother like you. They'll never amount to anything.'

'Oh, yeah?' Lucy shouted into his face. 'Watch this space!'

She turned, swung the buggy out of the front door and marched down the driveway. I'll show you, Gabriel, she thought. I'll make you regret your words. I'll raise the two most amazing kids in the world. Just you wait and see.

PART TWO

2016

14

Billy was worried. He knew this was a great opportunity for the twins, but he thought Lucy was too invested in it. He was also worried the kids might not fit in. They were happy in their current schools. Of course he was proud of Dylan. What an amazing kid he was! To think of what he'd achieved – Billy couldn't believe a grandson of his was so gifted.

Also, Billy had to admit, it was lovely to see Lucy so excited about something. She was so happy, like a young girl again. Billy was glad of that. She deserved to be happy – she'd had a lot of heartache and disappointment.

'Dad?' Lucy asked. 'Should we get another pizza? I think we might need one more.'

'Lucy.' Billy took his daughter by the shoulders. 'We have enough food for the feckin' cast of *Gandhi* and *Titanic* combined. Will you stop fussing?'

Lucy smiled. 'You're right. I'm just so happy, Dad.'

'You don't say!' Billy smiled back at her.

'I'm so proud of them. Can you imagine? My twins going to the best school in Ireland! Dylan is incredible, isn't he?'

'Did I hear my godson's name?' Sarah came into the kitchen holding a big chocolate cake. *Congratulations* was written across the middle.

Lucy hugged her. 'It's gorgeous, thank you.'

'I suppose it'll have to be battle of the godmothers,' Jenny said, as she strolled in holding up an equally large cake. 'They can have one each. Mine's for Kelly, though, because it's got white icing, which is her favourite.'

Lucy took it from her sister. 'Thanks, Jenny. She'll be thrilled.'

'Nice to see you out of the shed, Dad,' Jenny said. 'The last two times I've called in you've been hiding in there.'

'Sure I see you all the time, these days. You're never out of the place since you bought that apartment down the road. It's like you never left. Besides, every man needs a room of his own,' Billy said, 'away from all the women's talk.'

'You could learn a lot from women's talk, old man,' Jenny teased. 'I like living nearby – it's nice to be able to drop in anytime I fancy and keep an eye on you.' She picked up an olive and popped it into her mouth. 'I hope the twins don't become all stuck-up and annoying in St Jude's. I like them just the way they are.'

Lucy bristled. 'Of course they won't. They're very grounded, but it's an incredible opportunity. A scholarship for the final two years of their education at the best school in Dublin will set them up for life.'

'None of us went to St Jude's and we all turned out okay,' Jenny pointed out. 'Sarah and I run our own businesses, and you help Dad with the shop and do all our accounts.'

Lucy muttered, 'Not exactly my career goal. I was supposed to be a top lawyer, remember?'

'Hey.' Sarah leant over. 'You have succeeded at the most important job of all, bringing up two amazing kids.'

Lucy smiled. Yes, they were amazing and they had saved her when times were tough. When she looked at them, the disappointment of her life not turning out as she had hoped faded away. Dylan and Kelly were her life. 'They're good kids, but they're by no means perfect.'

'Compared to my two, yours are angels,' Sarah said.

'Come on, Shannon and Ollie are great,' Lucy said.

Jenny coughed as she poured them all a glass of wine.

'They're lively anyway,' she said, handing Sarah and Lucy a glass each.

'I'm grand here, don't mind me,' Billy grumbled.

'Sorry, Dad. Do you want a beer?' Lucy asked, opening the fridge door.

'Don't mind if I do. I've been slaving away here all afternoon and, in case you've forgotten, I'm sixty-four, not seventeen.'

'You've moved a bit of furniture around. It's not exactly slave labour,' Jenny noted.

Lucy handed her father his beer. 'Darren, would you like one?'

'Yes, Darren, you must be worn out over there watching the football,' Sarah drawled at her husband.

'I'm keeping Billy company. Isn't that right?' Darren waved from the sofa at the other end of the kitchen extension.

'Too right, Darren. It's nice to have some male company. Too many bloody women in this house,' Billy grumbled. 'Thank God for Dylan.'

'You love it, Dad. You love having Lucy and Kelly to look after you,' Jenny said.

'Well, I'd be waiting a long time for you to do it,' Billy said.

Jenny grinned. 'Consider me the son you never had. Cheers.'

A teenage girl wearing a very short, tight skirt rushed into the kitchen, followed by a ten-year-old dressed from head to toe in camouflage. 'They're about three minutes away,' the girl shrilled.

'Thanks, Shannon,' Lucy said.

'What in the name of God are you wearing? A face cloth?' Darren asked.

'It's called fashion, Dad. Not that you'd know anything about that. FYI, cords went out in the seventies.'

'I like my cords and no one's going to tell me different.'

'I agree with Shannon. They're horrific and should be burnt,' Jenny said. 'Sarah, seriously, they have to go.'

Sarah shrugged. 'He likes them and he's happy.'

'Yeah, but we have to look at them and they're an eyesore. You're not even forty yet, Darren, so stop dressing like my dad.'

'It's no wonder she hasn't a husband the way she goes on,' Billy said. 'No lad could listen to that kind of abuse.' To his younger daughter, he said, 'You'd want to tone your opinions down or you'll never get a lad to marry you.'

'It's 2016, Dad. Women are allowed to have opinions now, and jobs and the vote.'

'You were born with opinions,' Billy retorted.

'So, Jenny, tell me, what was Elle Sapphire like? Was she nice?' Shannon asked.

Jenny took a sip of her wine. 'She was a total diva. The hotel manager told me that she'd demanded her room be filled with white orchids, Evian bottled water at room temperature, fresh mango, chocolate-covered strawberries and two bottles of Dom Pérignon on ice.'

'Is she stunning?'

'To be honest, she looked a bit rough when I got there. She's got bad skin, but obviously by the time I was finished with her she looked incredible.' Jenny grinned. 'She was tricky, though. She asked me to do her make-up one way and then said it was all wrong and I had to redo the whole thing. Mind you, she paid me a fortune so I'm not complaining.'

'Well, she looked fabulous on TV so you did a great job. Kelly and me wanted to go to her concert but the tickets sold out in seconds.'

'I know. I asked her manager if you two could come backstage with me, but he said no way. Her security is really tight since her kidnapping scare.'

'Did she say anything about Colin King? Are they together?'

'I don't know. I asked her if she was seeing anyone and her PR girl nearly had a seizure – she was all over me like a cheap suit. "No questions." I said, "Relax, I'm just making conversation." But there was no way Elle was going to tell me anything with the PR woman breathing down her neck. It's a pity because if I'd had her on my own I definitely would have got info.'

'You have such a cool job,' Shannon said. 'I bet Kelly ends up doing something creative too. I don't have a creative bone in my body.'

Lucy handed Shannon a party popper. 'Kelly's going to college to get a law degree.'

'Here we go with the law degree,' Jenny said.

Lucy glared at her. 'She's my daughter, Jenny, and she's really bright. There's no way I'm going to let her waste those brains. She's not going to make the mistakes I did. She's going to get a proper degree, and if she wants to do something creative in her spare time or later on in life, she can. But she'll get a solid foundation first.'

'They're here,' Ollie shouted, and ducked down from the window.

Billy switched off the TV and everyone stopped talking. The kitchen door opened, and as the teenagers walked in, everyone jumped up and cheered.

Kelly grabbed Dylan's arm. 'Jesus, guys, you nearly gave me a heart attack,' she gasped.

Dylan grinned. 'Wow, this is great, thanks.'

Lucy went over to hug him. 'I'm so proud of you.'

'Thanks, Mum.'

She turned to Kelly, who was talking to Shannon and Jenny. 'Congratulations,' she said to her daughter.

Kelly shrugged. 'It's Dylan who deserves to be congratulated. He got the scholarship. I'm just part of the package.'

'Yes, but you're really smart and it's a fantastic school and a brilliant opportunity for you.'

'So you keep saying.' Kelly sighed. 'I'm perfectly happy in Woodside. I don't see why Dylan can't go to fancy St Jude's on his own.'

'Can we please not have this argument again?' Lucy said wearily. 'It's the best school in Dublin and tons of really successful lawyers have come out of there. You'll be in good company. I'd appreciate it if you could try to be happy about it.'

'Why should I when I don't want to go?'

'Hey, guys, let's not argue now. Come on, it's a celebration. Look, Kelly, I got you your favourite cake.' Jenny pulled her niece over to look at it. She wanted to get her away from Lucy before another argument blew up. Those two had been fighting since Kelly was born. They were too alike, strong-minded and smart. But Jenny knew that, underneath, Kelly was just a ball of teenage mush and insecurity. She was a lot less confident than Lucy had been at that age, less sure of herself.

Jenny couldn't remember a time when Lucy wasn't banging on about studying law. From a very young age it was all she had ever wanted to do. She was so focused and studious, it had made Jenny's life much harder. Lucy had set the bloody bar so high, and Jenny was never going to come close. It was a good thing Jenny hadn't wanted to do law or anything bookish because she'd always have been second best.

But Kelly was different. She hadn't had an adoring father, like Lucy had. Kelly had no dad – she didn't even know his name. Lucy had told the twins she'd had a fling with a boy in college and that he'd left the country as soon as he'd found out she was pregnant. She had been honest from the beginning but had never told them his name.

Kelly had asked Jenny recently who her dad was. She'd

said she wanted to try to find him, but Jenny had respected her sister's wishes and said she didn't know his name. She'd lied to protect Kelly, too. Tom had made it obvious he wanted nothing to do with them and she couldn't bear her niece to be hurt again.

To be fair, Lucy had been a fantastic mother, but sometimes Jenny wished her sister would go a bit easier on the twins, especially Kelly. She was a great kid and didn't need all that pressure.

Lucy was definitely tougher on Kelly about getting top marks than she was with Dylan. It was as if she saw herself in her and was determined that her daughter would succeed and be the woman Lucy had always wanted to be. But Jenny could see that Kelly was struggling under the weight of expectation. It wasn't fair to put so much on a seventeen-year-old's shoulders. Kelly was smart, and she studied harder than any other teenager Jenny knew. Lucy had decided Kelly was going to be a successful lawyer and that was that. Jenny worried that Kelly would end up being forced into a career that she would hate, just to please her mum.

A glass tinkled. It was Billy. 'If I could have your attention, please.'

Everyone turned to him.

'Get down out of that, Ollie.' Darren pulled his son off the kitchen counter, where he was trying to do a headstand.

'I just want to say a few words to mark this day. First of all, congratulations to Dylan for winning a sports scholarship to St Jude's. I hope you and your sister won't disown us when you start hanging about with the posh set up there.'

'You'd better not.' Shannon nudged Kelly, who rolled her eyes.

'No, but seriously, I want to congratulate Lucy. From the day you twins were born, she's done everything in her power to make your lives the best they can be. She has worked harder than any other mother I know to give you the best life possible and she had to do it on her own. It's not been easy, she's had to dig deep, and I'm very proud of her. She has raised two fantastic young people who are a credit to her.'

'Hear, hear,' Sarah shouted.

'And not only that, but soon after you were born, when your granny Tina got cancer, Lucy had to help nurse her and look after me and Jenny too. She's been the rock in our family. When Tina died I fell apart, but it was Lucy who got me back on my feet. You were only toddlers so you won't remember, but it was your mum who helped me to keep the business afloat and carry on. She's an amazing woman and she has sacrificed so much for this family. We owe her a deep debt of gratitude.'

Lucy brushed a tear away. Dylan put his arm around her. 'He's right. You are brilliant,' he whispered.

'What about me? Remember your other daughter?' Jenny joked to hide the hurt. It stung that Billy only remembered Lucy being brilliant and Lucy nursing Tina. It had been hell for Jenny to watch her mum die and have to sit her Leaving Cert exams while her mother lay in the next room, pumped so full of morphine that she didn't know if it was day or night.

Okay, Lucy had done a lot of the caring, but Jenny had looked after the twins while her sister and her dad had tended Tina. Jenny had also worked in the shop when Lucy was too busy with the kids and Billy was ferrying Tina to and from chemo appointments. Jenny was the one who had made Tina laugh during those awful years, always telling her silly stories to make her smile. But Billy never seemed to remember that. It was always Lucy.

Jenny knew how Kelly felt, having Dylan as the star of the

family, the favourite child. Jenny had always come second, too. Most of the time she hadn't cared but sometimes, like now, it stung a little.

'I'll get to you in a minute.' Billy smiled.

'Dylan and Kelly, I know I'm only your granddad, but I've loved watching you grow up and being able to help out, especially with Dylan's football. My God, the fun I've had watching you become the star player you are. And, Kelly, you're a fantastic girl too, always with your head in your books, doing so well in school. You're a great girl.'

'Yes, she is,' Jenny agreed. 'And drop-dead gorgeous too.'

Kelly blushed. Jenny winked at her. Her niece had no idea how stunning she was. Kelly had really blossomed this summer, going from a tall, gangly teen to a slim, stunning young woman. Her face had fleshed out a little, her skin was tanned, she'd grown her dark hair long and she had those eyes! Lucy said they were Tom's, that Kelly was a beautiful female version of him. No wonder she'd fallen for him, Jenny thought. Those eyes were killer green and mesmerizing.

'I know it hasn't been easy for you both not having a dad around,' Billy continued, 'but your mum has managed to make up for that by being the best mother ever. You're lucky to have her. I thought she was mad when she decided to train as a humanist celebrant to earn more money to pay for all your extra-curricular activities and holidays in Spain, but she's done a great job. People are queuing up to have her marry or bury them.'

'Come on, the Vicar of Violet Road,' Darren heckled.

'She always liked to preach,' Jenny said.

'The ravishing reverend,' Sarah said.

'The pain-in-the-arse preacher,' Kelly muttered, as Shannon giggled beside her.

'I'm still waiting,' Jenny said to Billy.

Billy grinned. 'Twins, you were also very lucky to have an aunt like Jenny, who was living here for the first seven years of your lives and helped out a lot. Even since she moved out she's remained very hands-on with you and will be even more so now she's living in her apartment two minutes away. You'll probably be sick of seeing her.'

'Never,' the twins shouted.

'In all seriousness, it's good to have you so close by, Jenny. We're all delighted you're back in the neighbourhood, and you've been a wonderful aunt to these kids.'

Jenny smiled. Finally, praise from her dad. It felt good. It wasn't the ode-to-Lucy type of praise, but it was nice all the same.

'Well, that's it, really, so here's to you Dylan, Kelly and to my darling Lucy.'

Lucy went up and hugged him. She wiped the tears away with the back of her hand. 'Thanks, Dad, lovely words.'

'I meant every one. You've been incredible, Lucy, to all of us,' Billy whispered in her ear.

'I couldn't have done it without you, Dad. You've been a rock to me too. Especially with Dylan. If it wasn't for you, he'd never have played football – and look at him now, a star.'

'He's a great kid and I've loved watching him play.'

'Do you want some cake, Mum?' Dylan asked.

'Thanks, love.'

Sarah took photos of the twins beside their cakes and more as they rubbed icing into each other's faces.

While the kids stuffed themselves with cake, then watched funny, and inappropriate, videos on YouTube, Sarah and Lucy sat outside in the little front garden, eating cake and drinking wine.

'So, how does it feel for the twins to be going to Tom's old school?' Sarah asked tentatively. Any mention of Tom and Lucy tensed, so she had to tread carefully.

'Weird and wonderful.' Lucy smiled. 'It's a brilliant school and gets the best results in the country year on year, but it also feels like justice that they're ending up there. My abandoned kids will end up in the school their father went to. It's bizarre, but great too. The best part is that they'll get a fantastic education for the last two years of their school lives and the facilities are state-of-the-art. We were all blown away by the sports pitches and gym, the pool, science labs and music rooms.'

'Sounds a lot better than Woodside.'

Lucy put down her wine glass. 'It isn't better, it's just got more to offer. I guess I feel the twins always missed out not having a dad, and now they're getting the chance to finish their education somewhere special. They deserve it.'

Sarah leant over and squeezed her friend's hand. 'They do, and so do you.'

'I know I'm a bit pushy and probably over-ambitious for them, but I messed up so badly and blew my chance at success. I want so much more for them.' Lucy grinned at her. 'Do you want to see something really crazy?'

'What?'

Lucy pulled the letter of confirmation out of her pocket. 'Look.' She pointed to the names of the board of management. There, in black and white, was G. Harrington-Black.

'No way!' Sarah gasped. 'Gabriel's one of the board members who signed off the scholarship?'

'Yes!'

'Do you think he knows?'

'Are you nuts? He'd never have let them in.'

They burst out laughing.

'That's poetic justice,' Sarah said. 'I love it. Do you think Gabriel has any idea at all they are his grandchildren?'

'None. He never knew their Christian names and Murphy, as he so sweetly pointed out, is a common name. So he has no idea that he signed off on allowing the slut's offspring into his posh alma mater.'

They laughed again and clinked glasses, then sat sipping their wine in companionable silence. Lucy was in such a good mood that Sarah decided to chance asking a question she'd been mulling over for a while.

'Lucy, do you think the twins might want to look for Tom when they leave school?'

Lucy sat up in her chair and frowned. 'No, I don't. They know how much he hurt me and that he wanted nothing to do with them. Why the hell would they look for him? He didn't want them. He's dead to them.'

'Okay.' Sarah took a large gulp of wine.

'Sorry, I didn't mean to snap.'

'It's fine. I understand.'

'Dad forgot to mention you in his speech. You've been so good to me, Sarah. Really, I couldn't have done it without your shoulder to cry on and your ear to bash and your kindness and help with babysitting, and taking us on holidays with you and, well, all of it. So, thank you.'

Sarah waved a hand. 'Stop, you'll have me bawling. Besides, I love you and your kids. Kelly is like the sister Shannon never had – the sensible sister she never had – and Dylan is so patient with Ollie and his madness. He's a saint.'

Jenny came out. 'When you two are finished gossiping, Ollie's just karate-chopped Dad in the nuts and knocked over Kelly's cake.'

Sarah groaned. 'Every time! Every bloody time we leave the house he causes mayhem. Stay there. I'll see you later.'

'Thanks for coming, and bringing the cake.'

Lucy sat back and raised her face to the sun. Inside the

house she could hear Darren and Sarah giving out to Ollie and the poor boy trying to defend himself.

She heard someone come out and sit beside her. She opened one eye. It was Dylan.

'Ollie's a nutter.'

'I know, but he's a good kid. He just has a lot of energy.' Ollie was a handful, but Lucy loved him and would defend him to the end.

'Thanks for the surprise party,' Dylan said.

'You're welcome. Thanks for making me so proud.'

'Mum.'

'Yes?'

'Granddad's right. You're a brilliant mum. Thanks for everything. I love you.'

Lucy closed her eyes and let the warmth of his affection wash over her body and soul. She could feel it – this was the start of something special. The best part of their lives was just about to begin.

15

Lucy hummed as she stirred the scrambled eggs. Beside her, Billy popped four slices of bread into the toaster and set four plates on the kitchen table. Lucy's stomach was doing little flips of excitement and anticipation.

'Mum.'

She looked around. There he stood, her pride and joy, dressed in his new school uniform, grey trousers, white shirt and a red and navy striped tie. She tried to control them, but tears sprang into her eyes.

'Oh, God, you're not going to cry, are you?' Dylan asked.

She mopped her eyes and went over to fix his slightly crooked tie.

'You look so . . . well, wonderful,' she said, kissing his cheek before he had time to duck.

'Enough of the emotional stuff.' He grinned. 'I'm starving.'

'You look the part and, remember, they're lucky to have you. Don't ever forget that,' Billy said.

Lucy piled scrambled eggs on top of the toast and handed it to Dylan. At seventeen he was permanently hungry. It amazed her how much food he could consume. Then again, he did train non-stop.

She sat opposite him and stared at his handsome face. He looked like her mum, his granny Tina – blond hair and big brown eyes that would melt chocolate.

Dylan caught her staring. 'What?'

'I'm just so proud of you,' she gushed. 'Getting that scholarship for you and Kelly, it's really amazing.'

'I'm just good at football, Mum, and the new headmaster wants to win the all-Ireland schools cup.'

She shook her head. 'No, it's more than that. This scholarship isn't just about football, it's about who you are, too. They chose you because you're a great kid who has never given any coach or teacher a day's trouble. You're smart too.'

Dylan shovelled more food into his mouth and chewed. Lucy wanted to reach out and touch his face, but she resisted. When he was young he'd loved her hugs. He'd throw his arms around her all the time. She'd snuggle her head into his warm neck and kiss him as he giggled. She could still feel the sensation of his sticky fingers on her skin and his hot cheek beside hers. She closed her eyes and savoured the memory.

'What are you doing, Mum? You look weird.' Kelly's voice cut through the moment.

Lucy stood up. 'I was just remembering when Dylan was small.'

'Whatever, can you do this stupid tie? I have no idea how it works.'

'I'll do it. Come here to me.' Billy did up Kelly's tie and kissed her forehead. 'Now you're perfect.'

'Thanks, Granddad.'

Lucy put a plate of scrambled eggs and toast in front of her.

Kelly frowned. 'I hate scrambled eggs.'

'No, you don't.'

'Yes, I bloody do.'

'Language,' Billy warned.

'I'm not eating this.' Kelly pushed her plate away.

Lucy willed herself to be calm and not lose her temper. 'Eat up, Kelly, or you'll be hungry in school.'

Kelly handed her plate to Dylan. 'You can have it, seeing as you actually like it. I'll pass.'

'Kelly,' Lucy snapped. 'You need a good breakfast.'

'Well, why didn't you make me something I actually like?'

'Stop it, Kelly. You do like scrambled eggs. Don't be difficult.'

'No, I don't. You make them for Saint Dylan because he loves them and occasionally when I'm so hungry I think I'm going to die I eat some just to keep me alive.'

Lucy didn't want an argument, not today, on their first day at their new school. 'Fine, have cereal, then.'

Kelly grabbed a box, filled a bowl to the top, poured in some milk and began to eat. She was hunched over it with one arm protectively around the bowl as if she was afraid someone was going to steal it. She was like a cat, always ready to pounce, Lucy thought.

Kelly tugged at her tie, then spilt milk on it.

'Kelly, love, be careful, you don't want to look a mess on your first day.'

'What? It's just a bit of milk, no big deal.' She wiped it with a napkin.

Lucy felt her shoulders tense. Why couldn't Kelly just behave? Why did she have to cause trouble on this special day? 'It is a big deal,' Lucy said. 'It's your first day at St Jude's. This is an incredible opportunity for you and you need to make a good impression.'

Kelly slammed her napkin down and spun around to face her mother. 'Oh, I know, Mum. I have to be the perfect student in this stupid posh school that you're forcing me to go to.'

'Forcing you?' Lucy spluttered. 'Do you have any idea how lucky you are? Because of your brilliant brother, you are now going to the best school in Dublin for free.'

'Lucky?' Kelly shouted. 'I never wanted to go there. I was happy in my old school. I don't want to be a charity-case scholarship student just because my twin brother's brilliant at football.'

'Ah, now, come on. We're all a bit uptight because it's a big day. Let's calm down,' Billy suggested. 'Kelly, finish up your breakfast and, Lucy, you have some coffee.' Billy poured her a cup.

'Relax, Kelly,' Dylan said, looking at her with concern. 'It's all good.'

Kelly bent her head low and finished her cereal. She said nothing, but Lucy could feel her daughter's rage. She prayed Kelly would try her best and not let herself or Dylan down. She had to behave and do well. She had to show everyone how great she was and how smart. Lucy wanted everyone in that stuck-up school to see how wonderful her kids were and what a bloody great job she'd done bringing them up on her own. She wanted Gabriel to hear about the Murphy twins and what a credit they were to St Jude's, and she wanted to be there when he realized they were his grandchildren and that Lucy, the gold-digging whore, had done it – she'd raised two incredible children.

Lucy went up to her bedroom and took her best navy jacket from the hanger. She put it on over her navy shift dress, the one she wore to celebrate a lot of her humanist ceremonies. She looked in the mirror on the back of the door. The outfit was a bit boring and conservative, but she wanted to blend into the background.

She was a bit nervous about meeting the other parents. What if one of them recognized her? What if she bumped into one of Tom's old friends, like Andy or Olivia? She'd changed her hair – it was honey-coloured and short now, 'gamine style', Sarah had said when she'd cut it. It had been seventeen years but, still, they might recognize her and she wasn't sure how she'd handle it.

Dylan knocked gently on the door and came in. He had his navy school blazer on and looked so handsome. He was born to go to a school like St Jude's. He'd fit in, no problem. Billy was right: they were lucky to have him.

'Ready, Mum?' he asked.

'Yes. You okay?'

He smiled. 'Keen to get in there and meet the other football players and classmates and all that.'

'Right, well, let's go, then.'

'You look lovely, Mum,' he said. 'A bit square, but nice.'

Lucy beamed at him. 'Where's your sister?'

'Here.' Kelly slouched outside the door, her school skirt rolled up and her tie askew. Her hair was tied up in a messy bun, the way she liked it. Lucy wanted to pull down her daughter's skirt and brush her hair, but she resisted. They didn't have time for an argument now.

In the twenty-five minutes it took to drive to school, Lucy and Kelly had two arguments. They never stopped sniping at each other.

Dylan felt bad for Kelly. He knew she loved her old school and her friends and that she wasn't thrilled about going to St Jude's. But it was the best school in the country and it was making their mum so happy. He wished she'd go with it. He wanted his twin to settle in and enjoy St Jude's. She was so smart, he knew that even in this posh school Kelly would be top of the class. Dylan was always amazed at how hard she studied. He was middle of the class. He did enough to keep his mother off his case but never exactly killed himself. Besides, his mother didn't seem to expect too much of him in terms of study and books – that was Kelly's role. He was sport, Kelly was law: that was how it had always been.

Dylan was psyched about the new coach at St Jude's, Jordan Green, who was top class. They'd poached him from

Plymouth Argyle – an actual professional club. All right, it was a second-division club and he'd been the assistant coach but, still, he was the real deal. Dylan couldn't wait to train under him.

It was Jordan who had come to see Dylan play for his old club and approached his mum about a scholarship. The best part about winning it was that Dylan could see he was making his mum happy. She was obsessed with education and getting a degree. She kept telling him and Kelly, 'Don't end up like me. Finish your degree and get a proper profession.'

Dylan knew she'd had to give it all up for him and Kelly, then to nurse Granny when she was sick and afterwards to look after Granddad and the shop. His mum had never really been able to do what she wanted. Dylan had always felt he had to succeed. With his dad legging it before they were even born, he felt the pressure to make up for that somehow. He wanted to prove to his mum that she had raised a decent son, not someone who would run away from his responsibilities. He had always wanted to make her happy and proud and make up for his deadbeat dad.

His mum barely mentioned his dad, and Jenny had given him and Kelly the tiny amount of info they had. Jenny had said Lucy had been really smart in school and top of her law class in Trinity. But then she'd met their dad, got pregnant, and her dreams were shattered.

Dylan was sorry things hadn't worked out for his mum. He thought his dad was a total prick. Life had been hard for Lucy. But since he'd got the scholarship, she had been really happy, which made him feel good too. Now his mother and sister were bickering about how short Kelly's skirt was. Dylan was ready and raring to go. He just wanted to get out of the car and not have to listen to them arguing. He was keen to meet his teammates and, most of all, to impress Jordan. He'd been working on his fitness all summer, when he wasn't helping out in the shop, and he felt really good.

Lucy pulled up at the back of the car park and got out. She gave Dylan a hug. 'Good luck today, you'll be great.'

Dylan put his school bag and kit bag over his shoulder. Lucy tried to hug Kelly but she squirmed. 'Stop, you're embarrassing me.'

'Bye, Kelly, try smiling. It might help not to scare the other kids off. You have a beautiful smile.'

'Bye, Mum. Thanks for ruining my life.' Kelly spun on her heels and walked up to her twin.

Dylan put his arm around her. 'Give her a break, Kelly. You might actually like it here.'

Kelly shrugged him off. 'I liked my old school. This is all your fault. You and your stupid bloody football.'

'I'm not going to apologize for being a legend on the soccer pitch.' Dylan grinned.

'Oh, sod off, Ronaldo.' Kelly half smiled.

'Hi, it's Dylan, right?'

They turned, and a boy of Dylan's age was standing behind them.

'I'm Conor, the goalie. We're stoked to have you on the team, dude.'

'Thanks.' Dylan shook his hand. 'This is my sister, Kelly.'

'Hi,' Conor said, looking Kelly up and down admiringly. 'Great to meet you.'

Kelly muttered, 'Hello.'

Dylan had noticed that recently guys were looking at his sister in a very you-are-so-hot kind of way and it made him uncomfortable. He didn't want them ogling her.

'So, are you twins?'

'Yeah, the least identical ones in the world,' Kelly said.

'It worked out pretty well for you, though.' Conor grinned and Kelly blushed.

A girl came up to say hello to Conor. 'Guys, this is Chloë. Chloë, this is Dylan and Kelly Murphy.'

'Oh, right, you're the scholarship kids. I think you're in my house, Kelly – I'm vice-captain. All the students are divided into one of four houses – Knights, Spartans, Samurai and Trojans. We're Trojans. Two of my best friends, Melissa and Alicia, are in it too. Give me your number and I'll add you to the WhatsApp group. If you're not on it you'll be, like, a total outcast.'

Kelly gave Chloë her number. Her phone pinged instantly. The Trojans group. Messages began flashing up, her classmates saying, 'Hi,' which was nice.

'Where do we go?' Dylan asked.

'Fifth-year corridor is through that door and it's the first on your right, but why don't you come with me, Dylan? I'm heading to the locker room first to dump my goalie gear. I'll introduce you to the rest of the team.'

Dylan followed Conor and glanced back over his shoulder. Kelly was talking to Chloë. He hoped she'd be all right.

At lunchtime, Conor walked Dylan down to the canteen. They sat with the other football players. Dylan said little and observed them. They seemed like a tight bunch. There was lots of slagging and talk about previous games.

'So, Dylan, what was your goal-scoring average last year?' Conor asked.

'It worked out two point four goals per game,' he said.

'Not bad.'

'I hope you're as good as everyone says you are,' a guy called Jackson said, glaring at Dylan. 'Because my best mate, Nathan, got dropped for you and he's not happy. Nor am

I. He's played with us all the way until now and then he just got dumped.'

The rest of the team looked at Dylan. He chewed his pasta slowly. It was sticking to the roof of his mouth. He tried to swallow it. He needed to get this guy onside. He didn't want any aggro. He just wanted to play football, but he had to tread carefully. The guy was angry.

He raised his hands. 'Look, mate, I don't want to step on anyone's toes here. Jordan came to see me play and he liked what he saw. He's a class coach. I came here because of him. I want to improve and hopefully help St Jude's win the cup. I'm sorry about your mate, but football is all about moving forward and making the team stronger.'

'Well, I hope you bring your A game to practice. I'd like to be impressed,' Jackson said.

Dylan nodded. 'I always do.' He held Jackson's gaze.

'Don't mind him. He's just pissed off about Nathan being dropped,' Conor whispered.

Dylan smiled. Jackson was a pussy cat compared to some of the nutters he'd had to deal with in his old school. Generally, people left him alone because he was a local football hero, but there had still been a few lads who were always looking for a fight. Dylan could look after himself.

As they were finishing their lunch a stunning blonde girl, with tanned skin, sparkling blue eyes and a very short uniform skirt, strutted by their table.

'Hi, Taylor,' one of the lads said.

'Oh, hi, David.' She stopped and turned to face them. Her blouse was open so you could just see the top of her bra. Man, she had a great set of boobs. Dylan could feel his temperature rising.

'How was your summer?' David asked.

'Amazeballs. We went to St Tropez and partied hard.'

'You look good, nice tan.'

'Thanks, I worked hard on it.' Turning to Dylan, she asked, 'Who's this?'

'Dylan's the new striker.'

Taylor's eyes locked with Dylan's. 'What's a striker?'

Dylan gave her his best smile. He hoped it was sexy and not creepy. 'The striker is the guy who scores all the goals.'

She smiled back at him. 'Well, good luck with your striking.' She swung her hips away from the table, and as she got to the door she turned, obviously to check if he was still looking at her. Dylan wasn't looking, he was staring.

'Dude, you're dribbling,' Conor said, with a laugh.

'Who is she?' Dylan asked.

'Taylor Lyons.'

'She's –'

'Sizzling.' Conor grinned.

'Is she going out with anyone?'

'She was with an older guy who was in first-year medicine, but they broke up over the summer.'

Dylan smiled. 'So she's single.'

'I guess so.'

Today just kept getting better. Dylan finished his pasta and hoped Taylor would turn up in some of his classes.

As he was walking across the yard to the science lab he caught a glimpse of Kelly. She was sitting in a corner, half hidden by a tree, with her headphones on. He was about to go over to her when Conor grabbed his sleeve. 'Come on, Mrs Long goes mad if you're late.'

Dylan felt bad seeing his sister like that, all alone. He hoped she'd settle in. He knew she missed her old pals, but this school was pretty amazing, and if she gave it a go, he reckoned she'd enjoy it. After only half a day he loved it. Besides, she could go and see them all after school and at weekends. He missed his old teammates, who had been in school with him too, but he'd make new friends.

That's what you did. You moved on, you looked forward, you went for your goals. Dylan reckoned it was simple – life was like football: you could never sit still, you had to keep moving.

16

Kelly swept the hair from under the chairs in the salon. She listened to the chatter of the women and the stylists – holidays, news stories, local gossip, sick husbands, troublesome children, you heard it all in Sarah's salon.

Sarah finished her last highlight and set the timer. She nodded to Kelly and made a drinking gesture. Kelly put the broom away and followed her into the back room. She sat on the small orange couch while Sarah pressed buttons on the coffee machine.

'Ah, for the love of God, I can't work this fancy thing out at all. Darren keeps buying these complicated machines. I was happy with my kettle and instant coffee.'

Kelly grinned and got up. She took the cup from Sarah. 'I'll do it.'

'Thanks, love.' Sarah perched on the arm of the couch. She was very different from Lucy – they were like opposites.

While Lucy was thin, bony, all sharp edges and huge brown eyes, Sarah was soft and cuddly. She had kind blue eyes and a gorgeous smile. She was a few sizes bigger than Lucy, but she was taller so she carried it well. Lucy was better-looking, if Kelly was being honest, but everyone loved Sarah because she was so kind and almost always in a good mood, except when Ollie did something totally mad or Shannon was being bolshie.

Sarah changed her hair colour all the time. It had been red for a while, but when she'd turned thirty-eight last month she'd dyed it peroxide blonde. Kelly thought she looked cool.

She always wore black, 'because it makes me look thinner', but usually with bright lipstick so she looked cheerful.

Kelly handed her a cappuccino.

'You're a wonder with that machine. Thank you,' Sarah said. 'Now, tell me, how are you finding the new school?'

Kelly tried to sip her latte, but it stuck in her throat. She felt a lump forming and then, without seeing it coming, she burst into tears. She covered her face. She was mortified. She never cried.

'Ah, now, come here to me.' Sarah put her sturdy arms around Kelly and patted her on the back. 'It can't be that bad after only a week.'

'It is.' Kelly sniffed. 'I hate it.'

'Moving to a new school at seventeen is hard. It's normal that you're finding it tough. But don't worry, pet, it'll get easier.'

Kelly wiped her eyes with the sleeve of her jumper. 'I don't think it will, Sarah. They all have their own groups – they've been friends for years. I'm a total outsider. There's this one girl Chloë who was all friendly and added me to the house WhatsApp group, but she has me down as "Kelly Scholarship". It's like I have a tattoo on my head – SCHOLARSHIP GIRL. Her friend Melissa seems like a real bitch. She looks at me like I'm scum.'

'There are mean kids in every school. Sure, a boy in Ollie's class asked him if he was retarded. Imagine, at ten years of age!'

'What?'

'I know, the cheek of him.' Sarah blew on her hot coffee. 'Now, come on, they can't all be rotten like Melissa. What are the other kids like?'

Kelly shrugged. 'Some of them seem okay, I guess, but they all have friends already. I haven't really got to know any of them. I just want to go back to Woodside and hang out with Shannon and Mandy. I wish Dylan had never got that scholarship.'

'It's a fantastic opportunity for him to train with a great coach, and it's a brilliant school. A lot of very successful people went to St Jude's and, soon enough, you'll be one of them.'

Sarah felt she had to say what Lucy would want her to say. She knew how much all this meant to her friend, but it was hard to see poor Kelly so upset. If only she'd left Kelly at Woodside and just sent Dylan to St Jude's, everything would be fine.

Kelly threw her hands into the air. 'I'm no good at sport so the "amazing facilities" Mum keeps banging on about make no difference to me, and I can work hard in any school. The Leaving Cert curriculum is the same. Besides,' Kelly exhaled deeply, 'don't tell Mum because she'll actually have a full-on heart attack and probably kill me, but I don't want to study law. I want to go to art college and study fashion and design.'

Sarah took a sip of coffee to gather her thoughts. Lucy *would* have a heart attack if she thought Kelly wasn't going to study law. Her heart and soul were set on it. Kelly was going to have the life Lucy should have had, and Lucy was incapable of seeing any other path for her. Sarah chose her words carefully. 'Okay, pet, but you might change your mind. Shannon has a new plan every second day. And even if you do decide not to study law, although I really think you shouldn't rule it out, you're still getting a great education. And . . . well . . . it's really important that you try your best. It means the world to your mum and you should show the St Jude's teachers how great you are. Let all of them and the headmaster, all of the parents and kids at the school, see what a fantastic girl Lucy raised.'

Kelly sighed. 'You sound like Mum now. She keeps going on about how I have to shine and be perfect. It's just a stupid school.'

Sarah paused. 'Well, it's not just any old school. It's pretty special, so why not do your best and make yourself and your mum proud? Give it your best shot, Kelly, for your own sake.'

Kelly put her coffee down. 'Okay, I'll try.'

'Good for you, and remember, the first week of anything new is difficult. You'll be okay. Just keep smiling your beautiful smile and they'll all fall in love with you – the boys definitely will anyway. Are there any cute ones?'

Kelly smiled. 'Well, yes, actually. There's one guy, William, who's pretty gorgeous.'

'See? It's not all bad.' Sarah grinned. 'Now I've to go and wash the colour out of Mrs Kilmore's hair. No doubt it'll be wrong – there's no pleasing that one. But she always comes back.'

Kelly washed and dried the mugs and leant against the sink. She knew Sarah was right – she should try – but she was still furious that her life had been turned upside-down for Dylan. No one had asked her what she wanted. The decision was made and she was supposed to just suck it up. She wondered what her mother's life would have been like if she hadn't got pregnant. Would she have become a successful lawyer? Would she have got married? Would she be happy? Would she have had kids?

Her phone beeped. It was a message from Lucy: *Are u on ur way home?* Kelly knew her mum loved her, but she wished she'd back off and let her breathe. She was always on her case, checking where she was, who she was with and what she was doing. Jenny said it was because she was afraid Kelly might make the 'same mistake'.

But Kelly wasn't stupid: she wouldn't have unprotected

sex with anyone. She knew the risks – she'd heard her mum talk about them often enough. But obviously Lucy didn't think so and was planning to stalk her until she got married. Even Shannon thought Lucy was ridiculously over-protective. She'd nicknamed her the Jailer.

The really annoying thing was that Lucy wasn't as hard on Dylan. She kept a close eye on him, but nothing like the steel grip she had on Kelly. 'Dylan's a boy,' her mum had said, when Kelly complained. 'They get to walk away. Girls get left holding the babies.'

If Lucy didn't tell them so often how much she loved them and how they were her world, Kelly would have thought sometimes that she regretted having them, but she knew she didn't. On every Christmas, birthday and family occasion, Lucy would say the same thing: 'You two are my world and my life. I love you more than anything.' Then she'd get all choked up and cry. It was embarrassing and kind of awkward, but Kelly still liked her mum saying it. It made up for the feeling she had sometimes that Lucy had sacrificed so much for them that they had ruined her dreams.

Kelly wondered if Lucy was lonely. She had Billy, but your dad wasn't the same as a husband or boyfriend. Lucy was pretty, but she never seemed to date anyone. Kelly had asked her once if she'd like to meet a man, but she had laughed in a don't-be-ridiculous way and said, 'I don't have time for a man and, besides, I'm perfectly happy with you and Dylan.'

And she did seem happy. When they were younger, Saturday night was movie night. Billy would go to the pub with his friends, and Lucy, Kelly and Dylan would cuddle up on the couch under a big duvet with a box of chocolates and watch movies. Kelly always remembered her mum saying it was her favourite time of the week.

But when they'd got older Dylan had started going out

with his mates and Kelly usually called over to Shannon's house to watch a movie or do make-up and hair and try on each other's clothes. So, for the past few years, Lucy had been on her own every Saturday. Sometimes Kelly stayed in with her because she felt sorry for her and wanted to keep her company.

She was glad when her mum had trained as a humanist celebrant five years ago, although in the beginning they'd all thought Lucy had gone mad and wanted to be a vicar or a priest or something. But when she'd explained it to them, it sounded quite cool. Kelly didn't believe in God and thought the humanist way was brilliant. Humanists believe that the happiness of humans depends on people, rather than on religion, and Kelly one hundred per cent agreed. As Lucy had explained, 'It's about being good without God.'

Billy had been wary. He'd thought it was a cult and that Lucy was going to end up taking the twins to live in some commune. He was very against her doing it, but when she'd explained it to him and told him she'd be earning up to seven hundred euros per wedding, he'd come round to the idea.

Kelly thought it was kind of cool to have a mum who married gay people – almost half of her mum's weddings were gay couples – and she'd done naming ceremonies for gay couples with kids. It was weird, though: she was open-minded, accepting and kind to everyone except Kelly. With Kelly, Lucy was always super-strict and obsessed with her getting a good degree so she could always support herself.

As Kelly walked down the road from the salon to her house, she resolved to do what Sarah had said. She'd try to fit in at St Jude's and make her mum happy. But she had a feeling it wasn't going to be easy. Maybe if she worked hard and got good results, she could talk to her about not wanting to do law. If she showed her how hard she was willing to work and try to fit in at school, maybe they'd stop fighting and Kelly could explain to her that she really wanted a career in fashion.

When she was younger she'd played along with the law thing because she'd seen how proud and happy it made her mum. Every time Lucy had said, 'My Kelly's going to be a lawyer,' and beamed at her, it had made Kelly feel all warm inside. Lately, though, she'd tried dropping hints about fashion and showing her mum some of the clothes she'd made, but Lucy just treated it as a 'little hobby'.

Kelly had no idea how to explain to her mother that her 'little hobby' was her life's passion. If only she had finished her own stupid law degree, perhaps she wouldn't be trying to force Kelly to live the life she'd wanted. Kelly felt as if somehow she had to make up for her mother's mistakes and it was starting to get to her.

17

Sarah looked at the sign on Ollie's door and shook her head. *If you risk nothing, you gain nothing.* She turned the handle and went in to wake up her son, but he wasn't in his bed.

'Where the feck are my glasses?' Darren shouted, from their bedroom.

'You left them in the bathroom,' Sarah said.

'They're not there.'

'Try the chest of drawers.'

'I did.'

'Have you seen Ollie?' Sarah asked.

'I thought he was still asleep.'

'He's not in his bed.'

Sarah went into Shannon's room. Her sixteen-year-old was splayed across the bed, fast asleep. Clothes were strewn all over the floor.

Darren came up behind her. 'Ollie's not in his bed and it's quiet. Jesus, what's that nut-job up to now?'

They hurried downstairs. Ollie was nowhere to be seen. Sarah looked out of the kitchen window and saw a small dark figure in front of a . . . fire!

'Darren,' she shouted. 'He's out the back.'

She ran outside and towards the flames. 'What in the name of God, Ollie?' she roared.

Behind her, dragging the hose, was Darren.

Ollie turned around, eyes shining. 'I did it, Mum. It took a while, but I did it, just like Bear Grylls.'

Sarah dragged her ten-year-old son away from the flames. 'Are you stone mad? You could have burnt yourself alive.'

The fire was six foot high and the flames had set the hedge alight. Cursing, Darren hosed down the blaze.

'Ah, Dad, you've ruined it!' Ollie shouted. 'I wanted to roast these ants over it and eat them. Bear Grylls says they taste fine and are full of protein.'

Darren put the hose down. He was breathing heavily. 'For the love of Jesus, will you stop listening to that fecker?'

Ollie's face was black with smoke. 'Bear Grylls is a legend,' he said. 'It took me an hour to get that fire going and now you've drowned it.'

'I'll drown you in a minute,' Darren snapped.

Sarah put her hand on her son's shoulder. 'Ollie, we've told you a million times you can't play with fire. You could get burnt or die. You have to stop with all this madness.'

'It's not mad, it's survival. I'm learning how to survive in the wilderness.'

'You're lighting fires in the back garden of your house. We live in the centre of Dublin. It's not the Amazon jungle,' Darren roared. 'If I hadn't put that fire out the hedge would have gone up and the house and next door. How do you think Joe would like waking up to his house on fire? Why can't you just play football, like normal ten-year-olds?'

'Don't listen to dream-stealers, that's what Bear Grylls says, and you are a dream-stealer, Dad. One hundred per cent.'

'Dream-stealer? Are you joking me? We've been to hospital five times with you in the last eight months since you saw that feckin' eejit on YouTube and started trying to copy him.'

'His dad let him sky-dive.'

'Yes, Ollie, his dad did let him sky-dive, and then he nearly paralysed himself when his parachute ripped.' Sarah had been reading up on Bear Grylls to try to understand

Ollie's obsession and nip it in the bud before her son killed himself.

'Yeah, well, that was bad luck and, anyway, eighteen months later he climbed Mount Everest to the top!'

'He's a man, Ollie. He was trained by the British Army. You're just a kid. You can't be like him.'

'I can try. If you and Dad weren't so mean, I could be Ireland's Bear Grylls, but you never want me to do anything so I'll never make it.'

Beside them Darren was raking through the fire with a stick. 'You've got to be kidding me. You have got to be bloody kidding me!' he shouted, as he held up a pair of charred glasses. 'A hundred and fifty euros these cost me. What the hell?'

Ollie looked guilty. 'I was using them to start the fire. You need glasses and then you spit on the lens and use it to angle the sun and some dry leaves and twigs and that's how you start the fire. It took ages, but it worked, Dad. It actually worked.'

Darren threw his arms out. 'Ah, well, then, it was worth it. Using my very expensive glasses to spit on and start a fire at nine on a Sunday morning was worth it. That's just brilliant, Ollie, feckin' brilliant. And tell me now, how am I supposed to work when I can't see? How am I supposed to wire people's houses when everything's a blur?'

'Maybe I could fix them. I'll look it up on YouTube.'

'I'll tell you what you can do. You can stay the hell away from YouTube, Bear Grylls and anything to do with survival or fire or eating bugs or climbing mountains or any of it. Get up to your room and out of my sight.'

Ollie stomped off. 'Fine, I will,' he shouted, over his shoulder. 'But you're a dream-stealer, Dad, a big fat dream-stealer.'

'I'd rather be a dream-stealer than taking you to hospital

with third-degree burns.' Darren turned to his wife and sighed. 'What are we going to do with him?'

Sarah had no idea. Ollie had come into the world ten years ago kicking and screaming. When she'd got pregnant, they'd been overjoyed. She'd had two miscarriages after Shannon. But there had been a lot of complications during the pregnancy and Sarah had had to spend a lot of it on bedrest. Darren had barely let her move. And then Ollie had arrived eight weeks early. They'd nearly lost him, but he was a fighter. Sarah could still remember the first time she'd held his tiny body in her arms, her precious baby.

Ollie had spent eight weeks in the neo-natal ward being monitored. Darren had been incredible. He'd spent hours holding Ollie's hand through the hole in the incubator, willing him to grow and get stronger. Darren had more love to give than anyone else Sarah had ever met. She knew how lucky she was to have married him. Always there for her, her rock.

At first Ollie had seemed a quiet, content little baby, but when he'd figured out how to crawl, all hell had broken loose. He was so different from Shannon, who had sat and coloured or calmly watched cartoons. Ollie never, ever sat still. Not for a single second. He was like a Duracell bunny. He went and went. 'Lively', 'high-spirited' and 'energetic' were some of the words the neighbours used to describe him, often through gritted teeth.

They'd signed him up for football when he was five, but he wasn't interested. The coach said he'd spent the whole time climbing up the goalpost and hanging upside-down from it.

They'd put him in the Scouts, but he'd been kicked out: the boys had gone on a camping trip and Ollie had disappeared for four hours. When they'd found him, he was up a tree and refused to come down. He'd wanted to see if he could survive there for the night, eating mushrooms and drinking his own pee. The Scout leader had had to climb up and get him down, but Ollie had struggled with him and the leader had fallen and broken his arm. That had been the end of Scouts.

'Do you think he's normal?' Darren had asked one night, after they'd found Ollie microwaving a snail.

Sarah knew that Ollie was normal. He was just different-normal. He liked more extreme stuff than most kids his age. When Santa had brought him a skateboard last Christmas, in the hope that he'd go outside with the other kids to skate up and down the road, Ollie had had other ideas. He had put a ladder against the back wall of the house and tried to skateboard down it from his bedroom window. Thankfully, he'd only broken his wrist, not his neck.

The thing was, Sarah loved his adventurous spirit. That was who Ollie was. But it terrified her too. She'd wanted a big family, but Shannon and Ollie were all she'd ever have. They were her world. She wanted to protect Ollie but not stifle him.

Darren just wanted him to play football, tip-the-can and skateboard on horizontal surfaces. He wanted him to be a normal kid. He didn't understand Ollie's obsession with survival and danger. Sarah knew Darren was scared of something happening to Ollie. He adored his son, he just didn't share his idea of hobbies.

Darren sat in the kitchen looking at the charred mess that had once been his glasses.

'Cup of tea?' Sarah asked.

'I need a drink after that,' he said.

'It's half nine so tea will have to do.'

Shannon came in wearing her pink fluffy onesie. 'I presume Ollie's done something mad again.'

'Ah, nothing much, just started a fire in the garden with my glasses,' Darren said.

'He should be locked up. He's seriously mental in the head.' Shannon poured herself some tea.

'Don't say that, he's just curious,' Sarah said.

Shannon rolled her eyes. 'He's a lunatic, Mum, and you never say boo to him. If I started a fire in the garden, you'd kill me. He gets away with murder.'

'Do you think we could get Dylan to talk to him, maybe persuade him to give soccer another go?' Darren asked.

'Leave poor Dylan alone. He's enough going on in his posh new school,' Shannon said.

Darren blew on his tea and took a sip. 'How's he getting on anyway?'

'Dylan's flying, but Kelly hates it,' Shannon said. 'She says the girls in her class are bitches. I said they're just jealous because Kelly is so gorgeous and smart. It's a pain for me having a deranged lunatic for a brother, but I actually think it's worse for Kelly because Dylan is her twin and he's a star. I mean, she was basically forced to move to that stupid school because of him. I think it's a crime. Lucy didn't even ask Kelly, just told her she was going.'

'She'll settle soon. It's hard adjusting, that's all,' Sarah said.

'No, it isn't, Mum. She'll never like it there. You can't just go to a school in fifth year and find friends. The only kids without friends at our age are the geeks and freaks.'

'I'm sure when the other girls get to know her they'll hang out with her. These things take time, and it is a good opportunity.'

'For who?' Shannon demanded. 'For Dylan it is, because he has a great new coach, but for Kelly what's so great?'

'Well, the school has fantastic facilities,' Sarah said.

Shannon banged her mug down on the table. 'She hates sport and she doesn't play any instruments so she doesn't need a fancy gym or a stupid music school. And FYI, if Ollie has to go to a special school for mental cases, don't even think of moving me too because I amn't going and no one will make me. No one. I think Lucy is a mean cow for making Kelly move.' Shannon stormed out of the room, the fluffy backside of her onesie wriggling.

'She's a strong mind on her that one!' Darren said, shaking his head.

Ollie came into the kitchen wearing his army camouflage trousers and T-shirt. 'I'm sorry about your glasses, Dad. Here.' He thrust ten euros into Darren's hand. 'I don't have any more, but I'll do jobs for you. I'll cut the grass now if you want.'

'No need, son. You scorched it this morning. Besides, you might remember that the lawnmower is broken because you tried to ride it to school.'

'Oh, yeah, sorry about that. Well, I could . . .' Ollie looked around the kitchen for inspiration.

'Why don't you come down to visit Grandpa Brian with me?'

Ollie frowned. 'He keeps calling me the wrong name and the place stinks of wee.'

'Well, that shouldn't bother you. Doesn't your pal Bear Grylls drink his own wee all the time?'

'Not all the time, only when he's out of water.'

'Are you coming or not?'

'Can I get a can of Coke on the way back?'

'You don't want to drink your own urine then?'

'Shut up, Dad.'

'Come on, you messer.' Darren pulled Ollie to him in a hug.

Sarah watched them go and smiled, her two boys. She silently prayed that Ollie would not cause any trouble or break anything in the old folks' home.

18

Sarah handed Lucy a glass of wine.

'Thanks, I need this.'

'It's me who should be thanking you for doing my wages every month. You're a lifesaver. Can you believe the salon's been open fifteen and a half years?'

'It seems almost impossible,' Lucy said. 'I remember when you started – the twins were so small. That was a great party you had to celebrate fifteen years.'

'Yeah, it was, and you're very much part of the salon's success. Come to think of it, you've been doing my maths for me since school. Remember? You used to let me copy your homework every day so I wouldn't get into trouble.'

Lucy grinned. 'I do remember, and you helped me get my nose out of books and have a social life. If it wasn't for you, I'd probably never have kissed a boy.'

Sarah laughed. 'Oh, with those beautiful brown eyes you'd have melted a few hearts on your own. Speaking of school, how's Kelly? Shannon mentioned she was finding it a bit tough settling in.' Sarah went for a soft approach: she knew how prickly Lucy could be about St Jude's.

'She's fine. She's just being Kelly. She hates change. Remember when I moved her to Woodside? She went mad and hated it in the beginning, then loved it.'

That was true. Kelly had been furious when she was sent to Woodside Senior School and Dylan had gone to St Brendan's. But that was because she had been parted from Dylan for the first time in her life. At thirteen years of age she'd found that really difficult, but in St Jude's they were back together, so in theory it should be an easier transition.

'It's not easy moving school at this late stage, though,' Sarah said. 'Dylan has his football team as a ready-made group of friends, but it's probably harder for Kelly to fit in.'

Lucy sighed. 'If Kelly smiled once in a blue moon it might help her make friends. She seems determined not to like St Jude's just to spite me. I know she'll settle soon, though. She needs to knuckle down, show them how smart she is and prove to them how lucky they are to have a girl like her in the school too.'

'I suppose so, but maybe go easy on her for the first few months and help her settle.'

Lucy put her glass down with a bang. 'I'd have given my right arm to get a scholarship to the best school in Ireland. She's lucky, Sarah. Yes, there are some stupid snobby kids there, but there are some nice ones too.'

Sarah picked up the bottle to refill their glasses as the kitchen door opened.

'Look who I found.' Darren came in, followed by Jenny. 'She was looking for the two of you and I had a feeling you'd be here having your post-wage-day drinks.'

'Wine! Great.' Jenny shrugged off her coat and sat down.

'How was your wedding?' Lucy asked her sister.

'Fine, the usual. Nervous bride, psycho mother, drunk bridesmaid, grumpy father, who cursed under his breath when I told him how much he owed me, and sleazy uncle who tried to pinch my bum until I told him I'd twist his dick into a knot if he came any closer.'

'Ah, Jenny, you've such a lovely way with men.' Darren grinned at her.

Jenny waved an empty glass in his face. 'Shut up and pour.'

'I've a wedding coming up, too,' Lucy said. 'A lesbian

couple. They're lovely, and great together, but the mother of one bride is not happy with her daughter being gay and is causing ructions. She got hold of my number and asked me not to perform the ceremony. I tried talking to her and suggested it would be nice for her daughter if she got involved in it, but she kept saying awful things like "It's not normal" and "Women should be with men" and "It's not God's way." Honestly, I'm worried she'll turn up and cause a huge scene. I feel so sorry for Debbie. She's devastated that her mother won't accept her for who she is.'

'It's a lesson to us all to accept our kids as they are and not try to change them,' Sarah said, one eye on Lucy to see her reaction.

'She should just tell her mother to fuck off.'

'It's not that easy, Jenny,' Lucy said. 'The mother isn't a bad person – she loves her daughter very much. She's just old-fashioned and has different beliefs. Debbie and her partner can't dismiss her. They have to try to make her see that what matters is her daughter's happiness.'

'Yes, but if she keeps refusing to accept who her daughter is, she'll lose her,' Sarah said.

'That's what I said to her,' Lucy said.

Sarah wondered if Lucy could see the irony. She wasn't accepting who Kelly really was – a girl who didn't want to change school, a girl who wanted to be a designer, a girl who didn't want to study law. All she saw were the mistakes she'd made that could potentially ruin Kelly's life.

'She'll come around. If she loves her, she'll figure out a way to accept her,' Sarah said.

Darren refilled all their glasses. 'Dare I ask, how is your love life these days, Jenny?'

'Fine, thanks. I'm still seeing Frank, and I know none of you approves. Yes, he is still married and, yes, I know I should feel guilty, but I don't. We meet, we shag, the sex is good, he pays for nice hotels, champagne, chocolates, strawberries and all that stuff and we have a lot of fun. It's easy. No strings, no hassle, just fun.'

Sarah glanced at Lucy. They said nothing.

'I've got to say it sounds good,' Darren said.

Jenny smiled. 'It is.'

Darren seemed downcast. 'I'm afraid I've lost Sarah. We used to be close, we used to have regular sex, but then he came into our lives and ruined it.'

'What?' Jenny and Lucy said, shocked.

'Netflix,' Darren announced dramatically. 'Sarah prefers Netflix to me.'

Sarah laughed. 'It's true.'

'I tried to throw the leg over the other night when she was in the middle of watching *Poldark* for the tenth time and got punched. She actually punched me away and said, "What the hell are you doing? He's about to take his shirt off." '

They all burst out laughing.

'To be fair, he has a body to die for,' Sarah said, with a giggle.

Darren threw his hands into the air. 'You see what I'm against? Men all over the world are cursing Netflix because it's ruined our sex lives.'

'Netflix is my sex life,' Lucy muttered.

'Well, that's because you never go out. If you don't go out, how do you expect to meet someone?' Jenny reminded her.

'What about Damien?' Sarah asked. 'You're still seeing him, aren't you?'

'I see him the odd time, but he's been swamped working on the Lippet case and I haven't had a booty call in ages.'

Jenny crinkled her nose. 'Do you really want to be sleeping with him? He's not good enough for you. He's got no sex appeal and he's so serious and intense.'

'First of all, I don't think you're in any position to judge me. Besides, he's available, he likes me, he makes me feel good about myself and the sex is good.'

'Is it really?' Jenny asked.

'Well, it's fine,' Lucy said.

'I'm doing up a bachelor fella's house at the minute,' Darren said. 'Nice, decent-looking, about fifty. I could introduce you.'

'Define "decent-looking",' Jenny said. 'Are we talking Ryan Gosling or Will Ferrell?'

Darren paused. 'Well, he's kind of a bit like Wayne Rooney, but older.'

Jenny jumped up and pulled Lucy to her feet. 'Quick, grab your bag! It's your lucky day! Darren's going to set you up with Wayne Rooney's dad.'

'I don't know how to thank you, Darren,' Lucy said. 'I've always wanted to have sex with Wayne Rooney's dad. Thank you so much.'

Darren laughed. 'All right, maybe he's not a good match.'

'For the love of Jesus, Darren, she's not interested in sleeping with some ugly footballer's lookalike dad. Find her an Aidan Turner clone,' Sarah said.

Darren turned to her. 'If I did that, she'd have to fight you off him first.'

Sarah threw her head back and laughed. 'Very true.'

Darren topped up their glasses.

'Did you ever look up your exes on Facebook?' Jenny asked.

Lucy, Sarah and Darren shook their heads.

'I've been with Darren since I was fifteen,' Sarah said. 'I don't really have any exes.'

'I'm basically a nun,' Lucy said.

'God, you're hopeless,' Jenny said, taking out her iPad. 'Okay, what about people we were in school with?'

They spent the next hour looking up everyone they

remembered and laughing or ogling at their lives. Some looked the same, some looked awful and some looked amazing.

'Wow! Fiona Keane must have had work done.' Sarah peered at the screen over Jenny's shoulder.

'Definitely a lip job, a nose job and Botox,' Jenny agreed.

'How can you tell?' Lucy asked.

'I work with people's faces every day. I can always tell when they've had work done.'

'Well, she looks good,' Sarah said.

'She looks weird,' Darren said. 'Her lips are too big.'

'Really? I think she looks great. Maybe I should get a lip job.' Sarah put her hand up to her small, thin lips.

'Don't even think about it. Guys like natural, not fake,' Darren said. 'I like you the way you are.'

He leaned over and kissed her as Jenny made vomit noises.

Lucy thought it was lovely that Sarah and Darren were still so in love – he was mad about her. She missed that sometimes. Mostly she was too busy to think about men, with the twins, her dad and the shop, doing Sarah's wages and her accounts, but sometimes she'd feel a huge wave of loneliness wash over her. She'd never known love. Not since Tom. She doubted she ever would now. Her kids filled her heart with love, and she was grateful for that, but if she was honest, she sometimes craved male love and companionship. To have someone look at her the way Darren looked at Sarah, it was . . . well, it was beautiful.

'Actually, Darren, I think some guys like fake,' Jenny said. 'I doubt Pamela Anderson sleeps alone.'

'Well, she had a lot of very good natural ingredients to work with,' Darren said, with a grin.

Jenny looked back at her iPad. 'Lucy, have you ever looked up Tom?'

Lucy froze. Sarah held her breath.

Through gritted teeth, Lucy hissed, 'No, I haven't, and I never will. I don't want to know or hear about him. Ever. Why the hell would I want to see how great his life is on Facebook? Jesus, Jenny, have you forgotten what he did to me? To my children? They have never had a father. There is a huge hole in their lives where Tom was supposed to be. I hate him. I fucking hate him.' Lucy stood up and grabbed her coat. 'I need to go home. I've got a headache.'

'Lucy, I'm sorry,' Jenny said. 'Come on, don't go.'

'It's fine. I'm just tired and the wine's gone to my head. But please do not ever mention his name again.'

Sarah walked her out to the front door. 'Are you really okay?'

Lucy's eyes filled with tears. 'Yes – I shouldn't have drunk so much. It's ridiculous, but even after all these years when I hear his name, it's like a dagger in my stomach. I still can't believe he did that to me and the kids. I guess I'll never get over it.'

'Don't go. Stay, and we'll talk nonsense again.'

Lucy shook her head. 'No, I want to sleep this off. I'll see you tomorrow.'

'Okay. Love you.' They hugged and Lucy wandered off into the night.

Sarah went back into the kitchen.

'Is she all right?' Jenny was worried.

'Yeah. Too much wine and the mention of Tom is a bad combination.'

'I shouldn't have suggested looking him up, that was stupid of me. I know how much she hates him.'

'Ah, come on!' Darren said. 'I get that she's still furious, but she doesn't have to go off the deep end at the mention of his name. It's been nearly twenty years. That's a lot of water under the bridge.'

'It's the twins missing out on a dad that hurts her most,

and I get that,' Sarah said. 'Imagine life for our two with no dad. It would break my heart.'

'Yeah, but I'm Superdad.'

'Go on, Superdad, open another bottle there.' Sarah winked at him.

Darren didn't need to be persuaded. 'Will we look him up anyway?'

'Tom?' Jenny said.

'Yeah, why not?' He poured them all another glass.

'I dunno. It feels a bit like betraying Lucy.'

'Don't be ridiculous. Here, give me that.' Darren pulled the iPad towards him and began typing. 'What's his surname again? Some stupid double-barrel thing, isn't it?'

'Harrington-Black,' Jenny said.

'Well, the good thing about having a ridiculous name is that you're easy to find.' Darren grinned and the two women rushed to his side to get a look at Tom's Facebook page.

Tom Harrington-Black. Married. There were a few photos of him and a good-looking blonde woman, at a baseball game, walking on a beach with two dogs and skiing.

'He's not exactly Mr Facebook,' Jenny noted. 'The last time he posted was eight months ago.'

'Interesting that he seems to have no kids,' Darren said.

'Well, he's clearly not father material, so that's a good thing,' Sarah replied.

'The wife's not bad.'

Jenny slapped Darren on the arm. 'She's not a patch on my sister.'

'No, obviously, I'm just saying.'

'Zip it, Darren,' Sarah warned him.

Jenny sat back. 'Lucy needs more in her life.'

'Lucy needs to get laid,' Darren said.

'No, that's not it. Lucy needs love,' Sarah said. 'She needs someone to put their arm around her at night and tell her how wonderful she is, how well she's doing raising two kids on her own, how she works too hard and needs to give herself a break, how she needs to start living her own life because the kids will be gone soon and she'll be alone.'

'I keep hoping she'll meet someone at one of the ceremonies she does, uncle of the bride or cute groomsman or maybe even a hot brother,' Jenny said. 'I'd love to see her meet a really nice guy who'd sweep her off her feet and make her happy again. Like proper happy, giddy and silly. She's too serious and too focused on the twins. I know she keeps saying, "When they're in college, I'll get my life back and I'll travel," but I bet she doesn't. She'll be making Dylan's lunch for him and checking who Kelly's out with when they're thirty.'

Sarah nodded. 'It's just that she feels she has to be so perfect, always trying to prove that fecker Gabriel wrong. I wish she'd just forget about him and Tom. Put it behind her. They're like a poison inside her. It's not healthy. And now the twins going to St Jude's seems to have brought all the old wounds back. I've seen such a change in her in the last few weeks.'

'I know what you mean,' Jenny agreed. 'She's so tense and uptight, these days, trying to make sure the twins prove themselves at St Jude's. To who? What for? Gabriel is a dickhead and Tom is a pathetic coward. I wish Dylan hadn't got that scholarship. It's unsettled all of them.'

Sarah, too, was worried about how the three of them were coping with the new move. The pain and humiliation of Gabriel kicking her out of the house with the twins that day seventeen years ago had bubbled back up, she could see. Lucy seemed so raw with emotion, these days. Sarah thought her best friend was getting far too caught up in proving herself to the world and missing out on what was really going on with the twins, especially Kelly.

'Do you think we should try to say something?' Sarah said to Jenny.

'And be shot down and maimed?' Jenny said. 'No, thanks. Lucy is going to have to work through this herself. All we can do is be there for her and keep an eye out for the twins.'

19

Lucy sat in her little Nissan and looked around the car park, which was full of big flashy cars. Hers seemed out of place. She felt a bit intimidated. She watched as men in expensive jackets and women in designer coats walked towards the football pitch.

She had a flashback to her days with Tom, sitting in silence as his St Jude's friends talked about holidays in Barbados and skiing in the Alps. Lucy had always felt slightly out of her depth with them. She was feeling the same now.

She took a deep breath. *Get out of the car and go and watch your son play. You're just as good as them.* She reminded herself that St Jude's had begged her to send her children there.

Her eyes darted from side to side, making sure she didn't recognize anyone from the old days, but no one was familiar. Thank God. She breathed a sigh of relief and got out of her car.

She looked up at the huge stone building with 'St Jude's' carved in a semi-circle at the top and smiled. Her twins, stars of St Jude's. Every time she thought of Gabriel now, she grinned. Little did he know that his grandson was the sports star of the school and his granddaughter would probably come top of her class. How do you like them apples, Gabriel? She chuckled to herself.

Lucy walked to the pitch and stood at the side. It was St Jude's first match of the season. She had watched Dylan play hundreds of times, and now he kept pulling up his socks, which was what he always did when he was nervous.

'Leave your bloody socks alone and focus,' Jordan shouted at him, from the sideline.

Lucy held her breath and prayed Dylan would have a good game. She wanted him to show them how brilliant he was, to impress Jordan and the headmaster, who was watching from the corner of the pitch. Lucy waved to catch Dylan's eye. When he looked over, she pointed at his boots and smiled.

He nodded. It was their sign. She'd first done it at a game when he was about seven. He'd been playing badly and had turned to her in tears. She'd been close enough to him that he could hear her. She'd pointed at his boots and said, 'Trust your feet.' He'd gone on to score two goals. Since then it had been their signal.

Dylan relaxed and played out of his skin. He scored a hat-trick. When he put the third goal in the top left corner of the net, he'd run back down the line close enough to Lucy to high-five her. She'd almost burst with pride. Everyone had turned to look. They now knew she was the mother of the star of the team. Lucy felt ten feet tall.

After the match, parents came over to say hello and congratulate her on her 'amazing son'. She almost felt like she belonged.

Then one mother asked, 'Any plans for midterm?'

'Taking the kids to London.'

'We're off to Paris. Rupert can take ours to the art galleries while I shop,' a mother in a long cream suede coat said. She reminded Lucy of Tom's annoying St Jude's friend, Olivia, privileged and not much substance.

'We'll head to our place in Connemara.'

'How about you, Lucy?'

'I'll be working,' Lucy said.

'Me too,' another mother said, sighing. 'Medical conference.

Mind you, it's in Chicago so it could be worse. The last one was in Frankfurt.'

'Lucky you, I'm stuck here defending Jenson,' a father said.

Lucy had been following that trial. Harold Jenson, a well-known businessman, was accused of murdering his business partner, then trying to make it look like a break-in. He'd found out his partner had misappropriated the company funds and had allegedly gone mad and stabbed him.

This must be Jenson's defence barrister, John Madden. He was very highly regarded. Lucy remembered him from college. He was in the year ahead of her, and even back then the other students were talking about how brilliant he was. She felt the old regret sweeping through her, like a physical pain. If only . . . It might have been her defending Jenson.

'Do you think Jenson's brother's testimony about the funds in Turks and Caicos will save him?' she asked.

John turned to her. 'Ah, a fellow lawyer?'

'Oh, gosh, no, I'm not . . . I'm, well, just interested.' She blushed.

'I'm hoping the brother's testimony will be enough. We'll see how it goes next week. What do you do?' he asked.

'I work in my father's business, a grocery shop.' Lucy wanted to shout, *But I studied law and I could have been good – I could have been great. I was smart enough . . .*

'Good business to be in,' John said.

'What? Oh, yes, I suppose it is.' Not half as bloody good as yours, though, she thought. Still, Kelly would do it. She'd be the first woman in the Murphy family to be a lawyer. She'd be the one defending the Jensons of the world. Kelly would do it and make them all proud, like Lucy was supposed to.

'And you've raised one hell of a footballer. Does his father play?' John asked.

Lucy flinched. She could feel everyone looking at her. Act

natural, she willed herself. 'Uhm, no, it was actually my father, Dylan's granddad, who got him into it.'

'Good old Granddad! He's certainly done St Jude's a favour.' John turned, called to his son and strode off towards the car park.

'Right. I'd better grab Lorcan – he has a violin lesson at three,' the doctor said, waving to her son.

'Declan has a maths grind,' someone said.

'Chemistry,' another chipped in.

Wow! Violin, maths and chemistry grinds – these parents were really pushing their kids. Lucy would have to keep on top of Dylan and his studies. As they all began to disperse, a small dark-haired woman came over to her.

'Hi, I'm Heather, Conor's mum. Conor's told me all about Dylan. He was fantastic today.'

'Thanks.' Lucy smiled. 'Conor was great too.'

'Is Dylan settling in well?'

'Yes, he loves it.'

'It's a great school, and they're obsessed with winning this football trophy. The old headmaster was all about rugby, but Mr Gough is mad keen on football. I'm thrilled because Conor is rubbish at rugby.'

'Well, it's certainly good for Dylan,' Lucy said.

'We're lucky to have him,' Heather said. 'He's fantastic. Everyone thinks so. I was going to ask you for your number for our football WhatsApp group. I know they can be a bit of a pain, but it's the best and easiest way to get information about games and training sessions.'

'Sure, of course.' Lucy gave it to her.

'Great, thanks. See you next week.' Heather walked over to her son, leaving Lucy feeling warm and happy.

Lucy was about to go back to the car to wait for Dylan, who was talking to the coach, when Mr Gough approached her.

'Wonderful start to the season, Ms Murphy, what a performance by Dylan.'

Lucy beamed. 'Yes, he was on form today.'

'We really are so pleased he decided to come to St Jude's. He seems to be settling in well.'

'He loves it here,' Lucy said. 'Thanks, Mr Gough.'

'Not at all, thank you for raising such a fine young man. And how is Kelly finding it?'

Lucy chose her words carefully. 'I think it might take her a little longer to settle in, but she is very happy to be here.'

'Good, excellent. Glad to hear it.' He walked off to talk to some other parents.

Lucy watched Dylan, surrounded by his teammates, all clapping him on the back. He was the centre of attention, the star. She savoured the moment.

A group of girls approached the team. A very pretty blonde went over to Dylan and, judging by her body language, was doing some serious flirting. There was lots of hair-flicking and giggling and eyelid-batting. She was a real pro, and Dylan seemed to be enjoying the attention.

Any girl would be lucky to have Dylan, but he deserved a smart, kind, decent one. That blonde seemed very into herself – Lucy wasn't sure she liked the look of her. Besides, she wanted Dylan to focus on football and his schoolwork, not girls. He couldn't put a foot wrong: he had to show them all that he merited the scholarship and do himself proud.

Dylan came over to her, smiling.

Lucy hugged him. 'Well played. Everyone was congratulating me on my son being the star of the team. You were wonderful.'

'Thanks. I'm just glad it went well. I really wanted to impress Jordan and the headmaster. I feel like it's all okay now. I was worried if I played badly, they might take away the scholarship.'

'Don't be silly. They've given it to you and they won't take it away even if you break your leg and can't play at all. But it's brilliant that you played so well. They were seriously impressed. Even the headmaster came over to me.'

Dylan smiled. 'I feel like I can relax now that I've proven myself.'

'I'm so proud of you,' Lucy said.

'Oh, God, Mum, don't get emotional.'

'I won't, but I'm really proud of you. You didn't have it easy with no father in your life, but you've never let that hold you back. You're just brilliant.'

Dylan put his arm around her. 'You're not so bad yourself, Mum.'

'See you on Monday, Dylan,' the blonde called.

Lucy saw her waving at him.

'See you, Taylor.'

'Who's she?' Lucy asked.

'A girl in my year.'

'She's very pretty.'

'And smoking hot.'

Lucy laughed. 'Well, yes, I suppose that too. She seems to like you, from the number of times she flicked her hair when she was talking to you earlier.'

'Do you think so? Really?'

'Yes.'

He grinned. 'I thought I was getting some good signals, but she's kind of flirty with all the guys.'

'No, she definitely likes you. Trust me, I'm a woman. I know these things.'

Dylan's grin broadened. 'Cool.'

'Just be careful to choose the right girl, you deserve someone really special.'

Dylan snorted. 'I'm not looking for a wife, Mum, just a bit of fun.'

'But not too much. You need to focus on football and your books.'

'Did you say football and boobs?'

Lucy hit him playfully with her handbag and they walked to the car laughing.

20

Mr Flanagan read out the results of the tests. Kelly was top of the class. 'Congratulations, Kelly, you certainly seem to have an aptitude for maths.'

'Thanks,' Kelly said quietly.

Behind her she heard Ted hiss, 'Looks like you've got competition, Melissa.'

Kelly watched Melissa's face redden. 'Shut up, you retard.'

Melissa gripped her exam sheet and stared at the result – ninety-five per cent. How the hell had this stupid scholarship loser beaten her? Maths was her thing. Being smart was her USP. She wasn't beautiful like Taylor, she was smart.

It was bad enough having to look at Taylor's perfect face and body every morning at breakfast these past six months, now that her mum had married Taylor's dad, but to have her place at the top of the class threatened was too much.

Even Taylor's dad, Stephen, had been impressed with her results in her summer tests – she'd got over ninety in every subject. He'd told Taylor to try to be more like her step-sister, which was ironic because Melissa's mother, Patrice, spent her whole time telling Melissa to try to be more like Taylor.

'Maybe if you stuck to rice cakes and cut out sugar and carbohydrates you could be svelte like Taylor,' Patrice had told her, as she'd admired her own slim figure in her dressing-room mirror. Melissa had inherited her father's figure, short and square. She was never going to be thin or beautiful like Taylor. No matter how hard she dieted, her thighs remained chunky, and no amount of mascara or eyeshadow made her small eyes look bigger.

Melissa wanted to shout at her mother, 'You didn't look so great before all the liposuction and the Botox and the eye lift and the nose job transformed your face, so give me a break!'

But she never disagreed with her mother. Patrice was not someone you crossed. She was razor sharp and very successful. When Melissa's dad had died suddenly of a heart attack fifteen years ago, Patrice had taken over his property company and grown it into a multi-million-euro empire. She worked incredibly hard and was always impeccably groomed. She expected Melissa to do and be the same.

Melissa knew that, but it wasn't easy and sometimes she just wished her mother could say, 'Well done,' but whatever she did was never enough. Melissa knew her mother was proud to have a smart daughter, but she wanted perfection, and it was exhausting.

Once, last year, when Melissa had complained that Patrice was too hard on her, her mother had grabbed her shoulder and shaken her hard.

'Listen to me. When your father died I had a choice. Sink or swim. I was devastated, but I dragged myself out and went into that company knowing nothing. I didn't just keep it going, I made it bigger and better. I wasn't beautiful either, but I made the most of myself. When you're not good-looking, you need to be smart so you can take on whatever life throws at you. That's why I push you so hard. If you're successful, men will find you a lot more attractive, believe me. Stephen Lyons wouldn't have looked at me if I was just another forty-year-old woman, but he admired me because of what I've achieved and then he fell in love with me. I want that for you, Melissa, so stop complaining and work harder.'

Now bloody Kelly was threatening her position. She

shouldn't even be in this school – she was just a charity case. Everyone knew she was only there because her brother was good at football.

Melissa felt a hand on her arm. 'Don't worry, I'm sure you'll come first in the midterms,' Alicia said.

Melissa jerked away. 'I know that. I got one question wrong because I misread it,' she lied, and crumpled the test paper in her hand.

She'd make damn sure she came first in the midterm tests. Getting straight As was the only thing that made her feel good about herself. She'd always been top of the class at St Jude's and no one, least of all some scholarship scumbag, was going to take that from her, not if she had anything to do with it.

Kelly tried to stop the hockey ball but it whizzed past her.

'Come on, Kelly, stick down. It's not complicated,' Mrs Parson shouted.

'It's a stupid bloody game,' Kelly muttered. Who the hell wanted to run around chasing a small ball with a stupid curly stick? Kelly hated hockey. She didn't see the point of it and she was rubbish at it.

'What games do you like, Kelly? Football like your brother? You know football is for lowlifes and knackers,' Melissa said. Her two stupid sidekicks, Lara and Grace, laughed.

'Well, then, you should be good at it,' Kelly snapped. She wanted to smack her over the head with the hockey stick. She was sick of Melissa needling her all the time and constantly reminding everyone that she was a scholarship girl. It had been non-stop for the past month. Everywhere she went, Melissa was there with some catty remark or sending WhatsApp messages with comments like 'Just sending this out so our new scholarship girl will know what's going on.' Kelly wanted to tell her to fuck right off, but she knew that if she got into trouble it could affect the scholarship, and her mum would go mental.

'We also wear trainers that don't look like we have special needs. Yours look like you got them in a skip. Then again, charity cases obviously have to shop in charity shops or dumpsters.' Melissa turned away just as Mrs Parson came over to see what was going on.

The bitch. Kelly's face burnt with rage and embarrassment. She muttered to Mrs Parson that she'd twisted her ankle and fake-hobbled off the pitch.

Kelly went straight to the changing room, ripped off her hockey skirt and top and put on her uniform. Then she headed out of the school. She'd had enough humiliation. She needed to get as far away as she could from those vicious cows.

Kelly got off the bus and took the long way around to Woodside. She couldn't go anywhere near the salon in case Sarah saw her, and she avoided the shop in case Mum or Granddad spotted her. There would be hell to pay if Lucy found out she had mitched off school. She'd only skipped double gym, so she was hoping she'd get away with it.

The problem was, there was no hiding here. Kelly kept bumping into people she knew.

'Ah, there she is. Hi, Kelly, how's the posh new school going? Your mum is very proud of you. Do you like it?' Mary Harris asked.

Kelly didn't want to let Mum down but Mrs Harris had known her since she was born. 'I'm not that keen to be honest.'

'Ah, well, takes a while to settle into anything new. You're a great girl, Kelly, you'll be all right. The uniform is lovely on you. The blazer looks very smart.'

'Thanks.'

'My Mandy misses you. She says school isn't the same since you left. Herself and Shannon miss the craic with you. I think they're worried you'll get all posh and won't have time for them. But I said to Mandy, "Kelly Murphy will never change. She's as solid as they come."'

'I miss Shannon and Mandy too. Big-time. I'm off to meet them,' Kelly said.

'Sure they'll be only thrilled to see you. Here.' Mary Harris handed her a tenner. 'Get yourselves a hot chocolate or something.'

'Ah, no, it's fine, Mary.' Kelly handed her back the money. She knew things in the Harris house were tight with Mandy's dad being sick and not able to work. Lucy sent over a hamper of food for them every week. She was very kind, and Kelly loved that about her. 'I've money from working in the shop last Saturday, so I'll treat the girls,' she said.

'Well, if you're sure?' Mary put the money into her pocket. 'I'd best be off. I've to get Larry's medicine.'

'How's he doing?'

'Getting better, thank God. Hopefully he'll be back at work soon, not driving me mad at home and me running around like a slave for him.'

'I'm glad to hear he's on the mend. Will you tell him I said hello?'

'Course I will. He always liked you, did Larry. Always said, "That Kelly has her head screwed on, unlike our Mandy!"'

Kelly smiled as she watched Mandy's mum bustle off up the road. She headed up to the school to wait for her mates.

She heard a wolf-whistle.

'Hey.'

It was Sean Whelan! Kelly tried not to blush, but she knew her cheeks were going red. Sean was a year older than her, the coolest guy in the neighbourhood, and the cutest. He hadn't seemed to notice Kelly, until suddenly this summer she had felt his eyes on her whenever she passed him. She always seemed to get tongue-tied around him. It was so embarrassing – whenever he spoke to her, she acted like an idiot.

'Hi, Sean,' was all she could manage to say.

She tried to calm down. She'd fancied him for ever, but Lucy had warned her to stay well away from him because his family were trouble. It was totally unfair. His older brother, Gavin, had got into trouble for selling cocaine at a nightclub, but Sean was nice. Still, once Lucy had heard about Gavin and the drugs that had been it. Kelly and Dylan were warned to stay away from the Whelan family.

She was ridiculously over-protective, but any time Kelly complained, her mum would just say, 'Look what happened to me and I was the smartest girl in my law class. It's my job to keep you safe and out of trouble.'

Kelly really liked Sean. Apart from being good-looking, he was sound and smart and funny.

'I heard you moved school,' Sean said.

'Yeah.' Kelly sighed.

'Not keen on it?'

'Not really.'

Sean stood close to her. Kelly's heart was pounding. 'So, have you hooked up with some posh bloke who has a mansion and a trust fund?'

'Maybe.'

'Maybe yes or maybe no?'

Kelly smiled. 'Maybe no.'

'Glad to hear it. What are you doing on Saturday?'

'Nothing.'

A slow, sexy smile spread across his face. 'Good. That new Ryan Gosling movie is on in the Odeon in town on Saturday night. I was thinking of going, you free?'

Did he just ask her on a date? Kelly's face lit up. 'Cool. Yeah, I should be.'

'See you there at eight. Nice trainers by the way.'

Kelly's heart soared. Sean liked her and he even liked her trainers, the ones Melissa had sneered at.

She heard shouting and turned around. Shannon was running towards her. She hugged her. Today had gone from awful to brilliant.

'What are you doing here?' Shannon asked. 'Did you get out early?'

Kelly grinned. 'Something like that. Where's Mandy?'

'She got detention.'

'What for?'

'She told Keelan that her face looked like a pizza and she should ask her zits for rent.'

Kelly laughed. 'She never?'

'Yeah, and Mr Byrne overheard her and you know the way he has loads of zits too, so he gave her detention. It was totally unfair because Mandy was only getting back at Keelan because Keelan had told Mandy that Kevin Dolan said her boobs were like udders, but Mandy was too embarrassed to say that to Mr Byrne.'

'Poor Mandy.'

'School sucks.'

'You can say that again. I mitched off early.'

'What? I thought they Tasered you in St Jude's if you tried to leave, and had electric fences and sniffer dogs to keep you in and the riff-raff out.' Shannon giggled.

Kelly loved this. She loved the banter and the fun and being able to be herself. She hugged her friend again.

'Jeez, Kelly, it must be bad. You're not really a hugger.'

'You have no idea. But forget about that, guess who I met on my way here?'

'Frank?'

'No.'

'Oh, Gary.'

'No.'

'Your man Simon?'

'No, you thick, Sean Whelan.'

'*Oooooh*, wow! He is hot.'

'*Soooo* hot, and he chatted to me.'

'And?'

'And he asked me to go to the cinema with him on Saturday if I was around!'

'That's so cool. What will you wear?'

'God, I don't know, we need to discuss it.'

'Let's go to the salon and get free coffees and talk about outfits.'

Kelly stopped walking. 'I can't. I shouldn't be out of school this early. Sarah might say it to Mum and then she'll know I mitched off and she'll kill me.'

'It's fine. Mum won't even notice. I'll say I asked you to come straight to the salon because I desperately needed you to help me with a science project and you came over because you're such a kind friend.'

When they reached the salon, they hurried through into the back room. Sarah came in after them. 'What are you two up to?'

'Kelly's helping me with my science project and we need caffeine to help us concentrate.'

'What science project?' she asked, arms folded, staring at her daughter.

'The one I'm doing for next week.'

'You never mentioned it before.'

'I did, actually, but you were too busy with Ollie as usual, probably peeling him off a wall somewhere, to listen.'

'Really?' Sarah smiled. 'What's it about, then?'

'It's about the science of . . . of . . .'

'The planets and how they work,' Kelly fudged.

'That's a big subject.'

'Which is why I need Kelly's help,' Shannon said. 'Now go away, Mum. We need to work.'

Sarah left them, muttering, 'Likely story.'

Kelly made them both cappuccinos and they sat on the couch chatting about what Kelly should wear on Saturday to the cinema.

'I think you should wear your red dress with the denim jacket and those cool black boots. You're a ride in that. He won't be able to keep his hands off you. Mind you, you're a stunner in anything you wear, you lucky cow.'

Kelly smiled. She liked that dress and knew she looked good in it. People told her all the time that she was good-looking, but Kelly had never felt it. She'd always been tall and scrawny, not a bit sexy like Shannon, who was all curves and boobs.

'Come over to me early on Saturday and I'll help you get ready, okay?' Shannon suggested.

Kelly finished her coffee. 'Cool. I can't wait!'

A date with Sean. Kelly had kissed a few boys, but never really fancied anyone except Sean. She'd liked him for nearly a year. She'd never admitted it to anyone but Shannon. She preferred to keep things private – it was better that way: there was less chance of getting hurt.

21

Billy tidied up the vegetables, taking out the wilting ones and putting them into a box to bring inside. Lucy would make a soup or magic something else out of them. She was a wonder, that Lucy. She could make a silk purse out of a pig's ear, that was for sure.

Billy pressed the button to bring down the shutters and soon the shop was in darkness. He went into the kitchen, then closed and locked the door that led from the shop into the house. He placed the wilting veg on the kitchen counter and stretched his arms over his head. He caught his reflection in the kitchen window. He'd have to cut back on the chocolate biscuits with his tea. His trousers were definitely a bit tighter. Still, he wasn't in bad shape for almost sixty-five. Mind you, the long hours in the shop had definitely taken more out of him lately, but Billy didn't trust anyone except Lucy to look after it properly. Over the years he'd tried hiring staff, but they were never good enough or they left or they turned up late . . . It drove him nuts.

'Why bother paying someone else to do the work when you can do it better yourself?' he'd always said to Tina, when yet another employee left or was fired.

Tina had wanted him to take more time off. Relax more, have more holidays. But how could Billy relax if he thought the shop wasn't being properly run? He was happy to work hard and provide for his family. He wanted the girls to have a good life, a safe and comfortable life. What Billy remembered most about growing up was being hungry. Money was always tight, food was always short and every winter the gas was cut off because they couldn't pay the bill and they'd be cold all the time.

Working hard and keeping on top of things was what made Billy happy, not holidays. He looked at the photo of his wedding day on the shelf above the dishwasher. Tina looked so young, beautiful and healthy. God, he missed her. She was his one true love. She'd died too young. It made him sad to think of her missing the twins growing up. She was crazy about those kids, but she'd never really got to enjoy them. Cancer had robbed her of that, and so much more.

Billy knew he would have sunk into a deep depression and probably taken to the drink if it hadn't been for Lucy and the babies. She had sat him down one morning after finding him passed out on the couch, bottle of whiskey empty beside him. 'Dad, this has to stop. Mum's been gone two months and you have barely eaten, spoken or gone into the shop. Jenny and I can't do this alone. I'm looking after two small kids, the shop, and trying to keep an eye on Jenny, too. We're all heart-broken, we lost our mum. But you getting drunk every day and night can't continue. It's not healthy for you, or for Jenny and my kids to see. I need you, Dad. Jenny needs you and so do your grandchildren. I know you're devastated, but Mum would not be a bit pleased to see you like this. In fact, she'd be bloody furious and you know it. I've tried to be patient, but I'm drowning under all the responsibility. I need your help. Now get up, shower and be in the shop at eight thirty sharp.'

Billy had stopped drinking whiskey that day. He'd drunk enough in the previous two months to fill a boat. From that day onwards he drank only beer, and even that in small amounts. Lucy had saved him from himself.

He'd found comfort in the familiarity of the shop, and working hard was a good distraction from pain. And the twins, well, they were the light of his life. He hoped poor Kelly would settle into that new school soon – he hated seeing her in bad form and she was quieter these days, too. Not the usual Kelly, full of chat. She was always in her bedroom now or looking at her phone. Still, he supposed that was what most teenagers were like, always staring at their phones. Even when they came into the shop, they wouldn't look at you, they'd pay while typing messages with one hand. Billy felt sorry for them. They were like robots. Where had the art of conversation gone?

Lucy was strict about no phones at the table. She was strict about a lot of things. Billy thought she was too hard on Kelly sometimes. She needed to give the girl a bit of freedom or else she'd rebel.

Billy stretched his back. It had been a long and busy day. He needed an evening in the shed. He pulled on his coat and headed out into the cold autumn air.

Within ten minutes Billy was nestled in his chair. The heat was on and Sinatra was crooning 'I Get A Kick Out Of You' on his turntable. Billy loved the sound of vinyl. None of this iPod stuff for him. The crackle of the records as they spun was beautiful.

He leant his head back and took a long sip of his cool beer. Bliss.

'Billy!' A voice interrupted his reverie.

Who the hell? Billy struggled out of the chair and went to open the door.

'What are you doing here?'

'I need your help,' Ollie said.

'With what?'

'These.' Ollie held up a mangled pair of glasses.

'Can you come back tomorrow?' Billy wanted peace and quiet.

Ollie shuffled about on his feet. 'I tried to fix them myself, but I think I made them worse. Dad said it doesn't matter, but I know they cost loads cos he has mad eyes where one sees far away and the other sees close. I feel really bad.'

'How did it happen?'

Ollie peered behind Billy's arm. 'Can I tell you inside?'

Billy sighed. 'Go on, then.'

Ollie rushed in and Billy closed the door behind them.

'Oooh, it's deadly in here.' Ollie put his hands up to the heater and rubbed them together. 'Do you have any food?'

Billy pointed to a cupboard in the corner. 'Biscuits in the tin in there. Help yourself.'

'Can I have two?'

'Have one and let's see if the sugar makes you hyper.'

Ollie pulled a chocolate biscuit out of the tin and bit into it. 'Sure I'm always hyper. The teachers think I have ADHD, but I was tested for it and I don't. Mum says I just have a lot of energy and a curious mind. Dad says I'm mad. Shannon says I'm a psycho who should be in a special school.' He shrugged. 'I don't know what I am, really. I'm not smart in school like Kelly. I find it hard to listen all day long. I think Dad's fed up with me. Me wrecking his glasses really pissed – oops, sorry – cheesed him off.'

The boy's voice quivered. Billy's heart went out to him. He was a good kid, just had a lot of energy that needed to be channelled. Billy had known kids like Ollie growing up – kids who'd had more energy than they knew what to do with. Kids who'd hated sitting at a desk for six hours a day. A lot of them had got into trouble in later life. You had to harness the energy in a positive way. The kid needed to focus on something, occupy his mind.

'Lookit, Ollie, you're a good lad. I was a bit like you when I was a boy,' Billy lied. 'My uncle Johnny, who was a carpenter, taught me how to make things. It helped me to focus my mind. Why don't I teach you a few basics? Stand here beside me at this workbench.'

Billy showed Ollie how to cut plywood with a handsaw, supervising him like a hawk while he did it. Ollie still ended up sawing through the sleeve of Billy's jumper and almost his skin. Luckily, Billy pulled his arm away just in time.

They managed to make a lopsided box. Billy decided to glue it together rather than involve nails or hammers or any other implements that could cause serious bodily harm.

Ollie held up the finished box and beamed. 'Deadly!'

'What will you do with it?'

'I'll give it to Dad to put stuff in.'

'Good idea.'

'Maybe he'll forget about the glasses when he sees this.'

Billy patted his shoulder. 'I'm sure he will.'

'Is there anything to drink in there?' Ollie eyed up the small fridge.

'Only water for you and beer for me.'

'That's cool. I've given up fizzy drinks anyway. It's important to keep hydrated and water is the best thing for that. By the way, Billy, if you ever get locked in here and you have a heart attack or a stroke or one of those things that happens to old people, and you can't get out or call for help and you're stuck here for days and you run out of water, you can drink your own pee.'

Billy spluttered on his beer. 'Thanks for the heads-up. Hopefully, if I do have an old person's issue, one of my daughters or grandchildren would notice me missing.'

Ollie sipped his water. 'Maybe, but it's good to have a backup plan.'

Billy looked at his watch. 'It's nine o'clock. Shouldn't you be heading home?'

Ollie sighed. 'Not yet. Mum and Shannon are watching *Gossip Girl* again and it's so boring. Dad's working late on a job. Can I stay for a few more minutes?'

'Okay. Finish up your water and I'll see you home.'

'Billy?'

'Yes?'

'Do you think I could call in here sometimes, like, to hang out and stuff?'

Billy wanted to say no. In one hour the kid had nearly sawn his arm off. But his little face was eagerly staring up at him. 'Sure, Ollie. Not all the time, mind you, but maybe once a week. How does that sound?'

'Deadly.' Ollie beamed at him. 'I'll see you next week same time. We can make a skateboard or something cool.'

Billy walked him to the front gate, then watched him run up the road and into his house. So much for a quiet night. He turned and went back to his shed to have one more beer and listen to Frank's soothing voice.

22

Lucy held out the menus. 'So, what do you fancy tonight, Chinese or Indian? Kelly, that new legal drama is on BBC tonight. It's supposed to be really good.'

'Actually I'm going out,' Dylan said.

'So am I,' Kelly said.

'Oh.' Lucy's hands dropped to her sides. 'I thought you were both staying in for a change. Where are you going?'

'Just the cinema with Shannon,' Kelly said.

Lucy turned to Dylan. 'Where are you off to?'

He needed to play this down. He knew if he said it was a house party he'd get a lecture about being led astray and the evils of alcohol. 'I'm meeting up with a few of the lads on the team.'

'You're not going to be drinking, I hope,' his mum said. 'You know you can't get caught doing anything silly, Dylan. You don't want to get into any trouble, and Jordan would go mad if he found out you were drinking.'

'I'm not drinking, Mum. Relax.'

'Where are you meeting up?'

'In Justin's house,' he lied.

'Which one is he?'

'He's centre mid.'

'Oh, yes, he seems nice. Well, don't be late. You've got training at eleven tomorrow.'

Dylan left the kitchen and went into his room to get changed. Kelly came in and lay on the bed. 'Liar!' she said.

'What?' Dylan sprayed on some aftershave.

'I heard you tell Mum you're going to Justin's house. You're not wearing your best shirt and half a bottle of aftershave for the boys. You're going to Taylor's party, aren't you?'

Dylan fixed his hair in the mirror. 'Yep, and if all goes well, I'm planning on hooking up with the hostess.'

Kelly sat up, hugging her knees to her chest. 'I hope Taylor's nicer than her sister Melissa. She's a real bitch.'

'Taylor's great. Which one is Melissa? Is she the short dumpy one with the long blonde hair?'

'Yes.'

'They're sisters? Seriously?'

'Step-sisters.'

'Okay, cos they couldn't look less alike.'

'I hate St Jude's, Dylan.'

Dylan sighed. He just wanted to go to the party and hook up with Taylor. The last thing he needed was a big chat about how much Kelly hated St Jude's, but he loved his sister and could see she was struggling, so he sat down beside her.

'I don't fit in,' Kelly said, looking at her toes.

'Maybe if you tried a bit harder. They can't all be bad in your class. Come on, I know I'm not in the top stream for all subjects like you, but some of those nerdy swots must be decent.'

Kelly shrugged. 'Some of them seem okay, but Melissa is in all of my classes and she's constantly making horrible comments.'

'Just ignore her. A couple of the lads slagged me off about being new and the scholarship and all that stuff in the first week, but I just let it slide. There were some arseholes in our old schools too. If you walk around looking like you hate everyone, you won't make new mates.'

'I have great friends already. I don't need new ones,' Kelly muttered.

'Poor Kelly. Come on, give us a smile.' Dylan lay on top of her and forced his sister's mouth into a smile. Kelly squealed and tried to push him off, but he had her pinned down. 'One smile and I'll let you go. Come on, I want to get to the party before some other fella hops on Taylor.'

Kelly gave him a half-smile.

'That'll do. Wish me luck.' Dylan straightened his shirt.

'You don't need luck. You're Dylan the amazing striker,' Kelly said.

'Well, now that you mention it, I guess I am.' He grinned.

Dylan walked up the long driveway, following the sound of thumping music. When he turned the corner and saw the house, he stopped in his tracks. It was huge. Like, footballer's-crib massive. A black Ferrari and an Alfa Romeo were parked outside. Taylor's parents must be seriously minted.

Suddenly Dylan felt nervous. If she came from all this, would she really go for him? She could have any guy she wanted. He knew at least five on the football team who fancied her. He was pretty sure they all lived in mansions too.

You're brilliant, Dylan. Any girl would be lucky to have you. He heard his mother's voice in his head. Feck it, what did he have to lose? Dylan put his shoulders back and headed to the front door.

The party was in full swing. Kids he recognized from school and lots he'd never seen before were drinking, kissing and dancing all over the house. Four people were doing lines of cocaine on the hall table. One of them was the stepsister – what was her name? Melissa. That was it.

He tapped her on the shoulder. 'Melissa, right?'

'Yes.' Her eyes were drug-induced bright.

'I'm Dylan.'

'I know who you are, Dylan. Everyone's talking about you.'

He smiled. 'Right, so you're Taylor's step-sister.'

'Yeah. My mum and her dad married last year.'

'Cool. Nice house.'

'It's okay. You should see my mum's house in St Tropez, though. It's, like, twice the size.'

'Right.'

She batted her fake eyelashes at him. One had come unstuck. She looked ridiculous.

'So, do you want some?' She offered him cocaine.

'No, thanks.'

'Are you sure?' She put her hand on his chest. 'We could have some fun together.'

Dylan laughed. 'I don't think so. You're not my type.'

'Oh, yeah? What is your type, then?'

'Good-looking.'

Melissa took a step back from him. 'Prick.'

'Do me a favour, Shorty, lay off my sister.'

'Screw you,' Melissa shouted at his back, as he walked away.

Dylan made his way towards the kitchen, nodding to a few of the kids from school. He found Taylor perched on the edge of the marble counter, in a very tight mini-dress. She was surrounded by guys and girls all cheering as she threw back a Jägermeister shot. When she saw Dylan, her face lit up. 'Hey, you, come here.' She held out her hand and pulled Dylan towards her. She handed him a shot. 'Party time!'

Dylan hesitated. 'I don't really drink.'

'Come on, it's a party, for God's sake.'

He smiled at her. 'What the hell?' He knocked it back.

The others whooped and cheered him on.

'Can you help me down?' Taylor asked.

Dylan held out his arms and she swung into them. He put her down but kept his arms around her.

Taylor leant into him. 'Strong arms, I like that,' she said, and stumbled on her high heels. Dylan steadied her. She reached for his hand and pulled him towards the lounge where people were dancing in very dim light.

'Come on.' She pulled Dylan into the dark room. A disco ball bounced coloured lights around the ceiling. She wrapped her arms around his neck and snaked her body into his. He held her tight. Then he pulled her head up gently with his hand and pressed his lips to hers. She opened her mouth and let him in.

Kelly turned her back to the mirror and swivelled her head to check her bum.

Shannon sighed. 'For God's sake, you look amazing. Stop obsessing about your bum. It's half the size of mine.'

'Are the jeans too tight?'

'For the millionth time, no! You look amazing. He's going to hop on you when he sees you.'

Kelly bit her nail. 'He's just so gorgeous and I know loads of girls fancy him. I can't believe he likes me.'

'He's mad about you. I saw the way he looked at you last week in the park. He couldn't take his eyes off you.'

Kelly grinned. 'Really?'

Shannon was glad to see her smiling. She'd been so miserable since she'd gone to stupid St Jude's. 'Yes, really. Now, come on. We have to get past your psycho mother. She's better than the CIA at sniffing out lies. If she suspects anything, she'll probably waterboard me to 'fess up.'

Kelly giggled as she put on her leather jacket. She had one last look in the mirror. Shannon was right, she did look good – as good as she ever could. If Sean didn't fancy her, there was nothing more she could do.

They popped their heads into the lounge, where Lucy and Billy were watching TV.

'We're off to the cinema,' Kelly said.

Lucy looked round. 'Okay. Now, I want you straight home afterwards. No later than eleven and make sure you get the bus home together. It's dangerous on your own.'

'Don't worry, Lucy. I'll glue myself to her,' Shannon said.

'Have you enough money?' Billy asked.

'Yes, thanks, Granddad.'

'Here, take a few quid for sweets.' He handed Kelly ten euros.

'No, honestly, it's fine.'

'Take it, you're a great girl. You deserve a night out.'

'She'd love to, thanks, Billy.' Shannon took the money and shoved it into Kelly's hand.

'Will there be any boys?' Billy winked.

'You never mentioned boys.' Lucy looked at Kelly.

'I wish.' Shannon took control. 'Sure we don't know any decent boys. It's just me and Kelly. Right then, see you later.'

They scurried from the house and ran up the street. Kelly let out a deep breath. 'Thanks, you were great. I froze when Granddad mentioned boys.'

Shannon giggled. 'I couldn't believe he said it! Your mum went all squinty eyed and glary and I knew we had to get out of there before she sniffed out the lies.'

Kelly laughed.

Shannon linked her arm. 'Come on, I'll walk you down to the bus stop in case she's watching out the window.'

'Knowing my mum, she probably is.'

At the corner Shannon hugged her friend. 'Jesus, you're shaking.'

'I'm ridiculously nervous. I really like him.'

'And he likes you, remember that. He asked you out.'

'It's the only nice thing to happen in weeks. I really want it to go well.'

'It will, but you need to relax, Kelly. Seriously. If you arrive shaking like that, he'll think you have Parkinson's!'

Kelly giggled.

'Now go on, I'm going to hide in Mandy's house until you call me. I'll meet you back here and we can walk to your house together. Enjoy yourself and I can't wait for all the gory details.'

When Kelly got off the bus her stomach was fluttering. She saw him straight away, leaning against the wall, smoking. He looked so gorgeous. He caught her eye and a sexy smile lit his face. Kelly swallowed her nerves and walked over to him. Her legs were shaking.

'Hey,' he said, throwing his cigarette down and putting it out with his boot.

'Hi.' Kelly couldn't think of anything else to say.

Sean moved over to stand in front of her. 'You look great,' he said.

'Thanks, so do you.'

He grinned. 'I got us two seats at the back so I could do lots of this.' He leant in, put his hand on the back of her neck and kissed her.

Kelly felt herself melt. She leant against him and kissed him back.

'I've wanted to do that for a long time,' he murmured into her ear.

'Me too,' she whispered back.

He smiled at her. 'Come on, or it'll start without us.'

He led her into the cinema foyer and over to the machine, where he collected their tickets. They were the only people in the back row. All through the film they were kissing and groping each other. Kelly couldn't get enough of him. She wanted to kiss him all night. She felt as if she was floating on air.

When the film was over they stood outside, wrapped in each other's arms.

'Will we go for a drink?' Sean said.

Kelly winced. 'I can't. I have to be home by eleven. My mum's really strict. To be honest, I kind of lied about meeting you. She wants me to focus on studying, impress my new teachers and come top of the class. No distractions allowed.'

'Are you?'

'What?'

'Top of the class.'

'In some . . . in most of them.'

'Smart and gorgeous, lucky me.' He grinned.

She twirled her fingers around his.

'So, do you like the posh school?'

Kelly shook her head. 'I hate it.'

'Really? That bad?'

'Yes. Some of the girls are total bitches and the others all have their own groups of friends.'

'Sounds rough. Are the bitches giving you a hard time?'

Kelly nodded. 'There's this one girl, Melissa, who seems to hate me and she never lets up. She sent a WhatsApp yesterday asking if anyone had a decent pair of shoes to give to Kelly, the scholarship girl, because the ones I wear are so gross. She uploaded a photo of my shoes. Loads of people replied with laughing emojis, and LOLs.'

'Did you reply? Do you fight back?'

'I have to be careful. I can't get into trouble or I'll risk losing the scholarship and get Dylan into trouble too. I can't blow it for him. Besides, my mum will have an actual nervous breakdown if I mess up. She's obsessed with this school.'

'Why? Did she go there?'

'No. She just thinks it's an amazing opportunity and that we're incredibly lucky. She wants us to shine, Dylan in sports and me in study.'

Sean ran his hands through her hair. 'Sounds like a lot of pressure.'

'It is, but Mum gave up everything for us. She got pregnant and had to drop out of college, so I can't let her down.'

Sean frowned. 'You have to live your life, not hers. I mean, the fact that she blew her chances isn't your fault.'

Kelly lay back in his arms – she felt so safe with him. 'I know, but she wants the best for me. She wants me to have a great career and life.'

'I dunno . . . If you want it, fine, but don't do it for her. We can't live our parents' lives, we have to live our own. You know my brother Gavin ended up in prison for six months for selling cocaine? He really messed up and my parents were devastated, but they got over it. He's still their son and he's good now. He's working in a café and he's got mad into health and fitness. People make mistakes, but it doesn't mean your life is over. Your mum's life worked out okay, so she shouldn't put so much pressure on you.'

Kelly didn't want to talk about St Jude's, her mother or Gavin. She wanted more kissing. Sean was right, but he didn't understand. Lucy had been abandoned at twenty-one with twins and then her own mum had got cancer and died. Her whole life had been turned upside-down and she'd never got to do what she wanted. It was Kelly and Dylan's job to make her proud. They'd always known that. Lucy adored them, they were her life, and it was their duty to be the best they could be.

Kelly turned to face him. 'I've only got ten minutes. No more talking.' She smiled and leant in to kiss him.

*

Shannon was hopping from one foot to the other trying to keep warm. Kelly jumped off the bus and threw her arms around her.

'I take it the date went well, then?'

'It was amazing, he's amazing. Everything is –'

'Amazing?' Shannon laughed.

'Yes!' Kelly twirled around. 'God, Shannon, he's so sexy and gorgeous, really nice too.'

'Did you sit at the back of the cinema?'

Kelly grinned. 'Yes, we did, and we kissed the whole way through.'

'Anything else?'

Kelly blushed. 'He may have had his hand up my jumper and I may have had my hands all over his gorgeous chest, but nothing more. We were in public.'

Shannon laughed. 'It sounds brilliant. So are you seeing him again soon?'

'Yes, we're going to try to meet up next Saturday afternoon. I just need to come up with a good lie.'

'I'll help you.'

Kelly hugged her. 'Thanks, Shannon, you're the best. I love you.'

'I have a feeling you love someone else.' Shannon giggled.

They walked arm in arm up the road to Kelly's house. Sure enough, Lucy was waiting up when Kelly went through the front door. She was in her dressing-gown, holding a mug of tea.

'Good film?' Lucy asked.

'The best I've ever seen,' Kelly said.

'I'm glad you had a good night, pet. I know the last few weeks have been tough settling into St Jude's. I'm really proud of you, Kelly. I hope you know that. You're a fantastic girl and I love you so much. I know I'm hard on you sometimes, but I really want you to have the best opportunities and choices in life because you deserve it.' She kissed Kelly's forehead.

'It's okay, Mum, it'll all be fine,' Kelly said, as she skipped up the stairs to bed. Tonight everything was just perfect.

23

Lucy woke to the sound of her alarm. She reached for her phone to switch it off. She lay back in bed and checked her messages. Uh-oh, ten missed calls from Debbie. Five new text messages. The last one said: *CALL ME!!!!!*

Lucy sat up in bed and dialled Debbie's number.

'Oh, Lucy, it's a total fiasco. I thought my mother not coming to my wedding was bad, but now the bloody restaurant we're supposed to get married in has gone into receivership. They only told me last night. What the hell am I going to do? I have twenty guests coming to a wedding that now has no venue. They were organizing the hairdresser and the make-up artist and the flowers and . . .' Debbie trailed off as she began to weep.

Lucy had to think fast. She wanted to help Debbie, plus she was relying on the seven-hundred-euro fee to pay for her car insurance and she wanted to treat Kelly to a new outfit to cheer her up. She could see her daughter was struggling to get used to St Jude's, although she had been in much better form the last few days.

'Debbie, this wedding is going ahead. Leave it with me. I'll call you back in ten minutes. Sit tight.'

Lucy called Jenny.

'Somebody better be dead. It's eight thirty on a Sunday!'

'Are you free today?'

'I'm meeting Frank later, but I'm free until four.'

'I need your help. Remember the lesbian wedding I was telling you about?'

'No.'

'Never mind, I need you to do wedding make-up. I'll call you back with when and where.'

'Whatever. I'm going back to sleep now.'

Lucy hung up and rang Sarah.

'Hi.'

'Listen, I have a big favour to ask. The wedding I'm supposed to be doing today now has no venue. Is there any chance I could use the salon? You'll get a good fee for the day and I'll have Kelly and Shannon to help me do it up. I'll also need you to do the bride's hair – actually, it's the lesbian wedding I was telling you about, so two brides need their hair done.'

'Sure that's fine with me. But are you sure they'll be happy with getting married in a hairdresser's?'

'At this stage she'd be delighted to get married in a cow barn.'

'Well, I'm free this morning so I can help decorate too. What time is it at?'

'Two o'clock.'

'Grand. I'll drag Shannon out of bed and meet you in the salon at nine. We can decide what we need to do to dress it up.'

'You're an angel. Thank you. Tell Shannon she'll be paid well for her help.'

Sarah laughed. 'That'll certainly get her out of bed.'

'See you in half an hour.'

Lucy hung up, then called Debbie and filled her in.

'Oh, my God, you are a lifesaver. Thank you so much.'

'Now it is a hairdresser's salon, so it's not your ideal wedding venue, but we'll do it up nicely. We'll do hair and make-up there too, and I called Luigi's, our local Italian restaurant, and they said they can book you a table for after.'

'I'm so grateful, Lucy. Thank you.'

'Don't forget to tell all your guests about the change of venue. I'll meet you at the salon at midday. That gives us two hours to get you two ready and have a final run-through of the ceremony.'

Lucy ran into Kelly's room and shook her awake. 'I need your help.'

'What's going on?'

Lucy filled her in and Kelly threw on a tracksuit and hoodie and followed her up to the salon.

'How much exactly am I getting paid for slaving on a Sunday?' Shannon asked, as soon as they stepped through the door.

'If you do a good job, I'll give you fifty quid each,' Lucy said.

Shannon smiled. 'Fair enough, I can buy those boots I saw in Office.'

I can buy new school shoes that won't get photographed and slagged, Kelly thought.

'Right.' Sarah clapped her hands. 'Ideas?'

It was going to take a bit of creative thinking to make it wedding worthy.

'I think we should drape all the mirrors with tulle and white ribbons and fill the place with lots of flowers and candles,' Kelly suggested.

'Great idea,' Sarah said, nodding.

'Most people will have to stand, but we'll need chairs for the older guests. I have six in the kitchen at home, and with your six, that should be enough,' Lucy noted.

'We can dress the kitchen chairs up with tulle and bows too,' Kelly suggested.

'Yeah, and we should get white balloons and a congratulations banner.' Shannon was warming to the plans.

'Great ideas. Let's get to work,' Lucy said. 'The brides will be here at midday, so we're on the clock.'

'Brides?' said Shannon, cocking her eyebrow. 'Sorry, what?'

'It's a gay wedding,' Lucy said. 'We've two discerning women to satisfy, so chop-chop.'

'What's discerning? Is it a new LGBT word? A new weird type of gay?'

Lucy laughed. 'No, they're just regular lesbians.'

Shannon shrugged. 'Cool. It'll be my first gay wedding. Wait till I tell the girls at school. I'm going to get a selfie with the brides.'

Sarah rolled her eyes. 'Less selfies and more work.'

Sarah persuaded Darren to drive Shannon and Kelly into town to buy tulle and ribbon, balloons and banners, while she gave the salon a thorough clean. Lucy went home to get Dylan to help her carry over the chairs before he headed to training.

Within an hour the girls were back, laden with all the materials.

'The only tulle they had was pink. I know the lezzers are probably more into blue or black or whatever, but it's all they had. They were sold out of white,' Shannon said.

'Everything else is white, so that should tone it down a bit,' Kelly added.

The girls set to work blowing up balloons. Kelly then sewed white ribbons onto the tulle and dressed the mirrors and chairs.

'Great job.' Lucy admired her daughter's handiwork.

'She's so creative,' Shannon said pointedly. 'She has a gift.'

Lucy nodded but said nothing further. She went back to flower-arranging with Sarah. They made mini bouquets from white roses and lilies and tied them to the chairs with ribbon.

'Bloody hell, it's like Barbie's grotto in here.' Jenny had arrived. She laid her huge make-up case on a chair.

'We wanted white, but that was all we could get at such short notice,' Lucy said.

'Once you turn down the main lights and there's just the candles it won't be quite so pink,' Sarah said.

'To be fair, guys, I thought this was a really stupid idea, but the salon has been transformed. It looks fantastic.' Jenny was impressed.

'Shannon and Kelly have been a huge help,' Lucy said. 'We'd never have got it ready without them.'

Kelly came out of the back room carrying a tray of coffees. 'I thought you could use a break,' she said.

'Oh, you little star,' Sarah said. 'I need one of these badly.'

Lucy smiled at her daughter. 'Thanks, sweetheart, perfect timing.'

They sat down in the decorated kitchen chairs and sipped their drinks.

'Right, if you don't need us any more, I'll be happy to get paid now,' Shannon said. 'I want to get those new boots today.'

Lucy opened her wallet. 'You've earned it, girls. There you go.'

'I can stay if you need more help?' Kelly said.

'Come on, you bloody martyr. Let's get out of here before they ask us to clean the loo or something.' Shannon tugged at Kelly's arm.

Lucy laughed. 'Go off with Shannon and treat yourself. You deserve it.'

As the girls left, Debbie and Kerrie appeared. They stood on the threshold, their eyes wide.

'Wow!' Debbie said. 'Look what you've done!'

'Oh, my God, it looks fantastic,' said Kerrie, who was already in tears.

'Sorry about all the pink,' Lucy said, 'but they had no white tulle left.'

'Pink is Kerrie's favourite colour! We love it!'

'So who wants to be transformed into a goddess first?' Jenny asked.

'Me, please!' Debbie laughed. 'I'll need the most trowel work.'

'Excuse me, I'm an artist, not a plasterer,' Jenny said, pretending to be insulted.

The two brides laughed.

'Of course, I beg your pardon,' Debbie said, bowing to her. 'Just don't do one of those subtle, natural looks – I want to be transformed.'

'I'll do your hair, Kerrie, while she's getting her make-up done.' Sarah led Kerrie over to the basin and got her sitting comfortably.

An hour and a half later, the two brides were beautifully made-up, coiffed and dressed in their matching cream trouser suits.

'If I say so myself, you look sensational,' Jenny said.

'Gorgeous,' Sarah added.

'Just stunning.' Lucy smiled. 'And I can see the photographer pulling up outside, which is perfect timing. We can get the first shot of you two as brides.'

'Thanks, guys, you've been incredible. I've never looked this good in my life.' Kerrie beamed.

'Today started so badly,' Debbie said, her lip quivering. 'I was so upset when we got the news about the restaurant. All I want to do is marry this amazing woman. But you turned it around for us, Lucy. You're a force for good in the world, you really are.' She grabbed Lucy in a tight hug.

'I'm thrilled we could help,' Lucy said. 'This is going to be a day to remember, all the more so because of the drama.'

The photographer pushed open the door. 'Is this it?' he said, sounding puzzled.

'Yes,' said Debbie, grinning. 'This is the venue.'

'Right so,' he said. 'I have me work cut out to make it look good, but I'll manage.'

'Cheek of you!' Sarah said. 'The place looks bloody brilliant!'

'Come on,' Kerrie said. 'First picture is the whole team, all of you over here beside us.'

The photographer snapped away and would have had them there for a hundred photos if they'd let him, but Lucy checked her watch and said, 'Right, ladies. It's a quarter to one, so we need to run through the ceremony.'

She led them into the back room and took her folder from her bag. 'So, you two will hide out back here until all your guests are accounted for. I've set out twelve chairs for your older guests, then the others will have to stand or lean on counters. When they're all ready, I'll give you the nod to go around and come through the front door, so you can walk up the "aisle" together. I'll be waiting for you at the top of the room.'

'Right! That sounds like a grand entrance,' Kerrie said. 'We can manage that.'

'Then I'll do my introduction and welcome everyone,' Lucy went on. 'I've noted you've an aunt, Debbie, who's come all the way from America, so I'll give her a special mention. Then I'll ask you two to light a candle each. Please, God, they light and stay lit because at my last one the buggers refused to light and the bride ended up in tears thinking it signified the marriage wasn't meant to be.'

The brides laughed. 'Ah, we're not that particular,' Debbie said. 'I'm marrying this one, come hell or high water – cancelled venues or uncooperative candles be damned.'

Lucy laughed. 'That's the spirit! After that, your son is going to read the Pablo Neruda poem, Kerrie. And then

Debbie's niece is going to sing "I Would Rather Go Blind", accompanied by her boyfriend on the guitar.'

'I'd rather go blind than have to listen to it, but my sister thinks her daughter is very talented so we have to suck it up.'

'Is the boyfriend any good on the guitar?' Lucy asked.

'Horrendous.' Debbie rolled her eyes.

Lucy grinned. 'All weddings have these moments. I did one where the cousin did a fifteen-minute solo on the flute – it was pure torture. But it made everyone laugh afterwards. After the music I'm going to talk a bit about you two,' Lucy said, smiling. 'Nothing salacious, I promise. Just to say what it's been like to work with you and how touching it is to see how devoted and committed you are to each other.'

'You'll have us crying,' Kerrie said.

'Tears are always welcome.' Lucy winked. 'And then Debbie's uncle is performing the speech from *The Princess Bride* about marriage, yes?'

Debbie sighed. 'Yes, another mad relation. Poor Kerrie, all her family are normal. Ted is insisting on doing the speech in the silly voice. You know, "mawwiage, that bwessed awwangement".'

Lucy looked at her uncertainly. 'Can you live with that? I could try having a word with him?'

Debbie laughed. 'Asking him to tone it down will only make it worse, believe me. Let him at it.'

Nothing surprised Lucy any more. She'd seen it all in the last five years of ceremonies – cousins who 'played' the violin, crucifying songs, friends saying 'a few words' that went on for twenty-five minutes, and even one best man who turned up so drunk he passed out cold in the middle of the ceremony. A goofy uncle was no big deal. 'After your uncle, we get serious. I'll invite you both to say your vows. Have you learned them off or do you have them written down?'

'We learned them,' Kerrie said.

'So we can gaze lovingly at each other while we say them,' Debbie said.

'Don't mock, you,' Kerrie said, swatting her arm. 'It'll be gorgeous.'

'There won't be a dry eye in the house,' Lucy said.

'There'd better be,' Jenny said, coming into the back room. 'Don't you two dare ruin all my work by crying your mascara off.'

The women laughed. 'Ah, Jenny, will you stay for it?' Kerrie asked. 'We'd love you and Sarah to be here.'

Jenny grinned. 'I wouldn't miss it for anything. I've already told my fella he'll have to wait longer to see me today.'

'We're honoured,' Debbie said.

'Finally,' Lucy said, 'once you've said your vows, Kerrie's niece is going to sing "My Baby Just Cares For Me".'

'And she can actually sing. She has a gorgeous voice.' Kerrie smirked.

'Glad to hear it.' Lucy chuckled. 'Then I'll invite you two to blow out the individual candles you lit earlier and light the big one together. And then I'll let you kiss the bride and you'll be married.'

Kerrie grabbed Debbie's hand. 'Oh, God, I'm nervous, but I can't wait.'

'Now for the big question,' Lucy said. 'This is the most important thing I'll ask you today. Did you bring the marriage certificate I asked for one thousand times?'

'I nearly went mad you asked so often,' Debbie said, 'but, yes, I did bring it.'

She went over to her handbag and riffled through it. They all watched her. She continued searching. Lucy felt her heart skip a beat. Please, please, don't have forgotten it, she thought. This had happened before, and she'd been unable to marry the couple that day. The rule was unbreakable: she had to view the certificate before the ceremony, and all three of them had to sign it. Without that, there was no wedding.

'Debbie?' she said. 'Do you have it?'

'Oh, Christ, I definitely put it in,' Debbie said, her voice rising in panic. 'Jesus, where is it?'

'I thought you weren't allowed to ask Him for help,' Jenny said.

Lucy stifled a grin. 'It's okay, take a deep breath. It might be looking at you and you're not seeing it.'

Kerrie went over to help. They emptied the contents of the bag onto the table. No certificate.

'Oh, no!' Debbie said, a sob catching in her throat.

Kerrie hugged her. 'Don't worry, love. We'll find it.'

'But I put it in,' Debbie said. 'I'm sure of it.'

'Check the floor,' Jenny said, jumping into action. 'It might have fallen out.'

Darren walked into the room as they were all searching, Lucy and Jenny on all fours.

'Eh, what's going on?' he said.

'Missing marriage certificate,' Lucy said, as she crawled behind the cabinet. 'Can't do the ceremony without it.'

'Oh, no,' Darren said. 'Does the groom have it maybe?'

All four women looked up at him.

'Typical,' Jenny said. 'Always thinking a man will save the day.'

'Or maybe the best man?' Darren tried.

Debbie stood up. 'Hi, I'm the bride, and this is my wife-to-be.'

Darren looked so astonished that Lucy couldn't help laughing. 'It's a gay humanist wedding, Darren,' she said. 'This is Debbie and Kerrie.'

'Oh, right, yeah,' Darren said, trying to recover himself. 'Of course. Cool, yeah. Happy . . . em . . . wedding day, you two. Can I help?'

'We need to find a piece of paper that says these two have been to the registry office and done the deed,' Jenny said. 'So quit yapping and gawking and start searching.'

They searched every corner of the room, but there was no piece of paper. By now, both brides were near tears, and Jenny was pressing tissues to their eyes to stop their make-up running.

'Wait,' Lucy said. 'Debbie, sit down here for a second. Now, close your eyes, deep breath. Picture yourself with the certificate this morning. It was a busy morning, you were upset about the venue, lots of stuff on your mind. Now try to clear your mind and see yourself with the certificate. Where are you?'

Debbie sat still, eyes squeezed shut, brow furrowed in concentration.

'I'm in the kitchen,' she said slowly. 'I'm crying because of the venue and because my mum texted me to tell me she wouldn't come to the wedding. I have the certificate in my hand and I'm thinking I must put it away before I soak it with tears. So I think of somewhere safe. So I went to . . . to . . .' Her eyes shot open. 'Kerrie's bag!' she yelled. 'I knew I could trust her more than myself.'

Kerrie shot out into the other room and retrieved her bag. She yanked it open and a folded piece of paper fell out, fluttering to the floor like confetti.

'Oh, thank you, sweet Jesus!' Kerrie shouted. 'I have it.'

'What's with you two? I thought you humanists didn't thank Jesus, Mary or St Joseph for anything,' Jenny said drily.

They all burst out laughing.

'Quick,' said Lucy, 'give it to me.'

They finalized the paperwork, and by a quarter to two the guests were arriving, the scene was set and the two brides had calmed down after their fright. Darren had insisted on pouring them a glug of brandy each – 'Medicinal,' he assured them – so the atmosphere had mellowed considerably.

Debbie kept peeping out of the back room.

'She's not coming, Deb, you have to accept it,' Kerrie said.

'I'm sorry about your mum. It's tough on you.' Sarah patted Debbie on the back.

'Jesus, will you stop? She'll start crying again. I need dry make-up,' Jenny huffed.

'It's just the two of us. My dad died when I was ten. I thought she'd come around. Oh, well . . .' Debbie choked up again.

'I'm your family now, Deb.' Kerrie kissed her.

Lucy went out to the room to greet guests and ascertain how many were there. She checked the candles, made sure the niece and her boyfriend had all they needed, persuaded the uncle not to give her an early rendition of his speech and made sure Kerrie's great-aunt Maggie was seated comfortably. Then she asked the guests to take their seats, or perch, and be ready to greet the bride and bride.

In the back room, Debbie and Kerrie were hand in hand.

'Are you ready to get married?' Lucy asked.

They nodded.

'Right. Here we go.'

As Lucy stepped out from the back room, the front door of the salon burst open. A woman in her seventies tripped over the lip of the doorframe and stumbled in.

Lucy rushed over to help her to her feet. Debbie charged out of the back room. 'Mum? Are you okay?'

'It's bad enough that you're marrying a lesbian, but did you really have to get married in a hairdressing salon? Really and truly.'

'Hi. I'm Lucy, the celebrant. Can I get you a chair?'

The woman straightened up and brushed down her jacket. 'No, thank you. I'm going to be walking my daughter up the aisle, or the salon floor or whatever this is.'

Debbie's eyes filled with tears. 'Oh, Mum. That means the world to me.'

Her mother pursed her lips. 'You're all I've got, Debbie – I can't lose you. I don't like it, but I'll try.'

'That's all I'm asking, Mum.'

'Stop!' Jenny came over holding a make-up brush. 'Mum, step back, please. Debbie, look at me. Look up.' Jenny filled in the tear marks on Debbie's face. 'Right, ladies, no more tears. This is supposed to be a happy occasion.'

Lucy ushered Debbie and her mum to the back room and told Kerrie to come out and wait beside her. There wasn't a dry eye in the place as Debbie and her mum walked through the salon, arm in arm.

Lucy was reminded of something her mum, Tina, used to say: 'Love is family and family is love.'

24

Sarah opened her eyes and stared at the ceiling. Beside her, Darren was sleeping peacefully. She slid out of bed and grabbed her dressing-gown. Opening the bedroom door as quietly as she could, she tiptoed past Ollie's room, where she could hear him breathing deeply. Careful to avoid the creaky spot on the stairs, she made her way down and went into the kitchen.

From the window she could see the white blanket that the early-morning frost had left on the grass. The first day of November had always felt like 'proper winter' to her. She put some coffee into a mug and went to warm some milk.

'Jesus!' A dead slug lay in the middle of a plate in the microwave. Ollie. Would that boy ever stop trying crazy things? If he was like this at ten, what in God's name would he be like at fifteen? They'd never be able to control him. He'd be jumping off cliffs. She knew it was important not to stifle his zest for adventure, but he was her only son and if anything happened to him . . . Well, she'd never get over it. Ever.

Her kids meant the world to her. Sarah knew she was probably too lenient with them, but her own mother had been so cold and bitter. Sarah wanted her kids to have a life filled with love and warmth and laughter, not rules and regulations. Still, they were getting a little out of control – she might have to rein them in a bit. In Ollie's case, for his own safety, and in Shannon's because she was worried she was going to get herself pregnant. She was so voluptuous and looked much older than sixteen. Sarah had seen the way boys and men ogled her and it made her blood run cold.

Even though she was a year younger than Kelly, Shannon was in the same year in school. They had grown up like sisters, spending all of their time together as toddlers, with her in the salon or with Lucy in the shop. When Kelly had gone to school aged five, Shannon had cried so much that Sarah ended up sending her in with Kelly the next day. At four she'd been young, but she seemed well able to keep up and had continued to do so throughout school. Sarah had suggested holding her back in the first year of senior school because she was worried about her being younger than the others in her class when it came to discos and boys and sex and all that. Shannon had freaked and gone on hunger strike (although Darren had found biscuit crumbs under her bed) until Sarah said she could stay in the year she was in.

Sarah worried that Shannon would attract the wrong kind of boy. The very short skirts she wore didn't help, but all the girls wore them and Sarah had to choose her battles. She'd told Shannon the 'Lucy story' many times in an effort to drill it into Shannon's head that even super-smart college girls could get pregnant: she had to protect herself and be careful.

Sarah took the slug out of the microwave, washed the plate, and put in her jug of milk. She made her coffee, stepped out into the back garden and sipped it slowly. The sun was weak, but it warmed her face. She loved this time of the morning when everything was quiet. Her phone beeped, and she pulled it out of her dressing-gown. A private Facebook message.

She opened it and began to read. The mug slipped from her hand and fell onto the grass, coffee spilling everywhere.

Dear Sarah, my name is Tom Harrington-Black. I went out with Lucy Murphy a long time ago. I recently got divorced and was feeling nostalgic so I looked up people from my past. Lucy has no Facebook page, but I remembered her mentioning her friend Sarah who was a hairdresser. When I googled hairdressers on Violet Road, I saw Sarah's Salon and photos of its fifteenth birthday party. Lucy is standing beside two children. One of them, the girl, is the image of my mother and me. I'm trying not to freak out or jump to conclusions, but when I left, Lucy was pregnant but was going to have an abortion. I know the way I left was awful and cowardly and I have hated myself for it. But we'd agreed that she was going to have an abortion, and my dad told me she'd had it. So who is this girl? How can she look so like me and not be mine? Did Lucy have the baby? I'm so confused and frankly completely shocked and I'm trying to stay calm but not succeeding. Is she mine? Can you give me a contact number for Lucy? I need to know. I need to know if I have a daughter. I'm desperate to know. I've wanted kids so badly but my ex-wife and I couldn't have them. Please, Sarah, please let me know. Am I a father?

Sarah stared at her phone while her heart thumped in her chest. Tom didn't know? Gabriel told him Lucy had had the abortion? Oh, Jesus. Sarah's hand covered her mouth. Could this be true?

'You're a FREAAAAK.' Shannon's screech cut through the silence and the back door slammed. 'I've had it.' Shannon stomped over to her mother. 'I'm reporting him to social services for mental abuse. Do you know what he just did?'

'No.' Sarah shoved her phone into her pocket.

'He used my brand new black nail varnish and eyeliner to decorate his new trainers and make them look more "camouflage". I swear to God, I'm going to kill him. I saved for ages to buy that Mac nail varnish.'

'I'll talk to him.'

'Don't do your usual Look-Ollie-it-wasn't-very-nice crap. Tell him he has to buy me all new products and if he ever touches my stuff again, he's going to prison.'

Sarah looked at her daughter's red face. 'Calm down, I'll sort it out.'

'I'm sick of him, Mum. He's always taking my stuff and using it. If you don't seriously make him stop, I'm moving in with Kelly.'

'I'll talk to Ollie.'

'*Muuuum!*' they heard Ollie shout. They turned. 'If you see any snails, will you bring them in?'

'He's abnormal,' Shannon hissed. 'He should be living in some tribe in Africa or with one of those Aboriginals in Australia. Maybe I'll email them – they might take him.'

They went back inside and found Darren shouting at his son. 'Stop trying to microwave bugs and eat some bloody cereal like a normal kid.'

'I hate cereal. It tastes like cardboard.'

'It tastes better than bloody snails,' Darren told him.

'Did you find any snails?' Ollie asked Sarah.

'No, and I need to talk to you.'

'Is it about Shannon's make-up?'

'Yes, it bloody is,' Shannon snapped.

'Ollie, you can't keep taking her stuff and wrecking it. It's not fair. Besides, those are new trainers you've now ruined.'

'I did her a favour. Black nails are rubbish on girls – they look like witches.'

'He has a point there. I was never a fan of dark nails. Red is the colour fellas like,' Darren said.

'Guys who are a hundred years old maybe,' Shannon huffed. 'We've moved on since the nineteen forties, Dad. Besides, I paint my nails for me, not for boys.'

'Hang on now. I'm thirty-eight, not ninety. Besides, black is very . . . well . . . butch.'

Ollie giggled. 'Yeah, girls with black nails look like lezzers.'

'Shut up, Ollie, and thanks a lot, Dad. Fathers are supposed to tell their daughters that they're beautiful and fabulous, not that they look like butch lesbians!'

'I didn't say that!' Darren threw his arms up. 'I said dark nails were butch.'

'It's the same thing.'

'No, it isn't.'

'Mr McInteer said parents shouldn't lie to their kids,' Ollie piped up. 'He said parents should be honest and not tell them they're great all the time. He said you only have to look at *The X Factor* to see these saddos coming in who can't sing and they think they're gifted cos their parents told them they had amazing voices and they're actually crap.'

Shannon leant over the table and stuck her face close to Ollie's. 'So what are you saying? That Dad can't tell me I'm gorgeous because I'm ugly?'

'You're not ugly, but you're not gorgeous neither,' Ollie said.

'Well, you look like a cross between a ferret and a slug.'

'Enough,' Sarah said. 'Can we all please be nice to each other?'

'Dad started it.' Shannon glared at him.

'I give up,' Darren said, and picked up his tea.

They all ate in silence for a minute.

'Can I row down the Liffey in a bathtub naked?'

'What?' Sarah and Darren stared at their son.

'Here we go again with the madness.' Shannon sighed.

'Bear did it down the Thames in London for charity. It was deadly. I was going to do it for – for – I dunno, kids in hospital or something.'

Darren buttered his toast. 'Let me get this straight, you want to row down the river Liffey in the centre of Dublin, bollock naked, in November?'

Ollie nodded. 'Yeah. Deadly, isn't it?'

'Oh, it'll be deadly all right because you'll die of hypothermia,' Darren said.

Ollie frowned. 'I knew you'd try and stop me. I can cover my body in Vaseline to keep warm.'

Shannon put her face into her hands and groaned. 'If you let him do that, I am leaving this family for ever, I swear. I'd rather be homeless and live in a skip than suffer the mortification.'

'Why do you have to be naked?' Sarah asked.

'Because Bear was.'

'Why was he naked?' Darren asked.

'Dunno,' Ollie said.

'To show off his assets.' Sarah grinned. 'He's easy on the eye, I'll give him that. Very hunky.'

Darren put down his toast. 'Hunky? Is he? I thought he was an odd-looking yoke. I suppose he's muscly from all that climbing. Still, though, could he not have done it in a pair of shorts?'

'I'd say women donated more to see all of him.' Sarah giggled.

'OMG, you are so embarrassing, Mum,' Shannon said. 'And none of this is funny. If he does this, we'll be the butt of everyone's jokes.'

'Butt!' Darren cracked up laughing.

'So are you saying I can do it if I wear jocks?' Ollie asked.

'In your dreams, son.' Darren spread jam on his toast.

Ollie slammed his spoon onto the table. 'I don't have any more dreams, Dad. You've crushed them all.'

'Maybe if you had normal dreams, like being a doctor or a

fireman, Dad would support you, but rowing down a river in a bathtub with your willy hanging out is not NORMAL!' Shannon roared.

Sarah reached over and patted his arm. 'Ollie, there are lots of things you can do that don't involve rowing a bathtub down the Liffey in the middle of winter. We love you and we don't want you to die of cold. Maybe we could try talking to Vinny and see if we can get you back into the Scouts.'

Ollie snorted. 'The Scouts are a bunch of muppets who go camping two miles up the road, sit around a rubbish little fire toasting marshmallows and telling crap ghost stories.'

'Sounds all right to me,' Darren said. 'Better than freezing your bollocks off in a feckin' bathtub.'

'You just don't get it, Dad. I want adventure.'

Darren sighed. 'I know you do, son, but breaking bones and collecting scars isn't the way to go about it.'

'I can't wait to be eighteen, get out of Ireland and join the SAS.'

Darren spluttered over his tea. 'You can't just stroll over to England and join the SAS, Ollie.'

'Yes, you can. I looked it up. You start by joining one of the SAS reserve regiments, they recruit normal civilians, and you serve with them for eighteen months and then if you're good enough, which I would be if I was allowed to actually do stuff, you can get into the real SAS.'

'Great. Only eight more years to wait. Can they not take you sooner?' Shannon asked.

Sarah felt her heart tighten. Ollie was impulsive enough to do something like that. 'Ollie, there is no way you're joining the army and going to any war. I just can't let you, love. Rowing down the river in your birthday suit is one thing, guns and war is another.'

'But, Mum, the SAS kill the bad guys. They're heroes.'

'The ones that don't get killed are. What about the ones who die or come home with no legs?'

'No legs? Well, at least that'd stop you nicking my stuff and embarrassing me in public,' Shannon put in. 'Every cloud.'

'Shannon!' Sarah snapped.

Ollie rubbed his nose. 'Why would it stop me doing anything? Sure you can get false legs. Look at your man, Oscar Whatshisname?'

'Pistorius?' Darren said.

'Yeah, him, he runs like the wind on those fake legs.'

'Let me get this straight. You want to join the SAS to kill bad guys, and if you get your legs blown off, you'll be happy enough with the false ones?' Darren asked.

'Well, not happy, like I won't be having a party to celebrate losing my legs, but I'll be grand.'

Sarah slapped the table. 'Can we please stop talking about lost limbs? Now, you two, off upstairs. I need to talk to your father in private.'

Sarah closed the kitchen door and locked it.

'Jesus, what's going on? You haven't locked the kitchen door since you told me you were pregnant with Ollie. You're not pregnant, are you?'

'No. It's not about us. It's about Lucy. You are not going to believe this.' Sarah pulled her phone out of her pocket and showed Darren the message.

'What the hell?' Darren's mouth hung open like a fish's.

'I know.' Sarah sat down opposite him. 'What am I going to do?'

'So he never knew?'

'Looks that way.'

'All these years he had two kids and he never knew. Jesus, that's terrible. The poor fella must be demented.'

'I don't think he realizes Dylan is his. He just recognized Kelly because she obviously looks like him.'

'That Gabriel is some bastard, telling him Lucy had the abortion.'

'Yes, but Tom should never have run away like that. He should have stayed with Lucy and then he'd have known she'd changed her mind. He was a spineless git.'

'I know what he did was really low but, come on, Sarah. Look at it from his point of view. He wasn't able to have kids, his marriage broke down and then he goes on Facebook and sees his daughter looking back at him. I can't even imagine what that must feel like. I'd die if I found out I had kids I hadn't known for seventeen years. I actually feel sorry for him. He's missed out on their whole lives.'

Darren was right. It must be devastating for Tom, such a shock. But he should never have run away and abandoned Lucy like that. Still, what Gabriel had done was despicable. Lying to his own son about his kids.

'What am I going to do?'

'You'll have to tell him the truth.'

'Should I call Lucy?' Sarah asked.

Darren chewed his lip. 'I don't think so. Not yet. Tell him that he has two kids – that'll probably be enough to give the poor fella a heart attack. You'll have to explain that Lucy thinks he knew about the kids and didn't care.'

'What's Lucy going to say? This will kill her. He did leave her, Darren, whether he knew or not, he left her alone.'

'But the fact is, he's their dad and he deserves to know. I'd want to know.'

Sarah nodded. Tom should be told. Oh, God, what a mess. How was she going to tell Lucy?

'One step at a time, Sarah. Tell him he has two kids. Tell him Lucy thinks he knew all along and that he abandoned them all. Explain to him that he has to take this really, really slowly.'

Sarah sat down and began to compose her reply.

Dear Tom, this will come as a shock to you, but you do have children. Lucy couldn't go through with the abortion and gave birth to twins – Kelly and Dylan (who is the boy standing beside her in the photo). Running away like you did was unforgivable. You left Lucy alone to make all of these decisions. She thinks you know about the kids. She has no idea your father lied to you. Lucy has raised the twins alone and done an incredible job. She will not be happy to know I have been in touch with you. She feels betrayed by you. But I felt you should know the truth. I will not be giving you Lucy's number. She will not want to hear from you. I realize this is a huge shock to you, but it will be an even bigger shock to Lucy and the kids. They have to be protected from any hurt or distress. You need to think about what I've told you and take this very, very slowly. There are two innocent children involved here who must not be upset. Lucy is my best friend. I will not let you hurt her again. Sarah

Sarah's hand shook as she pressed Send. She had a horrible feeling things were never going to be the same again.

25

Lucy typed in the last figure and printed out the sheet. The shop was doing well, but she was keen for Billy to invest in a good coffee machine. The mark-up on hot drinks was huge, and as the only shop in a mile radius, with a huge footfall of locals passing on their way to the bus stop or railway station for work, or mothers heading to the park with young children or school kids coming in for coffees or hot chocolates, she reckoned they could make easy money.

But Billy was resistant to change. He said fancy coffee was a 'fad' and that he had no time for all that 'grande latte' nonsense. If Lucy had her way, she'd have a little deli counter in the shop selling takeout coffees, scones and rolls. They'd clean up. But Billy liked things the way they were, newspapers and groceries. She'd have to get Jenny and Sarah to help persuade him.

Lucy locked the shop and went upstairs to get changed. She was looking forward to seeing Damien. It was her little lifeline, and the sex wasn't bad either. She put on her red lacy underwear and the black dress that made her feel good.

All those years ago in college, when she was nice to him because she felt sorry for him, she'd never have imagined he'd end up being her casual-sex person. She'd never fancied him – she was far too busy ogling Tom and his green eyes, stupid girl that she was. She'd have been better off going out with Damien, marrying him, and them becoming the two top barristers in Dublin. Instead, she'd got herself pregnant and trapped in a corner shop while Damien had gone on to have a glittering career and was hugely respected in the legal field. She'd make damn sure that Kelly ended up with a smart man who was kind and decent and going places, not a pathetic coward who shirked his responsibilities.

When she'd left college to have the babies and never gone back, she'd hidden herself away, ashamed at her failure. She didn't want to keep in touch with her old classmates and hear how well they were doing. She was heartbroken, and devastated by her stupidity and failure. She'd wanted to cocoon herself in her new world of motherhood and nursing her dying mother.

Damien had tried to reach out to her, but she'd pushed him away. Then, five years ago, when she was celebrating her birthday in a bar in town with Sarah and Jenny, she'd bumped into him. Literally. She'd been on her way to the Ladies when she'd bumped into a tall, dark man in an expensive suit. He'd apologized and had turned to let her pass when he'd said her name.

Lucy had looked up and there was Damien. The same, but different. More confident, more self-assured. Not better-looking, but more groomed. They'd got chatting. Lucy was a bit drunk and lapped up his attention. She could see he still fancied her. He kept complimenting her. It was like rain during a drought. Lucy had gone for so long without male attention and affection that she didn't realize how much she craved it. She flirted and giggled and touched his arm. At one in the morning when he'd asked her to come home with him, she'd gone willingly. The sex had been good. Lucy wasn't looking for the universe to shake, she just wanted decent sex and companionship.

Damien was single, incredibly busy, and happy to have Lucy in his life. He didn't want a wife or nagging girlfriend, he wanted Lucy.

Lucy loved listening to Damien talk about his cases. She soaked up the world he lived in, the one she'd wanted so badly. He sometimes asked her advice, which made her feel ten feet tall, and as if she was still a tiny bit involved in the legal world.

Lucy looked at her roots in the mirror. She'd need to book in with Sarah next week: the grey was beginning to show. She heard Dylan walking down the stairs, and put her head around the door. 'Hey, where are you off to?'

'Just meeting some of the lads.'

'From the football team?'

'Yeah.'

'Okay, but you've got a match tomorrow. Make sure you're home early.'

'Relax, Mum. It's fine.'

Dylan raced down the stairs, almost knocking Jenny over.

'Easy there, tiger, where's the rush?'

'Sorry,' he said, giving her a peck on the cheek. 'I'm late.'

'Don't let me keep you from whoever she is,' Jenny said.

Dylan raced out of the door without replying.

Lucy was putting on her mascara when Jenny came in. 'Who's the girl?' Jenny asked.

'What girl?'

'The girl Dylan's gone to meet.'

Lucy frowned. 'He's just seeing some of the football guys.'

Jenny snorted. 'Yeah, right. With half a bottle of aftershave on him, I doubt it.'

Lucy ignored her sister. Jenny didn't have a clue. Dylan was at the age where boys overdid the aftershave all the time. It was new to them and they hadn't learnt the art of subtlety. Besides, Dylan never lied to her.

Kelly, on the other hand, had been lying. Mrs Moran, the nosy cow, had come into the shop and told Lucy she'd seen Kelly with Sean at the cinema.

Lucy applied some more lipstick. Jenny took it from her and threw it in the wastepaper basket.

'Stop that. I like it.'

'Your lipstick is something a granny would wear. Put this on instead.' She handed her sister a red one. 'I got loads of new stuff in New York – I'll bring some over tomorrow.'

'Fine. Am I okay or do you need to change my whole face?'

Jenny looked her up and down. 'You're pretty good for a thirty-eight-year-old mother of twins.'

'Gee, thanks.'

'Tell me why I'm babysitting a seventeen-year-old again? I love Kelly, but isn't she old enough to stay at home for a few hours by herself?' Jenny asked.

'I found out she's been lying to me about seeing Sean Whelan. I don't like him. His brother is wild – he got caught selling drugs in a nightclub and ended up in prison. I don't want her getting involved with anyone who will lead her astray.'

Jenny laughed. 'Come on, Lucy, she's seventeen. We all lied at seventeen and dated boys our parents might not have approved of. Besides, just because Sean's brother is wild doesn't mean he is. I've seen him around and he seems like a nice kid.'

'I don't like her lying to me, Jenny. She never used to lie. He's obviously a bad influence. I need to protect her. I don't want her to make any stupid mistakes.'

Jenny put her hands up. 'Fine. But don't be too hard on her, she's a great kid. Now off you go and get laid. You need it. It'll de-stress you.'

'Do I look okay?'

'You look gorgeous. Enjoy yourself. Try not to let him talk too much about boring law.'

Lucy laughed. 'I like talking about boring law.'

'If that's your idea of foreplay, go for it. Just make sure you leave time for sex.'

'We always do.' Lucy winked.

'Woo-hoo, my sister's libido is alive.' Jenny grinned.

'Sssh, Kelly might hear you.'

'And what? Die of shock that her mother has occasional sex? Lucy, you're a grown-up, you're allowed to have a sex life.'

Lucy rolled her eyes. 'I'm off. Remember, Kelly is not allowed out, not even to Shannon's because it's probably a lie and she'll go and meet Sean.'

'Fine. Just go and get naked.'

While Lucy went downstairs, Jenny knocked on Kelly's door. It was her own old bedroom. 'Open up. It's me, Jenny.'

No answer. Jenny tried again. Nothing. Jenny took out a credit card and shimmied the door open – it was a trick she'd used as a teenager. Kelly wasn't in her room and her window was open.

Damn. Jenny texted her. *I'm in ur bedroom, yr mum doesn't know uv snuck out. Get your arse back here now b4 she finds out. I'll cover for u. Text me when you get back in.*

A text came straight back. *F**k, I locked the door.*

It used to be my room. I know how to break in.

On way home now. Tx for covering.

No prob, but don't do it again. I'll try to talk to your mum about Sean.

Pleeeeeease do, he's really great.

Is he nice to u? Does he treat u like the rock star u are?

YES, he really does.

OK then. U've 30 mins to get home.

Jenny went downstairs to make herself a coffee. She'd say nothing to Lucy. Kelly was a normal teenage girl, and Lucy was over-protective. Jenny understood Lucy's motives, but it was hard on Kelly. Her sister needed to lighten up or the already fragile relationship she had with her daughter would break.

She hoped Lucy would have lots of sex tonight. She needed to relax and have some fun. She was always so stressed about the kids. They were amazing, she'd done an incredible job, but now she needed to get a life for herself. Mind you, that Damien wasn't very sexy. Jenny reckoned Lucy could do a lot better. But, then, Lucy thought Jenny's love life was wrong.

In the beginning, Lucy had begged her to stop seeing Frank. She'd kept reminding her that he was married with a son. But he was the sexiest, most confident man Jenny had ever met, and the richest too. They'd met a year ago when she'd gone to Cannes to do make-up for an Irish actress who was starring in one of the nominated movies. Frank had been staying in the same hotel. Jenny had met him in the bar and sparks had flown.

In the first six months he'd wined and dined her. Weekends in Paris and London, hotel suites, vintage champagne. Jenny had loved it. It was the high life with none of the hassle. But Lucy had kept at her: it was wrong, it was immoral, he was using her, she deserved better . . .

Life with Frank was so much more fun than without. She wanted adventure and excitement and he gave it to her.

Jenny heard a noise from upstairs. She went up to the bedroom. Kelly was closing the window. 'You could have come in the front door. Your mum's gone out and Billy's in the pub.'

'I was afraid she might have changed her mind or gone out later.'

'You can't climb out of the window at night, Kelly. Your mum will freak if she finds out.'

Kelly bit her thumbnail. 'I can't do anything right anyway.'

'Come on, you know she loves you and she's just a bit over-protective.'

'She's a jailer. She wants to lock me up until I'm thirty. All she cares about is my exam results and fitting in at bloody St Jude's.'

'I take it it's not going any better?'

'I hate it.'

'It can't be that bad, and you hated Woodside at first too.'

'This is different. I only hated Woodside cos I missed Dylan. I hate St Jude's because the girls are bitches.'

'Is that Melissa cow still giving you hassle?'

'Yes, and it's worse now because Dylan told her to leave me alone.'

'Oh, God, bad idea.'

'Yeah, and he's going out with her step-sister, Taylor. They're all over each other. I think Melissa is jealous, so she's even more vicious to me.'

'Fight back. Don't take any crap from her.'

'I can't. If I get into trouble in school, Mum will kill me. She keeps banging on about how important it is that I behave impeccably and not put a foot wrong or I'll jeopardize the scholarship and let the family down, blah-blah-blah. She's obsessed with this stupid school. Did she want to go there when she was a kid or something?'

If only you knew, Jenny thought. Your dickhead of a father and bastard of a grandfather went there. 'Uhm, no. She just wants them to see how great you are. Look, you're entitled to defend yourself, so if Melissa is being mean to you, you're allowed to fight back and no one is going to blame you. Just don't punch her or send any mad texts. Do it verbally so it's your word against hers.'

'Sean's the only good thing in my life.'

'How long have you been seeing him?'

'Three weeks.'

Jenny grinned. 'And it's love?'

Kelly blushed. 'No, well . . . I mean . . . maybe . . . I really like him and he's really nice to me and right now I need that, Jenny. School is so horrible. Will you talk to Mum and see if you can make her understand that it's okay for me to see Sean? Please?'

Jenny smiled. 'I'll try, but you know how stubborn Lucy is.'

Kelly sighed. 'I certainly do.'

'Do you want to hear good news?' Jenny asked.

'Obvs.'

'I wore the dress you made me and everyone on the shoot in New York was asking me where I got it. It's really gorgeous. You're very creative as well as being intelligent – you lucky thing. It's rare to get both.'

'Did they really?' Kelly was clearly thrilled.

'Yes.'

'Cool, thanks, Jenny.'

'You're welcome. Now, come on downstairs and watch a movie with me.'

'Okay, but I'm not watching *Magic Mike* again.'

'But they're all so hot.'

'We've watched it tons of times. I'm choosing tonight.'

'No mushy rom-coms,' Jenny pleaded. 'By the way, what's up with your Facebook page? You never post anything, and when you do it's really boring. You need to shake it up a bit . . . or is it a cover?'

'Of course it's not my real Facebook page. I have a different one, a proper one. The boring one is to keep Mum from snooping into my life.'

'Will you accept me as your friend on your real one?'

'No. It's private. I'm seventeen and I need some privacy, Jenny!'

'Fair enough. I thought I was your cool aunt.'

'You are, but you're still old and Mum's sister.'

'Right, that's it. We're watching *Magic Mike*.'

'*Nooooo!*' Kelly laughed and threw a cushion at her.

Halfway through the movie, Kelly looked at Jenny. 'Can I ask you something?'

Jenny paused the film. 'Sure.'

'I've been thinking about my dad a lot lately. I don't know why, I guess maybe when things aren't great you start thinking about stuff more. Anyway, I really want to try to find him when I turn eighteen. I'll be an adult and Mum can't stop me. I need to know who he is. You can track anyone down if you know their full name. Do you think Mum will ever tell me his name?'

Jenny swallowed. 'To be honest, Kelly, I don't think she will. Look, I know it's really hard on you not having a dad or even knowing who he is. It must hurt like hell that he left you before you were even born, but I think he made it kind of clear that he didn't want to be a father. He's never come looking for you. I'm sorry, Kelly. I know you want to find him, but even I don't know his name, and if you did persuade Lucy to tell you, all you'd find is heartache. You may not have a dad, but you have a family who adore you. I really think you need to find a way to make peace with that.' Jenny reached over and put her arm around Kelly. 'I love you and I think you rock. Try focusing on this hot new guy Sean. Show me a photo of him – I want to see him close up.'

Kelly laid her head on Jenny's shoulder and flicked through her phone.

'OMG, he is gorgeous. Go, Kelly! Now I understand why you're sneaking out of windows to meet him.'

'Will you talk to Mum about letting me see him?' Kelly asked.

'Of course I will. I'll do my very best.'

Jenny meant it. She was going to try to talk Lucy around. Even though she knew it wouldn't be easy. Kelly needed some fun in her life, and some distraction from her grief about her absent father.

26

Lucy sat back and smiled across the table at Damien. 'This is so lovely. Thank you.'

'You are exactly what the doctor ordered,' he said. 'I've had a godawful week with the press crawling all over the case. The thought of a Friday unwind with you was all that kept me going.'

Damien was possibly the kindest man Lucy had ever met. All through college, he had been her friend and confidant, always there when she needed a shoulder to cry on, never asking anything in return. She'd known that he liked her, wanted to be her boyfriend, but he'd never pushed it. In truth, his social skills had been so minimal then that he'd never have had the guts to act on his feelings but, still, he'd respected their friendship and she had always appreciated that. These meet-ups were the only chance she got to be just Lucy, not Mum, not daughter, not shopkeeper, not worrier, just Lucy. She had Damien to thank for that.

Damien's phone buzzed and he looked at the screen. 'Damn. It's my junior counsel. Must be about the case. I'm sorry, Lucy, will you excuse me for a few minutes while I take this?'

Lucy waved her hand. 'Of course. I've got the bottle of wine to keep me company, so don't worry about it.'

Damien grinned at her and stood up, walking outside while talking urgently into his mobile.

Lucy envied him that, being important, being someone whose opinion was required, whose expertise was essential to resolve cases. That must feel wonderful, she thought, as she poured more wine into her glass. Her head was pulling her in the direction of 'If only' so she pushed against it. What was the point? That part of her life was shut down for good.

Sarah, Jenny and Billy had all tried to get her to go back and finish her degree, but Lucy had said no. She'd said it was because she was too busy with the kids and the shop and looking after Billy. All of that was true, she didn't have the time to study, but if she'd really wanted to, she could have studied at night. Deep down, she knew the real reason was that she was scared. Her confidence in her ability to study and do well in exams was gone. She'd never be top of the class or get a first. That Lucy was gone. The new Lucy was someone who hadn't really challenged her mind in years.

When the mums at the school gate had laughed about 'baby brain' and losing touch, she'd laughed with them, but really it had hurt like hell that she was no longer smart. Jenny used to tease her for being 'genius Lucy', but no one could say that now. Today she could barely finish a novel without falling asleep. In her heart, she believed that if she tried to finish her degree, she'd most likely fail the exams. And even if she did manage to scrape a pass, who would hire a woman in her late thirties with no experience? No, that part of her life was over for good.

Damien returned to the table and apologized. 'Sorry, this bloody Lippet case is proving very difficult.' He sat down and smiled at her. 'By the way, I took your advice and changed my opening statement to include the Churchill quote, "The scrutiny of twelve honest jurors provides defendants and plaintiffs alike a safeguard from arbitrary perversion of the law." It went down a treat with the jury.'

Lucy beamed. 'Really?'

He nodded. 'They loved it, made them feel important,

valued, and hopefully more sympathetic to me and my client, so thank you very much.'

Lucy reached over and squeezed his hand. 'I'm glad I could be of some little help. You know how much I love hearing you discuss your cases.'

He lifted her hand and kissed it. 'I know. It's a strange form of verbal foreplay for you! Although that's good news for me because I'm sure I fall down a bit on the other kind.'

'You're absolutely fine in that department too. A man of many talents,' she said, winking at him.

Damien picked up his knife and fork and began cutting his steak. 'So, how are things with you?'

'Same old, same old. Dylan is being his usual easy self and Kelly is pushing all my buttons. I found out she's been seeing this boy, Sean, whose brother got caught selling cocaine.'

Damien raised an eyebrow. 'Not great. Not what you want for her. But did this boy, Sean, ever get into trouble himself?'

'No,' Lucy admitted. 'But I still don't want Kelly hanging around with a kid from a bad family.'

'That's understandable,' Damien said. Lucy loved that he got it. He knew that she just wanted the best for her kids.

'Damien O'Neill. Is that you?'

Lucy and Damien looked up in surprise. A sweaty, overweight, bald man in a pinstripe suit was moving towards them across the room.

Lucy heard Damien sigh. Then he stood to greet the man. 'Leslie, nice to see you,' he said stiffly.

'You too,' the man bellowed. 'And who is this lovely lady?'

'You remember Lucy Murphy from college.'

'My God, there's a blast from the past. How are you?' Leslie asked. Then, tilting his head sideways, he added, 'Such a pity you had to drop out like that. I always thought you were the one to watch, top of the class and all that.'

'Lucy, do you remember Leslie Henshaw? He was in our class in college,' Damien said.

Lucy did remember him: he was one of the St Jude's crowd she'd hated. One of the people who whispered about her behind her back and gossiped. My God, he had changed. He used to be slim with a mop of brown curly hair. 'Oh, of course,' she said. 'It must be almost twenty years since I've seen you. How are you?'

'Fantastic,' he said loudly. 'Made a killing on property in the boom, solid property investments and all that, and of course I'm senior counsel now. Married Aoife White, do you remember her? Smart and good-looking. Three kids, house in the South of France, et cetera. How about you, Lucy? What have you been up to? Did that bolter Tom ever come back?'

Lucy could feel her face burning, and her throat was so dry she didn't trust herself to speak. How could she respond? No the 'bolter' hadn't come back. I'm a single mother who barely makes enough to pay the bills, never married, never bought my own house, didn't actually achieve anything. She wanted the ground to swallow her.

'Lucy has two wonderful children and helps me out from time to time,' Damien said smoothly. 'I'm with Fenman, Stein and McCall now, as you know, and Lucy has been assisting me with the Lippet case.'

Leslie looked from Lucy to Damien and grinned. 'Just helping you out in work, eh?' He winked.

'No, not just in work.' Damien put his arm around Lucy.

'Well, well, Lucy, I didn't think Damien was your type. We all used to feel sorry for Damien. The way he followed you around in college when everyone could see you only had eyes for Tom.'

Leslie had always been a spiteful oaf. It was like they were back in college, with the 'cool' kid trying to get one over on Damien and make him feel small.

'I was young and stupid back then, but I'm not any more, thank goodness,' Lucy said, her voice dripping with ice. 'I realize now that Damien was the real catch. He was the one I should have been looking at.'

Leslie cackled. 'You women are all the same. When you reach a certain age still single, you're suddenly a lot more receptive to the men you ignored in college.'

Lucy felt Damien flinch beside her. She was furious. 'I think you'll find that women, no matter what age, are discerning when it comes to men. I would rather die alone than spend a night with a self-satisfied, smug, ignorant prick like you. Little bald fat men like you, with ridiculous egos, make women sick. So why don't you take your senior-counsel arse the hell away and let us get back to our romantic dinner, which you so rudely interrupted?'

Leslie's eyes bulged. 'How dare you insult me? Just because you slept around and made a mess of your life doesn't give you the right to insult those of us who have made a success of ours. You're just a pathetic, bitter college drop-out. Tom was right to run a mile. I feel sorry for you, Damien. You could do a lot better than this.'

'You're making a show of yourself, Leslie. Please fuck off,' Damien said, with an icy smile.

Leslie stormed back to his table of colleagues, ready to slate Damien and Lucy, no doubt.

Lucy and Damien burst out laughing.

'You were incredible,' Damien managed to say at last. 'That's the absolute highlight of my week – no, my year. Christ, I've always wanted to say something like that to him, and the many others like him. "Self-satisfied, smug, ignorant prick". Jesus, Lucy, that's just priceless. And so true.'

Lucy looked over her shoulder towards Leslie's table, then smiled at Damien. 'I'll probably live to regret it,' she said, 'but he deserved it, the arrogant shit.'

'I know you always say you wished things had been different and you'd done law,' Damien said, 'but you would have had to deal with a whole world of Leslies. It might not have made you as happy as you think.'

'Is it really like that?' Lucy asked.

Damien nodded. 'Obviously there are lots of decent people too, but there are still far too many of his sort. Little men with huge egos and a ridiculous sense of entitlement.'

'That's a shame. If I'd made it, I've have enjoyed defeating him and others like him in court.'

'And judging by that performance, you'd have been bloody good at it.' Damien laughed.

Perhaps, but I never made it, Lucy thought sadly, and I never will. Lucy looked at her plate and realized she'd lost her appetite. She wanted to get out of here, away from Leslie, and be alone with Damien. She wanted to lie down, close her eyes and forget about everything.

Damien always made her feel so good about herself. With him she didn't feel like a washed-up mother of two, who worked in a shop and married or buried people for money. He made her feel like the old Lucy – intelligent, attractive, and as if she mattered in the world.

She smiled at him. 'How about we get out of here?'

'Wouldn't you like dessert?' he asked.

'Yes,' she said, kicking off her high heel and rubbing his leg with her foot. 'I really, really want dessert, something sinful.'

He reached under the table to stroke her foot. 'That's a coincidence,' he said quietly. 'That's exactly what I want, too.'

Lucy felt the heat building in her body and suddenly wanted him urgently. Now. 'Let's go,' she whispered.

Damien paid the bill quickly and helped her into her coat. She linked his arm as they headed outside and walked the short distance to his penthouse apartment. In the lift to the eighth floor, Lucy nuzzled his neck and he stroked her back.

'I want you,' Lucy said, into his ear.

He groaned. 'Oh, God, Lucy, you're so sexy,' he said, his hand dropping down to cup her bum. 'Come on, lift.'

Once inside the apartment, they were pulling at each other's clothes. Lucy felt a tear as he yanked down the zip on her dress, but she didn't care. Once they were naked, they fell onto the rug on the floor of the sitting room. And, finally, Lucy had her oblivion. There was nothing but his body, his breath against her cheek, the weight of him on top of her. She closed her eyes and gave herself over to it, letting it blot out everything else in her life. Everything.

Damien clicked the fire on and fetched a blanket, two glasses and a bottle of wine. They stayed on the floor, blanket over them, glasses filled, giggling like teenagers.

'That was fantastic,' he said, kissing her neck.

'Oh, God, I needed it so badly,' Lucy said. 'There's so much going on at the moment, I don't have a second for myself. Being with you is my only escape.'

Damien lit a cigarette. 'I love this,' he said. 'Let's never stop.'

She smiled at him and took the cigarette from him. She never smoked except when she was with him. He was her outlet. She drank too much wine as well when they were together. It was like a release. But she also had to be careful: this wasn't love. She knew that. It was wonderful, it got her through, and she knew he relished it too, but she wasn't in love with him and never would be. She didn't think he was in love with her either: he just thought he was because things were easy between them in a way he had never experienced with anyone else. She had to mind his feelings, though, and make sure he was always aware that while this was a wonderful arrangement, it would never become anything else.

'We'll keep doing it until you find the one,' Lucy said lightly. 'Then I'll let you go.'

Damien looked at the fire and said nothing. She felt a flash of guilt, but it was better to be honest.

He looked up and smiled. 'New conversation,' he said. 'How is the alma mater of our friend Leslie working out for Kelly and Dylan?'

Lucy passed him the cigarette. 'It's mad, isn't it, that they're going to St Jude's, of all places? I'd never have thought it possible. But they're both doing well. Dylan is flying it, of course. He was straight in with his team, making friends, so he's loving it. It's such a fantastic opportunity.'

'And Kelly?' Damien asked.

Lucy sighed. 'She's taking longer to settle. She keeps going on about her old school, but all I can tell her is that this is the best thing that's ever happened to her, to us, and hope that she makes the most of it.'

'It's a big change at that age,' Damien said. 'Going into a place where everyone has their cliques. Has to be hard on her.'

'I know,' Lucy said. 'But she's nearly an adult so, really, she has to get on with it. The good thing is, she's very bright. I'm really hoping she'll choose law. I'm sort of quietly pushing it every chance I get. The problem is she's into clothes designing and fashion, and that's distracting her. But I've told her it's best kept as a hobby, that there's no money or decent career opportunities in it.'

'I wouldn't say that,' Damien said gently. 'If Kelly has the brains to match her creative interest, she could be one of those designers who go far. You can be sure Victoria Beckham makes far more than your average lawyer,' he said, passing the cigarette back for Lucy to finish.

Lucy shook her head. 'I want her to use her brilliant mind, Damien. If she becomes a lawyer, she'll have a good solid career and will never need to depend on any man. It'll give her independence, which is what I want for her.'

Damien nodded. 'I understand where you're coming from with that,' he said.

Lucy stubbed out the cigarette. 'I won't let her end up like me.'

He looked at her. 'You don't really mean that, do you?'

'Of course,' Lucy said. 'I'm nothing. A failure. I want so much more for Kelly.'

'I don't see you like that,' he said.

'That,' Lucy said, rolling on top of him, 'is because you are a wonderful man and I'm pretty damn good in bed.'

He took her face in his hands. 'Stop doing that, Lucy. Stop putting yourself down. You're not a failure, you're absolutely fantastic.'

Lucy kissed him. He was sweet and kind. But Leslie's words had stung deeply because she believed them. She was a pathetic college drop-out.

27

Dylan's legs felt heavy. Damn, he shouldn't have stayed out so late with Taylor last night. He shouldn't have had the champagne and the cocaine. What the hell was he thinking? He'd never gone near drugs before. But Taylor was snorting a few lines and they were drunk and she was very persuasive and they'd had fun.

He'd tried to leave at eleven, but she'd changed into a gold bikini and dragged him into the hot tub in her garden. He hadn't been able to take his eyes or his hands off her.

They'd ended up drinking until two a.m. between making out. She was like a drug, fun, sexy and with a body to die for.

He'd only gone home when the ugly step-sister had come in and screamed at them to turn the music down because she had some maths exam to study for and she was trying to sleep.

His head pounded. He tried to shake off his tiredness and sprinted towards the ball Harry had just passed him, but he didn't make it. The defender got there first and passed it behind Dylan to the winger.

'Come on, Dylan, look lively,' Jordan roared from the sideline.

Dylan was sweating way more than normal. It was the bloody booze. He knew he shouldn't have drunk so much, but he was seventeen. Wasn't he allowed to have a blow-out now and then?

He'd stumbled home after two and had had to throw pebbles at Kelly's window to wake her up to let him in. She was not happy and had hissed at him that he was an idiot to be out so late before a big game. She said she'd lied when Lucy came in from her night out and told her that Dylan was already home and asleep.

He tried to jump for a header but missed it. Normally he would have easily put it away, but he had no spring in his legs. His heart sank and Jordan flung his arms into the air and cursed.

He saw his mother pointing urgently to his boots, but her signal wouldn't work this time. It wasn't nerves. Dylan wiped sweat from his brow. He was finding it difficult to concentrate. How many drinks had he had? He tried to think back. A bottle? Two? Too bloody much.

The half-time whistle blew and he jogged slowly over to the sideline. He knew he was in for a roasting. Before he'd even picked up his water, Jordan was on his case.

'What the hell is going on, Dylan? Your legs look like lead. Your head's not in the game. Get some water into you and get it together. We need a bloody goal, lads. We can beat these guys – they're not up to our standard. Now go out there and get one in the back of the net.'

Dylan could see his mother's worried face under her woolly hat. He didn't want to let anyone down. He poured water over his head in an effort to wake himself up.

The second half was worse. The little energy Dylan had was used up. He was outrun, out-skilled and out-defended. Paul, the right winger, sent in a beautiful pass, all Dylan had to do was pop it into the goal, but he missed. He could hear the groans of the St Jude's crowd.

They were one–nil down with ten minutes to go. Jordan pulled Dylan off the pitch and replaced him with Alex. Dylan jogged off, head down. Jordan ignored him as he went past.

With three minutes to go, Paul came sprinting up the

wing and chipped the ball over the left back's head. Alex deftly controlled the ball with his chest, and volleyed it towards the goal. It went in.

The crowd cheered loudly. The team rushed over to congratulate Alex. Dylan thought he might throw up.

'Brilliant, Alex, bloody brilliant,' Jordan shouted from the sideline. 'What a strike.'

Dylan glanced up and saw his mother standing at the halfway line. She was clapping and had a smile fixed on her face, but he knew she was upset. She'd be worried now that Alex would take his place, that he was blowing his opportunity.

Why had he been so stupid? Why had he got drunk and done cocaine the night before a game? Football was his life. Football was what had got him here.

The referee blew the final whistle. It was a draw. Alex had saved them from a loss. He was beaming from ear to ear. Dylan wanted to punch him, but went over and shook his hand instead. 'Well done, mate.'

'Thanks.' Alex's smile was huge.

After they'd shaken hands with the opposition, they huddled in for the usual post-game talk. Dylan, usually in the thick of it, stood slightly back. Jordan praised Peter and Alex and a few of the other players, but said nothing to Dylan. As the players walked off, he called him back.

Dylan walked towards his coach with a heavy heart. Jordan glared at him. 'I don't know what the hell you were up to last night, but you're a mess. I've seen players blow chances all my life. Don't be like them. Don't screw this up. Get your shit together and don't you ever turn up to a game again in that state. Whatever it is, or whoever she is, it's not worth it. You need to focus on your football. You've got a great opportunity here, son, so don't be an idiot. If you ever turn up in this state for a game again, you're off the team. Is that clear?'

Dylan nodded, unable to speak. He'd never let a team down before. He'd always been really professional. He could feel emotion welling inside him.

Jordan put his hand on Dylan's shoulder. 'You're a good kid, Dylan, but I've seen good kids get sidetracked and lose everything. Stay focused. Your team and this school are depending on you, and so am I. Now go home and sort yourself out. Get rid of all distractions, come back on Monday and show me the Dylan I know, the striker, the grafter. That's who I want to see.'

Dylan managed to croak, 'Yes, Coach. Sorry.'

Jordan strode off. Dylan's head hung low. He felt a hand on his back.

'Hey.'

'Sorry, Mum.' Dylan's emotions bubbled up.

'Into the car.' Lucy's voice was firm. 'You can fall apart in the car but not now. There are people still watching you. Head up, Dylan. Shoulders back. Don't let them see you down.'

When they got to the car, Dylan covered his face with his hands and wept. Lucy put the car into gear and drove quickly out of the huge black gates. Dylan wished she would shout at him. He wanted her to – he deserved to be shouted at.

She patted his leg. 'Calm down. It's okay, love. Everyone has a bad day. You just need to come back blazing in the next game and prove yourself. You can do it. You need to focus, though. No more going out with the boys until eleven the night before a game. Early nights, Dylan. One bad game is all right, two won't be. You know what you need to do, and you know how important this is.'

He nodded. 'I'm sorry, Mum,' he said again, and he was, he really was.

*

When Dylan woke up on Monday morning, after a night spent tossing and turning, he had decided what he had to do. He was dreading it. He didn't want to do it, but he knew he had to.

He smelt her before he saw her. Her perfume was expensive and sexy. He felt her arms around him as she hugged him from behind.

'Hey, you? Why didn't you answer my message yesterday?'

'I was just busy with the match and stuff.'

'How did it go? Did you win?' Taylor was examining a chipped nail.

'Not so good. I played badly.'

'Oh, well, I'm sure you'll play well in the next one. You're a superstar.' She leant in and kissed his neck.

Oh, God, this was going to be hard. Dylan pulled back from her embrace and walked her over to a bench in the corner of the school yard.

'Taylor, I played really badly and it's because I was drinking and all that. The coach went mad with me and told me he'd drop me if I don't focus properly on football.'

Taylor rolled her eyes. 'For goodness' sake, Dylan, it was one match. He's overreacting. All coaches do that. You're allowed to have fun. In fact, you're supposed to have fun. Lighten up.'

Dylan chose his words carefully. 'I know, but it's different for me. I can't get dropped. If I do, they might take away my scholarship. I have to put football first.'

He had her attention now. She was staring at him. 'What do you mean, put football first?'

Dylan took a deep breath. 'I mean I can't go out on Saturdays and Jordan said I can't be distracted by anything or anyone.'

Taylor's face darkened. 'Excuse me? Are you implying that I'm a distraction?'

Dylan smiled. 'You're the biggest distraction I've ever had, but I just need you to know that I won't be around much on the weekends or really during the week. I'm sorry, but I have to put football before anything.'

Two red spots appeared on Taylor's face. She stood up. 'If you're not going to be around, I guess I'll have to find someone else to distract.'

Dylan grabbed her arm. 'Hey, don't be like that. We can still hang out, just not as much.'

Taylor yanked her arm back. 'I have guys begging me to go out with them and you're telling me you might be able to squeeze me in for an hour here and there between football! I don't think so, Dylan. I thought we had something pretty great. Obviously I was wrong.' Taylor's eyes were wet as she stormed off.

Dylan called after her, but she didn't look back. What had he done?

28

Ollie answered the door, dressed in his usual camouflage outfit.

'Hey, Ollie, is Shannon upstairs?' Kelly asked.

'Yeah, she's locked in her bedroom. She locks it all the time in case I borrow her stuff for my experiments.'

'Well, it's probably for the best.'

'She's so mean. She never talks to me any more. She's always out with friends or locked in her room. She used to be fun, but now she's just narky.'

Kelly knew how he felt. 'She thinks you're great.'

'No, she doesn't. She thinks I'm a head-case.'

'She loves you, Ollie, just like Dylan loves me, but Dylan doesn't talk to me much either. He's always busy with football or out with his new friends. So I know how you feel. It's kind of lonely, isn't it?'

Ollie nodded. 'Yeah, and boring. Shannon used to play with me the odd time. Now she just roars at me to get out of her way.'

'Do you have any mates from school to play with?'

Ollie shook his head. 'Not really. Most of the lads in school think I'm too mad to hang out with. They only want to play football or tip-the-can. It's so boring. The parents don't want their kids being friends with me anyway, not since I set fire to Kevin's playroom carpet. It was an experiment that went a bit wrong, but Kevin's mum said I was a bad influence and the other mums agree.'

'Oh, Ollie, that's tough. To be honest, no one in my new school wants to hang out with me either.'

'Why? You're so normal and nice.'

Kelly smiled. 'Thanks, but the girls there think I'm a total loser and they tell me that all the time.'

'That's so mean. I think you're great, and so does Shannon – and Mum and Dad. Some of the boys in my class call me a retard in the yard when the teacher can't hear.'

'That's bullying. Did you tell your teacher?'

Ollie looked straight at her. 'Did you?'

'No, but I'm seventeen. I can handle it. You're only ten. It's wrong.'

'My teacher says bullying is wrong at any age. Teachers can't do much, though. They can't make kids like you, can they?'

'I suppose they can't. Do you have any friends at school?'

'I have Larry – he's my bezzie. He's got ADHD and loves doing fun stuff too.'

'I'm really glad you have him.'

'Do you have anyone in your new school?'

'Not really, but I have Shannon outside and she's great.'

'I'm glad she's nice to someone.'

Kelly smiled and ruffled his hair. 'I think you're great and so does Granddad. I hear you're visiting him in his shed now. He must really like you because no one gets into his shed.'

'Really?'

'Yes. Only *very* special guests.'

'Billy's cool.'

'Yeah, he is, very cool. Right, I'd better go up to Shannon. See you later, Ollie.'

'See you, Kelly, and I hope you make a friend soon.'

'Me too, Ollie.'

Shannon leant into the mirror and plucked an eyebrow. 'Ouch. God, boys are lucky they don't have to do this. Mind you, Kevin O'Loughlin should pluck – he has a full-on monobrow. He looks like that one, the painter, Fioda Kaloo.'

'Frida Kahlo,' Kelly said, laughing.

'Whatever. How are Melissa and all the witches of St Jude's?'

Kelly raised her thumb to bite her nail, but the big plaster stopped her. She hadn't realized how much she was biting it until the skin had started to bleed yesterday. It was completely raw. She pulled her jumper down to hide it. 'Same. Horrible, nasty, bitchy WhatsApp messages all day long, constantly making comments and putting me down.'

Shannon cursed as she plucked another hair. 'How do you stand it?'

Kelly shrugged. 'I don't have a choice. I can't let Mum and Dylan down. It's his dream to train under Jordan. I have to stay and stick it out.'

'Yeah, but it's your life too. Does Lucy know you're being bullied? I think you need to tell her. Seriously, Kelly, it's not right that you have to suffer.'

'No.' Kelly's voice was firm. 'I don't want her to know. The happiest I've ever seen her is when we got into that school. She knows I don't exactly love it there. She took me shopping last weekend and bought me a cool parka. She said she's really proud of me for getting such a good report. She's had a tough time and sacrificed a lot for us so I don't want to let her down. Anyway, it's only four weeks to the Christmas holidays. I'll be fine. Besides, I've found a new place to hide at lunchtime so at least I'm left alone then. And I have Sean.'

Shannon blasted her head with hairspray. 'He is pretty fab. It's so stupid that you have to lie about seeing him, though.'

'Jenny tried talking to Mum, but she said the fact that Sean's brother went to prison just freaks her out. She thinks Sean will lead me down a path to drugs and doom. It's easier for everyone if Mum doesn't know. Sean is the best thing in my life. He's just . . .' Kelly trailed off. She didn't want to admit how crazy she was about him. Being with Sean was keeping her sane. Meeting him after school, even though it was only for ten minutes sometimes, was the highlight of her day. When he put his arms around her and kissed her, she felt happy and safe. He was her sanctuary from all the bullying. She was nuts about him.

Shannon grinned. 'Ooh, Kelly's in love! But you need to do something about that Melissa one. If I could get my hands on her, I swear I'd kill her. You need to stand up to her more.'

'I've tried, Shannon. I've told her she's a rotten cow, but she has two best mates who literally follow her everywhere. I can't fight them all. Besides, I'm afraid to get into trouble because it might affect the scholarship.'

'Feckin' scholarship, it's the worst thing ever. They shouldn't be allowed. No one should ever get a scholarship. People should be left alone to go to the school they want and hang out with normal people and have friends they grew up with and not be forced to go to some la-di-dah place full of bitches. It's not right. We should start a campaign – Stop Scholarships Ruining Kids' Lives.'

Shannon applied eyeliner to her left eye. 'I'm telling you, we could get rid of them so other kids don't have to suffer. You could be the spokesperson for the group and go on radio and TV and tell everyone how crap scholarships are. You could send out loads of tweets and get everyone to follow you.'

Kelly took her hair out of its ponytail and shook it out. 'You're mad, Shannon.'

'Look at Donald Trump. He's a thick eejit and he won the election by tweeting and getting loads of people to follow him. Sure he can't even spell.'

'You'd think he'd have someone to check his spelling.'

'I heard he has people to, like, polish his shoes and taste his food in case it's poisoned, and staff to hairspray his big boofy hair and all, so you'd think they'd get someone to check his spelling.'

'Well, he can't ask his wife to check cos her English sounds crap.' Kelly giggled. 'Do you think she has sex with him?'

'Who?' Shannon said. 'Melanie or Meliana or whatever her name is?'

'Yeah.'

'No way.' Shannon was adamant.

'But they have a kid.'

'Yeah, but he's, like, eleven or something and I'd say she just did it the one time. Sure Trump is only shocking-looking. Imagine that big fat tangerine yoke lying on top of you.'

They both cracked up laughing.

'He'd crush her to death. Sure she's tiny.'

'I suppose the money helps her put up with him. She's from some mad country that no one's heard of and now she's married to the president of America,' Shannon said.

'I suppose, but still, could you do it? He's so ugly.'

'Whereas Shocko is only gorgeous. Did you hear he broke up with Aisling?'

'No, that's brilliant news.'

Shannon grinned. 'I know.'

'What happened?'

'I reckon he got bored looking at her moany face, but apparently he sent her a photo of his dick and she forwarded it to her friend Janet, and Janet, the thick cow, sent it to a WhatsApp group and it was forwarded on and now everyone's looking at Shocko's dick.'

Kelly stared at her. 'That's terrible. Poor Shocko. Did he go mad?'

'Poor Shocko? What type of an idiot photographs his dick and sends it? It's a good thing he's so great-looking cos he's clearly thick. Anyway, he did go mad when he found out and he dumped her. Apparently he got all the dorky stuff she gave him, like cards and a big cuddly bear and earphones, and burnt them all in his front garden.'

'God, I feel a bit sorry for her. She sent it to one friend – I'm sure she didn't mean for it to go viral.'

Shannon waved a mascara wand at Kelly. 'She deserved it. She's as dumb as he is. Everyone knows if you send a photo to one person it's going to get passed on. Apparently she's devastated and begged him to forgive her and get back with her, but he's having none of it, which is very good news for me.'

'Do you really want to go out with someone who sends you photos of his willy?'

Shannon grinned. 'Well, at least I'll know what to expect when we get together – do you want to see it?'

'No, gross.' Kelly turned away.

'It's big.' Shannon held up her phone and waved at her, laughing.

'Stop! I don't want to see it,' Kelly shrieked.

'So what about you and Sean? Have you talked about sex?'

Kelly nodded. 'Yes, he really wants to, but every time I think about it, I hear my mother's voice warning me about pregnancy and all that.'

'Feck your mother. If you want to do it, do it. I've condoms here, take some.' Shannon rooted around in the back of her drawer and pulled out two. 'Seriously, Kelly, it's your life.'

'What if the condom bursts?'

'Go on the pill, then. We can go to the Well Woman centre this weekend and get you on it.'

Kelly looked at the condoms. She wanted to have sex but

she was terrified. What if something went wrong? She just wasn't ready yet. She'd asked Sean to wait a few more weeks. She'd said she wanted to spend more time with him and sort out her birth control. She'd bought herself some time. She needed to think about it. Besides, she wanted it to be special. Not behind a hedge in the park or something awful like that. She wanted candles and a proper bed. She wanted her first time to be romantic.

'I can't this weekend – I have to help in the shop because Mum has two weddings to do – but maybe next.'

Shannon finished applying a thick layer of mascara to her eyes. She looked lovely, Kelly thought. Her blue eyes really stood out. Shannon was curvy like Sarah – she had big boobs too. Kelly wished she could fill out a bit. She was still so skinny and had two fried eggs for boobs. She envied Shannon her curves – she was very sexy.

Kelly didn't really need a bra. She wore one but only because everyone else did. Last week, Melissa had shouted across the changing room after swimming, 'Look, Kelly's wearing a bra! How pointless is that!' Everyone had laughed.

Kelly felt her cheeks redden every time she thought of it. She wished she could come up with something cutting to say back, but she never did. She only thought of things afterwards. Shannon would have had a quick response – she was much better at fast comebacks than Kelly was.

'You should have said, "At least I don't look like my stepsister's afterbirth,"' Shannon had told her when she'd heard.

Kelly had laughed. That would have been too mean to say, but it was funny.

She picked up Shannon's big bra and held it up to herself. 'I'll never have cleavage,' she said, with a sigh.

'Yeah, and I'll never see my feet again.' Shannon grinned.

*

Shannon sometimes wished she was thin and beautiful and smart like Kelly. Boys only talked to Shannon's chest, which was insulting. Shannon liked her curves and she knew boys did too, but there were loads of cool clothes she couldn't wear because her boobs were too big. Then again, she might not be book smart, but she wouldn't let some stupid little snob push her around. Kelly was too nice and too worried about everyone else's feelings. She was obsessed with making her mother happy. Shannon reckoned it was because Kelly had no dad and felt bad for Lucy being abandoned and all. She felt sorry for Lucy too, but there was a limit to how much you had to sacrifice because your wanker of a father left your mother.

But whenever Shannon gave out about it to her mum, Sarah said that Lucy had been on the road to a huge career and would have been seriously successful, but then the guy left her, broke Lucy's heart and crushed her dreams.

Shannon felt for her, it was a crap thing to happen, but surely seventeen years later Lucy should be over it and Kelly shouldn't still have to be doing everything to be the perfect child to make up for her dad being a loser. Why couldn't Lucy go to therapy or take Xanax, chill the hell out and stop putting so much pressure on Kelly? She thought the whole thing was way too unfair. Mind you, it did make her really thankful for her great dad. Although Darren could be embarrassing at times, he was a brilliant dad and Shannon knew how much he loved her.

All through her childhood Darren had told Shannon she was his princess, he was proud of her, she was gorgeous and funny, and any boy would be lucky to have her. He was a terrific hugger too. Shannon knew Darren adored her and that he'd do anything for her. It made her feel all warm inside. She felt bad for Kelly that she had never had that.

*

Shannon put more eyeshadow on. 'Thank God I have you, Kelly. You're the sister I'll never have.'

'Me too. Brothers are great, but there's a lot you can't talk to them about.'

Shannon snorted. 'I can't talk to Ollie about anything. He's deranged.'

'Dylan's good usually, but since he met Taylor he's just been out with her all the time. I'm worried – he's drinking and sneaking out at night. Mum said he played badly last week. I know it's because he got home really late. I had to let him in. If Mum finds out, she'll absolutely freak. If he plays badly and gets dropped from the team, he could lose the scholarship and Mum will die. Literally. You know how much she adores Dylan and how perfect she thinks he is.'

Shannon turned away from the mirror. 'For the love of Jesus, Kelly, will you stop worrying about everyone and obsessing about losing that bloody scholarship? Dylan is allowed to have a good time and you're allowed to defend yourself from bullies. From what I can see, this scholarship is ruining everyone's life.'

Kelly looked out of the window into the garden, where Ollie was digging a huge hole in the middle of the grass. The scholarship did feel like a noose around her neck, but her mum was so happy and proud. She had to make sure that neither she nor Dylan ruined it. They owed this to Lucy. She'd stick out St Jude's for her mother's sake, but she wasn't giving up Sean. No way.

29

Dylan sat hunched over his cereal bowl while Kelly played with her toast. Lucy was standing at the counter cutting fruit into a bowl and Billy was making coffee. The kitchen door opened and Jenny came in. 'Hey, I'm out of coffee and food, so I thought I'd call over. One of the many good things about living so close by is I can feed myself here.' Jenny plonked herself down between Dylan and Kelly.

'I told you to take some bread and coffee home with you yesterday when you called into the shop,' Billy grumbled.

'Yes, but I'd much rather call in and have it served to me.' Jenny winked at him. 'If you had a coffee machine you could sell really amazing coffee and make a huge profit.'

'Not this again.' Billy sighed. 'She's been tormenting me all week about it,' he said, pointing at Lucy.

Jenny pretended to be surprised. 'Really?'

'It's been non-stop about the bloody coffee machine.'

'Well, she's right. Think of the profit you could make. Everyone wants good take-out coffee now,' Jenny said.

Lucy could have kissed her sister.

'She has a point, Granddad. Even kids my age would buy cappuccinos and lattes,' Kelly said.

Lucy wanted to kiss Kelly too.

'Cappuccinos at your age? It's ridiculous.'

'Maybe, but it's how things are today,' Lucy said. 'I guarantee you'll be jumping for joy after a month when you see the profits, Dad.'

Billy turned to Dylan. 'What do you think?'

Dylan shrugged. 'Whatever.'

Lucy looked at him. 'Whatever? Is that all you have to contribute?'

Dylan went back to his cereal.

'Someone's got out of the wrong side of bed today,' Jenny said. 'What's up with you?'

'Nothing,' Dylan muttered.

'Are you all right, pet? You look exhausted.' Lucy was worried about him. He'd been in rotten form since the match last week. She knew he hated playing badly, but this was much worse than normal: he'd barely spoken in the last few days.

'Do you feel ill?' She put her hand to his forehead.

He pulled away. 'I'm fine, leave it.'

'It's probably a girl,' Billy said, pouring himself a coffee. 'Girls are usually the root of teenage-boy problems.'

'And boys are the root of all teenage-girl problems.' Jenny smirked at her father.

'Is that it, Dylan?' Lucy asked. 'Is it girl trouble?'

'Jesus, Mum, I said I'm fine.' Dylan stood up and stormed out of the room.

In shock, Lucy watched him go. He'd never snapped at her like that. Dylan was the easy-going child, the one who never answered back.

'Jeez, whatever it is, he's taken it badly,' Jenny said.

'I'm worried about him. He's in terrible form.'

Billy patted Lucy's shoulder. 'Relax, sure it's only hormones. Some silly girlfriend problem, I reckon.'

'But he doesn't have a girlfriend,' Lucy said.

Jenny laughed. 'Judging by the amount of aftershave he's been wearing lately, I'd say he does.'

Lucy decided to ask the one person who would know. 'Kelly, is Dylan seeing someone?'

'Uhm, I'm not sure,' she lied. The last thing Kelly wanted

was to get into a conversation about Taylor. She knew her mother would think she was unsuitable because she was a party girl. To be fair, she'd be right. Taylor was bad for Dylan, but Kelly wasn't going to snitch on her brother. They always had each other's backs. Well . . . they used to. Anyway, she wasn't going to fail him now.

But her mother wasn't letting it go. 'Well, have you heard anything? Has he said anything to you? Have you seen him in school with anyone? I wonder if it's that blonde girl I saw at the football match.'

Kelly got up and rinsed her plate. 'I don't know, Mum. I don't really see Dylan in school. We're in different classes for everything.' She wanted to get out of the kitchen and away from all the questions. It was funny that her mum was so worried about Dylan, Kelly thought bitterly, when she herself was the one being bullied relentlessly.

'Will you talk to him and find out?' Lucy asked her. 'I hate to see him upset.'

I'm upset too, Kelly wanted to shout. Instead she said, 'Okay,' and left the kitchen.

Billy sniffed. 'You were the same when you were his age, always some kind of drama about a boy.'

'No, there wasn't!' Lucy protested.

'I was,' Jenny said. 'I had lots of boyfriend drama.'

Billy rolled his eyes. 'Sure there was nothing but drama with you. You were always getting into trouble. I never had a day's trouble with Lucy, but you . . .'

Except when she got pregnant and dropped out of college, Jenny wanted to say, but she bit her tongue. It was amazing that, even after everything that had happened with Lucy, Billy still saw Jenny as the difficult child.

Mind you, it was the same with Dylan. It was like history repeating itself. Dylan was perfect in Lucy's eyes and Kelly could do nothing right. It pained Jenny to see her sister being so hard on Kelly. It reminded her of how her dad had been with her. Maybe that was just what happened with kids: you had one you naturally loved more.

Billy wasn't going to change now. Lucy would always be his favourite, no matter what Jenny achieved in her life. She'd given up trying to impress him.

'Nothing wrong with a bit of drama. Dylan will be fine, Lucy. He's probably just had a fight with the girl he's seeing, or maybe he got dumped. He'll bounce back. Sure they'll be queuing up to go out with him – gorgeous and a superstar.'

'I suppose so. I'm probably fussing. I just hate to see him down – he's always so sunny.'

'He'll be grand. He's a great fellow,' Billy said. 'Right, I'm off to open the shop. I'll get a bag of groceries for you to take home, Jenny.'

'Thanks, Dad.'

'If you had a husband, he'd look after you. How did I end up looking after everyone?'

'You love it,' Jenny said.

'My arse I do. I should be gardening or playing golf.'

'You hate gardening and golf. We know you love that shop,' Lucy said. 'Sure it's your third child.'

'And the only one who never answers me back.'

'Now,' Jenny said, 'on to something more important than coffee machines. What are we doing for your sixty-fifth?'

'Dinner here with the family is plenty,' Billy said.

Jenny sighed. 'Come on. It's a chance for a night out. Live a little. How about dinner out?'

'I don't want a fuss.'

'If I promise not to book a stripper, can we go out to dinner?'

'Okay, but if you found a stripper who looked like Ursula Andress in the bikini in James Bond, I'd be fine with it.' Billy winked at her.

'I'll see what I can do.'

Billy unlocked the door into the shop and disappeared.

'I'll book Chez Marco – he likes it there and it's got a family vibe. That suit you?'

Lucy spread some jam on her toast. 'Sounds great. Will we say it to Sarah and Darren and the kids?'

'Yeah.' Jenny paused. 'Does that mean Ollie too?'

Lucy smiled. 'Maybe, but I'd say Sarah will probably leave him at home with a babysitter. Actually, Dad and Ollie have become quite the pals. Ollie has been calling into the shed and hanging out for hours making things out of wood. Dad's great with him.'

'That's nice to hear, as long as Ollie doesn't lose control of the nail gun and shoot Dad in the heart,' Jenny said.

Lucy laughed. 'I was a bit worried about all the tools in there. Dad did say there was a hairy moment the first night Ollie called in where he nearly sawed Dad's arm off.'

They cracked up laughing. 'I hope Dad knows what he's doing. Of all the places for a hyper accident-prone kid to hang out, a shed full of tools seems nuts,' Jenny said. Her phone beeped. She read the message and gasped. 'Oh, shit.'

'What's wrong?'

'Frank's wife found out he's got another woman.'

'Oh, God, Jenny.'

'He said she's gone totally ape-shit and broken every plate and glass in the house.'

'Well, you can hardly be surprised that she's upset.'

'Damn it.'

'What are you going to do?'

'He said he'll be in touch when things calm down.'

Lucy put down her mug of coffee. 'I'm sorry, Jenny. I never approved, but I know you liked him.'

Jenny sighed. 'If anyone can talk his way out of something, it's Frank. We'll just have to wait and see what happens.'

Lucy was secretly glad. Maybe now Jenny could meet a nice man, single, devoted to her. She deserved it, and Lucy wanted only the best for her little sister.

30

Kelly was getting really worried about Dylan. She'd tried talking to him and asking him what was wrong, but he kept fobbing her off and saying he was fine. It hurt, because they'd always been so close in the past.

Kelly and Dylan, Dylan and Kelly. Peas in a pod. It was Kelly's hand that Dylan had reached for when the teacher asked them to make a Father's Day card, aged five. He'd squeezed it so tight, it hurt. Kelly had put up her hand and asked, 'Can we make one for our granddad instead?' It was on Kelly's bed that Dylan had cried when one of the guys on the opposition football team had called him an illegitimate bastard before he was about to take a penalty to win the match. It was Kelly whom Dylan had come to aged thirteen when he'd felt sudden blind rage at his father for leaving them. It was Kelly who had calmed him down and told him not to ask Lucy for information. Kelly had made him see that Lucy didn't want them to ask about their father.

Lucy always got this really awful look on her face whenever anyone mentioned their father. When someone asked if Kelly looked like 'her dad', Lucy's face would kind of crumple. Kelly always held her breath when it happened. She could see how hard her mother struggled with it. There was no way Dylan could go in and demand to know what his dad's name was so he could track him down and tell him how much he hated him. Kelly wanted to ask him why he'd left them, why he'd never cared or wanted to know them. But she knew that asking Lucy for his name would make her face crumple and Kelly didn't want that to happen. She wanted to protect her mum from all the pain.

It was Kelly who had sat up with Dylan late into the night, going over every single second of the all-Ireland final that his team had won last year. But just as she had been there for him, so he had been for her. Dylan had punched John Long when he'd called Kelly 'skinny freak' in third class. Dylan had handed her tissues and held her hand when the headmistress gave the maths prize to the girl who had come second in the exams. It was Dylan who'd always acted as the mediator when she argued with Mum.

Kelly hardly saw him now – he was busier than ever. She missed her brother. She felt left out. While he was thriving at St Jude's, she was drowning. They were drifting apart and it frightened her.

Kelly knew that either football or Taylor was upsetting Dylan. It was Melissa who ended up telling her the truth.

'Thank God Taylor's finally free of your brother. She can get a decent boyfriend now, not some charity-case footballer.'

'I can't believe he dumped her. Is he insane or blind?' Alicia asked Kelly.

Melissa glared at her friend. 'My sister did not get dumped,' she hissed.

Wow, Kelly thought. Dylan had dumped Taylor. But he'd seemed so into her. And if he was the one who broke up with her, then why was he so miserable?

Kelly spent the day trying to catch sight of Dylan. After lunch she saw him. He went over to talk to Taylor in the corridor, but she completely blanked him. She looked straight through him as if he didn't exist. Kelly could see he was crushed. Why had he broken up with her if he still liked her? Kelly didn't get it.

That night, Kelly waited in Dylan's bedroom for him to get home from training.

'What are you doing?' he snapped, when he saw her sitting on his bed.

'Waiting to talk to you about Taylor. I heard you broke up with her.'

'Yeah, and it fucking sucks.'

'Why did you do it?'

Dylan wiped sweat from his face with a towel and threw himself into the chair beside his desk. 'Because, as you know, she's a party girl and I was staying out late and drinking and playing badly. Jordan pulled me aside and told me I was risking everything and to cop on. He said he'd drop me if I turned up and played badly again. He knew I was hung-over. I can't let him down. I love training under him.'

Kelly felt her stomach drop – risking everything? He must have played really badly. 'You did the right thing. To be honest, I'm relieved. I was worried about all the late nights and lying to Mum. You know she'd go insane if she knew you were drinking till all hours.'

Dylan wrapped the towel around his neck. 'Yes, but that doesn't make it any easier. I still have to see Taylor every day in school and it's killing me.'

'Try to avoid her.'

'I go to the gym at lunchtime and pump weights so I don't have to see her in the canteen. But I can't totally avoid her. She's in three of my classes.'

'There are always ways to avoid people,' Kelly said quietly. She could tell him lots of places to hide. Kelly was an expert at being invisible in school.

'I don't want to avoid her. I like seeing her. I want to see her. I want . . . God, I don't know.'

'She's not worth it, Dylan. Focus on your football and school. You can't mess up. St Dylan can't blow this.'

'Stop calling me that.' Dylan threw the towel at his sister.

'You know how proud Mum is of you and how much this scholarship means to her.'

'I do.' Dylan stared up at the ceiling. 'Sometimes I wish it didn't mean so much.'

'Tell me about it.' Kelly exhaled deeply. She wished every bloody day that the scholarship had never happened. 'I wish Mum could be happy with her life, like Sarah. Why is she so obsessed with us being successful?'

Dylan moved over and lay down on his bed, groaning as his aching muscles sank into the mattress. 'I guess she had to give up her life for us when our dad buggered off and she wants us to have a better life.'

'Do you ever wonder what he's like? Where he is? If he had other kids?'

Dylan's face darkened. 'I never think about him, just like he never thinks about us.' Kelly rolled over and propped herself up on her elbow. 'Sometimes I wish he hadn't abandoned us – that he'd stayed and supported Mum. Things could have been so different.'

Dylan turned his pillow over. 'Who knows? They'd probably have split up and we'd have been with Mum anyway.'

He was right, Kelly thought. Still, she didn't believe Dylan never thought about their dad. She knew he did – she'd seen him over the years, watching the other players on his team when a father ran over to hug his son after a big win, or walked off the pitch with an arm around his shoulders, laughing together. Dylan would get this look of longing on his face, which gave Kelly a pain in her stomach when she saw it. She knew how much he wanted that too.

But then Lucy would rush over, hug him and tell him how wonderful he was, and if Billy could leave the shop, he'd be there to pat him on the back too. Dylan was surrounded by love, but having your dad there . . . He'd always missed that.

She'd missed it too. At her school plays, her mum would always be in the front row, cheering her on. But beside her, behind her and everywhere else, there were mums and dads together. Dads taking time out from work, sitting in their suits and ties, filming their little darlings. Kelly saw their eyes shining with pride as they clapped and cheered. Fathers besotted with their daughters – 'Daddy's little princess'. It hurt like hell.

'Don't get back with Taylor, Dylan. I understand it's hard for you, but she is a bad influence. I didn't mind covering for you and lying about what time you came in, but I knew it would affect your football. Taylor's a party girl. You can't keep up with her and the late nights.'

'I know,' Dylan said. 'But I really like her, and now the word's got out that she's available the guys are all over her.' He was gritting his teeth.

'It hasn't even been a week. It'll get easier. Things always do,' Kelly lied. It had been over two months and school had not got any easier for her. Every day felt like an eternity.

'It feels like a year,' Dylan muttered.

'You'd better try to get some sleep – you have a big game tomorrow.'

'Night, Kelly.'

'Night, Dylan.'

She walked out of the room and said a silent prayer that Dylan would get over Taylor soon and concentrate on living up to their mother's expectations of them.

31

Sarah handed Mrs Kinavan her credit card and showed her to the door, then locked it, and went into the back room to get a cup of coffee.

She put her phone on silent, sat on the couch and took her laptop out of her bag. She needed full concentration for this. She opened her emails. Tom had sent several, begging for information about the twins. He'd been deeply shocked to find out he had two children. He'd explained how sorry he was and how much he regretted his decision to leave all those years ago. He said he hadn't been able to sleep since her message telling him he had twins.

> Please, Sarah, I am begging you to tell me about Dylan and Kelly. Tell me what they're like. Are they happy? What are their interests? Please, tell me about my children. When Susie, my ex-wife, and I weren't able to have any, I thought it was God's way of cursing me because I'd got rid of the baby with Lucy. I felt so completely alone in the world after my divorce, but now I know that I have two children, I feel as if I've been given a second chance. I can't sleep or concentrate in work. I'm so excited and shocked, and also really angry that my father deprived me of knowing my children. I will never, ever forgive him for this. We barely speak any more anyway but this is a betrayal I can never forgive.
>
> I hate myself for what I did, running away like a coward. I allowed my father to bully me and I've regretted it every day. But now I have these children, two amazing human beings. I

understand it's too soon to get in touch with Lucy, but please, Sarah, tell me about my children. I'm desperate to know more – nothing is too little or insignificant, any scrap of news will do. I've missed so much of their lives, it's killing me.

Sarah could feel his pain and guilt jumping off the screen. She knew what he had done was truly awful, but he certainly seemed to be paying for it. While Lucy at least had had the joy of watching her kids grow up into wonderful people, Tom was alone in New York with nothing in his life except work. It all sounded so empty and hollow. Sarah wanted to reach into the computer and hug him.

He had done a terrible thing, running away like that, but should he spend the rest of his life suffering for it?

Sarah remembered Lucy sitting on the floor in her bedroom crying her eyes out, heartbroken, crushed and devastated. Sarah had genuinely thought she was going to have a nervous breakdown – she was utterly destroyed by Tom and his dad. But somehow her friend had dug deep, picked herself up and raised her kids. Sarah was so proud of her, and she'd hated Tom for hurting Lucy so much. But now it was different. He hadn't known about his children, so his running away had been cowardly but not cruel. And he was paying dearly for having missed out on his children's lives.

Still, Sarah had been afraid to write back. She never should have answered the first message but, then, he was their dad, he wanted to know them, and he had a right to. He'd been lied to. His children had been a secret kept from him for seventeen years. Sarah's head throbbed. Had she done the right thing? Darren said she had, and in her heart, she knew that no father should be lied to, as Gabriel had lied to Tom.

She sat down and began to write.

Hi Tom, I understand you want to know about the twins so I'll do my best to fill you in. Dylan is a tall, handsome fellow. Everyone likes him. He's easy-going and good-humoured. He's also a football star. He's been playing since Billy (Lucy's father) took him to the local club aged about six. He's incredible, a striker. Kelly is bright and smart like Lucy. She's an A student, always trying to please her mum and make her proud. She's best friends with my daughter, Shannon. Kelly is a lovely, kind, thoughtful girl. I'm absolutely mad about her. As you saw from the photo on Facebook, Dylan looks like Lucy and Kelly is like you, Lucy has devoted herself to raising them and has done an incredible job. Her mum got sick after she had the twins and she nursed her until her dying day. She never got the chance to go back to college and finish her law degree and I know that really hurts. She never got to have the life she wanted because you ran away and left her. I'm sorry, Tom, but that's the truth. If you had stayed and been a man, her life would be different. I'm not sure she will ever forgive you.

This year, in a weird twist of fate, Dylan got a football scholarship to St Jude's, which Lucy said is your old school. They gave one to Kelly too. So the twins are now at St Jude's and are doing well. Dylan is shining on the football team and Kelly is still trying to find her feet. It hasn't been easy for her, she was happy in her old school, but Lucy felt it was a great opportunity for them both to finish their last two years in a good school.

So there you have it, a brief summary of the twins. I'm sorry you never knew they existed. I can't imagine how angry and upset you are, but you have only your father to blame for that. I have to go now. Take care,

Sarah

PS I've attached some photos for you as I know you really wanted some.

Sarah logged out and had just lifted her coffee to her lips when she heard a loud banging on the shutters. She put down her cup, hid the laptop in her bag and went through the salon to see who it was.

She lifted the shutter, and Shannon stood there, in her school uniform, out of breath.

'Any chance you could answer your bloody phone? I've called you a zillion times.'

'Sorry, I had it on silent. What's up?'

'That freak of a son of yours has only bloody cut the top of his finger off.'

'What?' she gasped. 'Is he all right?'

'He's fine. Dad said not to panic. He was with Billy in the shed when it happened. Billy called over but saw the salon was shut and no one was at home, so he took Ollie straight to the hospital.'

Sarah ran to get her bag and find her car keys. She unlocked the door, went outside, locked up and yanked the shutter down. She grabbed her daughter's arm. 'Come on, hurry.'

Shannon pulled back. 'Why do I have to go? He's fine, and I said I'd go to Kelly's after school.'

Sarah glared at her. 'You're coming to the hospital to see if your brother's all right.'

'He'll be grand, like he always is. He's just mental.'

Sarah ran ahead of Shannon through the emergency doors and bumped into Darren, who was waiting for her.

'It's okay.' He hugged her. 'He's fine. Billy put the fingertip in a bag of frozen peas so they can sew it back on. He'll be taken down to surgery soon.'

Sarah needed to see her son. She went into his room. He was lying on a bed looking small and pale. 'Hiya, Mum.' He waved with his good hand.

Sarah threw her arms around him. 'You mad eejit, what the hell were you thinking?'

'I was making you a box for your jewellery.'

'Oh, love, that was very sweet of you.'

'Billy was helping me, but then his phone rang and he told me to stop cutting for a minute, but sure I know how to do it so I just kept going and then it slipped.'

'Oh, Ollie, you have to be more careful.'

Sarah heard a cough behind her. Billy was standing there, ashen-faced. 'I'm so sorry, Sarah. I'm completely responsible,' he said, in a strangled voice.

'Ah, Billy, will you stop? Ollie told me what happened. It's not your fault.'

'No, Billy,' Ollie said. 'It's not your fault at all.'

'Yes, it is. He was in my care, under my supervision. I told him to put down the saw, but then I turned away and didn't make sure he did it.'

'It's got nothing to do with you, Billy. You're a saint for letting him into your shed.'

Shannon took a selfie with the hospital-room background. 'I reckon he was dropped on his head when he was born. I bet Dad dropped him and is afraid to admit it.'

Darren came back into the room with three coffees. He handed one to Billy, another to Sarah and kept the last for himself.

'Did you, Dad?' Shannon asked.

'What?'

'Drop Ollie on his head when he was a kid?'

'No, and you can stop taking selfies. It's a hospital, not a nightclub.'

Shannon pouted and clicked. 'I know, but it's kind of cool to be in hospital.'

Billy put his coffee down. 'I'll leave you in peace. I'll wait outside.'

'Go home and get some rest, Billy. I'll call you when it's sewn back on and tell you how it went,' Darren said.

Billy looked shocked. 'There is no way I'm leaving this hospital until I know he's on the mend. It happened on my watch, Darren. I have to know the lad's finger is saved.'

'Billy,' Darren said, putting his hand on the older man's shoulder, 'Ollie has been in this hospital with two broken legs, three broken arms, four concussions and one broken nose. All of those accidents took place while he was on our watch.'

'I'd never forgive myself if his finger wasn't right.' Billy's voice shook.

'Billy, he'll be fine,' Sarah said. 'Honestly.'

'I feel terrible. I'm obviously too old to look after a young boy. I took my eye off the ball. I promise you he won't be allowed in the shed again. Not ever. It's too dangerous. I should have known better.'

'NO WAY!' Ollie roared, his eyes wild. 'I am *not* giving up the shed. Don't make me, Billy. Please!'

'Ah, now, Billy, don't say that. He loves being with you in the shed.' Darren looked alarmed. 'We've seen a huge difference in him – he's so much happier, these days.'

'He really is, Billy,' Sarah added. 'He loves that time with you and you're such a good influence on him. He's even going to bed earlier because you told him to. Please don't give up on him because of this.'

'Please, Billy,' Ollie pleaded. 'I will never, ever, ever, ever not do what you say again. I swear on my life and Mum and Dad's life and Shannon's life and –'

Billy smiled. 'Let's get through tonight, Ollie, and we can talk about it again. I'll wait outside. I need to stretch my legs.'

They watched as Billy left. Ollie turned to his parents, tears streaming down his face. 'I will not give up the shed. No way. You have to make Billy see it's not his fault. It's mine. I didn't listen to him. I'm a gobshite, I know I am. I love making stuff with Billy. Dad, Mum, you have to make Billy take me back. Please, I love it there, it's the best part of my week.'

Sarah sat down and took Ollie's hand. 'Ollie, we'll talk to Billy. But you have to stop doing dangerous things and taking risks with your safety. You are a ten-year-old boy, not an SAS soldier or Bear Grylls or any of them. You are Ollie McDaid, only son of Sarah and Darren, who love you and want you to remain in one piece.'

'I know, and I was being really careful with Billy's tools because he makes me be careful. He shows me how to do things properly and not rush.'

Shannon looked up from her phone. 'Maybe you should send him to one of those army schools. They make you get up at, like, four in the morning and shout at you and make you run up mountains with a flipping wardrobe on your back and then do push-ups in the mud, and then you have to eat crap food and go to bed at six. He'd be too tired to get into trouble.'

'Don't send me away. I just want to go home and see Billy in his shed every week. I'll be really good in school and I won't climb onto roofs or try to light fires or anything. I don't *mean* to mess in school, but it's so boring,' Ollie wailed.

'Ollie,' Darren said, 'I found school boring. In fact, ninety per cent of kids find it boring, but you have to go. It's the law.'

Ollie buzzed his bed up and down. 'Larry's started tae kwon do. They have a brilliant teacher over in Sandyford. Larry said he's the best and the classes are deadly fun.'

'Tae kwon do?' Sarah didn't like the sound of it.

'What's Tie-wandoo?' Shannon asked. 'Is it some kind of mad Chinese thing? Is he going to be kicking doors in and breaking the table with his fist?'

'No, you thick. Tae kwon do is a Korean martial art, and it's all about fast head-height kicks and spinning kicks.'

'Oh, brilliant. Yeah, that sounds like a great plan. Send Ollie to a class where he learns to do spin kicks and high kicks so he can kick us all in the head at breakfast. You know he's just going to end up knocking some kid unconscious in the yard and then you'll be sorry.'

'I won't – I swear I won't. And anyway, Shannon, at least I'll be learning something, unlike you who spends all day hanging around with Kelly talking about boys. You're pathetic.'

'I'm not the one who always ends up in hospital,' Shannon said, then turned her attention back to her phone.

'So, Dad, can I do it? Can I do tae kwon do?'

'I'll call the instructor and see if I can get you into that group. But this is your last chance. If you don't behave from now on and stop trying to injure and kill yourself and give me and your mum and poor Billy heart attacks, I'll kill you myself.'

Ollie jumped up and threw his arms into the air. 'Brilliant! Thanks, Dad and Mum. I promise I'll behave. I'm going to be the fastest kid in Ireland to go from white belt to black belt.'

'God save us all.' Darren reached out and squeezed Sarah's hand.

32

Dylan was up early the next morning. He went for a run and forced himself to think about the game, not Taylor. He had turned his phone off. He couldn't stand any more Facebook posts, Snapchat or Instagram pictures of Taylor. She'd posted one yesterday of her in a skin-tight red leather dress: *Ready for Sat night!!!!!*

She looked stunning. Dylan wanted to reach into the photo and touch her. Within minutes there were loads of comments on how incredible she looked, a lot of them from guys. Dylan's head was wrecked.

He turned up the music on his iPod to full volume and pounded his feet on the pavement. Soon he was dripping sweat and his chest was bursting with the speed he was going at. Faster and faster he ran. He had to get her out of his mind.

When he got home he found Kelly curled up on the couch, smiling at her phone. 'Wow, Kelly, I'd forgotten what your smile looked like,' he said. 'It's good to see. Is it a guy?'

'Maybe.' Kelly grinned.

'From St Jude's?'

Kelly rolled her eyes. 'As if.'

'Anyone I know?'

'Sean,' Kelly said, 'but don't tell Mum.'

'Aren't you supposed to have broken up with him?'

'Technically, yes.'

Dylan shrugged. 'I won't say a word. He seems okay. Brother's a tosser, though. I hope he treats you well. If he doesn't, dump him or tell me and I'll sort him out.'

'I don't need you to protect me. Go and shower, you stink.'

Dylan was glad Kelly looked happier. It had been a long time since he'd seen her smile like that.

He thought about Taylor in the shower, while having breakfast and all the way to the game. It was only when he was on the pitch that he stopped. It was tough. The guys from Daleside were very physical and tried to intimidate the St Jude's team. Some of his teammates were a bit distracted by the hacking, elbowing in the face, tackling off the ball, and one guy even got his balls squeezed.

'Referee!' Jordan roared. 'He grabbed his nuts! Come on, this is ridiculous. Whadda you want, for him to rip them off?'

At half-time they were two–nil down. Jordan called them over.

'Right, lads, you need to toughen the hell up. These guys are walking all over you. Stand tall, give as good as you get, but don't give away penalties. Watch Dylan. He knows how to handle himself. He pushes back, ducks and dives to avoid the elbows and gets in their face so they know they can't intimidate him. You need to do the same. Grow some balls, lads. Get out there and give it back. Get up in their faces. Show them who's boss.'

St Jude's played out of their skin in the second half. Dylan scored a hat-trick and won the match with a volley to the top right corner. The goalie hadn't a hope of saving it.

Jordan was thrilled with them, and all the parents came over to congratulate the team. Dylan was the star, though. He'd really shown his talent.

'I'm so proud of you,' Lucy whispered in his ear. Her eyes were filled with tears. Dylan hugged her. He wished Billy had been there to see it, but getting Billy out of the shop on a Saturday was a tall order.

Dylan basked in the praise of his peers, parents and the headmaster.

'Dylan, you are a credit to this school,' Mr Gough said, in front of everyone.

'Thank you, sir,' Dylan said, as Lucy beamed beside him.

He was glad to see his mum so happy and he felt good. He'd proven his place on the team today. As he walked towards Lucy's car, he saw Taylor and stopped.

She was talking to Josh. She threw her head back and laughed at something he'd said. She had her hand on his arm. He reached out and pulled her scarf so she moved closer to him. His tongue was practically hanging out. Dylan's blood boiled and he felt sick. He wanted to go over and punch Josh in the face. How dare he flirt with her like that? The prick.

'Dylan?' Lucy called him.

He peeled his eyes away from Taylor. 'What?'

'The car's over here.'

'I'll be with you in a minute.'

Dylan walked towards Taylor. She ignored him. He knew she'd seen him. She laughed even louder as he approached them.

'Hey, Dylan, great game,' Josh said.

'Thanks.' Dylan turned his back. 'Hi, Taylor.'

She looked over his shoulder. 'I have to go, Josh, but I'll see you tonight. It's going to be awesome.' She flicked her hair and strutted off. Josh and Dylan watched her as she walked away in her tight black jeans.

'I heard you guys broke up. Man, what did you do? She totally iced you out there.'

'Nothing. She's not available so hands off.' Dylan glared at him.

Josh put his hands up. 'Hey, no need to rip my head off. She told me she was single and that she was having a party tonight. She's hot and, if she's available, I'm going for it, man.'

Dylan grabbed Josh by the front of his jersey. 'Stay the hell away from her.'

Josh pulled away. 'I'll do what the hell I want. Now back off, Murphy.'

Dylan tried to calm his breathing. He heard a beep. It was his mum in the car, calling him over. He unclenched his fists, walked across to her and climbed in beside her.

'What was that all about? You look furious. You should be smiling from ear to ear after that game. Did something happen with that girl? Are you fighting with Josh over her? For God's sake, Dylan, don't let a girl come between you and your teammates. Forget about girls for now. You need to stay focused.'

Dylan didn't trust himself to speak. He was trying to work out what the hell to do. He'd played out of his skin today because he'd been in bed early and focused on football, but the thought of Taylor with anyone else made him want to throw up.

As they drove home his mum talked about the game and how brilliant he was, but Dylan was thinking, Taylor, Taylor, Taylor.

Dylan put on some of the designer aftershave Taylor had given him and the blue shirt she said was gorgeous on him. If she was having a party, he was bloody well going to it. No one was getting their hands on her. He couldn't stay away. He had to be with her.

'Where are you going?' Kelly asked.

She watched him pulling on an old sweatshirt over his good shirt.

'Out with a few of the lads on the team to celebrate the win.'

'We both know that's a lie. Don't go to her party.'

Dylan looked at her. 'What party?'

'Come on, Dylan, it's all over Facebook. Taylor's free house party. Don't go. Look how well you played today without her distracting you. Mum is on a high. Do you know what she said to me? "He's nailed it. He's shown them all how much he deserves to be in that school." I found her dancing around the kitchen to the radio earlier. Mum, dancing!'

Dylan ran his hands through his hair. 'I tried, but I can't, Kelly. I can't do it. I want to be with her and it's driving me nuts.'

'Come on. It hasn't even been a week,' Kelly reminded him.

'I know, and I'm miserable. Life's too short. I have to get her back. I'll make sure I focus on football and school too. I'll work it out. I might be late tonight, though, so cover for me, okay?'

'I really wish you'd leave it, Dylan. She's not good for you.'

'She's what I want.' Dylan walked out of the door.

He cycled over to Taylor's house and could hear the music from halfway down the road. Cars were parked all over the driveway and he could see people streaming through the front door holding bottles of beer, wine, vodka and gin under their arms.

He waved at a few but didn't want to get caught up in chat. He was on a mission. The front door was open and the music was blaring out from huge speakers. Dylan went into the kitchen looking for Taylor, but there was no sign of her.

He went through to the living room, but she wasn't there either. He went across the hall and into the room with the big snooker table. There she was, cheering as Josh hoovered up a line of cocaine. She was wearing a tight sparkly silver dress and her hair was all wavy, like she'd just been surfing.

She looked up and saw him. Her eyes widened in surprise.

Then she turned away and put her arms around Josh. 'I'll have some, please.'

'Anything for you, babe,' he said, and cut her a line of coke.

Dylan watched. Taylor snorted and wiped her nose, laughing. 'Dylan doesn't approve of having fun. I'm glad you do, Joshie.'

Dylan was over like a shot. He grabbed Taylor by the waist.

'Hey, get your hands off me.' She squirmed in his arms.

'Dude, let her go,' Josh said.

'Get out of my way.' Dylan elbowed Josh sideways and lifted Taylor over his shoulder. He carried her upstairs.

'Let me go, you pig.'

'Not until we've talked.'

'I've got nothing to say to you. You made your choice very clear. Football over me.'

Dylan placed Taylor on her bed and locked the bedroom door.

'This is my house and my party and no one invited you. Open that door,' she shouted.

'Not until you listen to me.'

Taylor stood up and turned her back to him. 'You dumped me. I don't ever want to see you again. End of.'

Dylan went over and put his arms around her. She shrugged him off and wiped her eyes. 'I'm sorry, babe, I freaked out. I was worried about the scholarship and all that, but I made a mistake, a huge mistake. I miss you.'

Taylor turned to face him. 'You can't just dump me then change your mind, click your fingers and expect me to fall into your arms. I'm Taylor Lyons. Guys beg me to go out with them and you . . . you just come into the school and use me, then break up with me. You hurt me, Dylan. I thought things were going really well and then out of the blue you blow me off.'

Dylan reached out to take her hand, but she pulled it away. 'I didn't use you, Taylor. I'm crazy about you. You're the most beautiful, sexy, amazing girl I've ever met. I'm sorry about ending it like that. I made a big mistake.'

Taylor twirled a strand of hair around her finger. 'Yeah, well, I am pretty amazing. Josh keeps telling me how fab I am and trying to stick his tongue down my throat.'

'I'll kill him. I want you back. I need you in my life.'

'What about football and me distracting you?'

'I'll work it out.'

'How do I know you're not going to dump me again if you lose your next match?'

Dylan went over and put his arms around her. 'I will never, ever break up with you again. I'm nuts about you. Come here.'

She punched him playfully in the chest. 'If you weren't so bloody gorgeous and strong and sexy and . . .'

Dylan leant down and kissed her, deeply and passionately. He felt her melt into his arms. He held her tight, wanting never to let go.

33

Kelly took the tub of ice cream from the huge supermarket freezer and put it in her basket beside the chocolate and popcorn. As she headed down the aisle towards the checkout, her way was blocked.

'Look who it is. Kelly Murphy, the biggest loser in St Jude's,' Melissa sneered. 'We thought we'd find you in this dump. We came to see how you lowlifes live. We saw your granddad's crappy shop. What a kip.'

Kelly's heart sank. It was bad enough to have to deal with Melissa in school, but to have her here, in her neighbourhood, insulting Billy's shop, was too much. She felt tears of rage and hurt well up. 'Why don't you fuck off home, then?' Kelly hissed.

'OMG, have you no shame? You look like a hobo,' Alicia said.

'I have to post this.' Melissa took a photo of Kelly.

Kelly tried to push past them, but they shoved her back.

'Charity cases like you shouldn't be allowed to go to St Jude's. You're dragging the school down,' Chloe said.

'You look like you've just climbed out of a dumpster.' Melissa wrinkled her nose.

'Where did you get that jumper? It's, like, the ugliest thing I've ever seen. I'd rather die than wear that,' Alicia said, snapping another photo of her.

'Please borrow it and die,' Kelly snapped.

'You're so pathetic,' Melissa said. 'Everyone thinks you're such a loser. And I mean everyone. Why don't you just do us all a favour and go back to your old school and scummy friends?'

'What's going on here?' Shannon appeared from behind Kelly, holding a two-litre bottle of Coke and a six-pack of crisps. 'Are these girls bothering you, Kelly?'

'Oh, my God, is this one of your friends from Scumtown?' Melissa snorted.

'I'm Shannon, and you're Melissa. I recognize your ugly mug from Instagram. You're actually even more vile-looking in real life, you poor cow.'

Melissa's face went bright red. 'How dare you speak to me, you lowlife? You should put the crisps down – you're obese.'

Shannon roared laughing. 'Obese? I'm curvy, love, and the fellas love it.'

'Maybe the boys in this crappy neighbourhood do,' Chloe said, 'but not at St Jude's, where people have taste and class.'

'Class!' Shannon whooped. 'You're a bunch of vicious bitches who eat each other for breakfast. You should lay off Kelly, otherwise me and my mates will have to come up there and sort you all out.'

Melissa shook her hands in the air. 'Oooh, I'm shaking in my boots. The only thing you could do is crush us with your revolting flabby body. Does everyone in your area look this gross?'

Shannon grinned. 'If I'm not mistaken, your sister is shagging Dylan morning, noon and night. So someone in your family can't get enough of us.'

'She's just . . . going through a phase. She's being a rebel, but it won't last.'

'I dunno, she seems very keen. All of her Instagram photos are of her wrapped around him. You and Kelly here are almost related.' Shannon chortled. 'Dylan is probably sticking his big dick into your sister right now.'

'Fuck off, you scumbag!' Melissa roared.

'Dear, oh dear, I'm very surprised that a lady like yourself would curse. What would Mummy and Daddy think?'

Kelly laughed. She couldn't help it – Melissa looked so out of her depth.

Melissa glared at Kelly. 'I'll get you for this.'

'Don't you threaten Kelly.' Shannon put her face right into Melissa's. 'If you hurt her, I'll come up to that school and give you a good seeing-to. I hate bullies.'

'Come on, Melissa.' Alicia pulled her friend away.

Shannon turned to Kelly. 'What a shower of bitches.'

'They make my life hell.'

'You need to stand up to them, Kelly. I know it's hard when you're on your own, but if you let them think you're in any way weak, they'll get worse.'

'I do try but I have to be careful not to get into trouble in school. If I tell them where to go, I'll end up in the headmaster's office.'

Shannon was so frustrated for Kelly. Putting up with that kind of abuse all the time must be a nightmare. 'It's really crap for you, Kelly. You need to tell Lucy.'

'I can't, Shannon. I don't want to burst her happy bubble.'

Shannon handed the crisps to the checkout lady. 'Well, at least we sorted them out today and gave them a bit of a scare. Hopefully I'll have made them think before they're horrible to you again.'

Kelly smiled, but she knew nothing had been sorted out. She knew she'd pay for this in school.

They went back to Shannon's house and set up the coffee-table with drinks, crisps, chocolate and popcorn.

'Right,' Shannon said, coming in with two glasses and curling up on the couch in her zebra-print onesie. 'Let's watch *Gossip Girl*. I love that Chuck Bass, he's so fit.'

Kelly sat back and tried to block out the supermarket incident, but she was already dreading the fallout.

Kelly trudged out of the school gate, head down, after a day of taunting from Melissa and Co, slagging off her 'fat friend'.

'No wonder you don't fit in here. You clearly like hanging around with foul-mouthed, obese lowlifes.'

It had taken all of Kelly's resolve not to punch Melissa in the face. She could handle people being mean about her, but not about her friend. She had tried to avoid them as much as possible, but Melissa was relentless. Kelly was never so glad that school was over. She wanted to kick the wall and scream.

She kept her head low and hurried down the road to the bus stop. Then she heard a familiar whistle. She looked up from beneath the hood of her uniform coat. 'Sean?'

'Hey, gorgeous, I thought I'd come and meet you. I missed you.'

Kelly wanted to weep. Sean had cycled miles to see her. He'd missed her. His timing couldn't have been more perfect. Kelly ran over and threw her arms around him.

'Woah, careful, you'll knock me over.' Sean steadied himself and hugged her back. 'Bad day?' She nodded into his neck. 'Poor Kelly. Don't let those bitches get to you.'

A car pulled up. 'OMG, is this your boyfriend?' Melissa squealed.

Kelly's heart sank. Melissa was leaning out of her car window, Alicia was in the passenger seat and Chloe was in the back, sniggering.

'Nice bike. I think I saw one like it in a skip,' Melissa said.

'What is that uniform, Scumtown National?' Alicia laughed, taking a photo of Sean.

Sean let go of Kelly and walked over to the window.

Leaning in, he said, 'Hello, bitches. How'd you like to climb out of the car and say that to my face?'

'Why? Are you going to beat us up? Is that how boys behave in Scumtown? Beat their women?' Melissa said.

'Oh, no, love, we're really nice to the good-looking ones, but ugly girls like you and your two mates, well, we set them on fire. We can't have ugly birds messing up our view.'

'How dare you, I'm –'

Sean leaned in further. 'What are you going to do? Run to Daddy and Mummy? Take another photo of my bike? Seriously, you're pathetic. Piss off and leave Kelly alone.'

Melissa drove off, shouting out of the window, 'Nice boyfriend, Kelly, a lowlife just like you.'

Sean turned to Kelly. 'Are you okay?'

She nodded. 'Yeah.' She was lying. Melissa had seen Sean. He was her other life, her private life. She didn't want them to know what he looked like or the bicycle he rode. She was proud of him and he was gorgeous. But she knew they'd say horrible things about him to hurt her and it would hurt. It would hurt so badly because Sean was so special to her. She was thrilled he'd come all the way to meet her after school, but now she kind of wished he hadn't.

'Hey.' Sean lifted her chin to look into her eyes. 'Don't let them get to you. They're jealous of you because you're gorgeous and you have a hot boyfriend. Just ignore them.'

Kelly gave him a smile. He didn't get it. No one did. You can't ignore girls who torment you all day long. It's not that easy. It was so bloody hard to deal with it day in, day out, and now they would be cruel about Sean and she couldn't bear that. She swallowed back her tears. 'Come on, let's get away from here. I hate this place.'

'Your wish is my command. Hop up,' Sean said.

She sat on the crossbar, holding him tightly as they cycled

home. He kissed her neck and slowly the tension began to fade.

When she got home, she checked WhatsApp and her heart sank. There was a string of photos of her and Sean, then the inevitable list of comments, going on and on . . . Kelly's boyfriend and his Ferrari . . . Kelly's boyfriend the thug . . . Kelly's boyfriend goes to Scumtown National School . . . Kelly and Scumbag, a match made in Heaven!

Kelly switched her phone off and tried not to cry, but she couldn't help it. It felt like Melissa had reached into her life and taken possession of the one thing that she really, truly cared about. She didn't want those cows anywhere near Sean, and now the whole class was staring at him and judging him. Kelly sobbed into her pillow to muffle the noise. She felt like she was being dragged lower and lower. If this didn't stop, she didn't know what she'd do.

34

Jenny threw open Lucy's bedroom door and twirled.

'Nice dress.'

'Made by your very clever daughter. She really is a wonder with clothes.'

Lucy ignored her. The dress was lovely, but she didn't want to get into an argument about Kelly's talent for clothes designing and that she should pursue it as a career. It wasn't stable enough. So few people made a living from it. Lucy wanted Kelly to be independent and financially secure. For every Victoria Beckham, there were millions of designers earning peanuts. Lucy didn't want Kelly to live hand-to-mouth, she wanted her to have a comfortable life where money wasn't a constant source of worry. She could design in her spare time.

'Hey.' Jenny came over and zipped up her sister's dress. 'Why the long face?'

Lucy fiddled with her earring. 'Dad's sixty-five and I'm not that far off forty. It's just, well, I thought my life would be different.'

Jenny hugged her. 'Don't look back and say "What if", look back and say, "Wow, good job." Picture watching Dylan scoring goals and Kelly graduating and you meeting some gorgeous divorcee who'll sweep you off your feet, and when the kids are gone you can go back and study or, I don't know, take up skydiving. Look at what you have achieved instead of what you haven't.'

Lucy's life had been full of love, laughter, clapping and crying with pride because of the twins. She had loved wiping their tears, putting plasters on their knees, cuddling up with them and watching movies, adoring them . . . Much as she hated to admit it, her sister was right. She needed to look at the wonder that the twins were and how they had made her life very special. 'I'm lucky, very lucky. Thanks for reminding me, sis.'

'Any time. You look gorgeous, total MILF. If you dressed up like that more often, you certainly wouldn't grow old alone or have to have sex with Damien any more. You could actually meet a really hot guy and have steaming sex. Come on, let's have lots of drinks and some fun.'

Lucy grinned. 'Yes! I feel like getting tipsy and misbehaving, but I'll have to wait until the twins go home to really let loose. Let's go clubbing later.'

'Woo-hoo, now you're talking.'

Billy knocked on the door. 'Are you two ready yet? I'd like to eat before the restaurant closes.'

'Keep your hair on, we're coming.' Jenny opened the door and went downstairs.

Lucy followed and whistled when she saw her father standing on the landing. 'You look nice, Dad.'

Billy grinned. 'Thanks. I decided to dress up.'

Lucy kissed his cheek. 'Happy birthday. Actually, hang on a sec. I have your gift here. I wanted to give this to you when it was quiet.'

She went into her bedroom and grabbed a photo album from the chair, then went out and handed it to him. Billy opened it. It started with an old black-and-white photo of his parents on their wedding day. Photos of Billy on the day he'd bought the shop. Photos of him and Tina on their honeymoon, of Lucy as a baby, of Lucy holding Jenny's hand at the seaside, behind the counter in the shop, photos of Billy holding Dylan's hand as he proudly stood in his first football kit,

Billy with Kelly wearing a tutu in his arms, her little hands wrapped around his neck . . .

Billy got choked up. 'This is wonderful.'

'It took a while to get all the photos together, but I thought it would be nice for you to have all those memories in one book.'

Billy cleared his throat. 'It's the best present you could have got me. As your mother always said, "Family is love, love is family." '

'God, stop, you'll have me crying now.' Lucy wiped a tear away.

'It's true, though. Losing your mum so young made me realize how important family is. Thank God you were here, Lucy, and thank God the twins were here too. You got me through those dark days. I couldn't have done it without you.'

Lucy blinked back more tears. 'I couldn't have managed without you, Dad. You've been a rock to me and an incredible father figure for the twins.'

'It's been wonderful for me watching them grow up. You did an amazing job, Lucy. I worried about you doing it on your own, but you've raised two incredible children. You should be very proud of yourself.'

Lucy couldn't stop the tears spilling down. 'Thanks, Dad. I did my best, and you played a big part in it too.'

'It's not been easy, you sacrificed a lot. But the pair of them are a credit to you.'

'I'm so proud of them,' Lucy said hoarsely. 'I really am. I worried that not having a dad would damage them, but it didn't.'

'It didn't because they had such a devoted mother,' Billy said.

'Let's go,' Jenny shouted up the stairs. 'We're all waiting for you two.'

Lucy kissed Billy's cheek, then they went down the stairs to join Jenny and the twins. Jenny flung open the front door and ushered them all outside. Kelly and Dylan were glued to their phones.

'I swear to God, they never look up from those phones.' Lucy sighed.

'It's called being a teenager.' Jenny followed the twins out.

'Let's go, I'm looking forward to a drink,' Billy said.

'We just have to go to Sarah and Darren's first,' Lucy said. 'Darren's friend with the minibus is collecting us from their house.'

Ollie was crouching behind the hedge waiting for them. As they pushed the garden gate open, a series of big bangs went off. Billy jumped backwards, stepping on Jenny's toe.

'Ouch!' Jenny squealed.

'What the hell?' Billy shouted.

'OLLIE!' Darren roared. 'I told you not to set those bangers off.'

Ollie giggled. 'Sorry, Billy, did I nearly give you a heart attack?'

'Yes, you bloody did.' Billy caught his breath. 'Well, I'm glad to see you're back to yourself after your accident.'

'Will I call over to the shed tomorrow? I know it's Sunday and I'm supposed to come on Mondays, but I have an idea of something cool I want to make.'

'Please say yes, Billy,' Darren begged.

'Of course you can.' Billy couldn't say no to the kid. He still felt terrible about the finger incident, although the surgeon had said it was as good as new.

'Sorry about the bangers,' Darren said. 'Come on in. My friend Mark is on his way to pick us up.'

They walked into the house to be greeted by birthday balloons.

'Happy birthday, Billy.' Sarah rushed over to kiss him.

'Thanks very much.'

Shannon came down the stairs.

'No way,' Darren said. 'It's Billy's birthday dinner, go and put on some clothes.'

'It's a dress,' Shannon hissed.

'It's a handkerchief, and you'll need it to wipe all that muck off your face. I want to see you in a dress that actually covers your arse.'

'Mum!' Shannon looked at Sarah.

'Dad's right, love, that's not the right dress for Billy's birthday dinner. Put on the red one with the black lace.'

'The one that makes me look like a granny.'

'Just put something on that doesn't make you look like you charge by the hour,' Darren said.

Kelly came out of the restaurant kitchen holding the birthday cake.

Billy grinned. 'My favourite chocolate cake, made by my favourite granddaughter.'

'She made it this morning and dropped it into the restaurant,' Lucy whispered to him.

Billy stood up and kissed Kelly. 'Thank you, pet, you're one in a million.'

'I'll have a large slice of that, thank you. I love Kelly's chocolate cake,' Darren said. 'Any chance you could teach Shannon the recipe? Mind you, she burns toast, so maybe not.'

'Thanks a lot, Dad. I may not be good at cooking, but I have many other talents.'

Darren put his arm around her. 'Sure don't I know it.'

Shannon shrugged him off. 'You're still in my bad books for saying I looked like a slapper in my other dress.'

'Ah, come on, you know I love you.' He kissed her forehead.

'Get off me, Dad,' she said, laughing.

Jenny tapped her glass. 'Speech time.'

Lucy stood up. 'Dad, Billy, Granddad – congratulations on making it to sixty-five. You look great and you've more energy than I do. Thanks for being a brilliant granddad. The twins have been so lucky to have you in their lives, and so have I. Thanks for letting us live with you and for being such a huge and integral part of our lives. Thanks for introducing Dylan to football. That day changed our lives – the twins wouldn't be in St Jude's if you hadn't brought Dylan down to the football club that day twelve years ago. Thanks for giving me work and a salary and a roof over our heads. Thanks for always having my back and never making me feel like I let you down. Thanks for supporting all of us through thick and thin but, most of all, thanks for being the best dad in the world.'

Billy got up and hugged Lucy tightly. He whispered, 'You've never let me down. I'm prouder of you than ever.'

'Enough of this lovey-dovey stuff. I'd like to say a few words.' Jenny stood up. 'Billy is the man who scared off every boy who ever came near me. He is also the man who told me that make-up wasn't a real job. Thanks for that, Dad, you made me determined to prove you wrong. Billy is also the man who told Mrs Fogerty to feck off when she called me a good-for-nothing. Billy is the man who gave me the money to pay the deposit on my apartment, which I'm going to pay back some day. Billy is the man who loved our mum more than life itself. He is the man who dragged himself out of his misery and heartbreak for me, for Lucy and for the twins. So, although you always made me feel like second best to perfect Lucy, I forgive you and I wish you a very happy birthday, Dad.'

'Come here to me, you.' Billy threw his arms around Jenny. She pretended to fight him off, but he held tight and kissed her.

'I want to say something.' Ollie stood up.

'Oh, Jesus, here we go.' Shannon rolled her eyes.

'I just want to say thanks to you, Billy, for letting me come to the shed. It's my favourite thing to do, even though the music's a bit rubbish. I'm sorry I cut my finger off and gave you a shock. I'll always listen to you, and I think you're deadly for an old man, not grumpy or narky, just really nice and funny too.'

'Well said.' Sarah patted him on the back.

'Ah, you're a great fella, Ollie.' Billy ruffled his hair.

Lucy looked around the room. How silly to feel melancholic about getting older. She was stupid, regretting all the things she hadn't done, when here she was, surrounded by love and support and kindness and generosity. These people were the people who had been there for her through thick and thin.

Jenny filled Lucy's wine glass. Lucy pretended to object, but then started giggling.

Dylan watched his mother. She was definitely a bit drunk. Good, that meant he might be able to sneak off and call into Taylor without her noticing. While his mum was distracted, Dylan slipped his phone out of his pocket and texted Taylor. She replied with a selfie of her in her underwear. *Hurry up!*

Kelly and Shannon sat at the end of the table, looking at the bitchy comments Melissa and her friends were still posting about Sean and Kelly. Lots of people had posted nasty remarks about Sean's old bike and how Kelly was 'bringing St Jude's down by dating outsider hobos'. There were so many such comments that Shannon was shocked.

'Who are these people?' she asked. 'I mean, seriously, it's a bike! He goes to a different school, so what?'

Kelly sighed. 'There are quite a lot of people in St Jude's who think they're superior to everyone else. They think that going to a posh private school somehow makes them better than the rest of us. It's pathetic, but that's how they see it. They're only delighted to slate me because I'm a scholarship student and they already think I'm scum. Sean and his bike just make it easier for them to vent their poison.'

Kelly turned to answer a question Billy asked her and Shannon quickly took photos of the WhatsApp comments.

Kelly turned back to her.

'It's just not right,' Shannon said. 'You really should tell your mum how bad it is. It's gone way beyond a joke now.'

Kelly snapped her phone off. 'No bloody way. She doesn't even know I'm seeing Sean. She'd freak. Shannon, you have to swear you won't say a word about this to anyone. Swear it?'

'I promise, but you need to fight back. Put up a post about Melissa having an STD or something.'

'I can't. If I get caught, I could get kicked out.'

'Well, go to the headmaster and talk to him privately, without getting your mum involved. You have to do something, Kelly.'

Kelly sat back and played with her slice of birthday cake. Shannon was right, she should go to the headmaster. Mr Gough was very nice. But what if he called Melissa in and it became a whole huge thing and then her parents got involved, and then Lucy would be dragged into it and she'd find out about Sean and be furious with Kelly for lying and everyone would know Kelly was a snitch and . . . Well, it was all too complicated. Kelly just needed to try to ignore it, like Sean and Dylan had told her to.

Suddenly the door of the restaurant burst open and a middle-aged woman, soaked from the rain, stormed in. 'Where's that bitch Jenny Murphy?'

Everyone froze. The other diners spun around. The woman stared around the room and then saw Jenny.

'There you are, you slut. I tracked you down via your Facebook page. Not very clever at hiding now, are you? So, how long have you been shagging my husband?'

'Mum, she just said –' Sarah clamped her hand over Ollie's gaping mouth.

'Is this your family? Did you all know Jenny was sleeping with my husband? The father of my child? Did you know your friend, daughter, whatever she is to you, is a whore?'

'OMG, this is unreal, total drama,' Shannon whispered. She reached out to squeeze Kelly's hand.

Lucy stood up. 'Whatever your issues are with my sister, there are children present.'

'Oh, I'm sorry, are your kids upset? Because my son is going to be heartbroken when he gets back from university in England and finds out his dad no longer lives at home because I've thrown him out. He's all yours now, you disgusting piece of work. When he comes back from his business trip, the locks will have changed. You are welcome to the cheating bastard. You deserve each other. And don't get too comfortable. You're not his first affair. He's had several and I stupidly believed that he'd changed. But once a cheating bastard, always a cheating bastard.' With that, the wife picked up a glass of red wine, threw it over Jenny and stormed back out into the rain.

Billy leant over. 'Would you like to tell me what the hell that was all about?'

'This is way better than *Gossip Girl*,' Shannon muttered.

'I'm sorry, Dad.' Jenny's hand shook as she wiped red wine off her arm with a napkin. 'It's complicated.'

'Is Jenny with that woman's husband?' Ollie's eyes were out on sticks.

'I think I'll take Ollie home,' Darren said. 'Why don't you come back to ours for a drink after . . . well, when you're finished up here?'

Darren ushered Ollie out of the restaurant. They could hear him pleading as he left: 'Ah, no, Dad, I want to see what happens next.'

'I'm going too, Mum. I've got training tomorrow and I'm kind of tired.' Dylan faked a yawn and followed Darren and Ollie out.

'I'm going nowhere. I want to hear everything,' Shannon said.

'Are you all right?' Kelly asked Jenny.

'I'm fine. I deserved that. I'm sorry you had to witness it, though.'

'Are you mad? It was brilliant,' Shannon said.

'So it's true.' Billy shook his head. 'You've been seeing another woman's husband?'

Jenny sighed. 'Yes, Dad, I have and I know it's nothing to be proud of, but . . . well . . . I don't have an excuse except that I really like him.'

'Oh, Jenny, when will you ever stop messing about and meet a decent man? It's time to grow up.'

'I'm sorry for ruining your party, Dad. But life isn't always straightforward. We aren't all lucky enough to meet the love of our lives at twenty-four. Some of us may never meet the one.'

'Lucky, my arse. It's called commitment. Your mother was the love of my life but we still had our ups and downs. We worked through them. That's the problem with all you modern people, you want the fairy-tale romance. Well, it doesn't exist. Real relationships take hard work and commitment, and they never start with being someone's mistress. This fella's a liar and a cheat. You deserve better.'

Lucy poured them all another drink. 'Let's forget about it for the moment. Back to you, Dad.'

Billy stood up. 'It's late. I think I'll head home. I'll take the girls with me. You stay and try to talk some sense into your sister.'

Jenny reached out to him. 'I really am sorry, Dad. I never meant to cause a scene on your birthday.'

He put his arm around her. 'Oh, Jenny, all I want is for you to be happy, love. But you have to start by making better choices.'

'Can I stay in case she comes back and has another freak attack?' Shannon asked. 'It was *sooooo* great.'

Sarah glared at her daughter. 'Go with Billy now. Tell your dad I'll be home in an hour.'

Kelly hugged Jenny. 'Night.'

'Night, beautiful. Please don't think badly of me. I'm really sorry and embarrassed that you witnessed that.'

'Jenny, I think you rock and I always will.'

Jenny kissed her and watched them leave.

'Well, we certainly won't forget tonight in a hurry.' Lucy drank deeply from her wine glass.

'Go on, tell me what a stupid slut I am and how I ruined Dad's birthday. I couldn't feel worse, so go ahead.'

'Enough has been said tonight.'

'What are you going to do about Frank being kicked out? Will he move in with you?' Sarah asked.

Jenny frowned. 'God, no. I mean, I don't think so. I doubt it. He said she kicks him out all the time but never for more than a few days, so it should be fine. She always takes him back. She likes the money, the house and the lifestyle too much to give it up.'

Lucy's phone buzzed. It was Damien. *Hope your dad's party going well. Call in on your way home. I'd love to see you.*

Lucy was a little drunk, a bit upset about the whole Jenny saga and badly in need of sex. She grabbed her coat. 'I've just had a booty call and I'm going. We'll talk about this tomorrow.'

Jenny watched her go, open-mouthed. 'Well, I didn't expect that,' she said, turning to Sarah.

Sarah laughed. 'You just lost out to Damien, of all people.'

'I want her to get laid! It might lighten her up,' Jenny said.

Sarah took Jenny's arm. 'Right, come on. You need a drink after that and I need to get out of this tight dress and these shoes. Back to my place. We can chat there.'

'I'm on.'

Darren was in the kitchen, eating crisps and drinking wine.

'Interesting night, ladies.' He grinned at Jenny.

'Just pour me a big glass of wine, please,' she growled.

Sarah took off her shoes, then left to change out of her dress.

'I hope this fella's worth it,' Darren commented.

Jenny put her feet up on the kitchen chair opposite her. 'God, can we please talk about something else, like Lucy? All of these bloody secrets coming out into the open tonight! Honestly, my head's spinning.'

'Ah, so Sarah told you about Tom getting in touch with her,' Darren said.

Jenny stared at him. 'What?'

'Darren!' Sarah stood frozen at the door in her dressing-gown.

Jenny's eyes narrowed. 'Did you just say something about Tom?'

'No.' Darren's face went bright red.

'He's drunk, don't mind him,' Sarah said.

'Bullshit. I'm not leaving until you tell me what's going on.' Jenny folded her arms over her chest. 'You know I won't, so you'd better spill the beans.'

'Jesus, Darren,' Sarah hissed.

'I'm sorry. She said something about Lucy and secrets, so

I thought you'd told her. And sure she might have a good insight into how to handle it all.'

'Can someone please tell me what the hell is going on?'

Sarah sat down and looked at Jenny. 'What do you think Lucy would do if Tom turned up and wanted to get involved with the kids?'

Jenny laughed. 'Do you really need to ask me that? You know she'd freak, probably have a nervous breakdown and then maybe stab him.'

Sarah didn't laugh. She looked worried. 'Look, I grew up with no dad and it hurt like hell. I've never said this to Lucy obviously, but it still hurts me that my dad didn't want to know me. I just wondered if maybe Tom didn't know about the twins. What if Gabriel lied and told him Lucy had the abortion?'

Jenny tied her hair up in a knot on top of her head. 'Even if Gabriel did lie to him, which is psychotic behaviour, Tom should never have run away and left Lucy in the first place. Technically, he abandoned her not actually knowing if she'd had the abortion or not. He left without checking, so he is a rat.'

'True, but if Tom was lied to by Gabriel, he's spent all of this time not knowing he was a dad, and maybe he would be a great one.'

Jenny grabbed Sarah's arm. 'What exactly is going on here?'

Sarah took a deep breath. 'A few weeks ago, Tom contacted me out of the blue.' She filled Jenny in on the whole story.

For once in her life, Jenny was utterly speechless. Tom never knew? Gabriel lied to him? He wanted to know his kids? He was heartbroken, divorced, childless . . . 'But he can't just waltz back in now. He just can't! It'd kill Lucy.'

'I know that. But he does have a right to meet his kids, Jenny. They'll be eighteen soon and they can make their own decisions. I've told him to stay away for the moment while I try to figure out a way to tell Lucy, but I'm finding it impossible.'

'Don't do it,' Jenny said. 'I'm sorry, but he doesn't get to run away like a coward and then come storming back into their lives.'

'That's how I felt at first too, but if you look at it from his point of view, he didn't know and he's heartbroken that he's missed out on their lives.'

Jenny thought about her sister. It had been a long uphill road for her. The twins were almost adults now. How could they let Tom crash in and turn their lives upside-down? No way. Parenthood was Lucy's life's work. Her self-worth was completely wrapped up in those twins. Tom would threaten everything she'd worked so hard to build if he turned up wanting to muscle in and be a dad to them.

'You have to keep him away, Sarah,' Jenny said urgently. 'He can't come back here now. Maybe when they've finished school, but not now.'

'I'll do my best, I promise, but I may need your help. He's absolutely desperate to see them.'

'If I have to go to America and tie him up, I will. He is not coming back now. I don't care how sad he is. He made his bed and he can bloody well lie in it for a bit longer.'

35

Taylor pulled back. 'Hey, I feel as if you're going to eat me.'

'I would if I could. You smell and taste so good.' He kissed her neck.

Taylor giggled. 'So the novelty of being back together hasn't worn off, then?'

'Nope, and it never will. I can't get enough of you.'

'Good, I feel the same way. Now, come on, let's get some more champagne.'

Taylor pulled him by the hand up to the bar of the nightclub. Dylan stopped her. 'Babe, I don't have any more money.'

She waved a credit card at him. 'That's what this is for.'

'I feel weird letting you pay.'

'It's my dad's card and he never notices what I use it for. Come on, let's just have fun.'

Dylan shrugged and let her order another bottle. The nightclub was way cooler than any he'd been in before. The DJ was playing great tunes, and he was having a ball. Taylor, champagne, good music . . . Life was great.

He glanced at his watch. It was one a.m. He had a match at eleven tomorrow morning. If he got to sleep by two, he should be okay. There was no way he was telling Taylor he had to go home early. She was still pretty touchy whenever he mentioned football. He knew she was worried that if he played badly he'd break up with her again, but he wouldn't – he couldn't. He was crazy about her. Besides, he could do both. He just needed to get to bed by two.

He texted Kelly. *Mum asleep?*

Yeah. Don't be 2 late, match 2morrow.

Chill.

Lucy pulled back the curtains and light flooded the room.

'Dylan, come on, up you get. It's nine o'clock.'

Dylan peeled his eyes open. Christ, his head hurt. He had a flashback to the nightclub and coming in at half past three. Damn, he felt awful.

Lucy peered at him. 'Look at the state of you. What time did you get in last night? Jesus, Dylan, the smell. Were you drinking?'

His mum's face was red. 'Only one beer, Mum. It was just with the lads.'

Lucy sat on the side of his bed and took a deep breath. He could see she was trying to control herself.

'Dylan, I know by your bloodshot eyes that you had a lot more than one beer.'

'Okay, I admit I had a few and I know it was stupid, but I'll be fine. I just need a shower.'

'Were you with that girl again? The blonde one? Taylor? I thought you'd broken up.'

Dylan paused. Should he lie or tell the half-truth? He decided to keep close to the truth. 'Yes, I'm kind of seeing her again.'

'Is she a drinker?' Lucy asked.

'Not really. I'm fine, Mum, everything's cool, relax.'

'It's not okay for you to drink, Dylan, and especially not before a game. She's obviously a bad influence. I don't like this. You need to get rid of her.'

'Calm down, Mum.' Dylan did not want to get into an argument about Taylor. He just wanted his mother to go so he could get himself together. He felt horrendous.

Lucy glared at him. 'Why did you drink before a big game, Dylan? Why would you risk it?'

Dylan pulled aside his covers and moved towards the bathroom. 'I know, Mum, believe me. I was just trying to be one of the lads.' He held up his hands. 'I won't make the mistake again. Now let me have a shower and get myself sorted for the game. If you fancied doing some scrambled eggs for me with wholemeal toast that would be great.' He tried smiling, even though his stomach lurched at the thought of food.

Lucy frowned. 'I'll make you breakfast, but you need to get it together, Dylan. Jordan will go nuts if he finds out you were partying last night.'

Dylan stood under the shower and cursed his stupidity. Why hadn't he stopped drinking earlier? Why hadn't he gone home earlier? His head ached, his legs felt like lead. Damn it, this was a big game. He had to play well. He'd be in huge trouble if anyone knew he was out drinking last night.

When he came out of the shower, Kelly held up her phone. 'You're in deep now.'

Dylan grabbed his sister's phone and groaned. Taylor had posted photos of them in the nightclub. In one, Dylan was holding a bottle of champagne and drinking from the neck. Jesus Christ.

'She has over a thousand Instagram followers. A lot of people are going to have seen those already,' Kelly said.

Dylan grabbed his own phone and rang Taylor. It went straight to voicemail. No doubt she was still in bed, sleeping off her hangover. He sent her a message: *Take down the pics of last night NOW.*

Dylan sat on the edge of his bed and put his head into his hands. He felt as if a bomb had exploded inside his head. He'd never drunk so much in his life. Most of his teammates followed Taylor on Instagram. They would be seriously unimpressed, and what if one of them slagged him in front of Jordan?

Kelly stood in front of him, arms folded. 'You need to cop on, Dylan. You were absolutely plastered last night. I had to drag you to bed. It was after four when you came in. You're so lucky Mum or Granddad didn't wake up and see you.'

'It all got a bit out of control. Taylor wanted one more drink and then . . . I don't really remember after that.'

'You have to learn to say no to Taylor. She's going to get you into trouble, Dylan. Mum'll freak if Jordan benches you or drops you.'

Dylan looked at his shaky hands and felt a surge of anger. 'Stop blaming Taylor. She didn't force me to stay out. I wanted to be with her. I guess I just lost track of time.'

Kelly sighed. 'I know you're mad about her, but please don't mess up.'

Dylan turned his back on his sister. 'Can everyone just get off my back? Jesus, I had a good time, so shoot me.'

He grabbed his clothes and went into the bathroom.

Dylan examined his bloodshot eyes in the mirror. He'd make sure he didn't get too close to Jordan today so he might not notice them. He splashed some cold water on his face and jogged on the spot in an effort to get his energy flowing, but he just felt dizzy.

As he walked towards the kitchen and smelt eggs, the nausea rose again. He couldn't face food.

'Eat up.' Lucy put a big plate of eggs and toast in front of him. 'I won't go on about last night, but I'm very disappointed in you and you must understand that it can never happen again. Never.'

'I'm sorry, Mum.'

Dylan nibbled the toast, and as soon as Lucy left the room

to shout at Kelly to hurry up, he scraped the breakfast into the bin and hid it under a newspaper.

Dylan rubbed his aching eyes. He'd have to try his best to look fresh and full of energy today so no one would suspect how rotten he felt.

Lucy's heart sank as Dylan missed his third shot at goal. Jordan was going crazy on the side-line. She paced up and down, praying he would get it together.

'What the hell is going on with you? Come on, Dylan, look lively,' Jordan roared.

Dylan fumbled a beautiful pass from Nick and the opposition used his mistake to win the ball.

As Lucy paced back towards the parents, she heard them all groan as the opposition scored another goal. Lucy heard a few people cursing Dylan's bad play. She heard one father muttering, 'It was a waste of money bringing that fellow to St Jude's. Should have given the scholarship to someone more deserving.'

A mother defended Dylan. 'Hang on, he's been fantastic in almost all of the matches so far. Scored lots of goals.'

'Well, he sure as hell didn't turn up today,' the father snapped.

'Apparently he was out drinking last night,' another woman said.

'What?' The parents looked shocked.

'Oliver saw photos on Taylor's Instagram. Taylor and Dylan drinking champagne in a nightclub until the wee hours.'

'That's a bloody disgrace,' the angry father hissed. 'He should get dropped.'

Oh, God, Lucy tasted bile in her mouth. Drinking all night with Taylor. What had got into him?

'Champagne?' one of the women tutted. 'He's obviously

getting carried away. The scholarship boy's getting ahead of himself, I'd say.'

Lucy went from shame to rage. How dare they call her son 'the scholarship boy'? How dare they imply Dylan wasn't good enough for this school? How dare they say he was 'getting ahead of himself'? These people were like Gabriel, looking down on everyone, thinking they were better than her and her kids.

Just as Lucy was about to speak up, Conor's mother Teresa said loudly, 'Come on now. Dylan is the best thing to happen to this team. He's got us this far. He's human, he has the occasional bad day. But ninety-nine per cent of the time he's absolutely brilliant. Conor says Dylan trains harder than any of the others. So, he went out last night, big deal. He's no doubt learnt his lesson. Give him a break.'

Lucy could have hugged her. One of the mothers turned to reply to Teresa and saw Lucy. She gave her a fake-smile and indicated to the other parents that Dylan's mum was standing behind them. They all stopped slating her son. But it was too late: the insults had stung Lucy deeply.

Jordan pulled Dylan off the pitch and benched him. What would he do if he found out Dylan had been drinking? He would probably drop him. Lucy fiddled with her scarf and tried to control her breathing. She was panicking. If the headmaster found out about the drinking, would Dylan be expelled? Oh, God. She tried to count five breaths in, five breaths out. It didn't help. Panic was consuming her.

If Dylan got expelled, would Kelly too? Oh, the shame of it. Gabriel was bound to find out about the scholarship twins getting expelled – they'd be the talk of the school. Everyone on the board would hear of it. Gabriel would see photos of the terrible twins and then he'd know. He'd know the instant he saw Kelly – she was so uncannily like Tom. He'd know that they were his grandchildren and he'd know that Lucy had failed. That she had failed as a mother, just as he'd said she would.

For the first time in her life, Lucy felt ashamed of her son. Her beautiful, wonderful son had let himself and her down. And she knew why. Taylor. Lucy set her mouth in a determined line. They had to break up, and they had to break up for good.

Dylan sat at the kitchen table with his head in his hands. Lucy was furious. She'd told him that he had made a show of himself and everyone knew about the drinking.

'They're all talking about you and that girl, Taylor. They all saw you, Dylan, drinking champagne last night in a nightclub. Have you lost your mind?' she shouted.

Kelly came in from the shop where she was helping Billy. Lucy turned on her. 'Did you know about this?' she shrieked. 'Did you know your brother was out getting drunk with his girlfriend last night?'

'No,' Kelly lied, not knowing what Dylan had admitted to or denied.

'Well, apparently it's all over Instagram. All the parents were chatting about what a disgrace your brother is, how irresponsible. In all my life, I have only ever been proud of you until today. You let us all down, Dylan. You let your family down, your team, your coach and yourself.'

Kelly went over and sat beside Dylan. She put a hand on his shoulder. 'Are you okay?' she asked him.

He shook his head. 'I messed up badly.'

Kelly looked up at her mother. 'It was one mistake, Mum.'

Lucy put her hands on the table and tried to control the quiver in her voice. 'It was a mistake that could cost him, and you, the scholarship. Some of the parents were saying you should never have got it. Don't you see, Dylan? Your mistake could cost this family everything.'

Tears flowed then. Lucy couldn't hold them back any longer. She was as angry as hell, but she was also terrified. Had Dylan blown it? Would the twins be kicked out of school? Outcast because they weren't good enough – didn't fit in.

'Don't cry, Mum,' Kelly said. 'Everyone makes mistakes. There's no way Dylan will lose the scholarship. He's the best player on the team by miles. He'll score loads of goals next week and they'll all be saying how great he is again.'

Lucy shook her head. She wasn't sure. If the parents made a big fuss, maybe there would be no second chance. Scholarship kids weren't the same as fee-paying kids. They had to be better. They had to live up to all the expectations and even beyond them.

'I'm sorry, Mum,' Dylan said miserably. 'I know I let you down, but I'll make it up next week, you'll see.'

Lucy looked at her son. She knew what she had to say would upset him, but she was going to have to hold firm. 'You have to, Dylan, otherwise it'll all be ruined. You have to break up with that stupid girl, who is leading you astray, and keep your head down. There is no other choice.'

'Break up with Taylor?'

'Yes, Dylan. That girl is trouble.'

'No, Mum, she isn't. I was the idiot.'

'Listen to me carefully now. This is not a request. You are to dump that silly airhead and put an end to all this. I know you want to defend her, but the plain fact is that you never got into trouble before you met her. You are not to see her again, do you understand me?'

Kelly had never heard her mum like this before. She'd never spoken to Dylan like that, never ordered him about, never doubted him. She could see that Dylan was going to fight back, but with Lucy in this mood, it was madness.

'Yes, he does,' Kelly interjected, putting her hand over his to tell him to be quiet. 'It's all right, Mum. He knows what he has to do.'

36

Lucy fiddled with her napkin and tried not to cry as she explained the trouble Dylan was in because of his partying.

'He'll be fine,' Damien said. 'All kids make mistakes. It's part of growing up.'

Lucy frowned. 'No, it's really serious, Damien. The parents were going mad. He could lose –'

Damien's phone rang. He picked it up and looked at the screen, then mouthed an apology while taking the call. Lucy glared at him. He talked on and on about a case while Lucy simmered opposite him. Eventually he said goodbye to the caller and put his phone down.

'Sorry for being rude, Lucy, but it's a new case, a really juicy one. Paul Clark has been accused of –'

'Damien!' Lucy snapped. 'I was in the middle of telling you something really important to me and you still answered that call.'

Damien was clearly startled. 'But you never mind me taking work calls. You're usually so understanding about it.'

Lucy leant forward, her voice shaking, 'I'm really upset about Dylan. I'm terrified he's going to get kicked off the team and out of the school. This is a huge deal for me and you just dismissed it and took a call.'

Damien sighed. 'Don't you think you're overreacting a bit?'

Lucy gripped her napkin tightly. 'No, I do not, because it is really serious. The scholarship is a huge deal and it would be humiliating and mortifying for Dylan to blow it because he got drunk with some stupid party girl who is leading him astray.'

'To be fair,' Damien said, 'she didn't make him drink. He did that all by himself. You can't vilify her.'

'She's a bad influence. Before he met this girl, Taylor, Dylan was never in trouble in his life. She's going to ruin everything. He needs to get rid of her. He's going to break up with her. He has to. And I'm going to make sure he does.'

'But it was one mistake, Lucy. As you said, he's never been in trouble before, so that's reason enough to give him a break now.'

'You don't get it.' Lucy pushed her plate away, her appetite gone.

Damien stared at her for a few seconds, his mouth set in a line. 'I do actually get it,' he said quietly, his voice flint-edged. 'I get that you're completely obsessed with St Jude's because Gabriel and Tom went there. You are proud the twins got scholarships there and you want them to shine. You want to prove what wonderful children they are. If they fail, it puts you all in a bad light, proves Gabriel was right and you are a bad mother. That's wrong for a number of reasons, not least because Gabriel doesn't even know they're his grandchildren.'

'Yes, but he will. He's sure to be at one of the events, like the football final, if the team makes it, or the end-of-year prize-giving. He'll be at something, and when he is, I will rub his nose in it. I've been dreaming of it almost every night.'

Damien leant across the table. 'Listen to yourself, Lucy. This is crazy. Why are you wasting time even thinking about him? You've done a wonderful job raising two fine children. Why do you need a man you hate to tell you so before you'll believe it? Focus on your children and forget Gabriel and Tom.'

'How can I forget them?' she hissed. 'Tom's their bloody father. Every time I look at Kelly, I see Tom. Every time I see a father hug his son after a football match, I see the hole in Dylan's life. It's easy for you to sit there and say, "Forget about them," but I can't. They will always be part of my life, even though I don't want it.'

Damien reached over for her hand. 'Lucy, please, you've got to stop obsessing about Tom and Gabriel. They're the past. You have to let it go?'

She snatched her hand away. He just didn't get it. Tom had left the twins with no father; every single day she saw that yawning gap in their lives, and it hurt like hell. She wanted nothing more than for Dylan to have a dad hug him after a great game, or for Kelly to have a father cheer loudly as she won yet another class prize. Lucy wanted to look at her children's father and share the pride and the joy. She was always alone. Yes, Billy was there in the house, but he worked long hours so she was always at school and sports events on her own. She'd watch parents sharing the precious moments of celebration and pride, and feel desperately and acutely alone.

'I'm not hungry. I think I'll just go home.'

'Come on, Lucy, forget about all of it for one night. Have another glass of wine.'

'I don't want to drink. I need a clear head. I have to watch Dylan like a hawk now. I will not let him ruin this opportunity over some stupid girl. No way. I will do everything in my power to prevent that happening.'

'But you can't watch him twenty-four/seven,' Damien said, looking annoyed. 'Be realistic.'

'If I have to, I will. This is too important. To be honest, I shouldn't even be here tonight. I got Jenny to come over and make sure Dylan didn't go out. Billy is out with his friends. I should go home. I need to be there to keep an eye on things.'

Damien poured himself another glass of wine. 'Seriously, Lucy, you need to calm down. He's a seventeen-year-old boy, you can't stalk him. He's almost an adult, for God's sake. I'm sure he knows he's made a mistake. That's how we all learn, from making mistakes.'

'I'm aware of that,' Lucy said tersely, 'but my mistake cost me everything and I will not let that happen to Dylan, no bloody way.'

Damien looked at her for a moment, then he sat forward. 'That's a very extreme way to look at it. I mean, I've basically lived the life you say you wanted and it's by no means perfect. I go home to an empty apartment every night. You think being a Senior Counsel in a law firm would have given you the perfect life, but that's not reality. Life happens, and sometimes what you thought was going to be the perfect life really isn't, and sometimes the life you didn't plan is actually better.' Damien leant forward. 'Lucy, you're blessed to have a beautiful family, but if you over-parent Dylan you'll suffocate him. You could lose him if you go on like this.'

Lucy stared at Damien. How could he possibly understand the perspective of a parent? When you had children, it was your job to protect them and keep them on the right path. 'I don't expect you to understand, Damien, but if I have to stalk him for the next eighteen months until he leaves St Jude's, I will do that. I will do whatever it takes. Because my children are my priority, Damien. I'm really sorry, but I won't be able to see you for a while, probably a long while. I think we should just call it a day. It's been great fun, but I can't afford to have any distractions in my life right now. My focus must be one hundred per cent on the twins. I've taken my eye off the ball, and now Kelly is lying to me about seeing Sean, and Dylan is lying about drinking. I let my attention slip and look what happened.' She sat back in her chair and gestured to the waiter to bring her coat. 'I'm sorry, Damien, but my kids have to come first.'

Damien stared at her in disbelief. 'Now hang on a second,' he said. 'Lucy, I know I don't have children, but if you push them too hard they may react badly. Too much pressure is not good for teenagers. I had a case recently –'

'This is my *life*,' Lucy said. 'I have a responsibility to those kids to keep them safe from harm. I'm sorry but you don't get it. You can't. I'm all they have. I'm their mum and dad and I have to be better.'

'Jesus, Lucy, I'm trying to help here. I know I'm not a father, but I think I can still be a good sounding-board for you. And you need that balanced perspective, Lucy, you really do.'

She glared at him. 'Oh, really, and what's that supposed to mean?'

He took a deep breath. 'I don't want to lose you or fall out with you, Lucy, but I feel that, as a friend, I should be honest with you.'

Lucy folded her arms tight across her chest. 'Go on.'

'You need to stop obsessing about Gabriel and Tom. It's like you never moved on. It's what drives you, but you don't seem to see that it's also your Achilles heel. Since the twins went to St Jude's you've become even more fixated with proving them wrong and making sure your kids succeed. I'm genuinely worried about you, Lucy. If you keep pushing your children, you could break them. If you're always looking to prove something, you're going to miss what's going on right under your nose. It's completely unhealthy and I know you hate hearing this, but really, truly, I'm saying that out of love for you.'

The waiter interrupted by bringing Lucy's coat to the table. She stood up and allowed him to help her into it. Then she picked up her bag and turned to Damien.

'You just don't get it. I'm not obsessed with those two bastards. I just want the best for my kids and I'm going to make sure they get it. Dylan and Kelly are my world, and they will be everything I couldn't be. It might look pushy from where you're standing, but that's what real love is, Damien. It doesn't take a day off, it doesn't stop, it doesn't give in. I won't let the twins blow great opportunities. I know first-hand how that feels and how it ruins everything else. I have fought for them their entire lives, and I will not stop now. So while I'm sorry to end things like this, I have to put my family first, which means I can't see you any more.'

'Lucy . . .' Damien called, as she turned and walked out of the restaurant. The catch in his voice hurt her heart, but she kept walking. She had absolutely no choice.

37

Sarah looked at the photo. It was a picture of Beyoncé.

'That's what I want to look like tonight,' Janice said.

Sarah heard Lucy coughing beside her.

'What do you think, Lucy?'

'About what?' Lucy feigned ignorance.

'About Janice wanting to look like Beyoncé tonight. Any thoughts on how to achieve that look?' Sarah's eyes were twinkling.

Lucy chewed her lip to stop laughing out loud. Janice was a fifty-year-old woman, with shoulder-length black hair and skin as pale as a ghost.

'It's for me new fella's birthday. He's younger than me. I'm a cougar.' Janice cackled. 'He's mad about Beyoncé, so I thought I'd try and do myself up like her.'

'What's a cougar?' Ollie came out of the back room with his maths book.

'It's when an older woman goes out with a younger man,' Janice explained.

'What age is your boyfriend, then?'

'Thirty-five.'

'What? But you're about eighty.'

'Ollie!' Sarah glared at him.

'Feck off, you divil, I'm only forty-ish.'

'Well, you look way older.'

'Go and do your homework, Ollie,' Sarah hissed.

'I need Lucy to help with my maths.'

'I'll be with you in a minute. I'm just finishing the wages for your mum.'

'So what can youse do to turn me into Beyoncé?' Janice asked.

'Extensions will fill your hair out and lengthen it, and we can curl it to make it look wavy,' Sarah suggested.

'Beyoncé!' Ollie turned around. 'You're white.'

'Well, I know that, I'm not blind. I want to look like a white woman version.'

Ollie frowned. 'But you're old enough to be her granny.'

'No, she isn't. Now go.' Sarah pointed at the back room.

'Well, Janice mightn't be blind, but her fella must be,' Ollie muttered.

'Come on, Sarah, let's get going. Transform me.'

'I'll do my best, Janice, but you do know you won't look like Beyoncé? You'll look like Janice with long wavy hair.'

Janice beamed. 'Ah, yeah, but when I'm all dressed up and have me fake lashes on, I'll be pretty close.'

Sarah sighed. She knew Janice would be disappointed. The ones who brought in photos always were. They came in thinking that Sarah could turn them from themselves into supermodels and celebrities. She was a hairdresser, not a magician.

She wanted her customers to feel good leaving the salon. If they felt better, she felt better. But sometimes the ones who brought photos cried when they weren't transformed and she felt terrible.

Sarah went into the back room to get the hair extensions and found Ollie and Lucy bent over his maths book.

'Lucy's brilliant, Mum. She makes maths seem easy.' Ollie grinned.

'This young man will end up ruling the world, he has such

a quick mind. He just needs to focus it.' Lucy ruffled Ollie's hair.

He tried to duck away. 'Don't touch the hair. I spent ages gelling it.'

'What am I going to do about Janice?' Sarah asked.

'Women are mad,' Ollie piped up. 'Imagine a granny thinking she can look like a pop star.'

'Easy with the granny comments, sunshine. I'm not that much younger than Janice,' Lucy said.

'What? Well, you look thirty years younger.'

'Aww, thanks.' She kissed the top of his head.

'But, seriously, a granddad would never come in with a photo of Ronaldo and say, "I want to look like this." '

He had a point, thought Sarah. Men were less delusional about some things.

'Yeah, but a sixty-year-old man would buy a sports car that he can barely get in and out of and think he looks cool in it. One of the dads on Dylan's team bought some fancy sports car, but it's so low to the ground, he takes ages getting out. He has to open the door, grab on to the roof and heave himself up. It's hilarious to watch – he looks like such an idiot.'

'I heard Dylan scored a hat-trick on Saturday.'

Lucy smiled. 'Yes, he did. He was brilliant, if I say so myself.'

Sarah was glad to see Lucy smiling again. When she had called over to Sarah the night after Dylan had got benched for being hung-over, she was so upset Sarah had got a fright. Sarah hadn't seen her that upset in years. In fact, she didn't think she'd seen her that upset since Tom had left. Lucy was terrified that the twins were going to be expelled. It had taken Sarah ages to calm her down.

It was lovely to see Lucy back to her old self. The only problem was, Lucy thought Dylan wasn't seeing Taylor any more, but Shannon had told Sarah he was. Shannon had seen photos on Taylor's Instagram of the two of them drinking at a party only the week before. Shannon said Kelly was really worried about Dylan's partying too.

Sarah didn't know whether to tell Lucy or not. But Dylan had played well on Sunday, so maybe he had only had one drink and was able to manage it all. Sarah didn't want to upset Lucy or land Dylan in trouble unnecessarily. She'd asked Shannon – if truth be told she'd had to bribe Shannon by agreeing to do hair extensions for her – to keep her updated on Dylan's movements.

She'd play it by ear. If he did seem to be partying too much or going off the rails, she would have to tell Lucy. It might be only a matter of time, Sarah thought glumly. From what she had seen of Taylor's Instagram pics that Shannon had shown her, the girl liked to party all the time.

Sarah felt weighed down by all the secrets and lies. She was keeping the Tom secret from Lucy. Dylan was lying about Taylor. Kelly was lying about Sean. All of these family and friends lying and keeping secrets from each other – it was crazy. But that was what you had to do sometimes to protect people from hurt. Sarah was keeping the Tom messages secret because she didn't want to hurt Lucy. She still hadn't figured out a way to tell her, and things were about to get a whole lot more complicated. Her head hurt with all the information she was keeping inside. Every time she looked at Lucy she felt guilty. What would her best friend do when she found out Sarah was in touch with Tom? Sarah shuddered at the thought.

'Mum, hello?' Ollie waved his hand in front of his mother's face. 'I want my dinner now. I'm starving.'

'I have to finish Janice's hair, love.'

'I'll take him,' Lucy said. 'He can come back with me. I'll give him something to eat and he can finish his homework.'

'Great, and when Billy closes the shop we can go to the shed.'

'If it's not too late.' Lucy smiled at him.

'Are you sure?' Sarah asked.

'Of course.'

'That'd be great, thanks.'

As Ollie and Lucy left, Jenny came through the door. 'I just want to make an appointment for next week,' she said, winking at Sarah.

The door closed and Jenny rushed over. 'Well? What did he say? Your text sounded urgent.'

Sarah pulled her into the back room. 'He's coming over.'

'*What?*' Jenny gasped.

'I tried stopping him. I told him it was too soon, that Lucy would freak, that he should wait until the summer, but he said he can't wait any longer, he has to see his kids.'

'When?'

'In three weeks. At Christmas.'

'Let me talk to him. I'll set him straight.'

Sarah shook her head. 'There's no point, Jenny. He's their dad. He has a right to see them. He's devastated about not knowing all these years – and he's a lawyer. He knows his rights. We can't stop him. He said all he wants to do is meet them. He promised not to interfere with Lucy's parenting or anything like that, he just wants to meet his kids.'

'But how the hell are we going to break this to Lucy? Feck it anyway.' Jenny kicked the door. 'She's just got over the scare with Dylan and the drinking and is in good form again. This will kill her – seriously, Sarah.'

Sarah ran her hands through her hair. 'I know, but what can we do? He's their dad and they have a right to know him too. He wants to be in their lives . . . and maybe it'll be a good thing. He seems decent. We've been messaging back and forth. I've been filling him in a bit about the twins. Look.'

Jenny leant over as Sarah pulled up the message she'd received from Tom the day before.

> I can't believe the twins are in St Jude's! I feel quite emotional about it. I'm picturing them walking down the corridors I walked down and eating in the canteen and swimming in the pool. It makes me feel closer to them somehow.
>
> I'd rip my right arm off to see Dylan play. He must be awesome to have got a scholarship. I was sorry to hear Kelly is struggling a bit. It can't be easy for her being in her brother's shadow. I remember the girls at St Jude's only too well, and some of them can be catty. Lucy never liked any of my girlfriends from school. But some of them were nice. Hopefully Kelly will make some friends soon. She sounds like such a brilliant, ballsy, gorgeous girl.
>
> Thank you so much for sending photos. I have been staring at them for hours. Kelly looks so like my mother it's uncanny. Dylan is all Lucy – what a handsome guy he is too. God, I feel so proud of them I could burst. I just wish I'd known. I wish I hadn't missed all of their precious childhoods. I will never forgive my father, he robbed me of knowing my own children. I'm gutted by what he did.
>
> I know you said wait, but I can't, Sarah. I have to meet them. I'm going nuts here. I can't eat, sleep or concentrate. I didn't think it was possible to be so happy and devastated at the same time. I discover I have two wonderful children and they think I abandoned them. It's killing me. I promise not to cause any trouble, but I need to meet my children. I need to tell them I didn't know and, somehow, try to make it up to them. I also need to apologize to Lucy for leaving her that way. I will never forgive myself for that.
>
> I'm giving you three weeks' notice. My tickets are booked for the 19th. I know I won't sleep a wink until then.

Jenny pursed her lips. 'He sounds full of remorse, which is good, but it doesn't change the fact that Lucy is going to flip out. The shock could kill her.'

'I put him off as long as I could.'

'Look,' Jenny said, 'I'm going to Milan for a few days, and I don't want you saying anything to Lucy while I'm gone. Promise?'

Sarah nodded. 'Okay, but we have just three weeks to try to figure out how to tell her and keep her from going over the edge.'

Jenny's eyes welled up. 'Poor Lucy,' she whispered. 'Jesus, it's going to be one crazy Christmas this year.'

38

Kelly was smiling when she walked into the classroom. Sean had just called to say he missed her and was looking forward to seeing her later on. She'd have to pretend she was going to help Shannon with her homework. Lucy had got even stricter since the whole Dylan drinking episode. She barely let them out of her sight. Kelly had to be extra careful not to get seen or caught with Sean. He was too important to risk losing. He was her lifeline.

She walked over to her desk, and as she went to sit down, her chair was pulled from under her and she landed on the floor. She smacked her head on the desk behind.

'God, you're so clumsy.' Melissa giggled and took a photo of Kelly sprawled on the floor.

Kelly's head really hurt, but she refused to cry.

'You're probably used to sitting on the floor. I doubt your people have furniture,' Chloë said.

'Why don't you just leave and go back to the stinking dump you came from?' said Alicia.

Kelly scrambled to her feet. 'Piss off and leave me alone,' she hissed at them.

'Tut tut. That language isn't tolerated here. What would the headmaster say if he knew his charity case has a mouth like a sewer?' Chloë said.

Melissa sniffed the air. 'Urgh, what is that disgusting smell? It's . . . it's coming from you. Don't you wash? You're gross. You're stinking out our school. Just admit you'll never fit in and go home. No one wants you here. Take your brother with you and your scumbag boyfriend and your lowlife mother. Can you believe her mother works in a corner shop? It's so embarrassing!'

Kelly could stand herself being ripped apart, but not her mum. No way were they going to slag off her mum.

'Why don't you fuck off and die, you stupid bitch?' she screamed.

Unfortunately for Kelly, the teacher chose that moment to come around the corner. 'Kelly Murphy!' she roared. 'Outside now. And you three as well.'

Kelly stood outside the door, shaking with rage and fear, listening to Melissa's lies.

'She just attacked me verbally for no reason. That's what happens when you let unsuitable and violent people come to this school.'

Mrs Holland asked, 'So you're telling me Kelly shouted at you for no reason?'

'I think she's jealous of me.'

'She totally is,' Chloë said, nodding.

'Why would she be jealous of you?' Mrs Holland asked.

'Because Melissa is so popular and, like, cool,' Alicia gushed.

'Really?' Mrs Holland didn't sound convinced. 'So Kelly screamed obscenities at you because she's jealous of you?'

'I think so,' Melissa said. 'She's got a really bad temper. I just don't think she's right for this school. My parents are not going to be pleased to hear about this verbal abuse.'

'Let's not dramatize the issue.'

'A verbal attack is just as serious as a physical one. I insist on speaking to the headmaster. Kelly needs to be punished for attacking me like that.'

Mrs Holland sighed. 'I will inform the headmaster. He can decide what course of action to take. Girls, go back to class. Kelly, you stay here.'

Kelly began to shake. What had she done? She didn't want the headmaster hearing about this. Damn it, it would look really bad for her. She had to fix this. If she had to apologize to Melissa, she'd do it.

She began to cry. Why was life so unfair? Now she was going to be in trouble and it was all that bitch's fault.

'Right, Kelly, go to the headmaster and tell him what happened. I need to keep this unruly lot under control. I have no doubt you were provoked, but you cannot scream obscenities at another student. I'll talk to the headmaster after class.'

Kelly dragged her heels as she walked down the long corridor towards Mr Gough's office.

Her legs shook as she stood outside the door beside the brass plate with 'Headmaster' emblazoned across the middle. She knocked gently.

'Come in.'

Kelly took a deep breath and slowly entered the room.

Mr Gough was sitting at a large desk surrounded by papers and files. His office was lined with bookshelves filled with a mixture of old and modern books. The wall behind the desk was covered with framed photos of him with important-looking people. They were probably past pupils, Kelly thought – successful, amazing, brilliant past pupils, who weren't scholarship kids and didn't tell their classmates to eff off.

The headmaster looked up and smiled. 'Kelly, what a nice interruption from these reports. How can I help?'

He was so kind that Kelly felt emotion welling up. She stood in front of him and blurted out, 'I screamed at Melissa just now and kind of swore a lot. I'm sorry, I'll apologize. I don't want any trouble. She just . . . she . . . I'm sorry . . .' Kelly was sick of it. Sick of Melissa bullying her every day. It was relentless, and not being able to defend herself properly because she was afraid of getting into trouble was exhausting. She'd been biting her tongue and trying to avoid Melissa and her friends for weeks and weeks, but it never stopped. She began to sob.

Mr Gough jumped up and came around to her. He patted her shoulder and gently guided her to the leather chair opposite his desk. He handed her a tissue. 'There now, calm yourself and tell me everything. In my long experience as headmaster of many schools, problems can almost always be sorted out.'

Kelly blew her nose as he went back to his seat behind the desk and waited.

'Would you be more comfortable if I called my assistant Darina in to sit with us? Another female in the room, perhaps?'

'No, please. I just want to talk to you on your own. I don't want anyone else knowing about it.'

'Very well. In that case, I'll just need to leave the door ajar.'

She told him the story, and when she got to the part about Melissa being so horrible about her mum, she saw his face darken. 'So I just saw red and I told her to . . . well . . . eff off and stuff. I know it was wrong. I just . . . She was being so mean about my mum and . . . well, my mum is the best. You know, she's sacrificed everything for us.'

Mr Gough took his glasses off and wiped them. Kelly held her breath.

'Kelly, what Melissa said to you, about you and about your mother, was utterly unacceptable. She has let herself down by behaving in this way. Your mother is a lovely lady and her complete devotion to you and your brother is remarkable.' He paused. 'I completely understand why you said what you said, but I can't allow a student, no matter how much they have been provoked, to shout expletives at another student.

If I let it slide, the whole school would be shouting the F-word at each other morning, noon and night.'

Kelly put her hands over her face. 'I know you have to punish me, but please don't let my stupid anger hurt Dylan or the scholarship. Please.'

Mr Gough leant over and patted her hand. 'Don't worry about that. This incident won't affect the scholarship at all.'

Kelly looked at him. 'Really?'

'I'll have to give you detention to show that we don't accept verbal aggression, but that will be it. I think it's best if we keep this as quiet as possible. We don't want any fuss. St Jude's reputation is everything. We pride ourselves on having a zero tolerance to bullying.'

'Thank you.' Kelly gulped back tears. 'God, I was so scared I'd messed up. My friend Shannon said I should stop letting Melissa taunt me and stand up for myself and then when she said the thing about Mum . . . Well, anyway, I know it was a mistake and I promise I won't ever tell anyone to eff off again, no matter what they say to me.'

'Has Melissa's name-calling and bullying been going on a while?'

Kelly hesitated. She didn't want to make things worse by making a big deal of this. 'Occasionally,' she said. 'WhatsApp messages and stuff.'

Mr Gough nodded. 'I see. Well, no student in this school should have to suffer name-calling or bullying. I'll be having very stern words with Melissa.'

Kelly's head snapped up. 'Oh, no, don't. It'll just make it worse.'

'I promise you it won't. I've dealt with many bullies in my time. Melissa is nothing. Now, I will have to notify your mother of the incident and the detention, I'm afraid.'

Kelly pushed her hair out of her face. 'You've been so nice

already, but is there any way you could not do that? She'll worry that the scholarships will be taken away and she'll get herself into a state. Punish me, but don't tell Mum.'

Mr Gough studied her for a moment, then nodded again. 'All right, I understand. I won't call her. What I'm going to ask you to do now is not going to be easy, but I need you to apologize to Melissa. It'll help smooth things over. I'll bring her in here and you do it in front of me. It means that if she makes a fuss of the incident with her parents, I can tell them honestly that you have apologized and the matter is over. It also gives me a chance to make sure Melissa knows that I won't tolerate her nonsense. This argument really shouldn't escalate or cause any more trouble. We will nip it in the bud today and move on.'

'I'll do anything to protect Mum and Dylan.'

Mr Gough smiled at her. 'You are a very brave and selfless girl, Kelly, a credit to your mother. Don't ever forget that.'

Ten minutes later Melissa was standing in the headmaster's office with her arms folded, glaring at Kelly.

'It's a disgrace, Headmaster, she has a really violent temper. I thought she was going to punch me.'

'Melissa,' Mr Gough said, bending down so he was eye to eye with her, 'please refrain from dramatizing the incident. Now, Kelly has something she wants to say to you. But before she does I want you to remember this. We don't tolerate bullying in this school.'

'What? Did she accuse me of bullying? Seriously? Well, where's the proof? My friends will tell you I did nothing. She's just a freak with anger-management issues.'

'Melissa.' The headmaster's voice was cold. 'Let's not forget the incident last year with Naomi.'

'Yeah, well, I didn't think she'd be so sensitive about her weight, did I? Some people can't take a joke.'

'There is a very thin line between joking and being cruel. You need to remember that, Melissa. Please note that I will be keeping a very close eye on you from now on. Try being kind and sensitive to others. It costs nothing.'

Melissa's eyes narrowed. 'Excuse me, but why am I being lectured? She cursed at me! Why don't you talk to her about being sensitive?'

Mr Gough smiled. 'I have spoken at length to Kelly about what happened and she has something to say to you. I have no doubt that you will behave graciously.'

Kelly cleared her throat. Apologizing with the headmaster present was actually fine. She hated Melissa's guts but she wasn't in big trouble, she hadn't ruined everything and her mum would never know, so all in all it was a great outcome.

'I'm very sorry for shouting at you, Melissa. It was wrong and I promise it will never happen again. I really am so sorry and I hope that you will be kind enough to accept my apology and forgive me.' Kelly had laid it on thick, so Melissa would have to be nice in front of the headmaster.

'Well, it better not happen again,' Melissa snapped.

'And you accept Kelly's gracious apology, isn't that right?' the headmaster prompted.

Melissa shrugged.

'I'm sorry, I didn't hear you,' Mr Gough said.

'Yeah,' Melissa replied sulkily.

'Excellent. Let that be an end to the incident. I'd like no more said about it outside this room. Not a word. The matter is closed.' He looked straight at Melissa. 'Now, Melissa, you can go back to class. I want to have a final word with Kelly.'

Melissa turned to go and closed the door loudly behind her.

Mr Gough turned to Kelly. 'Well done, a very effusive apology.'

Kelly grinned. 'I didn't want her to be able to refuse it.'

'Hopefully, now that she knows I'm watching her, and I'll make sure all the teachers do the same, she'll leave you alone,' he said. 'If there are any inappropriate messages sent to you, please take screen shots and bring them to me. As I said, we do not tolerate bullies in St Jude's and we must avoid any negative media exposure for the school. So please don't discuss this with anyone else and come straight to me if there are any more issues.'

Kelly nodded. She knew Melissa would find ways to make her life hell – teachers had no clue about social media, whispers in the corridors and bullying in the toilets. Kelly's life was about to get worse, she knew that, but she'd suck it up.

'Thank you so much for everything. I'm sorry I let you down and I promise I'll be a perfect student from now on.'

Mr Gough opened the door to see her out. 'Kelly, you don't need to be the perfect anything, just be your lovely self.'

Kelly turned so he wouldn't see her tears.

39

Jenny emptied a packet of chilli-flavoured crisps into a bowl and put a plate with cheese and crackers on the kitchen counter beside it. Then she poured them all a large glass of red wine.

'Dinner!'

'You shouldn't have gone to so much trouble,' Lucy said, with a grin.

Sarah laughed. 'You must be worn out from cooking.'

'You know I don't cook and this is as good at it gets, so tuck in.' Jenny popped a crisp into her mouth.

'How is this place always so clean?' Sarah wondered. 'You put my housekeeping to shame.'

'Eh, because she has no kids messing it up and Jenny has OCD,' Lucy said.

'I don't have OCD. I just like things to be tidy.' Jenny handed them plates and napkins.

Sarah cut a chunk of Brie to put on her cracker. 'Yum.'

'So, what's happened while I've been away?' Jenny asked them.

'How was Milan?' Sarah asked.

'Fabulous,' Jenny said. 'I was wined and dined in the best restaurants by my very appreciative client and did loads of shopping. I'll show you the shoes I got later. They are to die for.'

Sarah groaned. 'I wish I hadn't asked. I can only dream of a break like that.'

'So any gossip?' Jenny said.

Sarah shook her head. 'Same old, same old at my house.'

Lucy sipped her wine. 'I broke up with Damien.'

'Really?' Sarah said. This was news to her.

'What? Why?' Jenny asked. 'I didn't see that coming.'

'Neither did he,' Lucy said drily. 'But I need to focus on the twins. I took my eye off Dylan and he got into trouble. He really came very close to getting dropped from the team. And also I think Kelly might be lying again about seeing that boy Sean. Anyway, I just realized that I've been too distracted and that I need to concentrate on them more.'

'I think you're mad,' Sarah said, reaching for more Brie. 'You didn't even see Damien that much. It was nice for you to have him there to go out for dinner with, and the rest.'

'Jesus, if you'd broken up with him because you'd met someone hotter, I'd be thrilled, but breaking up with him for the kids? It's mad, Lucy.' Jenny shook her head. 'For goodness' sake, you're already a total helicopter parent. The kids need to breathe. So what if Dylan had a few late nights? At his age, all boys do it. And as for Kelly lying about seeing Sean, I lied about every boyfriend I ever had. They're not doing drugs or robbing shops, they're just normal teenagers. Seriously, if anything, you need to give them more space, not less.'

Lucy gritted her teeth to prevent herself saying something she'd regret. What the hell did Jenny know? It was so easy for her to say Lucy was a helicopter parent. She didn't understand that Lucy had to be, that she had no choice. There was no dad to help out with discipline, so it was all down to her. It was all on her head. And, yes, she had been strict, but hadn't it proved the right decision, given all they'd achieved and what lovely kids they were?

'I haven't come this far to let them fall at the last hurdle, Jenny,' she said tightly. 'They've only got two more years of school and I want to make sure they get through them with flying colours, that's all.'

Jenny reached over for the bottle. 'You know what? Let's not talk about it tonight. You need an hour off being a parent, and we are here to do that for you, aren't we, Sarah?' She refilled their glasses. 'Get that down you and forget your woes.'

Lucy smiled. 'Sounds good to me. I'm happy to get away from being a mum for an hour.'

'So what about Christmas presents?' Jenny said. 'Anything the twins really want?'

'Ollie wants an archery set,' Sarah said. 'If you ever call round to find me face down on the path with an arrow through the back of my head, you'll know what's happened.'

Lucy and Jenny burst out laughing.

'Can you not fob him off with a bike, or a watch or something?' Jenny asked. 'He shouldn't own anything that can be weaponized.'

'Sure boys can turn anything into a weapon,' Lucy said. 'I remember Dylan stabbing Billy in the leg with a fork when he was five.'

'They were so cute when they were that age,' Jenny said. 'I used to love buying them little outfits and doing Kelly's hair.'

Lucy smiled. 'They were great fun. I used to love going into their bedrooms at night and kissing their warm sleepy faces. They were so adorable.'

Sarah took a big sip of wine and tried to keep her voice even. 'I'd say if Tom knew how wonderful they are, he'd really regret leaving. They were, and still are, so lovable.' She shot a look at Jenny, who nodded slightly.

'Anyone would be proud to be their parent,' Jenny said. 'I've always hated Tom for leaving but you'd have to feel a bit sorry for him that he missed out on so much.'

Lucy's eyes narrowed. 'Feel sorry for Tom? Are you mad? He chose to abandon us.'

'But did he really, though?' Sarah said. 'I mean, do you think there's any chance he truly believed you'd had the abortion and had no idea he was a dad?'

'No,' Lucy said quickly. 'And even if he wasn't sure, if he'd bothered to contact me to see if I was okay, he'd have soon found out. But he didn't even do that much. Not even a lousy letter or email. He's an unfeeling bastard, as far as I'm concerned.'

'It's an interesting point, though,' Jenny said. 'I hadn't thought about that before. What if Tom didn't know the twins existed? It's possible, isn't it?'

Lucy stared at her in disbelief. 'Why the hell are you two suddenly talking about Tom?' she said, looking from her sister to Sarah. 'Where's all this coming from?'

'I'm just wondering if –' Jenny turned mid-sentence as the doorbell interrupted them. 'Who's that?' she asked, as she went to answer the intercom.

'Hello?'

'Hey, babe, it's me.'

'Frank?'

'Yeah.'

Jenny buzzed him in. 'What's he doing here? I wasn't expecting him.'

'We'll leave.' Lucy got up and Sarah did the same.

'No, stay and finish your wine. I want you to meet him.'

There was a knock on the door. Jenny went to answer it. She came back into the lounge followed by a man carrying a large suitcase.

Lucy and Sarah twirled around on their kitchen counter stools to look at him. He was tall, fit, tanned, had thick brown hair with flecks of grey, and was impeccably dressed.

'So, this is Frank. Frank, this is my sister Lucy and our friend Sarah.'

Frank shook their hands.

'Are you moving in?' Sarah laughed, pointing to his suitcase.

Jenny grinned. 'No, he's just back from Shanghai.'

'Well, yes, I am, but actually, babe, Barbara kicked me out. She's changed the locks and the gate code and . . . Well, she seems serious this time. So, it looks like I am moving in.'

Jenny's face fell. 'What do you mean?'

Frank put his arms around her. 'I'll be staying here until I get this sorted out. We can get a bigger place when I find out how much Barbara wants in maintenance.'

Jenny frowned. 'How long will that take?'

Frank laughed. 'Knowing Barbara, she'll try to take me to the cleaners, but I'm not having that so it could be a while.' Frank threw his jacket onto the couch. He picked up a cracker and put a huge chunk of cheese on top. 'Right, what's for dinner?'

Jenny pointed to his cracker. 'That's dinner.'

Frank laughed. 'I'm not a rabbit.'

'That's all I have,' Jenny said.

Frank went over to the fridge and opened it. It contained one carton of low-fat milk, two low-fat yoghurts, three bananas and a punnet of strawberries that had gone mouldy.

He looked around at Jenny. 'Seriously?'

'I don't cook. I travel a lot at short notice and I eat out a lot.'

'Right, I'll order take-out. Ladies, what can I get you?'

'We're fine, thanks. We're not staying. We'll leave you to it.' Sarah knocked back her wine and stood up.

'We all met your wife when she caused a major scene at my dad's birthday party.' Lucy looked Frank in the eye.

'Oh, yeah, Jenny told me. Sorry about that, she's a bit mad.'

'Is she? Or is she just humiliated and heartbroken by your affairs?'

'Lucy!' Jenny snapped.

Frank's smile faded slightly. 'Barbara is very good at playing the martyr. She's no angel. She's been shagging the golf pro at our club for the past three years.'

'Charming. Why are you still together if you're both unfaithful?' Lucy asked.

'Cheaper and a lot less hassle than a messy divorce.'

'I see.' Lucy tapped the countertop with her fingers. 'I presume you know how lucky you are that my sister is seeing you?'

Frank kissed Jenny. 'I certainly do.'

'Good. Well, just remember that and treat her properly.'

'Lucy, I'm not one of your kids.' Jenny squirmed.

Frank laughed. 'I haven't had a speech like that since I took Rosie Johnston to my debs and her dad said the same thing to me.'

'We'll head off now.' Sarah pulled Lucy down from her stool.

'Where's the best take-out around here? I need food.'

'We could go out?' Jenny suggested.

'Nah, I'm wrecked after my flight. Besides, Man U are playing at eight and I don't want to miss it. I'd love a glass of wine though, babe.' Frank kicked off his shoes and threw himself onto the couch, flinging Jenny's perfectly positioned cushions onto the floor. He picked up the TV remote control and began flicking channels.

Jenny walked Sarah and Lucy out.

'Good luck with your new flatmate,' Sarah said, grinning at her.

'He seems very at home already,' Lucy added.

'He'll be a great housemate,' Sarah said.

'You won't even notice he's here.' Lucy began to laugh.

'I'd say he's a whiz with a hoover and a mop,' Sarah said, and she and Lucy creased over with laughter.

'Stop it!' Jenny hissed. 'I don't want him living with me. That was never the plan. What the hell am I going to do?'

'Good *luuuuuuuck*.' Lucy and Sarah closed the front door behind them and laughed all the way down in the lift.

40

Dylan stared at the paper and sighed quietly. They were going over possible questions for the Christmas exams, and with every question he read, he realized how little he knew. Damn it, he should have studied harder these past few weeks. He'd been way too distracted by Taylor.

'Students, I want you to answer the following question. "Yeats uses evocative language to create poetry that includes both personal reflection and public commentary. Discuss this statement, supporting your answer with reference to both the themes and language found in the poetry of W. B. Yeats on your course."' Mr O'Casey glanced at the clock behind him. 'Right, you have fifteen minutes.'

There was an audible groan.

'We have spent hours and weeks studying Yeats's poetry. You are perfectly equipped to answer this question. Stop wasting time and get on with it.'

Dylan looked across at Taylor. She was staring at her nails. As if feeling his attention on her, she looked up and smiled. 'Boring,' she mouthed.

'Dylan, look at your paper not at Taylor, please,' Mr O'Casey snapped.

Dylan tried to concentrate on the question, but he had no answer. He hadn't studied Yeats. He hadn't really studied anything. His Christmas exams were starting next week and St Jude's took them very seriously.

Dylan felt the pressure to do well because, even though the scholarship was for football, he needed to prove he wasn't thick, that he could keep up with his classmates. He wanted to prove to the other kids that he wasn't just a football player: he had brains too.

Dylan tried to think of something to write, but he couldn't remember any detail about the poems they'd studied. There was the one about daffodils and saying goodbye so he tried to make up an answer around that, but he knew he was in trouble. He had only a week to cram for the exams and he had two training sessions after school this week, and Jordan wanted them to do two extra early-morning workouts in the gym before the final. After they'd beaten King's College in the semis, the pressure was really on. They had a shot at the cup, and Jordan was going to make sure they took it.

The bell went and they handed their papers to Mr O'Casey as they filed out of the classroom. Taylor came up behind Dylan and put her hand up his jumper. She whispered in his ear, 'Will you come over tonight? My parents are away.'

'I can't. My mum knows we have exams next week and she's really on my case. She'll go mad if I head out.'

Taylor's hand headed down towards the belt of his trousers. 'Tell your mum I'm hosting a study group. See you later.' She pulled her hand away.

'You are one lucky dude.' Conor came up beside him. 'She is a fox.'

Dylan grinned. 'I know.' He felt proud to be Taylor's boyfriend. All the other guys fancied her but she only had eyes for him. It made him feel like the king of the school, not just a scholarship boy.

'How's the study going? It's hard to fit it all in, isn't it?' Conor said, as they walked towards their maths class.

'The extra training sessions aren't helping.'

'Yeah, I only manage to cram in two hours' study on the nights we train,' Conor complained.

Two hours? Dylan did no study on football training nights. 'How do you manage two hours?' he asked.

'I try to do nine thirty to eleven thirty.'

'I'm so wrecked after training I can barely read,' Dylan admitted.

Conor shrugged. 'I have to put in the hours. My parents are paying a fortune to send me here. I have to get good results or they'll be really disappointed.'

Not as disappointed as my mum, Dylan thought grimly. He'd have to get up early and go to bed late, cram in as much study as he could. He'd tell Taylor later that he couldn't come over. Kelly could help him: she was a world-class studier.

Dylan sat in front of Kelly while she peppered him with questions. So far he'd got one right out of six. His phone pinged. *Hey babe what time are you coming over? The sooner the better.*

He looked at his watch. It was nine. He'd only just sat down to study because he'd got caught up talking to Billy and helping stock shelves in the shop. He'd have to put her off. *Sry babe Im WAY behind on study, gotta get my head down. C u 2mrw.*

So ur not interested in these. Taylor had sent a photo of her naked breasts. *Or this.* Another photo, this time of her lace knickers.

Stop ur killing me, u know I'm interested in all of it, but I have to study.

Fine. I'll have to find someone else to play with. So . . . who will I send these pics to next????

'Dylan!' Kelly snapped. 'Stop staring at your bloody phone. You asked me to help you, so you could at least concentrate.'

'Sorry, it's Taylor. She's sending me photos of her body parts.'

Dylan quickly texted back: *Don't even think about showing those pics to anyone else. That body is for my eyes only.*

'Dylan!' Kelly stood up and threw the book on the bed. 'You're going to fail. History is supposed to be your good subject and you've got almost all the answers wrong. You haven't a clue about any of the chapters you're supposed to have studied. You're going to fail and Mum will go mad and so will Mr Gough. How can you know so little? Have you not studied at all?'

He shrugged. 'I've been distracted with football training and stuff.'

'Taylor, you mean. Seriously, Dylan, she's not worth risking everything for.'

Dylan slammed his book on his desk. 'I am so sick of you and Mum being on my case. I'm having fun. Since when has that become a crime? Jesus, I've always done everything right to please Mum. I've been the peacemaker between the two of you when you get into your fights, I've helped Granddad out in the shop. I've been the perfect bloody son and now, finally, I'm having some fun and everyone is on my case. I'm sick of it.' He grabbed his jacket and headed out of the door.

Kelly called him back. 'Don't go out! Come on, I'll help you study – you need it.'

'To hell with it, I'm going to see Taylor.'

Dylan ran down the stairs and out of the front door. Kelly tore after him to try to stop him, but he was gone.

Lucy came in. 'Where's Dylan? He's not in his room.'

Kelly froze. Did she tell the truth or lie to protect him? She had to protect him: he was her twin. 'Uhm, I think he just popped out for a sec.'

'Where?'

'To . . . to get a –' Damn, Kelly couldn't think of anything.

It was a dark, cold night in December. What the hell would Dylan be popping out for? Her mind was blank. Damnit.

Her mother's eyes narrowed. 'Has he gone to see Taylor?'

Kelly hesitated. 'I don't know.'

'Don't lie, Kelly. It's obvious he has. I can't believe it. He has exams coming up and a big game on Saturday. That girl is going to destroy him.' Lucy's voice cracked.

Kelly hated seeing her mother upset. It was so rare that Lucy cried. All their lives Lucy had been so strong and only ever cried with joy, like when Dylan won a football cup or Kelly got first prize at school. Otherwise she was steely and tough and never let things get to her. Lucy was the rock of the family, the one who kept everything going, the one who looked after everyone. Kelly had never seen her like this.

'Why is he being so stupid? Doesn't he see? He's going to ruin everything.' Lucy began to cry. 'One person can ruin your life. Taylor could ruin his.'

Kelly didn't know what to do. She took a step forward and patted her mother's shoulder. 'Mum, he'll probably be back soon. Dylan won't let you down, he never does. He's just having a bit of fun. But he knows what matters.'

Lucy wiped away her tears with the back of her hand. 'Fun?' she croaked. 'Fun is what got me into trouble. Fun with the wrong person will be his downfall.'

She turned away from Kelly, took her phone out of her back pocket and called Dylan's mobile. Kelly could hear it go to voicemail. Lucy cursed. She texted him to come home *IMMEDIATELY*. He didn't reply.

'Look, Mum, why don't you go to bed? Have an early night. I'll bring you up a cup of tea. Dylan will be home soon, I'm sure of it.'

Lucy gave her a watery smile. 'Thanks, Kelly, you're a star. I don't tell you that enough. But I won't be able to sleep. I'll wait for him downstairs. I want to speak to him when he gets in. I can't believe he's back with her. Taylor has to go.'

Lucy went back downstairs and Kelly texted Dylan: *Get home NOW. Mum on warpath, waiting up 4 u.*

He didn't reply.

Kelly lay awake, staring at the ceiling, exhausted. It was one a.m. and Dylan still wasn't home. He'd never stayed out so late on a school night before. He was really pushing it this time.

Kelly texted Sean. *U up?*

Yep. U still free on Sat for David's party?

Yes, need to work out a lie to tell mum, but I'll be there.

Cool. I want some alone time!!! Wear that denim mini, u look hot in it.

Kelly's stomach did a little flip. *K.* She wanted to be alone with him, but she was worried about sex. She had Shannon's condoms, but she hadn't gone to get the pill yet. She kept finding excuses not to go to the clinic because she still wasn't sure about it. Should she warn Sean she wasn't ready, or wait and just talk to him on Saturday? She knew he wanted to have sex, but she was scared. Her mother had done a good job of freaking her out about getting pregnant.

Can't wait to see you.

Me too, Kelly replied.

K. C u gorgeous. xx

Kelly smiled at her screen. *C u. xx*

She lay back on her pillow. How was she going to get out on Saturday without her mother finding out? Dylan's late night would set Lucy off again, and she'd be breathing down their necks. She'd have asked Jenny for help, but since Frank had moved in she hadn't seen her, and when she'd spoken to her on the phone two days ago, her aunt had sounded really grumpy and stressed. She'd have to ask Shannon for advice. She had to make absolutely sure her mother didn't find out about Sean. She'd freak anyway, but now that she was so wound up about Dylan she'd double-freak. Sean and the party had to remain a secret.

Kelly tossed and turned, unable to sleep. She was worried about Dylan. Finally, she heard the front door open. Dylan was home. She heard him trip and then curse. She looked at her phone: 2.07 a.m.

'Dylan!' her mother's voice cried. 'Are you drunk?'

Kelly held her breath. Drunk! How could he be so stupid? She'd told him Lucy was waiting up for him. She reckoned Billy was staying well out of it. He hadn't moved from his room since ten o'clock. She couldn't blame him.

Kelly could hear Dylan giggling. Oh, God, he must be really pissed. This was bad.

She could only catch some of what her mother was saying because Lucy was crying. 'How could you . . . stupid . . . irresponsible . . . opportunity . . . ruin everything . . . why . . . please don't do this . . . sacrificed . . . have to stop seeing her . . . you have to.'

Dylan's voice was louder. 'I love Taylor and I'm never, ever going to break up with her, so get that into your head. She's the best thing that's happened to me. I feel brilliant when I'm with her. Free from all the pressure and hassle. Nothing you can say will make me dump her. She's the best thing in my life.'

Kelly could hear her mother properly now: she was shouting and crying. 'Don't ruin your life like I did. Please, Dylan, no one is worth it. Taylor is just one girl – you'll meet plenty of others. You have to stop seeing her. Jordan won't give you a second chance. He'll know you were drinking again. Look at you, you're absolutely plastered. Taylor is bad for you. If you don't break up with her, I'll bloody well do it for you. I'll make sure she stays the hell away from you. Over my dead body is that girl messing up your life.'

'Stop going on and on. Jesus, Mum, I'm not going to get her pregnant. I'm just having fun. Stop suffocating me. Stop trying to control everything me and Kelly do. We're not stupid like you were.'

'You and Kelly are my life,' Lucy cried. 'You're everything to me. Please, Dylan, don't let Taylor drag you down. Trust me on this. She's already caused trouble with Jordan and school. Stop it now before it's too late. You can't behave like this – you'll get expelled and so will Kelly. The football parents are already talking about you. We have to be better than everyone. Scholarship students have to be perfectly behaved. You have to prove to them that you belong there. Please, Dylan . . .'

Kelly hated to hear Lucy so upset, her voice coming out in gulps and hiccups as she veered between crying and shouting.

'I don't have to prove anything to anyone,' Dylan roared. 'Leave me alone and do not mention Taylor again. I love her and I'm never breaking up with her. I don't give a shit what the other football parents think of me and neither should you. Fuck them and fuck St Jude's.'

Kelly heard Lucy gasp and then Dylan's footsteps on the stairs. He stumbled into his bedroom and locked the door. Kelly could hear her mother sobbing.

Oh, God, Dylan and her mum never fought. They'd barely ever had a cross word. It was Kelly and Lucy who had always clashed. That was normal. This was totally abnormal. Kelly felt sick.

She slowly opened her bedroom door and looked out. Lucy was sitting at the top of the stairs, crying against the banister.

'Mum?' Kelly whispered.

'Go back to bed,' Lucy said, rubbing her eyes roughly. 'It's okay, love. Go on.'

Kelly closed her door softly and stood there, wondering what to do. How could she or her mum make Dylan see what he was doing? There was no getting through to him. This was just going to get worse and worse, she could feel it. What could they do?

She opened her door again. 'We can talk to him tomorrow, Mum,' she said. 'Force him to see that he's making bad decisions.'

Lucy raised her head, her eyes red and sore. 'He's going to break up with that girl if I have to do it for him. There is no other solution.'

'I know,' Kelly whispered. 'I know.'

41

Dylan was first in for pre-school training. He was glad the locker room was empty. He threw his kit bag on the floor and sat down. It had nearly killed him to get up when his alarm clock went off, but he knew he was on thin ice with everyone – at home and at school. That thought alone had forced him out of bed. He felt hung-over and guilty about shouting at his mother. He'd never done that before and he felt terrible. She hadn't been up when he'd left the house. He'd apologize later. He swore to himself that he wouldn't drink any more with Taylor. He'd see her, but he wouldn't take anything. And he was going to spend the next six nights straight studying like demon. That would make his mum happy.

He gulped down more water and opened his kit bag. Three of the lads came in and whistled at him.

Guy slapped him on the back. 'Very decent of you, Dylan, sharing Taylor's assets with us all. I must say, it was a bloody nice image to wake up to.'

'What a rack. As good as I always imagined it would be.'

'You're a lucky man.'

Dylan frowned. What the hell were they on about?

Conor came in behind them and sat down beside Dylan. 'Dude, were you drunk? Taylor's going to freak out.'

'What are you all talking about?' Dylan asked.

'The photo you sent to the football WhatsApp group of Taylor topless.'

'What?' Dylan jumped up.

'How drunk were you?' Conor asked.

'I never sent that! There's no way . . . I . . .' Dylan stuttered. Had he? Did he send it out? No way. He hadn't been that drunk. No. There was no way in hell he would do that.

He pulled his phone out of the pocket of his kit bag. His hands were shaking. He had tons of messages. Oh, Jesus, it had been forwarded on. Shit. His phone flashed as more messages flooded in. He opened the photo and looked at the time it was sent, three a.m. He remembered going to bed, setting his alarm clock and thinking, Shit, it's half two and I'm up at six. He was fast asleep at three a.m. Someone else must have sent it. He'd found his phone on the kitchen table earlier.

Oh, my God. Dylan's jaw dropped open as the awful truth hit him. Mum.

He remembered how upset she'd been when he'd come home – she'd even cried, which she never did. Jesus, had his mother done this? Could she be that psycho? She was obsessed with St Jude's and she had been really upset last night, way more upset than he'd ever seen her before . . . Dylan sat down. He felt sick.

'Nice tits, dude! Thanks for sharing.' Josh slapped his back.

Dylan felt sweat trickling down his back. Panic was setting in. His phone flashed. It was Taylor calling. How the hell was he going to explain this?

He walked out of the dressing room and outside the building. 'Hi.'

'You lowlife scumbag. How could you do this? How could you humiliate me like this? That was private, Dylan, between you and me. My phone hasn't stopped since I woke up. It's gone viral,' Taylor screamed.

'I swear to you I didn't do this. I don't know how it

happened, but I'm going to find out. I'm taking it down now and deleting it.'

'It's too fucking late! It's out there now. The whole world is looking at my boobs. You're an arsehole. I trusted you. Melissa was right, you are a lowlife.'

'Taylor, please, I swear I didn't send it. I wouldn't do that.'

'At least have the balls to own up. It came from your phone and was sent to your football team!' Taylor shouted. 'I hate you! I will never ever speak to you again. You're dead to me.' She hung up.

Dylan ran over to a hedge and threw up. How could she do this to him? How could his mother do this to Taylor? Anger welled inside him. It was her, he was sure of it. She'd been so obsessed about him breaking up with Taylor. The anger surged through him as he ran to where he'd parked his bike. He yanked the key out of his pocket, unlocked it, flung the lock on the ground and jumped on, pedalling furiously.

They were finishing breakfast when the door burst open. Dylan stood there, sweat running down his face, panting. He held onto the countertop and caught his breath.

Lucy, Billy and Kelly stared at him.

'Did something happen?' Lucy asked, sounding worried. 'What's wrong?'

'How could you?' Dylan shouted. 'How could you do this to her?'

'What are you talking about?' Lucy had expected him to apologize to her this morning. What the hell was this?

'You bitch.'

'Dylan!' Billy stood up and shook a finger in his face. 'Don't you dare speak to your mother like that. Calm down and tell us what's going on.'

'She,' Dylan shouted, jabbing a finger towards Lucy, 'sent

a photo of Taylor topless from my phone to all my friends and it's gone viral. The whole fucking country is looking at it. Taylor hates me now.' His face crumpled. 'She doesn't believe it wasn't me. She's hurt and humiliated. How could you do this? You're a psycho.'

'Jesus, I barely understand the world any more.' Billy pulled Dylan into a chair and stood behind him. 'Now let's just take a minute and sort this out.'

Lucy was staring at her son. 'You're saying a photo of Taylor was sent from your phone and you're blaming me? You think I'd do that? Have you lost your mind?'

'I know you did it, Mum. You told me to break up with Taylor and you knew I wouldn't do it, so last night when I went to bed you sent the photo out. I know you did so you can stop lying now. You're so obsessed with me being the perfect scholarship student that you'd do anything to stop me messing up. I just never thought you'd stoop that low.'

'I didn't do it,' Lucy said. 'It's ridiculous. You must have done it by mistake or pressed the wrong button last night when you came in. You were drunk, after all.'

'I wasn't that drunk! I'd never ever hurt Taylor, but you would. You wanted to get rid of her. Well, congratulations, Mum, it worked. She hates me. She's sent me tons of messages letting me know how much she hates me and how devastated she is. I will never forgive you for this, never.'

'Stop it, Dylan,' Lucy snapped. 'You only have yourself to blame because I didn't touch your phone. Besides, the fact that Taylor is stupid enough to send photos of her breasts to you speaks for itself, doesn't it? I won't have you speaking to me like this. I didn't send any picture. You were drunk enough to do that all by yourself.'

'I didn't do it!' Dylan shouted. 'I'm mad about Taylor.'

Lucy folded her arms. 'Well, I feel sorry for Taylor and I'm sorry you're upset, but you know what? Maybe your drunk actions last night are going to save you from making a serious mistake. Now that Taylor's out of the picture, you can focus on what's important. This might actually be a blessing in disguise.'

Dylan's mouth fell open. He stared at his mother. Then he stood up and walked over to her. He put his face close to hers. 'I know you did it and I hope you're happy. You've ruined my life and hers. Well done.'

He stormed up to his bedroom.

'What in the name of God is going on?' Billy asked.

'Stupid teenage nonsense, Dad. Don't worry about it. It'll blow over. Go on and open up the shop. I'll be there in a minute,' Lucy told him.

'Bloody phones, they're the scourge of life, I tell you,' Billy muttered, as he unlocked the door leading from the kitchen into the shop.

Lucy turned to Kelly, who was sitting quietly at the table. She hadn't uttered a word. 'Are you all right?' she asked.

Kelly nodded.

'Don't worry, pet, he'll soon realize he sent it by mistake last night and hopefully he'll learn something from it. He'll stop drinking now he sees what stupid things he does when he's drunk. I do feel sorry for Taylor, but then again, she's very foolish to send photos of her body to anyone. Let this be a lesson to you too, Kelly. Never send anyone an intimate photo of yourself. Nothing is private.' She looked towards the stairs. 'Hopefully Dylan will calm down soon and apologize.'

Kelly said nothing. She got up and put her plate into the dishwasher. Lucy watched her go up the stairs as she finished tidying up the kitchen. She only realized her hands were shaking when she tried to put her coffee cup into the dishwasher. She'd tried to appear calm in front of Kelly and her dad, but she'd been thrown by the force of Dylan's rage. She'd give him a few more minutes to calm down and then she'd go up and try to talk to him reasonably.

She never got the chance. Five minutes later, Dylan thumped down the stairs carrying a suitcase and headed for the front door.

Lucy rushed into the hall. 'What on earth are you doing?'

'Leaving.' Dylan pushed past her. 'I'm not staying in this house with you.'

'Stop this nonsense, Dylan. I've had enough now. I did not send any photo to anyone. Calm down and stop behaving like a child. You obviously sent it by mistake last night and blaming me is ridiculous.'

Dylan shoved his finger into her face, his eyes blazing. 'I will never forgive you. I'm going to stay at Jenny's because I can't live under the same roof as someone who could be so cruel. I hate you. I really mean that. I hate you.'

Lucy gasped. 'Come on, Dylan, this is ridiculous. Stop now. Come back. We need to talk about this. Dylan, you can't leave.'

He shoved her out of the way and walked out of the door, his suitcase trailing behind him.

'Dylan,' she called. 'Dylan, come back.' She began to cry. 'Please. You sent it by mistake. Please, come back.'

'I'm never coming back. Don't try to contact to me. You're dead to me.'

42

Kelly's phone pinged constantly.

Melissa: *Ur brother is scum. Taylor is absolutely devastated. My stepdad is going mental!!!!! He's going to get u all kicked out.*

Alicia: *Good riddance. St Jude's shld never have allowed u scumbags in.*

Chloë: *Taylor is such a nice person ur brother is a dick.*

Melissa: *Pack ur bags u lowlife. Ur days at St Jude's are over.*

It wasn't just her tormentors: there were tons of messages from all the other students in her class.

Ur brother is a lowlife.

Taylor deserves better than that scumbag.

Fuck off back to your old school.

Never should have given scholarships to filth like u.

We'll get revenge for Taylor . . .

It was unrelenting, message after message after message. She didn't know how she'd got through the day in school. It had been hell. She'd sprinted for the gates at four o'clock, desperate to be out of there.

Lucy was pacing up and down the kitchen when Kelly got home.

'Did you see him? Is he okay? Did he speak to you? Is he sorry for being so rude? Does he realize now that he sent the photo?' Lucy peppered Kelly with questions.

Kelly's head was already splitting with the day she'd had. 'No, Mum, I didn't see Dylan today.'

'I've been thinking about it all day. It's going to look very bad for Dylan. If the school finds out, he'll be in big trouble.

I'm scared, Kelly. He could get expelled for this. Sending a compromising photo of a girl is a terrible thing to do. Oh, God, this is bad, really bad,' Lucy said. She was pale and looked worn out. 'The school hasn't been on to me. Do you think they know?'

Kelly swallowed back the terror she felt rising in her chest. 'I don't know. But Mr Gough is really nice. Hopefully, he will be fair about it.' Kelly said the words she hoped were true but she knew it was bad. Much worse than she had ever imagined. Everyone had seen the photo. It was a disaster.

'Maybe no one else apart from the team has seen the photo. Have they? Did you hear anything?'

Kelly struggled to control herself. 'Unfortunately a lot of people have seen it.'

Lucy's face crumpled. 'Oh, Jesus, Dylan, what have you done? I wanted him to break up with her but not humiliate her. Oh, Kelly, what a mess.' Lucy began to sob.

'They don't like any bad press for the school,' Kelly said, clutching at straws, trying to convince herself as much as her mother. 'I think Mr Gough will do everything he can to keep this quiet.'

Lucy's head snapped up and she looked hopefully at her daughter. 'Really? That would be brilliant, if it can just blow over. I mean, it was just a stupid mistake.'

Kelly nodded, but she felt sick inside. There was no way this wasn't going to have consequences, big ones.

Lucy grabbed her house keys from the counter. 'I'm going to Jenny's to see Dylan. I have to do something, I have to help him fix this. Maybe we can go to Mr Gough and explain it to him, make him see it was an innocent mistake. We have to try.' Lucy hugged Kelly, then rushed out of the door.

Kelly collapsed into a chair and sobbed into her hands.

*

Lucy rang the doorbell. Jenny answered it.

'Come on in.'

Lucy walked past her sister and straight to the spare bedroom. The door was locked. She stood outside and called Dylan's name. Silence.

Frank walked out in his boxer shorts. He was eating toast and scattering crumbs on Jenny's cream carpet.

'For God's sake, Frank, eat in the bloody kitchen,' Jenny snapped.

'Jesus, keep your hair on, Mrs Mop.'

Jenny pushed him towards the kitchen.

'Hi, Lucy, sorry to hear of your situation.'

'It's just a mistake,' Lucy said, embarrassed that he was getting to witness her family unravelling. 'It'll blow over quickly.'

Frank shook his head. 'I doubt it. He won't come out of there until you admit to sending that photo.'

'I can't admit to something I didn't do,' Lucy hissed.

Frank put his buttery knife down on the kitchen countertop. Jenny whipped it up and wiped away the butter marks.

'Eh, I was going to have more butter.'

'You've had enough. Go on, get yourself ready and meet Colin for a pint. He'll be waiting for you.'

'Where are my clean shirts?' Frank asked.

'What do you mean?'

'I put them beside the washing machine.'

'I saw them. They're still there.'

'Why didn't you wash them?'

'They're not mine.'

'But I need clean shirts.'

Jenny folded her arms. 'Well, I guess you'll have to wash them, won't you?'

'Are you serious? You just left them on the floor?'

'Yes, Frank, I did.'

'Thanks a bloody lot. What am I supposed to wear to go out?'

'I don't give a shit what you wear. I amn't your cook or your cleaner. If you want clean shirts, wash them. You're a big boy.'

'Jesus, Jenny.'

'Jesus what? You're a smelly, lazy, untidy git. I will never wash your clothes or cook your meals. If you don't like it, the front door is there. Feel free to leave.'

'Don't push me, Jenny. I just might.'

'Please do. You're driving me insane.'

Frank slammed down his plate and stormed into the bedroom. He came out a minute later wearing trousers and a crumpled T-shirt. 'I'll have to go out looking like this now, thank you very much.' He cursed as he slammed the front door behind him.

'I see the honeymoon period has worn off,' Lucy noted.

'It lasted about five minutes. I'm making it as unpleasant for him as possible so he moves out soon. I haven't even had sex with him since the first night. I bought these disgusting fleece pyjamas and I wear them every night.'

'I thought he seemed very frustrated and angry.'

Jenny grinned. 'Hopefully he'll be gone by the weekend.'

'Are you really all right?'

Jenny snorted. 'I'll be fine when he leaves. I now know that I am never meant to live with another human, and that includes Dylan. I want him out too. Go and talk to him.'

Lucy took a deep breath and knocked on the bedroom door again. 'Dylan, no matter how much you push me away, I won't ever stop trying to talk to you. I love you and I'm sorry that you're angry, but you're angry with the wrong person. I didn't send that photo. You have to stop this and go back to school.'

Silence.

'Dylan, please don't throw away this chance because you're angry with me. Maybe one of your friends did it as a joke, or you pressed the button by mistake. Look, it doesn't matter, you have to come out of there and come home, go back to school and stop this.'

Silence.

'Please, Dylan, please,' Lucy begged.

Jenny came out of the lounge. She led her sister away from the door and over to the couch. 'Give it a break. Have a coffee.' She handed her a mug.

Lucy held it between her hands. 'I have to get Dylan to see sense. It wasn't me, Jenny. I'd never humiliate a girl like that. I know how it feels to be shamed, and I would never do that to another person. How can Dylan think I'd do something so awful?'

Jenny looked at her. 'So you absolutely swear you didn't do it?'

'Yes,' Lucy said. She looked at her sister. 'My God, you actually think I'm capable of this, don't you?'

Jenny shrugged. 'You've been so obsessed with this whole scholarship thing, I just thought you might have had a moment of madness, yeah.'

Lucy was taken aback. 'Jesus, Jenny, I'm not a lunatic. I mean, yes, I'm delighted they've broken up, but this isn't the way I wanted it to happen.'

Jenny tucked her long legs under her. 'Look, he's angry and heartbroken. Maybe he did it himself when he was drunk, although it doesn't seem like him. He's clearly mad about Taylor and he's a gentleman. You brought him up to respect women, so I just don't think he'd have done it. He is adamant that he didn't send it. If it wasn't you, it must have been one of his mates. Whoever did it is a real scumbag. I feel very sorry for Taylor.'

Lucy sighed. How was she going to persuade Dylan to stop blaming her and go back to school? She'd had to call St Jude's and pretend he was sick today, but this couldn't go on. 'Will you try talking to him again?' Lucy pleaded. 'He has to go back to school. If he keeps this up, he'll be dropped from the team and expelled. All because of a stupid girl. God, I wish he'd never met her. Why couldn't he just focus on his football and schoolwork?'

'Because he's human, Lucy. He's a handsome seventeen-year-old with hormones. You're too hard on them sometimes.'

Lucy bristled. Yet again her sister was talking as if she knew something about raising children. The only person Jenny had ever had to look after was herself. After one measly week sharing the apartment with Frank, she wanted to kick him out. 'I'm just protective, Jenny, there's no crime in that. I screwed up my life and I don't want them to do the same. Dylan is now behaving like an idiot because of that girl. I want him back in school and back on track. So do me a favour, spare me the lectures and help me get my son out of that room.'

Jenny put the cushion down and stood up. 'You don't have to go all gritted teeth on me. I know Dylan needs to go back to school. I'm doing my best. I'm not a total moron. Go home and I'll call you later. I promise to do everything I can to persuade him to go.'

'Thanks, sis,' Lucy said, and left reluctantly.

She breathed deeply as she walked home, dragging the crisp, cold air deep into her lungs. A half-moon hung over the city. The Christmas trees twinkled in every window, and she felt a lump in her throat. Christmas Day was just over a week away, and look at the mess they were in. It would be the first time her family had an unhappy Christmas. She couldn't bear the idea of the decorations and the cooking, all the fuss. She wanted to bury her head in the sand and wait for it all to be over.

The sound of Justin Timberlake suddenly singing 'Can't Stop The Feeling' made her jump. What the . . .? It was her phone. She smiled. Dylan was forever giving her new ringtones when she wasn't looking – he thought it was hilarious.

'Hello?'

'Ms Murphy, it's Mr Gough here. I'm sorry to ring after school hours, but I'm afraid we seem to have a bit of a situation regarding Dylan, Taylor Lyons and a photograph.'

Lucy's heart sank. 'Yes, I know about it.'

'Well, Mr Lyons is most concerned about the leaking of the private photograph and has requested a meeting with Dylan to get to the bottom of it. I think it's important that you attend with your son. Perhaps we can clear this mess up quickly. We don't want it getting out in the media. We must protect the school from any negative press.'

'Yes, of course,' Lucy said, her voice shaking.

Mr Gough cleared his throat. 'I'm afraid Mr Lyons is most upset about the matter and he's talking about taking legal action, which I'm doing my utmost to dissuade him from. It's important that Dylan is prepared to give his side of the story. We're proposing ten o'clock tomorrow morning in my office. Can you make that?'

'Yes,' Lucy said. 'I'll be there.'

She hung up and began to cry. This was it: her worst nightmare was coming true. If Dylan couldn't tell them who had sent the photo, he'd be sent away from St Jude's in disgrace and possibly taken to court. Oh, God, Dylan. Lucy had to lean against a wall. She felt faint. Her entire life was coming apart at the seams. All her efforts, seventeen years of working hard, sacrificing – and one photo, one stupid, stupid mistake, was going to take it all away from her. From them. And what would they have left? Nothing.

43

The tension in the kitchen was almost unbearable. Jenny had walked Dylan around so he could get ready for the meeting. Kelly was in her uniform and at the table, pushing eggs around her plate and eating nothing. Billy was sitting at the table, too, with a full cup of coffee in front of him that he hadn't touched. He was upset and kept looking at Lucy, who was standing in the corner of the kitchen, sipping a strong coffee. She kept glancing at Dylan, who refused to meet her eye. Kelly couldn't recognize her own family. Things had never been like this before. It felt scary.

'Come on now. No one's dead. This will all sort itself out,' Billy said, in a fake-cheery voice.

Kelly peeped at her mum from under her hair. Lucy looked terrible. She clearly hadn't slept a wink. Her eyes were red from crying and she stood as if her body was too heavy for her, like she was going to topple over at any minute. She knew they were all dead nervous about the meeting and what would happen. But Mr Gough was a good person, a sensible person. He'd make this okay – he had to. He would know that Dylan could never do anything to hurt anyone, and surely Taylor's dad would see that Dylan was a good person. But Kelly had heard her mum telling Billy that Mr Lyons was thinking of taking legal action. She'd nearly been sick when she'd heard that. He wouldn't, though, would he?

No. Mr Gough wouldn't let that happen because it would look bad for St Jude's. It would be awful if the school ended up in a scandal splashed across the newspapers. There was no way Mr Gough would stand for it. He'd talk Mr Lyons round. It would be okay, Kelly told herself for the millionth time. It would all be okay.

'Dylan,' Billy said, 'they're going to ask you what happened, son, so you need to have your answer ready.'

Dylan looked at Lucy. 'My mother sent out a private photo of my girlfriend to split us up,' he said.

Billy looked at Jenny. 'That might not be the best way to put it.'

'He's right,' Jenny said. 'You say that, Taylor's dad can initiate proceedings against your mum. Do you want that?'

Dylan's lip curled. 'I really don't care what happens to her.'

Lucy flinched. 'Please don't say that,' she said quietly.

'Listen, Dylan,' Billy tried, 'you're angry as hell right now, but you won't always feel that way. If you say something today that lands your mother in court, there will come a day when you regret it, trust me.'

Dylan scowled and said nothing.

'It might be easier to say you were drunk when it happened,' Jenny said. 'That it was never your intention. I think that's plausible, and it means you aren't really to blame.'

'Will you say it?' Billy asked. 'Will you, son?'

Dylan left the room without speaking.

Kelly went ahead and got the bus to school because she had to be there for ten past nine and the meeting wasn't until ten. She dreaded the day ahead. The messages on her phone just kept flooding in, telling her that she and Dylan weren't fit to be in St Jude's. It took every ounce of strength she had just to walk through the gates and into the building.

She kept her head down as she made her way to her locker, not making eye contact with anyone. Her first class was maths, which was a good distraction because they were working on calculus, which was difficult. After class she went straight back to her locker, head down, moving quickly. As she rummaged for her English books, there was a loud bang and she jumped.

'Enjoy your last day.' Melissa was in her face, looking at her with such hatred that Kelly was frightened.

She tried to push past her, but Chloë and Alicia pinned her back. 'Get off me, you freaks,' she hissed.

Melissa put her face right up to Kelly's – she could smell the girl's breath. 'My stepdad was on to his lawyer last night and your brother is going to be taken to court for emotional abuse, breach of the Data Protection Act and loads of other things. He won't just be expelled, he'll probably go to prison too. Dad's lawyer said he had a very strong case and that judges are coming down really hard on kids sending out private naked photos now. Dylan is screwed. And it serves him right because he is an out-and-out bastard. I can't wait to hear the announcement that you two are expelled. I'm going to enjoy it. I can't wait not to see your ugly face every day. I'm going to –'

Kelly felt the blood rush to her head. She drove through the two girls, knocking them sideways, and sprinted away down the corridor. She could hear Melissa shouting something at her, but she just kept running. As she sped past the big clock in Reception it read ten twenty. Please still be there, she prayed.

Kelly didn't knock, she flung open the door to the headmaster's office and stumbled, breathless, into the room.

'Kelly?' Her mum stared at her in astonishment. Kelly saw that she had been crying.

She looked around the room. Taylor was sitting beside a big man who had his arm protectively around her. Dylan was sitting beside his mum, looking terrified.

'What is it, Kelly?' Mr Gough moved towards her.

Kelly tried to get the words out but no sound came. A wail escaped instead.

'Come and sit down,' Mr Gough said, leading her to a chair. Lucy jumped up, went over to her and knelt in front of her.

'What in the name of God is going on? We are in the middle of an important meeting,' Mr Lyons shouted. 'Who is this?'

'It's Dylan's twin sister,' Taylor said.

'What's wrong, pet?' Lucy asked, holding her daughter's hands.

Kelly caught her breath and looked at Mr Lyons. 'It was me,' she said. 'I did it.'

Everyone stared at her. There was a shocked silence.

'I sent out the photo.'

Dylan shook his head. 'Kelly, you can't take the blame for something you didn't do. I know you're trying to help, but not like this.'

Kelly began to sob. 'It really was me. When you and Mum both went to bed, I found your phone on the landing. You must have dropped it. I sent the photo out on WhatsApp.'

'Why?' Taylor's eyes were wide in disbelief. 'What did I ever do to you?'

Kelly looked at her mum. 'I was trying to help. I was trying to fix it. You were so worried Dylan was going to blow his scholarship. I thought if I could break Taylor and him up, everything would be okay.'

Lucy slowly stood up and took a step away from her daughter. 'My God, Kelly,' she whispered.

'What's going on here?' Mr Lyons demanded.

Kelly stood up, her legs were shaking but she felt calmer. 'I am so sorry, Taylor and Mr Lyons. I sent that photo out because my brother was staying out late drinking and partying and I was scared that he was going to fail his exams and get dropped from the football team. I thought if he broke up with Taylor, he'd get back on track. But he wouldn't break up with her because he's mad about her, so I did something really awful and I sent out the photo and I'm so, so sorry.'

'Jesus Christ, how could you?' Dylan said, his fists clenched on his knees. 'I can't believe you'd do that to me.'

'I'm sorrier than you'll ever know. I feel sick. I never thought the photo would get out and go viral. I'm sorry, Taylor – I never meant to hurt you. Mum, Dylan, Mr Gough, I'm sorry. I know what I did was wrong. I was just trying to fix everything, but it all spiralled out of control and I panicked and didn't know what to do.' Kelly fell back into her chair and put her hands over her face.

'Do you have any idea of the hell I've been through?' Taylor shouted at her. 'I've had perverts stalking me on Facebook and Instagram. I've had to shut down all my accounts. I've been in hell since you sent that photo. And I thought Dylan had done it. I thought he'd betrayed me. I'm sorry, babe,' she said, to Dylan.

'I'd never do that to you,' Dylan said.

Taylor came over and hugged him.

Lucy stood still, as if rooted to the spot. 'But . . . why didn't you . . . How could you . . . It's just not . . . Kelly, it's wrong.'

'I know, and I'm sorry. I hate myself.' Kelly's body was shaking. She felt as cold as ice.

Mr Gough came over and handed her a glass of water. 'We all need to take a deep breath. Kelly has bravely owned up to a mistake she made.'

'Mistake?' Mr Lyons snorted. 'A crime she committed is more like it. Taylor's been traumatized.'

Mr Gough held up his hand. 'I quite understand that Taylor has had a terrible time and I think Kelly is aware of the damage she has caused. However, she did it to protect someone she loves, and while her actions will have to be punished, her intentions were honourable.'

'I don't give a fig about her intentions,' Mr Lyons shouted. 'She humiliated Taylor, who is the innocent victim let's not forget, and she'll be sued for it.'

'I do see that,' Mr Gough said calmly. 'But Kelly is young and clearly repentant for the trouble she has caused. If you bring an action against her, it will drag the whole issue into the public arena, which is something the school is anxious to avoid.'

'I'm not going to stand back, let my daughter suffer and do nothing about it,' Mr Lyons said. 'This girl admitted she sent the photo and any court in the land will find her guilty.'

'I would be concerned that involving lawyers and the gardaí would expose these young people to a huge amount of scrutiny,' Mr Gough argued. 'The media backlash would be very hard on them all. I'm sure we can resolve the issue among ourselves.'

Taylor put her hand on her father's arm. 'It's all right, Dad,' she said. 'We should let it go. I don't want a big court case and have the whole thing brought up again and the photo being shown around and the papers talking about it. That would be even worse. I can cope with the kids in school knowing about it, but I don't want to end up on the nine o'clock news. Just leave it, okay? Now I know it wasn't Dylan, I care a lot less.'

Mr Lyons patted her hand. 'I can understand you don't want it going any further, sweetheart. But,' he said, turning to Mr Gough, 'there has to be serious disciplinary action against this girl. She can't just get a slap on the wrist.'

Lucy spoke up. 'I can promise you there will be serious repercussions for Kelly's actions at home. I am shocked and deeply ashamed.'

Kelly felt her heart ache. She knew it was silly, but she'd hoped her mother would defend her. Stupid of her to think that: Lucy always cared more about what other people thought.

Mr Gough nodded. 'I shall be suspending Kelly for three days and she shall come in an hour earlier every morning until the end of January to help the staff set up for the school day.'

'That doesn't sound like much,' Mr Lyons said, frowning at Kelly.

'I think it's fair,' Mr Gough replied.

'Leave it, Dad. Dylan didn't betray me and I'm so happy about that. I just want to forget it and move on. Come on, let's go,' Taylor said, standing up. She took her father's hand and led him from the room, flashing a wide smile at Dylan as she left.

When they were gone, there was silence.

'So,' Mr Gough said, 'that was a bit of a shock for everyone. Thank you for coming in, Ms Murphy, and I'm very glad we were able to settle things amicably. Kelly's three-day suspension will start from tomorrow. After that, I want to see her here at seven thirty sharp every morning.'

Lucy nodded. 'Absolutely. We'll comply with whatever conditions you set. I can't thank you enough, Mr Gough. You were a tremendous help in persuading Mr Lyons not to take this further. We're very grateful for the opportunity St Jude's has given us, and I'll make sure Kelly causes no more trouble in her time here.'

Mr Gough nodded. 'Kelly.' He looked into her eyes. 'What you did was very wrong, despite your reasons for doing it. It's important that you learn from this mistake. I'm afraid you'll need to be a model student from now on. Another step wrong and we'll have to take more drastic measures. But well done for owning up and taking responsibility for your actions. That is proof of a strong character. Now, if you'll excuse me, I have a meeting with the board.'

The Murphys stood in the corridor outside Mr Gough's office.

'Jesus, Kelly, why didn't you own up sooner?' Dylan said angrily. 'You caused so much trouble. You hurt Taylor and me and Mum.'

'I'm sorry,' Kelly said, as tears ran down her cheeks.

Lucy glared at her. 'I'm so disappointed in you.' She turned on her heels and walked away. Dylan followed his mother. Kelly was left alone, with her guilt and her sorrow.

44

Darren looked out of the kitchen window. Ollie was at the end of the garden digging furiously. 'What in the name of Jesus is he doing now?'

Sarah dipped a chocolate biscuit into her tea. 'Making a bomb shelter.'

Darren spun around. 'Tell me you're joking.'

'Nope. He came home from school and went straight to Billy's shed to borrow the spade. He's worried there's going to be a terrorist attack in Dublin and he wants to build a bomb shelter so we'll all be safe. Billy tried to stop him, but even he couldn't get through to him.'

'I told you he wasn't right in the head.' Shannon grabbed a biscuit from the packet and sat down opposite her mother.

'He'll be a long time digging a shelter that'll fit all of us,' Darren said.

'At least it'll keep him occupied for a few days and he isn't bothering anyone,' Sarah replied.

'He's bothering me, digging up my garden,' Darren said.

'It'll be feck-all use. Sure those mad terrorists come at you with knives and all sorts now – a rabbit hole isn't going to protect you.' Shannon reached for another biscuit.

'Leave him. He's happy and isn't a danger to himself or anyone else,' Sarah said.

'For the moment.' Shannon snorted.

Sarah put her mug of tea down. 'How is Kelly?' she asked.

'Shocking,' Shannon said. 'She's a mess.'

'Ah, God love her. Hopefully it'll settle down soon.'

Shannon glared at her mother. 'Settle down? Her mother and brother are barely speaking to her. The only one who's nice to her in that house now is Billy. Lucy keeps saying, "I'm so disappointed," and Dylan just completely ignores her. She's in bits.'

'I know, love, but it's only been a few days and what she did was wrong.' Sarah held up her hand. 'Before you jump down my throat, I know she did it because she was worried about Dylan and saw how upset her mum was, but she still did something very wrong and took her time owning up. It wasn't easy on Lucy having Dylan hate her for something she hadn't done. And poor Taylor had a tough time, too. So while Kelly's intentions were good, what she did caused an awful lot of hurt. They'll come round, but it'll take a bit of time.'

Shannon put down her half-eaten biscuit. 'She's really upset, Mum, like, really upset. Not only are her own family hating her but everyone in school does too. They all know it was her who sent the photo because that Melissa cow told them all. She's got nowhere to hide. Everyone hates her. She's on twenty-four-hour watch – it's like Guantánamo Bay in that house. And they took her phone so she can't even talk to Sean.'

'Poor Kelly. Lucy and Dylan don't hate her, they're just cross. I'll talk to Lucy again and try to smooth things over.'

Sarah had already tried talking to Lucy. But her best friend was as upset as she'd ever seen her. She couldn't believe Kelly would do something so stupid, then not own up to it straight away. She kept saying, 'How could she let me take the blame and have Dylan move out and almost get expelled?'

Sarah had pointed out that Kelly was only seventeen, had been trying to help them all and was just scared, but Lucy was too angry to see Kelly's side. Or that her own obsession with St Jude's had created a perfect storm in Kelly's head that made her think this was a good solution.

'She almost ruined everything,' Lucy had told Sarah. 'Dylan would have been expelled in shame and he'd have blamed me for ever. She left it until the very last second to own up. I just can't believe she'd behave like that. I'm so disappointed in her.'

Sarah knew Lucy would come around eventually – she loved her daughter. But in the meantime, Sarah felt for Kelly. The poor girl was already having a rotten time in school and now her home life was awful too. It was a lot of stress for a young girl. She'd told Shannon to check in with her every day. 'You can ask Kelly to tea tomorrow and she can stay the night if she likes,' Sarah said now.

Shannon rolled her eyes. 'Like Lucy's going to let her out of her sight. She's grounded until the summer. Her life is hell, Mum, literally hell. Sean called to her house yesterday because he'd heard and wanted to check she was okay. Lucy answered the door and went absolutely mental. She told him she'd have him arrested if he darkened her door again.'

'Oh, no.'

'Oh, yes. And Kelly heard the whole thing from her bedroom and now she's worried Sean'll go off with someone else, which he probably will because you can't go out with someone you never see or speak to or even text. She's like a prisoner in there.'

'If he likes her, he'll wait for her,' Sarah said.

'He's a hot teenage boy, Mum. He's hardly going to wait until she's allowed out in the summer!' Shannon said.

'Fair point,' Darren said.

'Come on now, Shannon, Lucy just said that in anger. Kelly will be out again soon, and I bet she gets her phone back next week.'

'Bet she doesn't. You need to talk to Lucy, Mum. It's not fair. Kelly's really down. It's horrible for her. And now she has to go back to school tomorrow and she's sick at the thought of it. They are going to crucify her.'

'Ever one for the drama,' Sarah said, smiling at her daughter. 'But I'll talk to Lucy.'

Later that day, Sarah called into the shop. It was empty and Lucy was behind the counter, tapping furiously on a calculator.

'Hey.'

Lucy looked up and smiled. 'Hey, there. Would you like a coffee from our fancy new machine?'

'I'd love one. So you finally got it?'

Lucy grinned. 'After the last few days of hell, I told Dad I was getting the machine and that was that. He knew not to say no. We've only had it two days and we've sold forty coffees, so I think he's happy enough.'

'Good for you.'

Sarah sat on a stool behind the counter while Lucy fiddled about making coffee. 'So, how are things?' she asked.

Lucy poured milk into a stainless-steel jug. 'Good, thanks. Dylan keeps following me around and hugging me, saying he's sorry he blamed me and left home. I have my lovely boy back, which is such a huge relief. It was just awful, Sarah. I was scared I'd lost him for good.' Lucy's eyes filled with tears. 'He was so angry. I was terrified he'd never realize it wasn't me who sent that bloody picture.'

'I know, but thankfully Kelly was brave enough to own up.'

'Brave.' Lucy frowned. 'She said nothing and let Dylan leave home and almost get expelled. I'm so angry with her, she almost destroyed everything.'

'Yes, but she did it out of concern and love.' Sarah's voice was firm. She wanted Lucy to see that Kelly had come from the right place.

'She should have talked to me, or at least to Dylan. What

she did was . . . It was so wrong and underhand, and then the lying afterwards. It's . . . Well, it reminds me of how Tom behaved. Lying and sneaking around. I worry she's going to turn out like him. I want more for Kelly. She's a good girl, but what if she has his character as well as his looks?' Lucy wiped a tear away.

Sarah took the coffee Lucy held out to her and put it on the counter. Her hand was shaking. She needed to tell Lucy about Tom. He was arriving so soon, but the whole Dylan drama had happened and now didn't seem like a good time either. 'Come on, Lucy. Don't even think that. Kelly's a really good person and a credit to you. She made a mistake.'

Lucy looked down at her coffee cup. 'I know, but she's changing, Sarah. It's not the only thing she lied about. That boy Sean came around looking for her. She's been seeing him and lying about it. So that's two huge lies. What else is she lying about? I feel like I don't know my daughter any more. She's changed. She's . . . she's . . . I don't know who she is. I'm really worried about her. I need to keep a close eye on her and make sure she doesn't turn into her father. I'm not letting her out of my sight.'

Sarah sighed. 'Kelly is a great girl. She's kind and generous, and she worries about her family and everyone around her. She's you. How can you not see that? She is exactly like you were.'

Lucy stiffened. 'Me? I would never have done something like that.'

Sarah eyeballed her friend. 'So you never lied to your parents about going away on a dirty weekend with Tom? You didn't lie about your pregnancy until you had to admit it? You never made a mistake as a teenager?'

'Well, I never . . . I mean, that's different.'

'No, it isn't. All young people make mistakes. Yes, Kelly's

was a very big one, but it wasn't done to save herself or for her own benefit. She did it to save you and Dylan. You have to give her a break, Lucy. Shannon said Kelly's desperately upset. Just try to let the anger go and look at the situation from her point of view. Will you do that?'

Lucy sighed. 'I'll try.'

'Okay, and now I've gotta fly – I've left the dinner in the oven.'

Sarah had reached the shop door when Lucy called, 'Thanks, Sarah. Only a best friend can make you see the other side of the story. Only best friends know all of each other's secrets.'

Sarah's heart sank as Tom popped into her mind. Not all of the secrets, she thought.

Later that night, when the kids were in bed and Darren was stuck into a football match on the TV, Sarah pulled out her laptop to check for messages from Tom. There was one, with his flight details, saying how excited and nervous he was.

Sarah had to stop him. Now was not a good time. Now was a disastrous time.

> Hi Tom, I'm sorry, but you have to postpone the visit. Things are not good here. There's been a lot of trouble and misunderstanding. Kelly did something pretty silly, although well intentioned, and has got into a lot of trouble. It's all sorted out now, but Lucy is still really upset and shaken. So, now is just about the worst time in the world for you to waltz back into their lives. Please just push the trip back by a month. Let this all settle down. Honestly, arriving now would be a really bad idea. I know you're excited and dying to meet the twins, but please trust me when I say do not come next week. Give them time to get over this hiccup. I'll be in touch, Sarah

45

Kelly pulled out her Kindle. It was the only piece of 'technology' she had left. She was hoping her mum would give her phone back soon. The three days at home on suspension had been awful, with Lucy not talking to her and no screens or any means of communicating with the outside world, but at the same time Kelly had been so glad not to be in school. She'd come back yesterday to find that everyone was freezing her out. No one spoke a word to her. In a way it was easier than the verbal abuse, so it wasn't too bad. At least today was Friday, just another few hours and she'd be out of there for two days.

Lucy had softened a little bit, but Sean calling over had definitely made things worse. Her mum now knew she'd been lying about that too. She'd gone mental. Kelly was sick of everything and everyone. Why couldn't they see she was only trying to help?

School and home were now a complete nightmare and she didn't even have Sean to call or text to make her feel better. She knew he'd move on to someone else. He had queues of girls waiting to go out with him. Her life was about as awful as it could get.

Kelly's tears splashed off the screen of her Kindle. She couldn't concentrate on anything these days. She couldn't sleep and was constantly exhausted.

She pulled her sandwich out of her bag and took a small bite. The cubicle door burst open. Kelly fell sideways in shock, but put her hand out quickly enough to steady herself.

'Look at this loser,' Melissa sneered, holding up her phone. 'Kelly the scholarship girl eating her lunch in the loo. Say hi, Kelly, you're live on Facebook. FYI, in this school we actually have a canteen. It's where normal people eat. Obviously someone like you, a freak, liar, shamer and loser, has to eat in here. Everyone in this school hates you, Kelly. Everyone knows what you did to my sister and they think you're scum. But look at you, Kelly, who's the loser now? You. St Jude's doesn't want lowlifes like you dragging the school down. We all hate you – even your own brother does. Why don't you do us all a favour and die?'

Alicia and Chloë tittered beside her.

Kelly stood up from the toilet and shoved Melissa out of the way. She bolted past the girls, running as fast as she could. Tears of anger, shame and humiliation streamed down her face. They had put it live on Facebook – people would see it and know she was a complete loser. Everyone would see it. Oh, God, what if Sean saw it? Kelly let out a sob.

She ran into the yard and tried to find somewhere to hide. She gulped back tears and ran towards the sports hall – she could hide behind the wall there.

'Kelly?'

Damn, it was Dylan. He was with Taylor. They were wrapped around each other. Kelly turned and ran the other way.

She heard footsteps behind her. 'Hey, Kelly.' Dylan reached out and turned her around by the shoulder. 'Jesus, what's wrong?'

Kelly couldn't control her tears. 'Your girlfriend's sister just put a live video of me eating lunch in the toilet on Facebook.'

'What?' Dylan's face darkened.

Kelly sobbed. 'Everyone in the world now knows what a

sad loser I am. It should make you happy seeing as you hate me too. Everyone hates me. I hate me.'

'Come on, Kelly, I don't hate you. I was just really pissed off with you. I'm sorry. I'll find that little bitch and sort her out.'

'Don't. You'll just make it worse.'

'I'm not letting her get away with it. But why were you –'

'What?' Kelly interrupted. 'Why was I eating my lunch in the toilet? Oh, let's see, because I have no friends. Because going to the canteen is a nightmare. I end up sitting on my own, listening to people whispering about me, laughing at me, slating me . . .'

Dylan looked at her kindly for the first time in days. 'I'm sorry, Kelly. I had no idea it was that bad.'

'It's always been bad but since . . . well, since the Taylor thing, it's much worse.'

'I'll sort it out, I promise. Leave Melissa to me. No one hurts my sister.'

Kelly began to bawl, but this time they were tears of relief. Dylan didn't hate her. The person she loved most in the world was still on her side.

Taylor came over to them. 'What's going on?'

'Your sister is bullying Kelly,' Dylan said.

'What did she do?'

Dylan filled her in.

Taylor looked at Kelly and raised an eyebrow. 'Kind of like what you did to me but not as bad because you had your clothes on.'

Kelly felt her face go bright red.

'Now you know what it feels like. It's not nice, is it?'

Kelly shook her head. 'I'm sorry, Taylor, I'm really so sorry about what happened. I swear I regret it every single day.'

Taylor sighed. 'I know, you've apologized loads of times,

but it doesn't take it away – it doesn't take away the shame of everyone looking at my boobs. I'm sorry Melissa is being a bitch, but maybe it's, like, poetic justice or something. It'll blow over. You just have to brave it out, like I did. If people think you don't care, they'll stop. Look, I'll talk to Melissa. I know she can be a bitch, but her mum is very hard on her so it's not always easy at home.'

Easy at home? Try living in my house, Kelly thought. 'Thanks, it's really nice of you.'

'Chin up, okay? You have to be ballsy.' Taylor gave her a half-smile.

'Thanks, and I'm sorry again for what I did.'

Taylor took Dylan's hand. 'Let's just move on. Come on, Dylan, let's go.'

'I'll see you later, Kelly. We can talk then,' Dylan said, as Taylor led him away.

Kelly watched her brother choose his girlfriend. She was alone again.

Shannon sat on the wall looking at her phone, her jaw slack with shock.

'Hi.'

Shannon jumped, she hadn't heard Kelly coming. She threw her phone into her school bag. 'Hi, Kelly.'

'Did you see it?' Kelly asked.

Shannon didn't want to admit it. 'No.'

'I know you did. Show me your phone.'

There was no way Shannon was going to let her see all the comments below the live Facebook stream. Thank God Kelly didn't have her phone – she'd die if she saw what people were writing. The messages were awful.

WTF? Is she insane?

What did she get a scholarship for – being a freak?

Pig
LOL, loser
Go back to where you came from scumbag
Dog
Go live in a skip

Shannon held her bag close to her chest. Kelly narrowed her eyes. 'You're supposed to be my best friend, I need to know the truth. Has everyone seen it?'

'No.'

'A lot of people?'

'Some people.'

'How many views and how many comments, Shannon?'

Shannon shrugged. How could she possibly tell her that there were three hundred views and about a hundred comments? 'Like, about twenty or so.'

Kelly bit her lip. 'It must be bad if you're lying to me.'

'Looking at it and reading messages from horrible people isn't going to make you feel better. It's a good thing you have no phone. It'll be yesterday's news tomorrow. Just try to forget about it. Come on, let's go to my house and I'll do your make-up. I got some really cool new Charlotte Tilbury eyeshadow.'

Kelly bit her raw thumbnail. 'No, thanks. I've got a splitting headache. I think I'll just go home.'

'Ah, come on, Kelly, come back with me. We'll put on some music and eat ice cream and have fun.'

Kelly picked up her bag. 'Thanks, maybe tomorrow. If Mum lets me.'

Shannon watched her friend walk towards her house. Her back was hunched, like she was a hundred-year-old woman with the troubles of the world on her shoulders. Shannon didn't know how Kelly was coping with all the crap that was being thrown at her. It was coming from every side. She was worried about her. Shannon pulled out her phone and took screen shots of all the nasty messages on Facebook. Just in case there was any trouble, she could help Kelly defend herself.

She'd call Kelly on the house phone later and check on her. House phone? It was like living in the Dark Ages.

46

It was the day of the final. Lucy was so nervous she could hardly stand still. If St Jude's won the cup it would cement Dylan's place in the school, and help put the events of the past week behind them for good.

She was on the sideline with Jenny, Sarah and Darren. Billy and Ollie stood apart, Billy telling Ollie who all the players were and what positions they played. Shannon and Kelly were a little away from them, chatting and staring at their phones.

'I see you gave Kelly back her phone,' Jenny noted.

Lucy sighed. 'She's been so unhappy and you, Sarah, Dylan and even Dad told me to give her a break, so I caved and gave it back to her. She's a good kid and I do realize that she did what she did for the right reasons. We all need to move on.'

'Good for you.' Jenny squeezed her arm. 'She still looks miserable, though. I'll try to get a chat with her later, see how she's doing.'

'How are things with you and Frank?' Darren asked. 'Has his mad ex been around to throw any more drink over you or torch the place?'

Jenny smiled. 'No – thanks for asking, though, Darren. Actually, Frank has decided to move out.'

'Why?' Darren asked.

'He said I was impossible to live with.' Jenny feigned shock.

'What tipped him over the edge?' Sarah grinned. 'The constant cleaning? The lack of food? The unwashed shirts?'

'All of those and the lack of sex, my constant "headaches" and my nagging.'

'Sounds like an average day in our house.' Darren laughed, as Sarah thumped his arm.

'Is he really going?' Lucy asked.

'Yes, big sister, he is and, yes, I am going to avoid falling for married men in the future. They are a lot less attractive when their smelly socks and jocks are all over your flat and they stink out your toilet.'

'Sounds familiar.' Sarah pinched Darren.

'So he goes tomorrow,' Jenny said, 'and I'm going to clean my place from top to bottom and luxuriate in being alone. If you don't see me for a few days, I'm just in blissful solitude!'

'Good for you,' Lucy said.

'I've realized I need to be with someone who has their own place, is completely independent and only comes over when it suits me.'

'Good luck with finding him.' Sarah laughed.

'Damien was like that,' Lucy noted.

'So why the hell did you break up with him?' Darren asked.

'I was wrong about him. He's perfect,' Jenny said.

'Call him,' Sarah urged.

'Don't be silly. It's over. I'm fine about it,' Lucy lied. She missed him and his company, the sex and the attention.

'Sssh, you lot, no more chat. The match is about to start. We need to concentrate,' Billy said.

Lucy crossed her fingers and the whistle blew. There was a big crowd at the match: St Jude's were playing the favourites, Celtic United. They were a very strong club.

Dylan bounced up and down on his toes and took off with the ball, but he was tackled by a big defender. The ball whizzed past as each team defended and attacked in equal measure. There was nothing in it: the teams were evenly matched.

Dylan struck the ball well, but the goalie saved it. A minute later, the striker on the other team belted a ball towards the St Jude's goal, but it hit the crossbar. On it went, up and down, until half-time.

'Jesus, my heart,' Billy said. 'This is some game.'

Lucy felt it too – the tension was unbelievable. Beside her, Sarah was taking photos and videos.

'Dylan's playing brilliantly – he's giving it everything,' Darren said. 'You can't ask for more than that.'

The second half was the same, and it was still nil–all with three minutes to go. Lucy could see Dylan was beginning to tire – he'd run his heart out. He looked at her. She pointed to his boots. He grinned.

The St Jude winger ran up and crossed a high ball in to Dylan. It was too high. Dylan began to run backwards to try to catch the ball as it came down. Lucy watched him as he flung himself into the air as high as he could and just managed to connect the top of his head with the ball. It sailed over the goalie's head and into the net.

The place erupted. Dylan's teammates all piled on top of him. One–nil and two minutes to go. Those two minutes seemed an eternity, but they got through it, defended well and came out winners.

People came over to hug Lucy and pat her on the back. Everyone was talking about the striker who had saved the day. Dylan was the hero of St Jude's, just like Lucy had dreamt he would be. She wanted to scream and jump and punch the air. He's my son, she wanted to shout. The boy I raised alone, a hero.

Lucy was surrounded and basking in the praise of all the parents, past pupils and students when she saw him. He was standing talking to Mr Gough.

Her heart stopped and everything went really still. Gabriel Harrington-Black. Lucy began to shake. He looked the same. Older, greyer, but the same arrogant face. The same expensive navy coat. The same loud voice.

Everything around her seemed to quieten and she could hear his voice: '. . . Marvellous footballer. Is that the scholarship boy?'

Mr Gough nodded. 'Yes, Dylan Murphy, a credit to the school and, indeed, his mother. She's a single parent, you know, not easy.'

Lucy's feet began to move towards them. She felt out of her body, as if she was watching it all from above. She stopped in front of the two men. Mr Gough shook her hand enthusiastically. 'What a wonderful performance. Dylan was incredible. I'm so proud of him, as I'm sure you are.'

Lucy was amazed at how calm her voice sounded when her insides were twisting and churning. 'Yes, I am, very proud of him.'

Mr Gough turned to Gabriel. 'Ms Murphy, this is Gabriel Harrington-Black, a former pupil of St Jude's and indeed one of the board members who signed off on the scholarship for Dylan. He was just saying what an incredible boy he is, a great addition to the school.'

Lucy smiled and looked directly at Gabriel. 'Oh, I know Gabriel. We met a long time ago, almost eighteen years ago, if memory serves me correctly. I was at university with his son, Tom.'

Lucy watched with glee as Gabriel's face changed. Slowly he realized who she was. As he began to put the pieces of the jigsaw together, his eyes got wider and his mouth fell open.

'Mr Gough,' a parent called, and the headmaster left them alone.

'You,' Gabriel spluttered.

'Yes, me. Lucy Murphy. Mother of the incredible Dylan Murphy. The boy everyone in St Jude's is hailing as a hero.'

'But how . . . I don't . . .'

'What? You never realized that this boy was your grandson? Why would you? You refused to look at him when you kicked me out of your house all those years ago. Well, it looks like Lucy Murphy, the slut, tart and hussy, turned out to be a pretty good mother after all. Pity you'll never get to know your grandson. You'd like him – he's pretty wonderful, and so is his twin sister. But only grandparents who acknowledge their grandchildren and don't treat them like filth on their shoe get the pleasure of knowing them. You'll never be able to boast about your talented grandson at the bar with your friends because you rejected him and you gave up the right even to look at him. You stupid, stupid man.'

'Mum.'

Lucy turned to see Kelly waving at her.

Gabriel gasped. 'My God, she's –'

'The image of her father? Yes, I know. Pity he'll never get to see her. That's what happens when you abandon your children and run away to America, like a spineless rat. Well, I'm off to celebrate with my hero son. You have two incredible grandchildren and you will never know them. And you can tell Tom they never missed having a dad because their "slut" of a mother turned out to be pretty damn good. Goodbye.'

Lucy turned on her heels and walked over to her children. She'd waited so long for that moment and it had felt so good.

'Come on,' she called to her family. 'Let's go and celebrate!'

47

Kelly opened the door of the storage cupboard and peered out. No one on the corridor. She wrapped up her uneaten sandwich and stepped out. At least she was able to be at peace in there during lunchtime. No doubt Melissa would find her new hiding place soon enough, but for now it was a safe haven.

The weekend had been good. Her mum had been in a great mood after Dylan and the team had won the cup, so she was talking normally to her again, smiling and laughing. Kelly was so glad the photo thing seemed to be over, but it was still going to be a long week in school. At least they got their Christmas holidays on Thursday – she was living for that. She could spend time with Shannon and try to meet up with Sean – get her life back. Four more days and she would be safe from the hell of school, and maybe by the time they came back after the holidays the whole Taylor thing would have been forgotten.

As she walked back to class she heard people nudging and whispering. She was used to it – it happened all the time, especially now. The entire school knew who she was and what she'd done. She ignored them and kept her head down.

When she got to her desk, William asked her if she'd 'sort him out'.

'What?' Kelly said.

'Oh, come on, don't play Miss Innocent with me. I saw the video. You're good, Kelly. A real pro.'

'What the hell are you talking about? What video?'

'Denial, okay, I get it. You don't want to talk about it in school. Why don't I call you later?' Brendan reached out and squeezed her bum.

'Sod off.' Kelly pushed him away.

She turned to sit down and saw Jonathan pointing to his crotch, mouthing, 'Me, please.'

What the hell?

Melissa strode into the classroom and sat down at her desk. 'Some girls are just complete whores,' she announced loudly.

'Slut,' Chloë hissed.

'BJQ.' Greg tried to high-five Kelly. All the guys cracked up.

'Nice video, really classy!' Nina said.

'I don't know what you're talking about,' Kelly said.

Mr Harrow came in and the whispers stopped. Kelly was sweating. What was going on? She asked to be excused and took her phone to the cloakroom.

When she opened it, there was a text from Shannon. *OMG, are you ok? WTF? Was it Melissa? Looks like fake account. Call me.*

Kelly's hands were shaking. She opened her Facebook account. There was a video of a girl giving a guy a blow job. The girl could only be seen from behind. She looked like Kelly.

Kelly gasped. *No, no, no, no, no.* She had to delete this. The video, which was linked to her Facebook page, had come from a blank Facebook page with the title 'Exposing whores'. Underneath the video on Kelly's page there were hundreds of messages from guys and girls. Kelly's phone was beeping and flashing. Messages were flooding in on Facebook.

Everyone was looking at 'Kelly' giving head to a guy online. Girls called her whore and bitch and slut. Guys asked her to call them – I want some, you're hot, come to our school, my place, I like slutty girls – and then BJQ. BLOW JOB QUEEN.

Kelly felt a tsunami of emotions crash over her. She leant against the cold tiled wall and wept. She was a joke, a laughing stock, charity case, slut shamer, and now a whore. This would go on and on. It would never, ever end. Everyone would think it was her in the video, no matter how much she denied it. She was now known all over the city as a whore. Kelly Murphy BJQ.

Kelly dragged herself up and ran out of the toilets, out of the building, out of the school gate. She had to get away from St Jude's and all the haters. She couldn't take it any more.

She pulled out her phone to call Shannon, see if she could meet her, when her phone beeped. Sean! She'd been texting him for two days but hadn't heard anything back. Thank God, something good.

Her eyes scanned the message: *Hey Kelly, really sorry to do this over text but I know you can't talk with your psycho mother stalking you. I got your messages and I've been thinking, it's just not going to work out. We're never going to be able to see each other properly and all the hiding and lying is doing my head in. Besides, your mother made it clear I'm never going to be welcome, so it's best we just leave it and move on. See you around, if you ever get out of prison! S x*

Kelly stared at the words. They began to blur as her tears fell onto the screen. Sean was breaking up with her. It was over.

She crossed the road, opened her backpack and pulled the Christmas present she'd bought for him out of her bag. She dropped it into the bin. The gold paper shone brightly among the banana peel and empty coffee cups. The little gold bow fell sideways into a half-eaten sandwich. Tears flowed out of her, like a river bursting its banks. She sobbed as her heart shattered into little pieces.

48

When Lucy got home the house was empty. She popped her head into the shop. It was quiet. Billy was drinking coffee and reading the newspaper.

'How was the naming ceremony?' he asked.

'Good, thanks, they're a lovely family. The baby was as good as gold throughout, which is rare. They were all delighted with themselves and even tipped me fifty extra euros. Are Dylan and Kelly not home yet?'

'Dylan's in the shower, I think. I haven't seen Kelly.'

'Okay. I'll have a coffee.' Lucy went to make herself a latte.

'Dylan told me he's going out to see Taylor this evening, just to forewarn you.'

'I'll talk to him,' Lucy said. 'As long as he's home by ten I don't mind.'

'I wish I'd seen that Gabriel's face when he realized who Dylan was,' Billy said, for the millionth time. 'I just wish you'd waited until I was there to sock it to him.'

'I had to take my opportunity, Dad. I'd waited years for it.'

'God, it must have felt good.'

'It did,' Lucy said. But the truth was, although it had felt wonderful to meet Gabriel and see his shocked face, when the euphoria of the confrontation had worn off, Lucy had felt kind of flat. She'd spent so much of her life full of rage with him and Tom and had waited so long to say those words to Gabriel that now it was all over she felt deflated. Like a popped balloon.

It was strange. She'd thought she'd be on a high for months, but it was just a moment, a good moment, but a moment that had now passed.

She still felt angry and she still resented and hated him, but the sting had gone out of it. The anger didn't well up in her like it used to. Gabriel was an old man now. He wasn't frightening or intimidating any more, just kind of pathetic.

It was his loss and her gain. If Gabriel hadn't been such a bastard, she'd probably have had the abortion. But because he'd been so awful, she'd changed her mind, and look at what she'd got. Instead of feeling triumphant, Lucy just felt really grateful to have the twins. Seeing Gabriel again had brought home to her that the decision she'd made had been the right one.

'Probably a good thing I didn't see him,' Billy muttered. 'I'd have punched his smug face for sure.'

Lucy smiled. 'Well, then, I'm glad you didn't spot him. I don't need you punching a board member in front of the headmaster. He thinks we're crazy enough. I've had enough drama in the last week to last me a lifetime.'

Lucy's phone buzzed. It was Sarah, the third message that day. She needed to talk to Lucy: it was nothing urgent and nothing was wrong, she just wanted a quick chat. Lucy took her coffee into the kitchen and put her phone on the table to remind her to call Sarah back.

She put her feet up on the opposite chair and sipped her hot coffee – bliss.

The front door opened and she heard slow footsteps down the hall. Kelly came into the room.

'There you are. I was about to send out a search party. I've just come from a gorgeous naming ceremony. It reminded me of your christening, actually. What would you like for dinner? I can make you spaghetti carbonara, if you like.'

'No, thanks.'

'Are you sure?'

'I don't feel very well.'

Lucy glanced up. 'You do look a bit pale. Let me get the thermometer and see if you have a temperature.'

'No, it's fine,' Kelly said.

Dylan came down the stairs and into the room. 'I'm off.'

Lucy pursed her lips. 'Okay, love, but remember it's a school night,' she said. 'What time will you be back at?'

'Mum,' Dylan said firmly. 'I'm not going to get drunk. I'm going over to meet Taylor and take her to a pizza place near her house. That's all. I'll be home after that. I won't be late. Chill out, you can trust me. Okay?'

'Fine, but be home no later than ten thirty. Do you need any money?'

'If you had a twenty, that would be great.'

'Okay,' Lucy said. 'Give me a sec. My bag is in the shop.'

She went through the door and Dylan looked at Kelly. 'You okay after today?' he said.

'What do you mean?' she asked.

'I saw that video,' he said, looking uncomfortable. 'You're still getting a bit of slagging, are you?'

Kelly couldn't believe he was so blind. A bit of slagging? Had he really no idea how bad it was? 'It's horrible, Dylan,' she said. 'The messages are vicious.'

His phone buzzed and he glanced down. 'It'll be grand,' he said. 'Ignore it. They just want to get a reaction out of you. Holidays are nearly here. It'll be yesterday's news, they'll leave you alone.'

'No, they won't,' Kelly said, struggling to hold back tears. 'They really hate me. All of them.' He didn't get it – no one did. She was in hell.

Lucy came back. 'Here you go, love. Enjoy yourself.'

'Thanks, Mum. See you later.' He turned to Kelly. 'You'll

be fine.' He zipped up his jacket and headed for the front door.

'Have a good time, but not too good,' Lucy called out. Sighing happily, she said, 'Isn't he just great?'

Kelly said nothing but moved towards the stairs. Her phone vibrated as she went.

'Oh, hang on, Kelly. I never took your temperature.'

'It's fine, Mum. I just have a headache. I'm going to have a bath and an early night.'

'I'll check in on you later. I'll make some dinner for Granddad now. If you change your mind let me know and I'll make something for you.'

Kelly silently left the room and walked up the stairs.

49

Shannon pushed her dinner around her plate.

'What's wrong with you, love? Not hungry?' Sarah asked.

'Shannon not hungry? That's hilarious, she never stops shoving food down her cake-hole.' Ollie sniggered.

'Shut up, you twat. At least I didn't get sent home from school for trying to barbecue snails with a lighter.'

'Let's all be nice to each other for a change,' Sarah pleaded.

Shannon pushed her dinner away. 'I can't eat.'

'What's up?' Darren asked.

Shannon looked around the table. She couldn't say it in front of Ollie and she was too embarrassed to say it in front of her dad. She looked at her mum. 'Can I talk to you for a minute in private?'

'Oh, Jesus.' Sarah's hand flew to her heart.

Shannon paused, then realized. 'For God's sake, I'm not pregnant.'

'Pregnant, you? Sure who'd ride you?' Ollie said.

'Loads of guys, actually,' Shannon hissed.

'For the love of God, I'm trying to eat my dinner,' Darren huffed.

'Come on.' Sarah pulled Shannon out and they sat down in the lounge. 'What's going on?'

Shannon tried to get the words out. 'It's Kelly. I'm worried about her. There was this video. It's . . . well, it's kind of a porn video and the girl in it is kind of, well, doing stuff, and she looks like Kelly, but obviously it isn't Kelly, and anyway it's gone viral and zillions of people are commenting and being horrible and she won't answer her phone.'

Sarah nodded. 'Did you speak to her at all today?'

Shannon shook her head and tears began to roll down her face. 'I've tried calling and texting all afternoon. I went into the shop earlier but Billy said she wasn't home. I'm really worried, Mum. She's having such a horrible time and she's been really low since the Taylor thing, and then I heard from Mandy who heard from Peter who heard from Jason that Sean broke up with Kelly today. I'm . . . I think she might do something stupid.'

Sarah stared at her. 'You mean hurt herself?'

Shannon nodded. 'Maybe. I mean, it's just too much, Mum.'

Sarah stood up and hugged her daughter. 'I'll run over to Lucy's now and see if she's there. You keep trying her phone. Call Dylan and see if he's spoken to her today.'

'I'm coming with you,' Shannon said.

Sarah and Shannon sprinted down the road to the shop. They ran in. Billy was behind the counter.

'What's wrong?'

'Is Kelly here?'

'Yes. She came home about forty minutes ago, said she wasn't feeling well.'

'Oh, good,' Sarah said, catching her breath.

'I'm going to check on her.' Shannon ran through the shop and into the kitchen.

Lucy was setting the table for dinner.

'I'm just checking on Kelly.'

'She's in the bath. She said she didn't feel too good so she didn't want anything to eat.'

Shannon ran upstairs and knocked on the bathroom door. 'Kelly? It's me. Are you okay?'

Silence.

'Kelly, please, let me in. I know you must be feeling crap, but we'll work it out. Just let me in so we can talk.'

Silence.

Shannon began to panic. 'Kelly!' She raised her voice. 'Come on, just tell me you're okay in there and I'll go away.'

Silence.

'Please, Kelly, you're freaking me out now! Tell me to go away – just speak to me! Say something!'

Silence.

Shannon rattled the door handle. 'If you don't speak to me, I'm going to have to get your mum and break the door down. Kelly, come on.'

Silence.

Shannon felt her blood run cold. 'Lucy!' she screamed. 'Mum! Come quick!'

Lucy and Sarah came running up the stairs.

'What's wrong?'

Shannon was crying. 'Break the door down – she's not okay. Please, I'm really scared. Break it down.'

'Shannon, love, calm down.' Lucy wriggled the door handle. 'Kelly, it's Mum. Are you all right in there?'

Silence.

'Kelly?'

Shannon grabbed Lucy's arm. 'We have to break the bloody door down. Something terrible happened at school – she's not okay.'

Lucy's face drained of colour. 'What happened?'

'It doesn't matter now. We just have to get in. Now. Please.'

'What's going on?' Lucy was beginning to panic.

'Lucy, just get the fucking door open,' Sarah shouted.

Lucy looked shocked. 'Okay.' She raced downstairs and called for Billy. Shannon tried to shoulder the door open, but just ended up hurting herself.

Billy and Lucy came up with a wrench from the shed. 'What's going –'

'Just do it!' Shannon shouted over Billy.

Billy put the wrench into the side of the door and heaved the lock back. The door flew open.

There was a moment of silence. Then Lucy's scream split it apart. *'Kelly!'*

'Oh, Jesus,' Billy shouted, staggering against the door frame. Shannon bent double, crying and wailing. Sarah was saying something to her, but she couldn't hear it. Lucy felt as if she was under water. The voices around her were muffled, distant. It was as if all the sound had been drained out of the world and there were only the images that she couldn't even begin to comprehend.

Kelly was slumped in the bath. The water was pink. The tiles were white. The bath towel on the hook was dark blue. The colours blurred and merged. Then the pink water came into sharp focus.

'Kelly! No!' The voice came from Lucy's own mouth, but it sounded far-off and hazy. She went into the bathroom, elbowing the others out of her way. She stood swaying at the side of the bath, looking down at the blood. My God, there was so much. Then she saw where it was coming from. Blood oozed out of Kelly's wrists. Her beautiful little wrists. In the water, on the bottom of the bath, Lucy could make out something metal and sharp.

'What have you done?' she wailed. She reached into the bloody water and pulled her daughter up and into her arms, cradling her limp body. She pushed her hair back from her face. Her eyes didn't open. Kelly hung from Lucy's embrace like a rag doll. It was as if she had gone, leaving her body behind.

Sounds came back into focus. Lucy could hear Billy

making a noise that sounded like keening. Sarah was weeping. Shannon was distraught.

'Is she dead? Is she dead?' Shannon screamed over and over again. 'Oh, God, it's my fault.'

Sarah pushed Shannon towards the door. She shook Billy's arm. 'Get your phone out,' she barked at him. 'Call an ambulance.'

Billy nodded and fumbled in his pockets.

'Use Shannon's!' Sarah roared. 'Shannon! Phone! Now!'

Shaking, Shannon took out her phone and handed it to Billy. He dialled and a moment later began reciting the address.

Sarah gently loosened Lucy's grip on her daughter and placed her fingers on Kelly's neck. 'She's got a pulse,' she said.

'Is she alive? Is she, Mum?' Shannon sobbed.

'Yes, she is. She needs us to be calm now. Hand me some towels, Shannon.' Sarah barked orders and her daughter obeyed her without thinking.

Lucy wrapped Kelly in the dark blue towel and rocked her. She kissed her face, she told her she loved her, she cried and prayed. She bargained with God. 'Don't take her, God, take me, strike me down, but please not Kelly. Please . . .'

Sarah ran out of the room and came back with a pair of socks. She tied them around Kelly's wrists to stem the flow of blood.

'It's okay, Lucy,' Sarah said. 'Deep breaths. Help is on the way.'

Lucy rocked her like a baby. 'I love you, Kelly, stay with me. I'm sorry, I'm sorry, I'm so sorry. Don't leave me.'

'It's here! The ambulance is here!' Billy roared, as a blue light lit up the room in intermittent bursts. He took the stairs two at a time and flung open the front door.

Two paramedics rushed through the house, up the stairs and into the bathroom. They had to prise Kelly from Lucy's arms. Useless now, Sarah, Lucy, Shannon and Billy held each other and cried as the crew lifted Kelly gently onto a stretcher on the floor. They checked her vitals, took off the socks and applied proper bandaging.

'We need to get her there quick,' one of them said. 'Can someone pack a bag for her? Then you can all follow us.'

'No way,' Lucy said. 'No, no, no, I'm not leaving her alone.'

The paramedic tried to persuade her, but they were losing precious minutes arguing.

'Fine,' he said. 'Just the mother. Quickly now.'

Within minutes Lucy was in the back of the ambulance, gripping the side of the stretcher as they raced through the streets, siren wailing. Grief and panic seared through her. She closed her eyes and the tears that escaped burnt too. She felt like she was on fire, the pain unbearable.

'Please, please, please,' she whispered. 'Please save her. Save my beautiful Kelly.'

50

Dylan and Jenny burst through the door of the family waiting room and looked around wildly. 'Where is she?' Dylan shouted.

Lucy threw her arms around her son. He held her tight. 'Is she okay, Mum?'

Lucy was crying too much to speak. Dylan held her and began to cry too.

'They're working on her now,' Darren said. 'She's in Intensive Care. They think she's going to be all right.'

'Think?' Jenny looked at Billy.

He put his arm around her. 'We don't know much yet. We're hoping and praying. They think we got to her in time. Jesus, Jenny, if you'd seen her.' Billy covered his eyes and began to weep.

She pulled him to her. 'It's okay, Dad, she'll make it.' She looked around at the others. 'What happened?'

'She did it in the bath,' Sarah said softly. 'Cut herself. She's lost a lot of blood.'

Jenny shook her head. 'I can't believe it,' she said. 'That she could do this to herself. Why didn't she come and talk to me? To any of us? We could have fixed whatever it was.'

Dylan paced the room. 'It's my fault. She told me she was being bullied, but I didn't think it was this bad.'

'No! It's my fault,' Shannon said, sniffing. 'I knew how bad it was, but I didn't say.'

'Shannon, you saved her life,' Sarah said. 'You saved her.'

'She's right,' Lucy said.

'None of this would have happened if I'd told you how

bad things were,' Shannon sobbed. 'I begged her to tell you, Lucy, but she was too afraid to upset you or to mess up the scholarship. She was so worried about everyone else – she never put herself first. But I should have told you anyway.'

'That's so Kelly,' Jenny said. 'Always thinking about other people's feelings.'

Billy wiped his eyes with a large handkerchief. 'Poor little mite. To think she was suffering so much and we didn't see it. How did we miss it? How?'

Lucy went over to sit beside Shannon and held her hand. 'Tell me everything. All of it. Don't spare me any details. I need to know what she's been going through. I need to know what I missed.'

They all sat down and everyone looked at Shannon, waiting. Darren sat on her other side and put his arm around her as she sobbed and spluttered her way through the last few months of Kelly's life.

'. . . and then today they send this video out of a girl that looked like Kelly doing . . . well . . . doing something . . .' Shannon looked at her dad.

'Doing what?' Lucy asked.

'Just say it, love,' Billy said.

'I can't,' Shannon said.

'What was it, Shannon?' Jenny asked. 'It's okay, you're not in trouble. We need to know.'

'It was . . . she was . . . the girl in the video was . . .'

'Kicking?' Ollie asked.

'No.'

'Punching?'

'No.'

'Stabbing?'

'Shut up, Ollie,' Shannon shouted. 'She was giving a blow job.'

'Kelly?' Billy gasped.

'No! The other woman who looked like her.'

'Oh, right,' Billy said, his hand on his heart.

'Jesus Christ,' Jenny spluttered. 'That's a whole new level of vicious. Those little bitches.'

'Oh, my God, poor Kelly,' Lucy said, her face white with shock. 'I had no idea. I can't believe the things they said, the shaming and slandering . . . It's . . . it's horrific.'

'I swear to God I will kill those bitches,' Dylan said, through gritted teeth. 'I could rip them apart with my bare hands. How could they?'

Billy went over and put his arm around his grandson. 'Easy,' he said to him. 'Don't let the anger take over.'

'But I was in school with her,' Dylan said, blinking back tears. 'I should have seen it. I was right there. But I was too busy with my own stuff. Jesus, I'm so selfish. I'm –' A sob caught in his throat and he leant against Billy and wept. Lucy thought her heart would fall right out of her chest.

'It's the worst I ever heard,' Darren said, shaking his head. 'Poor Kelly.'

'I should have told you,' Shannon sobbed. 'If she dies, it's my fault.'

'STOP!' roared Ollie. 'It's not your fault, Shannon. You're a brilliant friend. Kelly always said it, "Shannon is my best friend." She's not going to die. She's an outsider like me, but that makes us strong and brave. She won't die. She'll live and she'll get better and go back and fight those bullies and stand up to them and not let them call her names and send videos and all that. Kelly's brilliant and kind and smart and she won't die.' Ollie began to cry.

Shannon leant over and hugged her brother, their two heads bent together, shoulders shaking. Sarah came over to hug her children. 'Now, now,' she whispered. 'You have to stay strong. Kelly will pull through. And she'd be so upset to hear you sitting here blaming yourselves. I know she would.'

It's not your fault, Shannon, Lucy thought. It's mine. All mine. I am to blame for this, for my daughter's despair. I did this to her. I pushed her and pushed her and I didn't listen.

Jenny put her hand on Lucy's arm. 'Don't.'

'Don't what?'

'Don't blame yourself. I can see it on your face.'

Lucy gulped back tears. 'I did this, Jenny. I forced her to go to that school. I told her to try harder when she told me she hated it. I told her to be friendlier, to make more of an effort. Oh, Jesus, I sent her into that lions' den every day. I didn't listen. I was so wrapped up in St Jude's and what it means to me. What kind of mother does that? I'm a monster, Jenny. I did this. Oh, Jesus . . . I did this to her.'

Jenny grabbed Lucy's shoulders and shook her. 'Stop it. You didn't make this happen. Those disgusting vile bitches did. We all saw Kelly was unhappy, and we all missed just how bad it was. But that doesn't mean we're uncaring. It's just that none of us could have imagined this was going on. No way.'

Lucy gripped Jenny's arm. 'She's my daughter, my flesh and blood. I saw her every day. I knew she was unhappy, but I dismissed it as settling-in issues. I never in my wildest dreams imagined she was being tormented. Every day in school must have been a living hell. What if she dies, Jenny? What if I never get to tell her how sorry I am? She can't die, Jenny, she's my life.'

Jenny threw her arms around her sister and they cried together. Dylan came over and wrapped his arms around his mum. His phone began to ring. He looked at it.

'It's Taylor,' he said.

'Don't answer it,' Lucy said.

'But, Mum, she only wants to –'

'No, I mean, don't tell her what's happened,' Lucy said, rubbing her face roughly with her hand. 'I don't want any of those bullies to be forewarned and able to get rid of evidence or come up with a story or whatever. Just not yet, Dylan. Hold off for now.'

Dylan put his phone away. Lucy reached up to touch his face. 'I love you, Dylan.'

'I know, Mum.'

'Does Kelly know I love her?'

Dylan's face crumpled. 'Yes. I just hope she knows I love her because I haven't been acting like it. She's my twin, she's part of me, and I've just been pushing her away. I thought the video was nothing, a sick joke. I told her to ignore it. Jesus, what kind of a brother am I?' He was crying again, and all Lucy could do was hold him.

They sat in silence for another half-hour. The tension in the room was suffocating. Ollie dozed off against Billy's shoulder. Eventually, the door opened and a doctor in scrubs appeared. 'I'm Dr Caffrey. Can I speak to Kelly's parents, please?'

Lucy stepped forward. 'I'm her mother.'

'Perhaps you could step outside so we can talk in private?'

'Oh, no!' Shannon cried. 'Oh, Jesus! Kelly's dead!'

Sarah grabbed her daughter by the shoulders. 'She didn't say that. Get a grip. She didn't say that.'

'We're all beside ourselves,' Lucy said. 'Please just tell us all. It's fine to talk here.'

The doctor nodded. 'Okay. The good news is that although Kelly is critical she's stable. The chances she'll fully recover are very good. She's weak and needs lots of rest. We'll be monitoring her closely in the ICU for the next twenty-four hours, at which point we hope to be able to move her to a ward. You can see her in a little while, but it's probably best to keep visitors to a minimum for the moment.'

Lucy blinked. 'So you're telling me she's going to be okay?'

The doctor smiled. 'All going well, it looks that way. The incisions were quite deep and there was significant blood loss, but you found her in good time and got her here, which made all the difference. I'm sure it's been a huge shock for all of you,' she said, looking around at their stricken faces, 'but I think she'll recover physically. It'll be the emotional wounds you're really going to have to deal with. But we can direct you towards help.' Her beeper went off and she looked at it. 'Sorry, have to go. I'll be back later to let Mum in for a visit.'

She left the room. It was like everyone exhaled at once. Kelly wasn't going to die.

Lucy walked over to Shannon and grabbed her in a tight hug. 'Thank you,' she said. 'You really did save her life. I wouldn't have gone to check on her for ages. If it wasn't for your quick thinking, Shannon . . .'

'Oh, God, don't say it,' Shannon said. 'I'm so sorry. I adore her, and I didn't help her.'

'You were her lifeline,' Lucy said. 'The rest of us failed to help her, but you didn't. You are an amazing friend, Shannon. Just amazing.'

Sarah put her arms around the two of them. 'One big family,' she said, smiling through tears.

'That's exactly what Kelly's going to need to get through this,' Jenny said. 'And we'll all be there for her. And for you and Dylan.'

Lucy knew they would, but she also knew that what lay ahead wouldn't be easy. The doctor was right: there were going to be all sorts of wounds from this, and they would take time to heal.

51

The Intensive Care Unit was very quiet. It was eleven p.m. and the night staff had come on duty. The lights were low. Sarah and her family had gone home some time ago, after it became clear that Kelly's condition was improving but they wouldn't be allowed to see her that night. Ollie and Shannon were drooping with exhaustion, so Sarah and Darren had bundled them up and taken them home.

It had been difficult to convince Jenny to leave, but eventually Lucy had persuaded her. She had an early shoot the following day, and there was nothing more she could do. It was just Lucy, Billy and Dylan left in the waiting room. Billy insisted he would stay to drive them home. None of them wanted to be anywhere else.

Lucy had drunk so much coffee, she could feel her heart racing. She couldn't face food. Billy had brought in sandwiches and chocolate bars, but she couldn't eat a thing. She just drank coffee and prayed.

The door of the waiting room opened and a nurse came in.

'Yours is a long vigil,' she said, smiling at them. 'You're Kelly's family, aren't you?'

'Yes,' Lucy said. 'Is there any news?'

'I'm Aideen, and I'll be minding Kelly for the night. She's doing well, vitals all good. She's young and strong, which helps a lot.'

'Is there any chance we could see her?' Dylan asked, stepping forward. 'Even just for a few minutes. I'd just love to . . .'

He bit his lip. 'Just to see her, touch her hand, let her know we're here.'

The nurse smiled at him. 'You've had a really bad day,' she said kindly. 'Look, let me check. Give me two minutes.' She went out and left them alone again.

'I'll let you two go in,' Billy said.

'What? Oh, no, Dad. You've waited just as long. And you adore her as much as we do.'

'I know,' Billy said. 'But they're probably doing us a favour to let us in at all at this hour. Three is a bit much. I want you two to see her. Just tell her I love her, and that I'm here.'

Lucy squeezed his hand. 'Thanks, Dad.'

'Right,' Aideen said, coming back into the room. 'I've checked and you can go in. Not for long, but we know how important it is for you to see her. Follow me, and if you can go quietly, please. Most of the patients are sleeping now.'

Lucy and Dylan walked along the quiet corridors. The bluish glow of the night lights made it feel like a dream. Lucy felt almost disoriented, as if she was in a halfway world, between real and not-real, felt like a ghost.

'Here we are,' Aideen said, pushing through a set of double doors. 'She's in here.' She turned right, walked past a nurses' station, and in through a door.

Lucy held her breath, almost afraid to see her daughter. Dylan took her hand and they went into the room together.

Kelly was lying on the bed on her back, breathing steadily. The machine beside her beeped quietly, and she was hooked up to a drip. She looked incredibly peaceful. There were two other women in the room, both sleeping. Aideen pulled the curtain around Kelly's bed and gestured to the chairs on either side of it. 'Sit down there now and let her hear your voices,' she said. 'I'll give you ten minutes, okay?'

'Thank you so very much,' Lucy said.

They approached the bed and went either side to sit down. Kelly seemed so pale and young – Lucy was afraid that if she touched her, she would disappear.

Dylan reached out and stroked her face. 'Kelly,' he whispered. 'I'm here.'

Lucy swallowed the lump in her throat as she watched him look tenderly at his sister. He brushed her hair back from her forehead, then bent to kiss the top of her head.

'I'm so sorry, Kelly,' he murmured. 'I didn't understand. I was useless to you. I wasn't there when you needed me. But I will be from now on. I promise.' He was still stroking her face. 'I'll be here properly for you, Kelly,' he said. 'Like you've been for me since the day we were born.'

A small sound came from the bed. Kelly stirred slightly, then her eyelids fluttered. Dylan and Lucy sat forwards, staring intently at her. Slowly, her eyes opened. She looked at them tiredly. Then she smiled.

'Kelly,' Lucy said, reaching to take her hand. 'Can you hear us?'

Kelly nodded slightly, as if the effort was almost too much.

'Oh, Kelly, I love you and I'm so sorry.' Lucy kissed her forehead. 'I'd better get the nurse and tell her you're awake.' She jumped up and walked quickly out onto the corridor.

Kelly whispered something. Dylan didn't catch it. He leant down, putting his ear to her lips.

'I'm sorry.'

'I'm the one that's sorry,' he said. 'We thought we'd lost you. Jesus, Kelly, I couldn't be in the world without you. You're the other half of me. I love you.'

Kelly smiled at him. 'I love you, too,' she said, and her voice was a little stronger this time.

Lucy came back through the door with Aideen at her heels.

'Well, that's a good sight,' the nurse said, as she moved quickly to check Kelly's pulse and the machine beside her. 'Kelly, you cut your wrists quite badly. But your family got you here quickly and the doctors think you'll make a full recovery. But we need you to rest and not talk too much, okay? Is there anything I can get you?'

'Water,' Kelly said.

'No problem. Be with you in a moment.' She turned to Lucy and Dylan. 'You can stay while I fetch the jug, but I'll have to ask you to leave then. She needs her rest.'

She left the room. Lucy leant over, laid her hand on Kelly's cheek and looked into her eyes. 'Oh, God, Kelly, I'm so glad you're okay. Once you're better, we can deal with anything. I love you so much, sweetheart. You're my world.'

Kelly's eyelids fluttered again. She was struggling to keep them open, but she couldn't. Her head dropped to the side and she was asleep again.

'She knows we love her, Mum,' Dylan murmured, 'and that we're here for her.'

Lucy nodded as tears slid down her cheeks. 'I just hope she can forgive me.'

52

Sarah looked up from her phone and beamed at Darren. 'Good news. They're letting Kelly out today. She's doing great, and they're happy for her to recuperate at home now.'

'Fantastic,' Darren said. 'I'm sure she can't wait to be back in her own bed. Thank God it worked out the way it did.'

Sarah nodded. 'I can't even allow myself to think of the alternative,' she said.

Darren hugged her. 'You don't have to. So don't. I wonder does Shannon know. She'll be straight over there.'

'I'll have to have a word with her. Kelly will need lots of rest. She can't camp out around there like old times.'

'I think our Shannon has grown up a lot in the last forty-eight hours,' Darren said. 'I'm sure she'll be fine about it. But she's also important for Kelly. It will do Kelly good to have time with her.'

'I need to ask you a favour,' Sarah said. 'Can you watch the kids and cover for me with Lucy for a while?'

'You're going for him, are you?' Darren asked.

'Yeah,' Sarah said. 'The timing is so crap, but what can I do, Darren? He's coming no matter what. At least if I bring him, I can try to smooth the path. A little.'

Darren kissed her. 'It's not your fault,' he said. 'And I'll stand by you, no matter what happens.'

'Thank you,' she said. 'I'm going to need all the support I can get.'

*

The airport was crowded with people coming and going. Sarah swallowed the panic rising in her throat. Had she done the right thing? Lucy would never forgive her. But she was doing this for Kelly and Dylan: she knew what it was like to have no father and believe he didn't care. She clung to that thought.

She saw him. It was easier than she'd ever imagined. He was Kelly, Kelly was him. The resemblance was so striking that it took her breath away. She waved. He rushed over to her and threw his arms around her. 'Thank you,' he muttered into her hair. 'Thank you for letting me know. How is she?'

'She's doing really well,' Sarah said. 'Out of the woods and recovering. She's on her way home now.'

'That's so good to hear,' Tom said. He looked exhausted. 'So can I see her at the house?'

Sarah bit her lip. 'I'll take you there, Tom, and I'll do my best, but don't be surprised if Lucy runs you out of the place. Your timing really isn't good. She'll hate that you're seeing her family at a low point. It's going to be tough.'

'That's all I expected,' he said. 'I'll have to take it on the chin and hope we can somehow move on from there.'

'Maybe,' Sarah said doubtfully.

'And what do we know about the circumstances?' he asked, as they walked to Sarah's car.

Sarah filled him in on the horror of the last forty-eight hours, and of the hell Kelly had been living through in the months prior to that.

'Those venomous bitches,' Tom cursed. 'Sorry, excuse my language, but how could they do that to her?'

'It's unthinkable, but kids can be incredibly cruel sometimes. Shannon has taken screen shots of everything, all the messages. She said she has lots of others from previous bullying and awful things posted. We had no idea Kelly was having such a terrible time.'

'And how's Dylan coping?' Tom asked.

'Devastated. He blames himself for not looking out for her more. Lucy blames herself for not being a better mother and Shannon blames herself for not being a better friend. Everyone's in shock and shattered.'

Tom nodded. He looked out of the window as Sarah drove away from the airport. His first time back in Ireland in almost eighteen years. It hadn't changed so much. More built up, but the same. He bit his knuckle. What would he say to her? What would he say to his little girl, his beautiful Kelly? How can you apologize for missing every second of your child's life? How do you explain why you ran away like a coward? He felt his heart tighten. He'd thought he was having a heart attack on the plane – they'd had to give him oxygen. A doctor on board said it was a panic attack and asked Tom if he had something on his mind. Tom had wanted to shout, Yes! Seventeen lost years!

They parked outside Sarah's house.

Sarah turned to him. 'Okay, here's what we'll do. I'll go in first. I've printed out your email, where you described how you didn't know and how sorry you are. It changed my mind so I'm hoping it will help now. I'll ask Lucy to read it, then tell her you're here and call you in. Okay?'

Tom nodded. He looked terrified.

Sarah gestured up the road towards Lucy's. 'When we walk into that house, both of our lives are going to change for ever. I'm going to lose my best friend and you're going to meet your children.'

Tom reached across and hugged her. 'I can never thank you enough for what you've done.'

Sarah exhaled deeply. 'It's the right thing to do and I have to cling to that. Okay,' she said, 'let's do it, or I'll lose my nerve.'

They walked down the road together, then Tom waited just out of sight of the house.

'Wish me luck,' Sarah said, and walked up the garden path.

'Does she want anything to eat?' Billy asked. 'I can make anything. Anything she likes.'

'I'm going to run into the shop and get some of those vitamin drinks she likes,' Jenny said, fussing around.

Billy was opening and closing cupboards, making a racket. 'I think we should go to the supermarket, Jenny, do a proper stock-up, so no matter what she wants, we'll have it.'

'Good idea,' Jenny said.

'Would you two please sit down and stop running about?' Lucy said. 'We're only in the door. She doesn't need anything right now. You're like headless chickens.'

'I just . . . Jesus, I don't know what to do with myself,' Jenny said. 'I want to help, but I've nothing to do.'

'She's upstairs with Shannon. Let's have a coffee while they have ten minutes together, then see if we can do anything for her.'

Billy and Jenny looked at each other, then reluctantly sat down.

'Are you doing okay?' Jenny asked her sister.

'I'm tired, still in shock, but yeah,' Lucy said. 'I was worried about that wedding I was meant to do, but the Humanist Association helped me out and found a replacement celebrant. The couple were very understanding.'

'That's good,' Jenny said, rubbing her sister's arm. 'Just put everything else out of your head now. We can even ignore Christmas. You don't need any more stress.'

*

Shortly after Sarah walked into the kitchen. 'Hi, guys,' she said. She gave Jenny a meaningful look. Jenny's hand flew to her mouth, her eyes wide. She gave a little shake of her head, and Sarah knew she was saying, 'Don't do it,' but it was too late now.

'Shannon's up with her,' Lucy said, smiling at her. 'Pour yourself a coffee and join us.'

'Lucy,' Sarah said, and the tone of her voice made Lucy look up. 'I have something I need to tell you. It's going to be difficult for you to hear, but I'm really hoping you can keep an open mind.'

Jenny reached over and took Lucy's hand.

'Oh, God, what now?' Lucy said, looking distressed.

'I need you to read this,' Sarah said, taking a sheet of paper from her bag and unfolding it. She placed it on the table in front of Lucy, who bent to read it.

As she read, Lucy began to gasp, 'No, no, no.' Then she bent her head down, right onto the table, and let out a wail, like that of an injured animal.

'Jesus Christ, what does it say?' Billy asked, jumping up in alarm.

Lucy raised her head. 'How could you, Sarah? How could you do this? He . . . he . . . I can't deal with this. He can't come back . . . He can't just turn up! What the hell are you doing to me?'

Sarah's eyes filled with tears. 'I'm sorry, Lucy. I tried to put him off, but he has a right to know them,' she said.

'He has no rights,' Lucy shouted. 'None.'

'Lucy,' Jenny pleaded, 'he's their dad. He didn't know they existed.'

'He didn't want to know!' Lucy screamed. 'You've both betrayed me, you know how much he hurt me. How could you? Now! When I'm on my knees. Now, with Kelly . . . How could you?'

'I'm sorry,' Sarah whispered. 'But there's never going to be a good time and he's here.' She walked to the front door and opened it.

'What the hell is going on?' Billy said.

Sarah came back into the kitchen with a tall man walking behind her. He stood before them, his face flushed, hands bunched together.

'Hello, Lucy,' he said.

'Who the hell is this?' Billy shouted. 'What is going on?'

'Dad,' Jenny said, holding his arm. 'This is Tom. The twins' father.'

Billy's mouth dropped open.

Lucy hadn't moved a muscle. She stared at Tom, unable to speak or move. It was surreal. Her brain couldn't take it in.

'Please,' Tom said, holding up his hands. 'I just want a chance to explain.'

'Get out of my house,' Lucy hissed. 'Go away and don't come back.'

There was a sudden movement, and before any of them realized what was happening, Billy was in front of Tom. He pulled his arm back and punched Tom across the left cheek. The sound made the three women jump. Tom fell sideways onto the floor, where he lay clutching his face. Slowly, he stood up. Billy was standing there, his breathing ragged, eyes full of tears.

'Stop!' Jenny shouted, running around to grab hold of her father.

'Well done, Dad. Now you can bugger off back to America,' Lucy shouted at Tom. 'You do not get to waltz back in here after all this time. No way. We don't want you here!'

Lucy turned to Sarah and shook a trembling finger in her face. 'As for you, you back-stabbing bitch, how could you bring him here? How could you let him come into our lives? I thought you were my friend. After everything I've been through!' Lucy began to cry.

Sarah tried to put her hand on Lucy's shoulder, but she brushed her off. 'Lucy, he didn't know they existed. He's their dad – he just wants to know them. You had a dad who loved you. I didn't and I missed it. I still miss never having had a dad who gave a damn about me. Tom wants to make amends. He's sorry.'

'Sorry!' Lucy shouted, glaring at Tom. 'Now? After abandoning us? Now he's sorry. It's too late.'

'Give him a chance to explain,' Jenny pleaded. 'He honestly didn't know about the twins.'

'How could you betray me?' Lucy said angrily. 'You're my sister. You saw what he did – you saw what I went through.' She sobbed.

'Jenny only found out recently. It was me who was in touch with Tom. If you want to blame someone, blame me,' Sarah said.

'What the hell is going on? Why is everyone shouting?' Dylan stood in the doorway between the kitchen and the shop, staring at them in confusion.

'No,' Lucy said, moving towards him.

'Dylan.' Tom's voice cracked. 'I'm –'

'Who is he?' Dylan's voice shook as he looked at Lucy, who was crying.

There was a silence, then Jenny said gently, 'He's your dad.'

Dylan recoiled in shock. 'What? I . . . how . . .'

'I'm so happy to meet you,' Tom said, walking towards him and proffering his hand.

'Get the fuck away from me.'

Tom held up his hands. 'Dylan, I know this is a huge shock to you. It is to me too. I had no idea that –'

Dylan jerked away from him and put his arm around Lucy's shoulders. 'You're not my dad. A dad is someone who shows up every day. Someone who actually gives a shit about you and doesn't run away like a coward before you're born. Piss off. I don't want anyone upsetting my mum.' His voice shook with emotion.

'Dylan, please.' Tom tried to suppress a sob. Even saying the name made him want to weep with joy. His son, his magnificent son, was standing in front of him. Tom wanted to reach out and pull him into his arms. His son.

But he knew he had to stay in control. 'Dylan, I swear to you, I do not want to upset anyone, least of all Lucy. I deeply regret leaving your mother that day. I was a coward and a fool and I hate myself for what I did. But I had no idea I had children. I didn't know you existed until recently, and when I found out . . .' Tom's voice cracked '. . . I had to come. I just had to.'

Billy stood between Dylan and Tom and eyeballed Tom. 'Listen here, sonny, you left my young daughter pregnant and heartbroken. You never came back and you never even had the decency to contact her. You deserted her and never bothered to ask what happened because you didn't care. Lucy raised those kids on her own and I couldn't be prouder of my grandkids. You don't get to come back in here and pretend it's all okay. Who the hell do you think you are to come in here now, when Lucy is on her knees with worry and stress about our Kelly? I will not have my daughter being upset by you or that prick of a father of yours. You've caused enough trouble in this family. So just get the hell out of here.'

'Please!' Tom said desperately.

'You're not my dad and I'm not your son. You mean nothing to me. These people are my family, not you,' Dylan choked out, as he looked around the room at the people who had raised him.

'Go away, Tom,' Lucy cried. 'No one wants you here. You're not welcome. Go, and you can go too, Sarah. Get out of this house. I never want to see either of you again.'

'Why the hell are you talking to my mum like that?' Shannon was standing at the door, holding Kelly, who was leaning on her friend and staring at them wide-eyed. 'What's going on?'

Beside her, Kelly was gazing at Tom. They had locked eyes.

'Oh, my God,' Kelly gasped. 'It's you, isn't it?'

Tom nodded.

'He's who?' Shannon said. Then she looked from Tom back to Kelly and back again. 'Bloody hell!' she shouted. 'You're the image of him! Are you her dad?'

'Yes, I'm her dad,' Tom said, his heart bursting with pride.

'No, no, no way,' Lucy said, rushing forward. 'Don't even look at her. Get out. Take him out, Sarah, and don't either of you ever come back. I won't let you rip my family apart.'

'Don't be mean to Mum,' Shannon said fiercely. 'She's been a great friend to you – always there for you and the twins. She's been a rock to you, Lucy, and don't you go forgetting that now.'

Lucy's face was flushed. 'But she lied to me and she betrayed me. I can't forgive that.'

'Well, try harder. Remember all the amazing things Mum has done. And by the way,' she looked at Tom, 'I think you're a total dickhead for running away.'

'I was,' Tom said. 'Really and truly. But I didn't know about the twins. My father told me Lucy had had an abortion. I had no idea he was lying. So I went away. I was a pathetic coward but I didn't know. I swear to you. To both of you,' he said, looking at Dylan. 'I wish so badly that things had been different. I've missed so much of your lives. I'm just so sorry.'

Tom began to sob. He covered his face with his hand. His shoulders shook. He sounded like a lost child.

Kelly stood up straight and took a few slow steps towards him. She reached out her hand and held his. 'Don't cry. It's okay. You're here now.'

53

'This family is going to end up on *Jeremy Kyle*,' Dylan said, as he lay down on the bed next to Kelly.

She shifted a little to make room for him.

'Everything is crazy right now,' she agreed. 'I could never have imagined any of this.'

Dylan rested his head against hers. 'I'm so glad you're here and still with me,' he said.

'Me too,' Kelly whispered.

'Can you tell me why you did it?' he asked.

Kelly stared at a little spider on the ceiling. It hurt her heart to talk about it, to think about it. She felt like she was going to have to say sorry for the rest of her life. 'I just felt trapped,' she said. 'I dreaded school every day because they were always looking for ways to humiliate me, and then when I wasn't at school it still didn't stop because my phone was always buzzing with messages. The whole class hated me, Dylan. Melissa was the ringleader, but it wasn't just her. Every post she put up got so many likes and comments. I was just a scholarship pig to them. I really tried, for Mum's sake and yours, but then there was that video, and Sean breaking up with me . . .'

'Jesus, Kelly, it must have been a nightmare,' Dylan said. 'I can't believe I didn't see it. I was so caught up in my own stuff.'

'That happens too,' Kelly said. 'I know we're twins and all, but we can't know everything each other is thinking. Life is going to get in the way.'

'I don't want it to,' he said, which made her smile because he sounded about seven years old again.

'I need to say sorry to you,' Kelly said, taking his hand. 'I hadn't planned to do it but I thought I could stop the pain. I just wanted it all to go away.' Kelly's voice shook. 'I know it was wrong and I gave everyone a terrible fright. I never meant to, honestly. I wasn't thinking straight.'

'You have nothing to be sorry for. You were in hell,' Dylan said.

She nodded. 'That's true, but my actions caused so much pain for all of you. That's what really kills me.'

'Everyone loves you, Kelly. They're just so relieved and happy that you're safe and well. All of that is over now. We're all looking at the future and how we can be better to each other.'

'What about Dad?' Kelly said.

'You mean Tom?'

'Yes,' Kelly said, smiling. 'Our father. What are you thinking now about all that? You've had a day to get over the shock. Where's your head at?'

Dylan's body tensed. 'He's nothing to me,' he said. 'I don't want to know.'

'Did you read the email?' Kelly asked.

'Yeah.'

'Well, didn't that explain it? I mean, it wasn't really his fault.'

'He never bothered to see if Mum was okay. He just left her to deal with everything – whether she had an abortion or not,' Dylan said. 'He's a selfish prick.'

'I'd like to get to know him,' Kelly said quietly.

'Well, you're a much better person than me. I don't want or need him in my life.'

'Liar,' Kelly said.

Dylan's head jerked back and he looked at her. 'What?'

'Liar,' Kelly repeated. 'I know you've missed having a dad as much as I have. There's a hole in your heart where a dad is supposed to be. You don't want to admit you need him, but you do.'

'No way,' Dylan said. 'Mum did a great job and we had Billy too. Tom can sod off back to America.'

Kelly was quiet for a moment. Then she said, 'Do you mind if I see him?'

'Of course not. It's your choice. I just want you to be happy. If that makes you happy, go for it.'

'I'm glad you don't mind,' Kelly said. 'I don't know about Mum, though. I think she's nearly having a breakdown at this stage.'

'Can you blame her?' Dylan said. 'It's been a hell of a shock. She's had a lot to deal with these past few days. She's freaking out about everything going wrong.'

'I know. But maybe things will get better now,' Kelly said. 'Maybe this is a new chapter in our lives.'

Dylan smiled at his sister. 'Good old Kelly, always hoping for the best.'

Kelly shrugged. 'I want to look forward now. I think we all need to. I've come back from the brink and I'm determined to live an honest and happy life from now on.'

Dylan squeezed her hand. 'You deserve it, sis.'

So do you, Kelly thought. So do all of us.

54

Kelly lay wrapped in blankets on the couch. Jenny stroked her forehead. 'How are you doing, sweetheart?'

'Good, thanks. I feel stronger each day.'

Jenny kissed her head. 'We're so glad to have you home. Do you need anything? Another duvet? Pillow? Tea?'

Kelly smiled. 'I'm fine, honestly. Mum's been fussing over me. I have everything I need.'

She seemed so young and frail, it was hard not to cry just looking at her. Jenny stood up to go. 'I'll let you have a little snooze.'

'Jenny?'

'Yes, love?'

'It feels like a kind of miracle that my dad turned up when I most needed him.'

Jenny smiled. 'I guess you could say that.'

'He seems really nice.'

Jenny picked up a magazine from the floor and put it on the coffee-table. 'Yes, he does.'

'Do you think Mum will let him come and visit me here? He's been texting me and I'd like to see him properly.'

'Well, it's been a shock to all of us, especially your mum. I think she just needs a little bit of time to get used to the idea that Tom is here.'

Kelly rubbed her eyes. 'Will you have a word with her? She listens to you. I don't want her to think I'm going to run off with him or anything. I'd just like to get to know him, that's all.'

Jenny stroked her cheek. 'I will, pet. I'll talk to her. But it has been a massive shock, so you might need to be patient, okay?'

Kelly nodded. Jenny went to stand up again, but Kelly reached out and took her hand. 'Jenny, I'm sorry,' she said. 'For the grief I caused. I'm really sorry.'

'Don't even think about it,' Jenny said, squeezing her hand. 'You never have to apologize for being sad and overwhelmed. I'm sorry I didn't see how bad it was.'

'But what I did . . . I shouldn't have. I should have talked to you, or someone. I didn't plan it, Jenny. I want you to know that.'

Jenny bit back tears. 'I'm really glad to hear that,' she said. 'But please, Kelly, don't ever let things get so bad again. I'm always here for you. Always. I'm Team Kelly, every step of the way.'

'I know that,' Kelly said. 'Thank you.'

Lucy was in the garden, sitting on the bench in the corner, her face up to the weak winter sun. Billy and Ollie were in the shed, banging and hammering. Whatever they were making involved a lot of noise and effort. Thankfully, Frank Sinatra singing 'Fly Me To The Moon' was drowning most of the noise.

'Penny for your thoughts?' Jenny asked, as she sat down next to her.

Lucy opened her eyes. 'I honestly don't know what my thoughts are any more.' She looked exhausted. Her skin was pale and black shadows hung under her eyes.

'It's been a crazy few days. You'll need a bit of time to process it all.'

'The important thing is that Kelly's home,' Lucy said.

'Absolutely. She said she feels a little stronger today, still wiped out, though.'

'The doctors said it'll take her weeks to get her strength back. We have to build her up – she isn't eating much.'

'She'll be okay. Kelly's a fighter, like her mother.'

'I feel like a loser, not a fighter,' Lucy said.

'Come on, stop beating yourself up.'

'I failed her, Jenny. What kind of mother doesn't see that her daughter is suicidal? I'm so ashamed of and angry with myself. I'll never forgive myself, never.'

'We all failed her, Lucy. None of us saw it.'

'But I'm her mother. I'm supposed to protect her and I didn't. I sent her into that school day after day to be bullied and humiliated. I ignored her when she told me she hated it. I forced her to go there, and all because I wanted her to be better than me. I destroyed her happiness because I was so hell bent on proving that I was the best mother in the world. What kind of person does that?'

Jenny exhaled deeply. 'The kind of person who wants the best for their kids. You did nothing wrong, Lucy. You took an opportunity and went with it. We all messed up. None of us listened to Kelly.'

'She tried to tell me, Jenny, but I didn't want to hear. I wanted her to shine in St Jude's more than for her to be happy.'

'Well, okay, your obsession with St Jude's was a little blinding, but Dylan loves it there and you presumed Kelly would settle in eventually.'

'How am I ever going to make it up to her?'

Jenny seized her opportunity. 'Kelly loves you and she knows you adore her. She's the most big-hearted person I know. I was just talking to her and she was saying she'd like to see Tom.'

Lucy groaned. 'I want him to go away. Why did he have to turn up now, in the middle of this crisis? He must think I'm a wretched person and the loser his father said I was. I certainly proved them right.'

'Stop it.' Jenny felt anger rising inside her. 'Jesus, Lucy, stop bloody obsessing about what they think. For Christ's sake, who gives a damn what Tom or Gabriel thinks? It's what Kelly and Dylan think that matters. Why do you still care? Have you not learnt anything from all this? For God's sake, let it go.'

Lucy sat back away from her. 'I just don't need Tom coming in here seeing us at our worst, and don't you dare lecture me. You lied to me and kept the secret that he was coming over. You went behind my back. You should have told me. You should have prepared me. And I can't help caring what they think of me. When someone humiliates you, treats you like dirt and makes you feel like scum, it hurts.' Lucy was crying. 'It hurts like hell.'

'I know it hurt you, but it was a long time ago and you raised two wonderful kids who love you and need you. Stop wasting your time thinking about bloody Gabriel. It's making you blind, Lucy, blind to your kids' needs. You're stuck in the past. Move on! We nearly lost Kelly. You have to stop being so hard on your kids and making them think they have to be the best and succeed all the time, not go out to parties and make mistakes like normal kids. Let them breathe. Stop micro-managing their lives. Listen to them. Listen to what they want. Kelly wants to know her dad, and if that's what she needs right now, then you're just going to bloody well have to suck it up and agree to it.'

Jenny was right. The only people whose opinion mattered about her mothering were the twins. Why had she let Gabriel and her anger towards him distract her so much? The twins were all that mattered. Their love and respect was all she should need. She had to start listening to them. Lucy's head throbbed. She'd been so foolish, spending all this time and energy being angry and stupid . . . really, really stupid.

'I just wanted to prove to them that I was a good mother. But you're right. I've wasted far too much time being angry with Tom and his rotten father. I'm such a fool. I just want everything to go back to normal.'

'There's going to be a new normal now,' Jenny said firmly. 'Whether you like it or not, Tom is here. We can't turn back the clock. You have to accept it and try to manage it. He didn't know about them, Lucy. He missed all those precious years that you had. You can't stop him seeing his kids. Don't drive a wedge between you. They have to be allowed to see him. If you try to block him, you'll hurt them and you may even lose them. This is not your decision to make. It's theirs. Stop trying to control everything. Step back and hand control to the twins. They're almost adults. Let Kelly see Tom. She wants it and she should be allowed to have whatever she wants.'

Lucy covered her face with her hands. 'It's just so hard. I'm afraid of letting him in. What if they prefer him to me? What if they choose him? Kelly should choose him – he'd probably have listened to her and protected her instead of pushing her into the lions' den every day.'

Jenny shook her head. 'Jesus, Lucy, listen to yourself. You're talking about how this affects you when the really important thing here is how it affects the twins. Look up, look around you! Those kids need to have a relationship with their dad.'

'I'm scared, Jenny. It's not easy.'

'Try harder,' Jenny said impatiently.

'You don't know what it's like! You don't have kids!' Lucy shouted. 'Don't you judge me!'

'Oh, for Christ's sake, Lucy. If you don't stop suffocating

and putting pressure on the twins, they're going to run a mile the minute they can. And that time is very close now. They're almost eighteen. Open your bloody eyes! Your daughter tried to kill herself. Something needs to change and that's *you*.'

Lucy looked as if she'd been slapped. 'How dare you say that to me? Don't you know how bad I feel?'

'There you go again,' Jenny said, throwing her hands up. 'Me, me, me. Stop talking about how bad *you* feel and start acting. Make it up to her! Let her do whatever the hell she wants, see who she wants, date who she wants, go to whatever sodding school she wants. And if she wants a career in fashion, then shut up about a bloody law degree and let her do it. Stop crying and start making real changes.'

'You don't have to be such a bitch,' Lucy cried.

'Get your head out of your arse before it's too late!' Jenny shouted. She got up and stormed off.

When Kelly opened her eyes, her mum was sitting in the armchair beside the couch. She looked like she'd been crying, but she looked like that all the time now.

'How do you feel?' Lucy asked her, for the millionth time.

'Good, thanks.'

'Ollie has something for you. Can he come in?'

'Of course.'

Lucy opened the door and called him.

'I made you this.' He held up a lopsided wooden cross.

'Oh, wow, thanks.' Kelly took it from him and turned it around in her hands.

'A big cross, how sweet of you, Ollie,' Lucy said.

'What?' He snorted. 'It's not a cross! It's a sword to fight off those bitches with. See?' He showed Kelly how to hold it. 'You can stab them with the end of it. Well, not really stab them. Billy said I couldn't make it too pointy or someone could get seriously injured, but I wanted to. I wanted to make it really spiky so you could stab those horrible girls and watch their blood gush out. Then school will be okay again because they won't be there to mess it up for you.'

'It's a wonderful present. Thanks so much, Ollie.' Kelly smiled at him.

'I want you to be safe in school, Kelly. I have kids call me names like "retard" and "special", and sometimes, if my friend Larry isn't in school, I eat my lunch in the toilet too. But I never had anyone video me and put up horrible things online. That's way worser. So I want you to be able to protect yourself.'

'I honestly think this is the best present I ever got. And if anyone is mean to you in school, please tell your mum and dad. They'll protect you, Ollie. That's what parents do.'

Lucy felt her heart twist. She hadn't protected Kelly. The pain of knowing that was excruciating.

'Well, I'll see you soon,' Ollie said. 'Billy's waiting for me, and we're going to make a big star for the top of your Christmas tree.'

'See you, Ollie, and remember, you're special in a brilliant way.'

He grinned. 'You too.'

Lucy smiled at Kelly. 'He's gas, isn't he?' she said. 'But his heart is very firmly in the right place.' She stroked her daughter's brow. 'Are you hungry?'

'Sure, I'll eat something.'

'What would you like? I'll make you anything. Anything you want, just name it.'

'Uhm, toast would be fine.'

'White? Brown? Gluten-free? Wholegrain? Sourdough?'

Kelly laughed. 'White is fine. Just one slice, thanks.'

Lucy smiled. 'Sorry. I know I'm probably driving you nuts, but I just want to look after you and help you to get your strength back.'

'I know, and I will.' She looked at her mother. 'I'm sorry, Mum. This has been a huge strain on you. Finding me like that must have been awful.'

Lucy sat on the edge of the couch. 'It was,' she said, 'but I don't think about that. I just think how glad I am that we got there in time. You have nothing to be sorry for, darling, not one tiny thing. I love you so much. You're the centre of this whole family. We'd all fall apart without you. I'm . . . I'm just so sorry for pushing you so hard that you broke.'

'I didn't break, Mum,' Kelly said. 'I know it might sound crazy, but all this has taught me that I'm stronger than I thought I was. Maybe stronger than any of you thought I was. And come on,' she said, poking Lucy playfully, 'Dylan is the centre of the family. We all know that.'

Lucy didn't smile. She took her daughter's face in her hands. 'No, Kelly, you are. You're the one who looks out for Granddad, Dylan and me. You spend your life trying to keep us all happy. You're the key to this family, the most important person by miles. Don't ever forget that. But now I want you to stop worrying about everyone else and just be a kid. Be a teenager, and let all of us look after you.'

Kelly smiled. 'That sounds good to me.'

Lucy kissed her cheek. She left the room to get her daughter some toast. It was up to Lucy to fix the damaged daughter that she had put in harm's way. She would spend the rest of her life making it up to Kelly, no matter what she had to do.

55

Lucy tossed and turned in her bed. She couldn't sleep. There was a text from Tom on her phone, which she hadn't answered, asking her to meet up with him, and Jenny's words kept ringing in her head.

If you don't stop suffocating the twins they're going to run a mile . . . Your daughter tried to kill herself. Something needs to change and that's you . . . Make it up to her, let her do whatever the hell she wants . . . Stop crying and start making real changes.

She threw off the duvet and stood up, opened the curtains and looked out at the cloudless sky. The moon shone brightly down. All of the houses were in darkness. All around her people slept. Families were in their beds. Did the parents who slept so soundly know what their children were thinking? Did they know that beside them, in the next room, a child could be contemplating killing herself? Was Lucy the only parent who had no idea what her child was suffering? The only blind fool?

What if Kelly had died? Lucy would have been responsible. One hundred per cent responsible for her daughter's death. 'Why did she do it?' people would have asked. Why? Her mother forced her to go to a posh school she hated because she wanted to impress some old bastard who'd shamed her nearly eighteen years ago. 'Is the mother insane?' people would have wondered.

Am I? Lucy thought. Jenny's words needled her and so did Damien's, from that awful night when she'd broken up with him. She pressed tears back into her eyes. Yes, I am, she thought. I'm crazy to have let this go on. I'm certifiable to have allowed Gabriel and his spineless son to continue to affect my life and the lives of my children. What have I done?

Lucy felt more lonely than she'd ever felt in her life. It was a sense of pure emptiness. She suddenly knew she needed to talk to the one person who knew her best, who was always there for her in a crisis. The person who had been with her on this journey from the day she'd done the pregnancy test.

Lucy peeped in and saw that Kelly was fast asleep. Dylan was snoring so loudly she didn't even have to look into his room. She tiptoed down the stairs, grabbed her coat and boots and headed up the road.

She went to the back of the house and threw a pebble at the bedroom window. It made her feel thirteen years old again. After the fourth pebble, the curtain was pulled back and a bleary face appeared at the window.

Darren peered down at Lucy, then his eyes went wide in shock. He yanked open the window and half whispered, half shouted, 'Jesus, Lucy, what's happened? Is everyone okay?'

Lucy held up her hands. 'Everyone's fine. I just . . . I need to talk to Sarah.'

He looked at her uncertainly. 'Look, if you're going to rip her to shreds for not telling you about Tom, can't it wait till the morning?'

Lucy shook her head. 'It's not like that, Darren. I need her advice. I just need to talk to my friend.'

He looked alarmed as she started to cry. 'Two seconds,' he called down. Then she heard him saying Sarah's name.

A few seconds later, the kitchen light flared on, then the door was unbolted and pulled open. Sarah stood there in her pyjamas, hair wild. 'Come on in,' she said quietly.

Lucy went over and looked at her friend. 'I know it's

the middle of the night, and I'm sorry, Sarah. I feel like I'm going mad.'

'It's okay,' Sarah said. 'I'll click on the kettle.'

Lucy cupped her hands around the warm mug and looked her friend in the eye. 'I need you to be honest with me. Really honest. Brutally honest.'

Sarah took a deep breath. 'Okay.'

'Jenny said some things to me today that hurt like hell.'

'What did she say?' Sarah asked.

'She said that the situation has to change, and that means I have to change. She said if I don't, I'll lose my kids. She said I have to start letting them go, trusting them to make good decisions.' Lucy looked at Sarah nervously. 'The night I broke up with Damien he said some stuff too. That I was letting Gabriel cast a shadow over my whole life and that I had to move on from it.'

'Are you asking me if I think the same thing?' Sarah said.

Lucy nodded miserably. 'If you agree with them, I'll know it's really true.'

Sarah sipped her tea. 'Yes, I do agree with them,' she said.

Lucy bent her head and began to cry softly.

'You asked me to be brutally honest,' Sarah said, 'so I'll throw in my two cents' worth. I think Jenny loves you so much that she's gone along with your decisions over the years, but I think she's always known in her heart that some of those decisions came from the wrong place. It sounds like Damien copped it too. You were dealt a hard hand, Lucy. Getting pregnant as a teenager is really tough, but you held your head high and you did it. You were lucky with the support you had. While you always acknowledge that support, you also have a tendency sometimes to talk like a victim.'

Lucy's head shot up, her mouth open to protest. Sarah

held up her hand. 'You've always described getting pregnant as this terrible thing that happened to you, that ruined all your plans, that was so hard for you. But it wasn't just you. Billy's life has been deeply affected, and Jenny's, to an extent. Some girls who get pregnant young have no help at all. You had a lot of help and support. But you've been so angry that sometimes I think you forget it wasn't just your life that was turned upside-down. You were so devastated by Tom's leaving and crushed by Gabriel that it ate you up inside. You've been angry for a long time, Lucy, and you need to let it go. You kept saying you couldn't go back to college or finish your degree, but if you'd really wanted to, you could have done. You know we would all have helped you. So, why didn't you? Why not?'

Lucy was shocked silent. She had never, ever heard Sarah speak like that before. Her voice was calm, but her words were like tiny cuts. 'Are you calling me self-pitying?' she finally managed to ask.

'At times you have been, yes,' Sarah said. 'You asked for brutal honesty, remember?'

'Jesus, I had no idea you thought about me like this.'

'I love you,' Sarah said matter-of-factly. 'You're like a sister to me, but that doesn't mean you're perfect. I'm sure if I asked you to be brutally honest about me, there'd be things you'd have to say. But right now we're dealing with a girl we all adore and who nearly lost her life. This is too serious for sugar-coating, Lucy. I'm going to be blunt.'

'I understand,' Lucy whispered. 'You're right.'

'So answer my question,' Sarah said. 'Why did you never go back to college?'

There was a long silence before Lucy raised her head again. 'I was scared,' she said quietly. 'I thought if I tried, I'd probably fail. The things Gabriel said about me, how he looked at me, they got under my skin. I couldn't stop thinking about it. I guess I started believing it. I felt like a failure, so his words just confirmed what I already thought about myself. I was terrified to go back to law and do badly. Everything that happened shattered my confidence, in myself and in life. I didn't want to prove him right.'

'You should never have let him hold that much power over you.' Sarah was upset too. 'You've allowed Gabriel to keep you from living your life.'

Lucy dragged her sleeve roughly across her face. 'I know,' she said. 'I couldn't let it go. But in a weird way, the hatred I felt for Gabriel and Tom drove me on. It kept me going on days when I wanted to curl up in a ball and cry. It kept me motivated when being a single mum felt like it was too much. I honestly thought that proving them wrong and making sure my kids succeeded was good motivation. Oh, God, I'm such an idiot. I let them control my life and my decisions. How could I be so stupid?' She groaned and began to cry again. 'I hurt Kelly. I hurt my daughter to prove a stupid point to people I hate. I'm a monster.'

'No, you're not,' Sarah said firmly. 'The Lucy I know and love is fair-minded, funny, loving and loyal. She is a wonderful friend, daughter and sister. She is the most devoted mother I've ever met. She is the heart of her family, the rock. Don't you see? You are such a beautiful person, Lucy, but this thorn in your side has been poisoning you and blinding you. But it's only a thorn. You can pull it out and throw it away. Now that you know it's there, and you can see it, you can get rid of it.'

'I have so much to change and make up for,' Lucy said, sniffing.

'You can do it, Lucy,' Sarah said. 'I think you know what your mum would say if she was here with us now.'

Lucy looked at her. 'Jesus, I'm so glad she isn't here to see this. I'd have broken her heart.'

'No, you wouldn't,' Sarah said, pushing her hair back from her forehead. 'She would be so proud of all you've done for your children, and she'd be even more proud of you sitting here admitting to your mistakes. That's way harder. But you're doing it. And you're going to make the changes. She'd tell you that life was short. Pick yourself up and start again.'

Lucy smiled weakly. 'She would,' she said. 'I miss her so much.'

'You were lucky to have two great parents,' Sarah said. 'Lucy, I really missed having a dad, it hurt like hell and my mother became so bitter. You grew up surrounded by love, which was why you were able to deal with everything life threw at you. Because of your parents' love and support, you were strong and able. Don't deprive Dylan and Kelly of a father who wants to know them and love them. You have a chance now to rise above the past, to be better than Gabriel.'

Lucy looked at her. 'Do you . . . do you think I've been like him?'

'No,' Sarah said, shaking her head. 'He's an ignorant sod who does things to hurt people. You only ever act out of good intentions. But if you allow his insults to hold any more power over you, it will affect your relationship with the twins – badly. Forget about the past, forget about hurt and revenge and proving anything to anyone. Just be yourself, trust yourself, let yourself breathe and love and live the way you want to. Stop pushing the twins and let them be who they're meant to be, not who you think they should be. If you don't, well, if you don't . . .'

'I'll lose them for ever,' Lucy said grimly. 'It hasn't been easy to hear this, but you and Jenny and Damien are right.

I'm actually exhausted from thinking about Gabriel and Tom and being fuelled by anger. It's worn me out.'

'So what are you going to do?' Sarah asked.

Lucy set her face into the determined expression Sarah knew so well. 'I'm going to think very carefully about everything you've said, and I'm going to start making some serious changes.'

'I hope I wasn't too hard on you?' Sarah asked.

'You said what I needed to hear. I came here because I trust you one hundred per cent.'

'Look, I'm sorry too. When Tom got in touch, I should have talked to you. I could never find the right time, but I should have tried harder.'

Lucy shook her head. 'It doesn't matter. I would just have gone off the deep end and ranted and raged. And I definitely wouldn't have given him a chance. I can see now why it was impossible for you to tell me about it.' She sighed deeply. 'I've made terrible mistakes, Sarah. If I'd lost Kelly, I'd have thrown myself off a bridge. But by some miracle she's still with us, which means I have a second chance.'

Sarah bit her lip, trying to stop the tears that were welling up. 'I know this has been a horrendous week for you. But you can change things and make them better for all of you. I'm here for you – we all are.'

'And if I do happen to bump into Gabriel I can always stab him with Ollie's revenge sword.' Lucy smiled.

Sarah looked at her, puzzled, and Lucy explained about Ollie's gift for Kelly.

'Oh, my God,' Sarah laughed, 'what am I raising?'

'He's absolutely wonderful,' Lucy said warmly.

'They all are,' Sarah said. 'We're doing a pretty good job, you and me. We may not ever get a mother-of-the-year award, but we're doing enough.'

Lucy couldn't see it that way, not right now. The scars on her daughter's wrists meant she could only feel sick dread at what had almost happened, and her role in it. The words of Sarah, Jenny and Damien were rolling around in her head, impossible to ignore. She knew they had all tried before, particularly Jenny, but she'd built a hard shell around her that meant nothing said could get through to her. But now it had.

She owed Damien an apology. When things calmed down, she'd call him and say she was sorry face to face. Maybe she could rebuild the bridges she'd burnt there too.

What Kelly had done had smashed through every defence Lucy had erected. Nothing would ever be the same again. She had to find the strength inside herself to make some tough changes. There was no other way forward now.

56

Lucy sat at the corner table in the hotel bar. To the right of them, a woman played traditional Christmas songs on the piano. A huge fir tree groaned under the weight of tinsel and baubles.

Lucy clenched her hands as a waiter placed their coffees on the table and a plate with two slices of chocolate cake between them. 'I told you not to order me food. I'm not hungry,' she said.

'I thought you might decide to have some. It doesn't matter.' Tom pushed the cake aside. 'I want to thank you for agreeing to meet me. I didn't hold out much hope, I can tell you.'

'It's not what I really want,' Lucy said, 'but this is where things are at and we have to deal with it.'

'I want to say a huge sorry to you,' Tom said. 'Before anything else, I'm so sorry. I was stupid and blind and too scared of my father to do what I should have done, to do the right thing. I'm really sorry about that. I pay for it every day of my life.'

Lucy thought about her own life and the effect Gabriel had had on her. In truth, she realized suddenly, she didn't have much of a leg to stand on when it came to judging Tom's behaviour. 'We've all done things we're not proud of, Tom,' she said. 'I wish you'd made different choices, but we can't rewrite the past, can we?'

'No,' he said. 'I can't change it, even though it kills me.' He looked up at her. 'But I'd like a chance to explain, if you'll listen. I know it doesn't matter in one way, but I'd love to describe what it was like from my side.'

Lucy nodded. 'I'll listen.'

'Thank you,' he said. 'I know what I did was unforgivable. I was so weak and pathetic. I let my dad bully me into abandoning you and then I didn't have the backbone to come home and fix things. I've tried to make sense of it, but the only excuse I have is that Dad was all I had. I never knew my mother and I spent my whole life craving Dad's approval and love. I know it's stupid, but he always made me feel inadequate, as if I was letting him down. I was desperate to make him proud of me and the only way I knew how to do that was to do as he told me. I hated my childhood – it was so lonely in that house. I think that's why I liked school so much, because I got to be with other kids. If I'd refused to go to New York, I knew Dad would never speak to me again and I was terrified of that.' He took a deep breath, closed his eyes for a moment, then opened them and looked at her.

'I'm so ashamed of what I did to you. I was mad about you. It hurt like hell to leave, but in the end I was too weak to choose you over him. I left you because I was scared of him. I honestly thought you'd have the abortion and move on. After going to New York and leaving you, I thought it was best to let you get on with your life. I figured you'd come out top of the class, marry some fellow genius lawyer and have a huge career. I messed everything up. I am completely to blame for all of it. I'm sorrier than I can ever say. If it's any consolation, my life has been empty and very lonely. I'm divorced and have no kids – I mean, no other kids. I hate myself for what I did. I really do, Lucy.'

Lucy took a sip of coffee, then cradled the cup in her hands. 'It does make me feel better that your life didn't turn out well. It may seem spiteful, but it does. I was twenty-one,

Tom, a young girl trying to make my way in the world, a girl with a bright future, and you destroyed that. If you'd stayed, we could have worked it out so we could both have stayed in college and, much more importantly, the kids would have known their father. I'm not saying we would have got married and lived happily ever after, but we would have muddled through, sharing custody at least. But you just walked away and never even had the balls to tell me to my face or to ask what happened. I could have died having the abortion or got an infection or changed my mind, as I did, but you never bothered to find out.

'My parents were heartbroken that I got pregnant and dropped out of college, but they supported me. If it wasn't for them, I'd have ended up on the street. You just left me and never looked back. When I saw your father to try to find you, he called me a slut and kicked me out of the house. Do you have any idea how humiliating that was? Do you have any idea how crushed I felt? How belittled and demeaned?

'Everything I wanted out of life was taken from me. I had to dig so deep to get through those first years with the twins. And then, just when I was beginning to see light at the end of the tunnel, Mum got cancer. I had to nurse her and watch her die. So while you were feeling lonely, I was being crushed under the weight of responsibility, grief and heartbreak.'

Tom rubbed his eyes. 'Lucy, I'm sorry. As I said, I thought I was doing you a favour by not contacting you. Dad told me you'd had the abortion and it all went well. I believed him. I guess I wanted to believe him. I know it sounds shallow and selfish, and it was – it is. I was a stupid kid who didn't have the balls to stand up to his tyrant of a father. And because of that you were left alone and abandoned and I missed out on my children's lives, which hurts like hell. I wish I could turn back the clock. I wish I could make it up to you and the twins somehow . . .' Tom wiped his eyes with a napkin.

Lucy knew there was nothing he could do to make up for what he had done. He'd lived with his mistake and, to be fair, he really did seem to have had a sad and empty life. Her life had been difficult, but she'd had the twins to bring her so much joy, to fill her days, her life and her heart. She had hated him for so long. But now as she looked at this thin man, weeping into a napkin, full of remorse and sorrow, she felt nothing. She kind of felt sorry for him. She thought about what Jenny had said. It wasn't about her, it was about the kids and what they wanted.

'So what do you want?' Lucy asked, even though part of her didn't want to know the answer. She took a deep breath and tried to control her emotions.

'I don't want anything,' Tom said. 'Well, I suppose I do, in that I'd like the chance to get to know the twins. If they'd like that.'

'Okay,' Lucy said. 'The only thing that matters now is the twins' happiness. Kelly wants you in her life, so you can see her whenever you like. Dylan doesn't want to see you – he's very angry. I won't have you stalking him. If he wants to talk to you, he'll do so in his own good time, but he may never want to, Tom. You have to face that fact.'

Tom looked at her gratefully. This was hard for him, Lucy could see. But it had been harder for Dylan to grow up with no dad.

'You were never in his life, never there. He has never needed you and he doesn't feel he needs you now. Maybe over time he'll soften, but if he doesn't, it's his decision. You do not get to come back here and start interfering in their lives. They will dictate if they want to see you, not me or you.'

'I totally agree,' Tom said. 'I swear I'll never push myself on them. I understand Dylan's anger – I'd have been angry if my dad was never around too. Mind you,' Tom laughed bitterly, 'I had a dad who was present and I hated him.'

'Yeah, well, you didn't get so lucky there.'

'I often wonder whether he would have been nicer if my mother hadn't died. Would she have made him let me stay and stand up to my responsibilities?'

Lucy pursed her lips. 'As a woman, I'm sure she would. Women don't run away. They stay and stick it out.'

'You've done an incredible job, Lucy. The twins are amazing. You're a wonderful mother. All credit to you.'

Lucy felt a lump building in her throat. 'I thought I was doing a good job too but now, well, I'm not so sure I'm Mother of the Year with a daughter who tried to kill herself. I failed, and failed badly.'

'Hey, this is not your fault. No one is to blame except those heartless bullies. I had no idea kids could be so cruel. It's mind-blowing to think they could hurt Kelly like that. She's so . . . she's so . . .'

'Wonderful?'

Tom smiled. 'Yes.'

'And kind and thoughtful and talented and sensitive and loving and caring and, underneath it all, thank God, she's also strong,' Lucy added.

'Like her mother. I'd like to see Kelly today, if that's okay.'

'If Kelly says it is, then it's fine with me.'

'Great. She asked if I could call over this afternoon, about four.'

'Fine.'

Lucy didn't want Tom in her house or near the kids, but if Kelly wanted to see him, she would say nothing. From now on Kelly would have whatever she wanted. Lucy had finished telling her what to do or trying to make decisions for her. She was a smart, sensible girl and she should be allowed to fly. Lucy would never clip her daughter's wings again. She'd been wrong about so many things and over-parenting was one of them.

'Just don't stay too long. She gets tired very easily. It's going to take a while to build her back up, physically and emotionally. Jesus, when I think . . . If you'd seen her . . . the blood . . .' Lucy began to cry. The image of Kelly lying in her own blood would haunt her for ever. 'How could I have missed it? I knew she wasn't mad about St Jude's, and then all the stuff with Taylor and the photo happened and we were all cross with her, but I had no idea about the bullying. I should have known. It's a mother's job to protect their kids from harm.'

'Has there been any word from the school?' Tom asked.

Lucy nodded. 'The headmaster called me and they're investigating. Poor Mr Gough is devastated too – he has a real soft spot for Kelly. I sent him all of Shannon's photos of the WhatsApps and Facebook posts. He has promised that all of the girls who were involved will be severely punished. He's very keen to keep it out of the media. I got the usual speech about "not wanting a few nasty girls destroying the reputation of the whole school". So I told him that if I wasn't satisfied with the punishments, I'd be going straight to the press. I reckon there will be quite a few empty desks at St Jude's in January. Taylor told Dylan that Melissa is already moving to a boarding school in England. Good riddance to her.'

'You do have grounds to press criminal charges,' Tom noted.

'I know,' Lucy sighed, 'but Kelly's begged me to leave it alone. She wants to put it behind her and move on. I promised I wouldn't go to the police, although I would dearly love to see those little bitches being cross-examined in a courtroom.'

'God, me too.'

'But Kelly wants it behind her, so we have to accept that. She doesn't want revenge, she wants peace. She said she wants to go back to Woodside, her old school, so I've set up a meeting with the headmistress. I'm hoping I can persuade her to take Kelly back. I know she'll be safe there with Shannon at her side. God, I owe Shannon so much. She's been a rock to Kelly.'

'She seems like a great girl and a really good friend.'

'She is, just like her mother was to me when I was at my lowest point in life.'

'Your friends are a reflection of you. I guess that's why my father has none,' Tom said.

After all these years of being the big looming shadow of her past, Lucy could now see Gabriel for what he was: a bully, who alienated everyone in his life and whose only son hated him. But, then, who was she to judge him? Gabriel had forced Tom to go to New York and Lucy had forced Kelly to go to St Jude's.

She had almost lost her daughter because she had bullied her into doing something she hadn't wanted to do. 'I'm like Gabriel,' she said, almost to herself, feeling sick to her stomach. 'I made Kelly go to that school against her will. Oh, my God, I'm just like him.' Her hand flew to her mouth.

Tom grabbed her arm. 'You're *nothing* like him. I lived with him but he never loved me or anyone else. He's incapable of love. You love Kelly so much it almost hurts to see. You adore her – you sacrificed everything for her. You have done nothing wrong. You were given an opportunity and you took it. Do not blame yourself for this. It's not your fault. You have raised a beautiful girl and I'm so proud to know her.

You're a brilliant mother, Lucy, despite all of the curve balls life threw at you. You made those kids what they are today and they are magnificent.'

'Thanks,' Lucy croaked. 'I do love them more than anything, but I have to admit my mistakes, learn from them and change. I'll never make them do anything against their will again. I thought I knew what was best for them, but I was wrong. I'll spend the rest of my life making it up to Kelly.'

Tom raised his coffee cup. 'A toast, to making up for our mistakes. May we both have happier futures, Lucy.'

That afternoon, Tom sat in a chair beside Kelly's bed. She pulled things out of the big bag he'd brought and laughed. 'Seriously, did you buy the whole shop?'

'I wasn't sure what to get, so I asked Shannon to come with me and told her to get everything and anything she thought you might like. She's a funny one that Shannon.'

'She's great – she's like my sister.'

'I can see that. She really loves you. She feels terrible that she didn't tell Lucy sooner that you were being bullied. But I told her she'd saved the day and to focus on that.'

'Good advice.' Kelly smiled.

Tom looked at her beautiful face, and then his gaze lowered to her thin arms with the bandages around the wrists. He wanted to wrap her in his arms and never let go. 'Thanks for seeing me,' he said. 'I know I can never make up seventeen lost years to you. But I want you to know I'm so sorry you had to go through such a terrible experience and I'm proud of you for trying so hard. If there's anything I can do for you, please just ask.'

Kelly twirled the sleeve of one of the Topshop tops Tom had bought around her fingers. 'There is one thing. Keep trying to talk to Dylan. He's angry and hurt, but he needs a dad, and I can see you're a nice person and that you regret leaving Mum.'

Tom reached out and gently took her hand. 'How did you get to be so wise and so wonderful? Your mum did an incredible job raising you. But I have to say, you look so like my mother, it's spooky. She was beautiful too.'

Kelly blushed. 'Do you have a photo of her?'

Tom smiled. 'I do, actually. She died when I was ten months old, so I never knew her. Her photos are my memories. I have a nice one here.' He pulled it out of his wallet.

Kelly gulped. 'Oh, my God, she's me.'

'Yes, and you're her.'

'And you.' Kelly smiled shyly. 'When I saw you in the kitchen that day, it was the first time I'd ever seen anyone who looked like me. I knew immediately you were my dad. Dylan is so like Mum and Mum is like Granddad and, well, it's nice to see where I come from.'

'You come from a long line of beautiful women. My mother was a lovely person by all accounts, just like you.'

'Oh, I'm not always lovely. Ask Mum – we fight a lot. I can be quite feisty when I want to be. I guess these last few months have just knocked my spirit a bit.' Kelly closed her eyes.

'Hey, I've stayed too long. You're tired and you need to rest.'

Kelly squeezed his hand. 'No, please don't go.'

'I'm here for as long as you want me, sweetie.'

'For ever?'

Tom caught his breath. 'If you'll have me.'

Kelly closed her eyes and went to sleep smiling.

57

Lucy sat in the hard-backed chair staring at the poster on the wall. *You can be all that you want to be. Anything is possible.* She'd always hated inspirational posters, usually with a sunset or a seascape, then some obvious caption that was supposed to blow your mind. This one seemed to be mocking her. She remembered having a similar poster in her bedroom at seventeen – 'Wish it, dream it, do it.' Back then she'd been so full of optimism and confidence.

Where had that girl gone? She'd been replaced by a woman who felt old, tired and a failure. Lucy held her handbag tightly on her lap and took a deep breath. She needed to be calm and dig deep. She felt sick. What if they refused?

'Mrs Donoghue will see you now,' the secretary said, smiling at her. She walked her to the door of the principal's office, knocked gently, then opened the door and guided Lucy inside.

'Good morning, Ms Murphy,' the principal said, standing up to shake her hand over the desk. 'Take a seat, please.'

'Thank you,' Lucy said, sitting down. 'And thank you for agreeing to see me at such short notice, Mrs Donoghue.'

'Please call me Laura,' she said. 'And I heard about Kelly. The school grapevine sends news fast. I was shocked and so sorry to hear it. Is she doing okay?'

Lucy nodded. 'Yes, very well. It was a horrendous shock to us all, but since it happened, Kelly has been able to talk about what was going on with her. I want to help her in any way I can, which is why I'm here.'

Laura nodded. 'I'm guessing you'd like her to return to Woodside to complete fifth and sixth year.'

'Yes,' Lucy said. 'That's exactly what I'm here to ask. I know it's a huge inconvenience, but I can't let her go back to St Jude's.'

'Was she unhappy there from the start?' Laura asked.

'Yes,' Lucy admitted.

'Poor Kelly. Were there warning signs? Did you notice the strain she was under?'

Lucy felt her face redden. She admired and respected the principal and she could see that Laura Donoghue was wondering how things had gone so wrong. Or, more to the point, how Lucy had got it all so wrong. She felt humiliated and stupid. It was like she had a sign over her head: 'Bad mother, shit mother, worst mother in the whole bloody world.' That was what everyone would think of her now.

'I did notice that she wasn't her usual self,' she said, 'but I didn't realize the extent of it. I thought she was just taking a little time to settle. She didn't tell me what was going on. I had no idea she was being bullied.' Lucy's voice caught. She cleared her throat. 'A lot of it happened online and I was clueless to it all. I realize that makes me sound like a really bad mother and, believe me, I feel like one. I should have been more vigilant of their social media lives, but when I checked the twins' Facebook pages they were totally innocent. I know now they were fake pages and that they had different ones where they socialized. As for WhatsApp, Kelly deleted the nasty messages – thank God Shannon took photos whenever she could.' Lucy sighed. 'I missed it, Laura. I missed my daughter's suffering and I will never forgive myself. I have to make it up to her and ensure she's safe and happy.'

'I'm a parent too,' Laura said kindly. 'I'm well aware that our children have ways and means of circumventing us. I'm not judging you, Lucy, but it is important that I understand what happened so that I can be aware of how Kelly is doing, of what might trigger her anxiety, and of how her family situation helps or hinders her. I'm sorry to be so blunt, but when a student tries to take their own life, it's a very serious situation.'

Lucy gripped the strap of her bag even tighter. She knew she had to be honest, even though it was the last thing she wanted. But it wasn't about her: it was only Kelly who mattered now.

'I understand,' she said, nodding. 'Well, as you know, I took Kelly out of Woodside because of Dylan's scholarship. That opportunity they were given meant more to me than anything else. I'm a single mother – their father left before they were born. I dropped out of college to look after them and I've spent the last two decades caught up in pushing them to do well, pushing them to live out my failed ambitions and dreams. I was so blinded that I didn't see Kelly was suffering much more than just new-school teething problems. I was so focused on my own hang-ups, I didn't see that my daughter was being pushed right to the edge by her classmates. I kept telling her to go in and do her best and get on with it. That was all she got from me. I just kept pushing her.' Her eyes filled. The shame of what she had done was acute. But somehow being honest, putting it all out there on the table, was a relief. No more lying and pretending and covering up. She was admitting to this woman that she had failed and why. How her ambition and disappointment in life had led her to put her own daughter's life in danger. It was like purging. Lucy felt as if she was shedding a layer of skin. A skin that she had used to protect her and drive her forward all these years, but a skin that had ultimately led her to be blind, stupid and reckless with her precious daughter's life.

She was removing it and stepping out of it, away from Gabriel and St Jude's and all of it.

Laura said nothing. She was watching Lucy with what seemed to be a mixture of surprise and sympathy.

'I've realized a huge amount about myself and how I parent over the last week,' Lucy said quietly. 'I've had to own up to a very difficult picture of who I am. While it's not easy to admit to these things, it's important for me to do so and move forward. I'm ready to change, to be a better mother to my children, and I'm hoping Woodside will help me to do that by letting Kelly come back and giving us both a second chance. Please, I'm begging you.'

The principal sat back in her chair. 'As a mother, I know it's horrible to have to admit to mistakes – especially when they have very bad outcomes – but I believe you when you say it's changed you. I admire your honesty.'

Lucy smiled weakly. 'It's been very hard won, and far too long in coming.'

'We all have blind spots,' Laura said. 'You shouldn't keep beating yourself up. The digital world is a huge challenge and most parents are a bit overwhelmed by it. Kelly's a great girl. I have no doubt she'll put this behind her and be back to her happy self in no time.'

Lucy gazed hopefully at her. 'So you'll take her back?'

'I'd be delighted to,' Laura said, smiling widely. 'We'll do it in baby steps, give her time to get over the incident and move on, and I'll keep a very close eye on her to make sure there's no relapse of any kind. But, yes, Woodside would be very pleased to count Kelly among its students again.'

The tears Lucy had been holding at bay slid down her cheeks. 'Thank you so much. Honestly.' She gulped. 'This means everything to me. To us. Thank you from the bottom of my heart.'

Laura stood up and held out her hand. Lucy stood up and shook it.

'I'll set the ball rolling at this end,' the principal said, 'and I'll be in touch with you very soon. I'll talk to the staff, explain things, and we'll have you and Kelly in for another chat before she starts her classes.'

Lucy left the school feeling lighter than she had in a long time. She took out her phone, meaning to text Sarah, but then she stood there staring at the screen. She fired off a text message: *Tom, I just had meeting at Woodside. They are taking Kelly back.*

It felt so odd to be involving him, but at the same time, it felt like the right thing to do.

Her phone pinged. *Am so happy to hear that news! Well done and thanks for letting me know.*

In spite of everything, Lucy felt things were starting to change for the better.

The shop was closed when she reached it, which confused her. There was a hastily scribbled sign on the door: *Closed for lunch.* Lucy looked at her watch. It was two thirty. What was Billy playing at?

She walked into the house and followed the sound of voices to the kitchen. Billy and Jenny were sitting at the table, deep in conversation. As soon as she saw Lucy, Jenny jumped to her feet and held up her hands. 'Lucy, I've been feeling terrible about all the things I said. I don't want to kick you when you're down. I'm just . . .'

Lucy strode straight across to her, and Billy leapt up in fright. 'Don't hit her!' he yelled. 'Don't fight! She didn't mean it!'

Lucy reached Jenny, and pulled her into a tight hug. 'Don't apologize,' Lucy said fiercely. 'You've saved my life. You told me the truth and I needed to hear it. It's me who's sorry. I've been so blinded by the past. I've been a complete idiot. I'm sorry to both of you,' she said, looking at Billy, who was standing stock still, his mouth open. 'I'm sorry, and I promise I'm going to change. You've both tried to say it to me over the years, and I couldn't hear you. But I'm hearing you now,' Lucy said. 'Thank you for keeping on trying to get through to me. I'm just so sorry it's taken so long.'

'Ah, now,' Billy said, coming over and hugging them both. 'That's wonderful, Lucy, my darling. Wherever Tina is, she's smiling down at us.'

'I feel like a huge, heavy cloud has been lifted and I can suddenly see clearly. And guess what? I've just come from Woodside, and they're taking Kelly back.'

'That's fantastic!' Jenny said. 'You're brilliant. She'll be so thrilled.'

Billy sniffled as he tried to hold back tears. 'I love you both like mad. You do know that, don't you?'

'Always, Dad,' Lucy said, kissing his cheek.

'It was all your mother and me ever wanted, that you two would be there for each other when we were gone.'

Jenny grinned at him. 'Well, now that Lucy's doing what I tell her, there shouldn't be a problem.'

'Hey,' Lucy said, punching her arm. 'I'm still the oldest, remember.'

Billy smiled. 'Magic,' he whispered, more to Tina than to himself.

58

Lucy placed two big red candles in the middle of the table and stood back. It was going to be a tight squeeze, but hopefully it would be a good day.

Billy came in with bottles of red wine, which he placed on the mantelpiece. 'It looks lovely, pet. You've done an amazing job. I never thought we'd be able to seat everyone in the lounge for Christmas dinner, but you did it.'

Lucy smiled. 'I want it to be perfect for Kelly.'

'It's fit for a queen.'

Ollie came in, carrying logs for the fire. 'I cut these myself with a saw! Billy let me.'

'Well done, Ollie. You're a little star.' Lucy beamed at him.

'I was there to supervise the whole time. I didn't turn my head for a millisecond.'

'Dad, we all know Ollie's safe with you,' Lucy reassured him.

'It all looks very fancy, Lucy.' Ollie admired the good china.

'Well, Christmas Day is an important day and today is very special because Kelly is home and feeling better.'

'I used to wish Kelly was my sister instead of Shannon, cos Kelly is always so nice to me. But Shannon saved Kelly's life so I think she's pretty cool.'

'She's a hero in my eyes,' Lucy said.

'Yeah, but don't tell her that. She's getting a really big head. She told Dad yesterday that she needed the full box of Milk Tray to herself because heroes need energy.'

Lucy giggled. 'What did he say?'

'He told her that she'd want to go easy on the chocolates or her arse might be too big for her superhero costume.'

They all laughed. The doorbell rang. Lucy went out to the hall to answer it.

'I know it's Christmas Day and I don't want to disturb you and I know you think I'm bad news, but I heard what happened and I just wanted to give this to Kelly.' Sean handed a beautifully wrapped gift to Lucy.

Lucy shook her head. 'No, I won't.'

'It's not drugs!' he said.

'I certainly hope not.' She smiled at him. 'I mean, no, I won't because I think you should come in and give it to Kelly yourself. She'd love to see you.'

Sean looked shocked. 'Really?'

'Yes, and I'm sorry for chasing you away before. You seem like a nice kid. But just so we're clear, if you hurt her, I will hunt you down and kill you.'

Sean grinned. 'I really like Kelly and I'd never hurt her, but it's good to know where I stand.'

'She's in the kitchen with Dylan and Jenny.' Lucy pointed to the door.

Sean went in, and Lucy watched Kelly's face light up. Sean handed her the gift. Kelly stood up and hugged him. She caught her mother's eye over his shoulder. 'Thank you,' she mouthed.

Lucy smiled and went to finish setting the table.

Two hours later Sarah, Darren, Shannon, Ollie, Billy, Jenny, Lucy and the twins were sitting at the table. Kelly kept fingering the necklace Sean had given her. It was a delicate silver chain with a K hanging from it.

Lucy went to sit down. 'You put out too many chairs,' Ollie said.

The doorbell rang. 'Who's that?' Billy asked.

'Kelly, why don't you go and see?' Lucy said.

Kelly found her dad on the doorstep, laden with gifts. 'Mum!' she squealed. 'You invited him.'

Jenny reached over and squeezed her sister's hand. 'Well done, you.'

Tom walked tentatively into the room. 'Merry Christmas,' he said.

They all greeted him, except Dylan, who said nothing. Lucy took his coat and Tom handed gifts to everyone.

'Even me?' Ollie said, looking surprised.

'I couldn't leave you out! You're the boy who made Kelly the sword. You're a very important person.'

Tom had brought bottles of wine for the adults, who all murmured their thanks.

Shannon opened her gift. It was a jacket. 'OMG, you remembered me saying I loved it when I took you shopping to get stuff for Kelly. Wow! Thank you – it's amazing.'

Ollie's was a Segway. 'This is so *coooool*!' He whooped.

'Way too generous, Tom, thanks,' Sarah said.

'I got a bit excited. I hope I haven't overdone it.'

'They're wonderful gifts, thank you.' Sarah patted his hand.

Kelly's gift was a thick silver charm bracelet with four charms – a heart, a dress, an angel and tiny sewing machine. She threw her arms around him. 'I love it.'

'What are the charms?' Shannon asked, from the other end of the table.

'A heart for . . . Well, I guess that's self-explanatory. The dress and sewing machine because your mum told me how talented you are at making clothes, and the angel is to watch over you.' Tom's voice cracked.

'It's beautiful, Tom.' Lucy touched his shoulder.

'Open yours, Dylan,' Ollie said.

'I'll leave it.' Dylan put it under his chair.

Jenny, who was sitting beside him, pulled the box out again. Dylan looked at Lucy. She nodded. 'Go ahead, love.'

He unwrapped the paper and opened the Nike box. Inside was a pair of football boots in his favourite colour, orange, and on the back, in gold lettering, his name, Dylan Murphy.

'They're the same boots Ronaldo has.' Darren whistled. 'Nice.'

'Thanks,' Dylan muttered.

'Right, Tom,' Lucy said. 'Sit there between Kelly and Sarah and we can eat.'

Everyone tucked into their food hungrily. Everyone except Kelly, who only ate a small amount of hers. Lucy watched as Tom gently encouraged her to eat more. Kelly was smiling and laughing, looking like the young girl she was supposed to be. Maybe Tom turning up was a blessing, she thought. He had lifted Kelly's spirits and made her so happy.

Dylan said little, letting the others around him chat. Lucy saw him watching Tom from under his fringe. He might pretend he didn't care, but she knew he did. He needed his dad. She'd have to encourage him to spend time with Tom.

Lucy waited for a lull in the conversation, then said, 'Dylan has a match on the twenty-seventh if you're free, Tom. You could come with me and Dad to see him play.'

There was silence at the table.

'I'd absolutely love to, if that's okay with Dylan,' Tom said, sounding nervous.

Dylan shrugged. 'Whatever.'

'I'll text you the details.'

'I'll come too,' Kelly said.

'Can I go?' Ollie asked.

'Sure I'd like to see it too,' Darren said.

'I'm free,' Jenny said.

'So we'll all go together, then,' Sarah said.

'I don't want to. Football is so boring,' Shannon complained.

'James will be playing.' Dylan smirked at her.

'Ooooh! Is he the hot one with the blond hair?' Shannon asked.

'Yep, and he's just broken up with his girlfriend.'

'I'm coming!' Shannon squeaked. 'What'll I wear, though?'

'Preferably something that covers your arse,' Darren muttered.

'Will you do my make-up?' Shannon asked Jenny.

'Jesus, Shannon, it's a football match,' Darren said, shaking his head.

'It might be a football match to you, Dad, but to me it's a potential meeting with my future husband.'

Everyone laughed.

'Ollie, will you help me with dessert?' Lucy said, when they had all finished eating.

'Really?' Ollie said. 'Sure.'

Lucy and Ollie went out to the kitchen. She poured brandy over the Christmas pudding and let Ollie light it. They walked from the kitchen into the lounge and placed the pudding in the middle of the table.

'It's a Christmas miracle,' Darren said. 'Ollie lit the cake and didn't set the house or himself on fire.'

'Shove off, Dad. I never mess up any more. I'm responsible now, aren't I, Billy?'

'You are, Ollie. You're a great lad.'

'See?' Ollie pointed at his father, knocking a glass of red wine all over Tom.

Sarah jumped up. 'Ah, Ollie.'

'You're a muppet,' Shannon shouted at him.

'So sorry, Tom.' Sarah handed him an extra napkin.

'You've been baptized, Tom,' Darren said, laughing. 'You're part of the family now, that's for sure.'

Silence.

'What I mean is –' Darren spluttered.

'Nice one, Dad,' Shannon drawled.

'It's okay, Darren.' Tom smiled at him. 'I hope, one day, to become part of this family, but I have to earn it. I know it's going to take a while for everyone to get used to me being around and I have a lot to do to make up for everything. I'm going to spend the rest of my life trying and, hopefully, some day in the future, I'll earn my children's forgiveness.'

'I hope you mean it,' Billy said.

Tom turned to face him. 'I do, Mr Murphy. I swear to you, all I want is to be a part of the twins' lives in whatever capacity they'll allow me. I'm going back to New York next week to sell my apartment and wrap up my work. I'm moving back to Dublin. This is where my children live and I want to be as near to them as I can be.'

'That's a good first step.' Billy nodded.

'Actually, I have some news too,' Lucy said.

Everyone stopped talking and looked at her.

Lucy felt really nervous. 'What I want to say is that Tom has decided to move back to Dublin and I'm glad because it'll give the twins a chance to get to know him in their own time. It'll be January soon, and I for one am making some serious New Year resolutions. First, Kelly, I promise never to mention the word "law" to you again. Be whoever and whatever you want to be. Whatever you decide, I know you'll be brilliant at what you do. Go out with Sean. He seems like a nice kid and he's clearly mad about you. Dylan, date Taylor and go to parties and have fun and enjoy being seventeen. I would still prefer if you didn't drink – but I'm not going to police you. I'm going to trust you both. You have grown up to be two wonderful people and I certainly don't take credit for it. Everyone here has helped raise you, even Tom. You have his DNA, so he is part of who you are.

'Dad, Jenny, Sarah, Darren, Shannon and Ollie, you have all been an integral part of the twins' lives. I don't thank you enough and I haven't properly acknowledged the huge part you've played in my children's lives. Thank you from the bottom of my heart. The twins turned out so well in large part because of you guys. You have stood by me through thick and thin, held me up on bad days, made me laugh on sad days, and supported me and the twins every step of the way. Most of all, in the last week you've been my rocks.

'Dylan and Kelly, I'm lucky to be your mum. I'm truly sorry for all the mistakes I've made. I promise you that I'm going to learn from them and be a better mother and person. I'm going to step back and let you fly.

'I've also decided to stop bemoaning the past and do something about it. I'm going back to college to finish my law degree. I may do nothing with it, I may fail, I may come bottom of the class, but I'm going to try to finish what I started.

'My mum always said, "Family is love and love is family," and if the last week has taught me anything, it's that that statement is so true.

'Kelly, I owe you such a huge apology. I'll never forgive myself for pushing you to go to St Jude's. I'll try to make it up to you. Please go and live your best life and be who you're supposed to be, not who I once thought you should be. I'll cheer you from the sideline, willing you on, wishing you happiness and success, but never, ever pushing you.

'I'd like to make a toast to my beautiful twins, loves of my life, who have taught me that love is not keeping your children close, it's allowing them to spread their wings. Just promise me you'll come back and visit me!'

They raised their glasses and clinked.

Kelly whispered in Lucy's ear, 'I love you, Mum, and I forgive you a thousand times over. Please forgive me for giving you such a fright.'

Lucy hugged her fragile daughter to her chest. 'I have nothing to forgive. You are perfect, Kelly Murphy, and don't ever forget it.'

'So, like, are we going to eat the flaming pudding or what?' Shannon asked.

59

The house was quiet. Sarah and Darren had taken Ollie home. Shannon was upstairs with Kelly. Dylan was in his bedroom on the phone to Taylor, and Billy had gone to the shed for a nightcap.

Lucy sat on the couch in front of the fire. Tom came into the room. 'I've just loaded the dishwasher and that should be the last of it.'

'Thanks for tidying up. I just have no energy left.'

'Not surprised after the week you've had, and the fact that you cooked a feast for all of us today.' He sat down beside her and picked up his wine glass. 'It was a perfect day. Thanks for including me. It was the best Christmas I've ever had, by miles.'

'It was lovely.'

'I can't wait for Dylan's match. I'm so keen to see him play.'

Lucy wriggled her toes, feeling the warmth of the fire sink into her feet. 'He's pretty amazing. You're in for a treat.'

Tom sighed happily. 'I still can't believe it. I'm a dad.'

'I still can't believe you're here.'

'It's all a bit surreal. Do you think Dylan liked his boots?'

'He loved them. He's just going to take a bit longer to warm to you. Give him space, Tom. Don't rush him – you'll only push him away.'

'I just want to hug him so badly.'

'Restrain yourself.' Lucy laughed. 'He'll run a mile if you do that.'

Tom smiled. 'There's something I really need to do this week.'

'What? Run Melissa over with your car?'

They both laughed.

'As tempting as that sounds, I'd rather not end up in prison after just finding my kids. No, I need to call up to my father and tell him face to face what a bastard he is.'

'Can I come?' Lucy asked.

'You'd want to?' Tom looked at her in surprise.

'Yes. I have a few things I'd like to say.'

'No time like the present. Do you want to run over there now?'

'What?' Lucy said.

'I've only had one glass today,' Tom said. 'I could drive us.'

Lucy sat up. 'You're on.'

Tom stood beside her before the imposing front door. Lucy was surprised at how calm she felt. She'd thought bad memories would rise up, but she felt no anger. Her mind was clear and she knew exactly what she wanted to say.

Tom rang the bell. They heard footsteps and then the door opened. Gabriel took a step back. 'Tom?'

'Hello, Dad.'

'When did you get back? I had no idea.' He looked at Lucy. 'What on earth is she doing here?'

'Lucy, the mother of my children and your grandchildren, is here because I invited her to come. We have a few things to say to you.'

Tom held his arm out and he and Lucy walked into the hall. An expensive artificial Christmas tree stood in the middle of the otherwise empty space. Their footsteps echoed as they walked across the marble floor. The house felt cold, Lucy thought. Cold and impersonal, like its owner.

She thought of her own home, full of people coming and going – presents, warm fires, decorations covering every surface, the kitchen groaning with food, music playing. It was by no means perfect, but it was full and alive. Full of love and friendship. This house was devoid of everything – people, warmth, life and love. It was an empty shell.

The hall didn't seem so big now, or daunting. A lot had happened since she'd stood here with her two tiny babies. She'd been so desperate, heartbroken and alone then. Now she was much stronger, happier and so lucky. Yes, she thought, I'm lucky. I'm the luckiest person in the world.

'What's all this about? I hope she's not here to cause a scene.' Gabriel crossed his arms and glared at Lucy.

'If by "she" you mean Lucy, no, she isn't,' Tom said firmly. 'I wanted to see you because I now know the truth. I was a stupid, spineless, weak fool to let you talk me into going to America rather than staying here and standing up to my responsibilities. I can't blame you for that, but I can blame you and I do blame you for not telling me the truth. How could you not tell me I had children?' Tom's voice croaked with raw emotion. 'How could you lie about my own flesh and blood? Because of you, my children grew up with no father and I had no children. Do you have any idea how that feels? *Do you?*' He was shouting.

'Calm down. I did what I thought best.'

'Best?' Tom hissed. 'Best to deny me the knowledge that I was a father to two amazing children? Who made you God? Who gave you the right to lie to me for all these years? I've missed out on so many precious moments. My children thought I didn't care. How could you? How could you do that? How do you sleep at night? You bastard.'

'How dare you speak to me like that? I'm your father. Have some respect.'

'Respect? You have to earn respect. I'll never forgive you

for this. And as for being my father, you were never a father to me. You were a bully and a dictator. I'm determined to make up for the lost years and be the best bloody father I can. And it's going to be easy because all I have to do is the exact opposite of how you parented me.'

Gabriel flushed and he shoved his finger in Tom's face. 'I gave you the best life a boy could want. How dare you come in here and insult me? I did what I thought was best. She would have dragged you down into the gutter with her. You've had an excellent career in America.'

Tom's eyes narrowed. 'I don't give a damn about my career. I care about my children and how the hell I'm going to make it up to them. I can't believe they've let me into their lives so generously. They're magnificent, and the reason they are is because they had an incredible mother.'

'Yes, well, the boy is talented enough, I suppose. Football, though, not my bag,' Gabriel said.

Tom snorted. 'God, you'll never change. Always looking down on everyone from your pedestal. How does it feel up there? Cold? Lonely? Look at you, living alone in this big house with no family or friends, a son who hates you and two grandchildren you don't even know.'

'Don't you dare come into my home and speak to me like that. I'm perfectly content, thank you very much.'

'If you are, then I pity you. Thank God my children have decided to let me try to rebuild the bridges I burnt.' Tom turned to Lucy, who was standing slightly to his left. 'Lucy has raised the twins and done the most terrific job. They're clever and talented and bright and smart. Most of all they're decent. Decent human beings with huge hearts.'

Gabriel rolled his eyes. 'Big hearts. Really, Tom, you've gone all American. Children need to be focused and disciplined to achieve success.'

Lucy stepped forward. 'Yes, I thought so too. And I pushed my children to succeed so I could prove what a good mother I was. My determination to prove you wrong, you, who called me a whore, gold-digger and unfit mother, almost ruined my daughter's life. But I have seen now that decency and a big heart is worth more than any amount of As in exams or success on the sports field. My kids are a credit to themselves. They came out into the world ready-made, full of love and life and goodness. They're not perfect, but they're pretty damn close. The sad thing is that when you threw me and my babies out of your house, you lost the right ever to know them. I feel sorry for you, Gabriel, because you don't know what you're missing.'

Gabriel took a step towards her. Lucy didn't flinch. 'I don't need your pity.'

Lucy smiled at him. 'But you have it. You're a bitter, twisted old man, and that's sad. I wish you no harm or hurt.'

'What's all this about, Tom? Why are you here? I don't want this awful woman in my house.'

'Don't you –'

Lucy held her hand up to stop Tom. 'I came here today for closure. It might be a bit American for you, but it's important to me. When you kicked me out seventeen years ago, I was utterly devastated. But I survived and I made it and so did my kids. I've come here to tell you that you were wrong about me. I'm not a gold-digger or a whore. I'm just Lucy Murphy, mother, daughter, sister, friend and survivor.'

Lucy looked at Tom and nodded.

'We're leaving now,' Tom said. 'This is the last time I'll ever speak to you, Dad. You stole seventeen years from me and I will never forgive you. You've lost your only son and the chance to get to know your two grandchildren. Don't try to contact me. You were never a father and you will never be one. It's up to me to change that cycle and be the best father possible.'

Gabriel stared after them in silence as they left, then slammed the door behind them. They climbed into Tom's car. Lucy leant her head back on the seat.

'You were amazing,' Tom said.

'Yes,' she said. 'I kind of was.'

They both laughed.

When they reached Lucy's house, Tom switched off the engine and turned to her. 'I've found a three-bedroom house near where you are. I was thinking of buying it. The twins could have a room each, if they ever wanted to stay over, not that I would push it, just if they wanted to and if you were happy for them to do that. How would you feel about it? Too close? Too much? Too soon?'

Lucy smiled. 'No, I think it's a good idea. The kids can see you whenever they want and I'll be happy to know they're close by.'

'Great.' Tom beamed. 'I wasn't sure how you'd react but now I know you're okay with it, I'll put a bid in.'

'The twins' happiness is my priority and you living near us will be good for them. Besides,' she grinned, 'I'll need you to help with them while I go back and finish my law degree.'

Tom nodded. 'I'd be glad to. I robbed you of that, among many other things.'

Lucy waved a hand. 'It's all in the past now, Tom. This is the new chapter in my life and all our lives. I'm determined to put the past behind me, change and grow and be a better person. No more anger, no more secrets and lies. Watch out, world, here I come.'

Acknowledgements

As a mother of three young children I found the research for this book eye-opening and at times truly alarming. Social media has given our teenagers so much more to deal with. Nowhere is a 'safe space' when you're being bullied online.

I dedicated this book to mothers because they are the centre of our worlds. Mothers try to be the best they can be but they are only human: they make mistakes and they say and do the wrong thing sometimes. But they are only ever trying their best for their children. We should judge less and support more. We're all just trying to muddle through and keep our children safe and happy.

As always I have many people to thank.

Biggest thank-you goes to Rachel Pierce, my editor, who held my hand through this book and helped to push me along when I was faltering; Patricia Deevy, for her great insight, ideas and cheerleading; Michael McLoughlin, Cliona Lewis, Patricia McVeigh, Carrie Anderson, Brian Walker and all the team at Penguin Ireland for their continued support and help. To all in the Penguin UK office, especially Tom Weldon, Joanna Prior and the fantastic sales, marketing and creative teams. To my agent Marianne Gunn O'Connor for being a great agent and a thoughtful and kind person. To Hazel Orme, for her wonderful copy-editing and for being such a positive force.

To Lia Moloney for giving me an eye-opening (and, at times, jaw-dropping) insight into the complicated minefield that is the world of teenagers today: thanks, Lia, you are a fantastic girl.

To the headmaster who patiently talked me through the very delicate and challenging job of dealing with parents and students over bullying. He explained that schools are doing their best to keep up with the constantly changing ways and platforms via which bullying now takes place. The safety and happiness of students is paramount.

To my fellow writers, thanks for your support, encouragement and for always reminding me that the important thing is to keep going!

To my mum, sister, brother and extended family: thanks for always being there.

To all of my friends, thanks for your support and love always.

To Hugo, Geordy and Amy: I hope I can be a good mother and let you be whoever you are meant to be.

To Troy, thanks for being my best friend.